SHADOW OF GOD

SHADOW OF GOD

Frank Rooney

Shadow
of God

HARCOURT, BRACE & WORLD, INC., NEW YORK

For Helen

God is truth and light his shadow.

—Plato, *The Republic*

FOREWORD

This book, it must be stated clearly, does not deal with real people or with real events. Although the events recounted in the book may have parallels—or even models—in history, they are neither bounded nor defined by history. So far as the writer knows, no Catholic order of nuns called the Sisters of the Order of St. Luke exists. Sister Esther's ordeal may be matched in some details by that of a real nun, but Sister Esther herself escapes historical accuracy. For that matter, in this book, history itself escapes historical accuracy. Only the human spirit, which may be damned but cannot be confined or defeated, is intended to be real.

The Peninsula

The Peninsula

CHAPTER I

First Sergeant Sam Goldman stood with his back to a fat-boled, many-twigged, semitropical tree and looked down the valley toward the two soldiers, Lewis and Kincaid, who in the protective twilight were moving toward the stone building that might or might not be occupied by the enemy. Searching for a refuge, had he found an obstacle?

"What do you think, Goldman?"

Goldman glanced at Captain Sterling's well-assembled profile, the right parts in the right places, before saying, "I'm not thinking, Captain, I'm hoping."

Sterling put the binoculars to his eyes, adjusting the lenses as if focusing on the kickoff of a football game between, say, Princeton and Harvard; Princeton to win. Bareheaded, freshly shaved and washed, his hair trimmed, his tailored fatigues clean, his half boots polished, his carbine oiled, Sterling appeared prepared for any of the evening's disappointments, whether K rations, command, or death. Goldman's powerful body, with its size seventeen neck and forty-eight-inch chest, encased in fatigues that were neither clean nor pressed (he became conscious of the smell of dried blood), did not diminish Sterling; it set him apart, the primitive of the fieldstone pointing the sophistication of marble.

"What's it look like in the binocs?" Goldman asked. Lewis and Kincaid were now no more than a hundred yards from the building. The eight other enlisted men in the company, survivors of the original one hundred and thirty-one, were spread out below Goldman, concealed but ready to provide Lewis and Kincaid with protective fire. Veterans to a man, they knew that "protective fire" meant immediate withdrawal from the valley if the enemy (in their language, Patty Lou or old Pat) appeared in force. Lewis and

3

Kincaid would then provide *them* with protective fire till old Pat either silenced them or permitted an unplanned withdrawal.

"Looks like a church," Sterling said. "Could it be a mission?"

"Well, if Pat's there, here's where he opens up, the lethal son of a bitch."

"Why not wait and get all of us?" Sterling said, and then paused, as if aware that he had not explained himself fully. "Including the girls."

Goldman looked back beyond the tree at the five nuns standing in a semicircle at the base of the slope that dropped to the north entrance of the valley. Their white tropical habits, faintly yellow, lacking starch, many times patched and mended, appeared in the heavy evening air rather like the cleaning housewife's apron and hood. Only Sister Agnes, their nominal superior, glanced at him, a nun's look—brief, impersonal, to the point. Noting that he had nothing to say to her, she resumed the reading of her breviary.

"They've gone inside," Sterling said. "Maybe we've found a home."

Goldman stretched and grunted, easing his taut muscles. On both sides of the slowly darkening valley the ground rose, in terraces, to the hills. After the heat and stench of the jungle, the languid cobras and the milky vines, the fabulous insects and the big dewy plants, the open valley offered the relief (and at the same time produced the ache) of the half-forgotten familiar—for Lewis, a farm in the Ozark Mountains; for Goldman, New York and Columbia College. Goldman, concentrating on the stone building, listening for the first burst of fire, pictured in his mind the movements of Lewis and Kincaid—the doors being kicked open, the pause, the sprint across the threshold, the body twisting against itself in anticipation of a bullet, a grenade, a bayonet, a knife.

Sterling, looking through the binoculars, said, "Lewis, by God."

"Intact?"

"Goddam it, why doesn't he signal the all clear?"

"Maybe Pat's got a gun at his back."

4

"Finally." Sterling lowered the binoculars. "Well, shall we go in?"

Goldman lifted an arm, and the five nuns, with packs strapped to their backs and carrying medical supplies, rations, sewing kits, and tools by hand, began to climb the slope toward him. At Sterling's signal, the eight men in front rose, slung their rifles, and formed two loose columns facing the stone building. Passing Goldman, the nuns positioned themselves between the two columns. Another hand signal from Sterling started the company toward the building. Goldman followed about ten paces back, looking at the crests of the hills on either side of him and occasionally to his rear, the Russian-made automatic rifle held loosely in his right hand, the barrel resting against his right shoulder. The men in the company carried the standard M-1 rifle, Sterling a carbine, but Goldman, the iconoclast, preferred his Russian beauty, liberated from the enemy on the last abortive offensive to the north and bedded with a fidelity he could not imagine inflicting on a native mistress—had he had one. They are, he thought, a beautiful people, gentle and considerate, and also tough and obdurate, not a nation, but a confederation of tribes, split in half by ideological doctrines incomprehensible to the men who believed them.

But he had not slept with any of the women of this divided country, enemy or ally; nor did he think he would. He could not be sure of the deterring force. It was there; he felt it—like a dying nerve in a tooth. During his two and a half years of active service (he was overdue for repatriation) he had gone through all the motions, from the jerky stumbling calisthenics of combat to the twilight sleep of a rest camp. Some actions, such as the accidental killing of children and the maiming of young mothers, could be neither reconciled through analogy nor justified by dialectic or a world view. You filed them for future analysis, hoping that you would lose the key to those archives.

He remembered, among others, the woman he had been forced to search for contraband, possibly radio-transmitter parts or a grenade. At his signal—his gun to her belly—she removed her hat. He felt her hair carefully with his left hand, pushing his fingers

5

into her scalp. When she took off her shirt she presented it to him with both hands. As he squeezed it he looked at her breasts, shocked that they were so much younger than her face. He looked briefly at her back, then pointed to her pants. With these squeezed and pressed, he stared at the naked woman, who, in response to what she interpreted as a command, moved her feet apart, thrusting her crotch forward. Goldman touched her quickly and drew his hand away without probing her vagina. When she took the clothes he offered her she moved her feet together and bowed to him. A physical grace note to Goldman's brutal pantomime, and a killing one, because he knew, even as he released her, that he was copping out on a cheap plea of molestation to escape the graver charge of negligence, the kind of narcissism for which other men die.

"Beautiful," Sterling said.

Walking through the double wooden gate that breached the seven-foot-high stone wall surrounding the building, he pointed at the long narrow stained-glass windows, and said in an aside to Goldman, "Couldn't be a monastery, could it?"

"I wouldn't know, Captain."

"What the hell," Sterling said, jerked from speculation to apprehension by the actions of Sister Roberta, the youngest—or at least the youngest-appearing—of the nuns, who was bent over the flagstones in the courtyard, coughing and retching, her hands pressing her abdomen. The other nuns quickly surrounded her, as if to hide this feminine indelicacy from their masculine escorts. Goldman moved toward Ahearn, a devout Catholic and a sensitive giant, but not quickly enough. Ahearn, his St. Christopher's medal visible on his collarbone, said, "She's sick."

"Let's hope it's a miscarriage," Koslow said.

Petroni, the smallest man in the company, standing between Ahearn and Koslow, appeared to rise off the ground and float toward the courtyard wall. Grabbing Koslow, Ahearn lifted him over his head and slammed him to the flagstones. He was lifting and slamming Koslow when Goldman hit him on the base of the skull with the barrel of Petroni's rifle, a weapon that made a better club than his own Russian beauty. Ahearn shuddered, staggered,

6

but did not let go of Koslow, who was bleeding heavily from the head. Goldman hit Ahearn again, again using the barrel of the rifle, knocking the man to his knees, and then, as Ahearn screamed, kicked him hard under the ribs, trying to ram the toe of his boot into the solar plexus. Ahearn, on his knees, twisted to get at Goldman, and Goldman, aiming his boot, kicked him a second time. His diaphragm frozen by the force of the kick, Ahearn rolled on his side, pulling his knees up to his chest. Suck your thumb, Goldman thought, before he said to Bolton, "Tie him up. Hands behind his back. Put a hobble on his feet. Twenty-inch spread. Use the slings off his and Petroni's rifles." He said to Corporal Plinnett, "Get a man up in the tower with the binocs. The rest of you stand by." Sister Esther was on her knees beside Koslow. Sister Agnes had moved to Petroni, who lay with his back arched from the base of the wall where Ahearn, in the ecstasy of a justifiable madness, had thrown him. Sister Catherine and Sister Mary, supporting Sister Roberta, walked up the three broad shallow steps toward the main door of the building.

Goldman pointed at Lewis. "Is there a room we can lock Ahearn in?"

"Cellar. But I didn't see any key to the door."

"We'll see what it looks like inside," Sterling said. "Come on, Goldman."

The other men, who had watched the action with the indifference of prisoners to whom this might happen tomorrow, settled themselves in the courtyard, awaiting further orders. When you know the future, the present is only a minor distraction.

CHAPTER II

GOLDMAN SAT AT A DESK in what must have been the reception room of the monastery, studying the company roster. If he included Sterling and himself—and he felt he should—there were nine able-bodied men: Sterling, Goldman, Corporal Plinnett, Lewis, Bolton, Kincaid, Francisco, Masters, and Schofield. On the sick list, Koslow and Petroni. In detention, Ahearn. Locked in a bin in the cellar. Locked in, but not tied.

The light from the single shielded candle on the desk created marvelous unstable shadows on the blanket-hung windows and on the wall to his left. Should he say suitable shadows? On his right as he sat at the desk he could see the big center hall through open double doors and, beyond the hall, part of the library. He could also see one edge of the straw mat hung from the arch through which you had to pass to reach the front door, the mat serving as a blackout curtain. Behind the desk and two paces to the right of it was the only unlocked door leading to the infirmary and nuns' quarters. Out of bounds, forbidden country, except to Sterling and himself. Above and behind Goldman hung a huge stone Jesus on a burly cross, blood congealed in realistic droplets on his skull, his hands and feet, and on his wounded side—an important atrocity, necessary and memorable. In the left front corner of the room, in white, blue, and gold, stood a life-size statue of the Virgin Mother with the God-Infant in her arms and Lucifer, in the form of an Asiatic cobra, under her heel.

As Goldman sat at the desk, the situation absolutely fouled up, actually hardly defined, Sterling came into the center hall from the courtyard, shutting the door tightly behind him before pushing aside the straw mat. Goldman stood when Sterling entered the reception room, offering the desk, but Sterling declined with a thrust of his shoulder and sat instead in a heavy dark chair near the statue of the Virgin. Laying his carbine on the floor, he lit a cigarette and stared over Goldman's head at the crucified Jesus.

"These icons get you, Goldman?"

"Not me, Captain."

Sterling smiled. "They get me, but I don't know why. Maybe it's the atmosphere. Stony and dismal."

"Lewis back yet?"

"No sign of Lewis." Sterling saw the roster on the desk. "How are Koslow and Petroni?"

"Koslow's in a coma he may never come out of. Petroni's busted up but ought to survive. Neither of them can be moved. And you know what that means, Captain."

"And Sister Mary?"

"No change. The bleeding's stopped, but she can't be moved, either."

"I have a contract with the U.S. Army, Goldman, not with God."

Goldman considered remarking that all contracts out here were renegotiable, but thought better of it. He stood. "Twenty-two hundred hours, sir. I'll make the rounds."

"Sit down, Sergeant. As you may have observed, I'm not much of a military man."

"Neither am I, Captain. What I really am is a Pfc."

"When we get back to the regiment, Goldman, I'm going to recommend you be given a battlefield commission."

"Captain, I don't even know how to keep a roster."

"How are you on close-order drill?" Sterling dropped his cigarette and put his heel on it. As if aware of his analogical movement, he half glanced over his shoulder at the statue of the Virgin. Then, observing the positive manner with which Goldman studied the papers on the desk, he added, "I'm a good Presbyterian, Goldman. File that."

"The grape-juice circuit."

"Yes. We don't use wine. How did you know?"

"I had a Presbyterian friend, Captain."

"Are you Orthodox or Reformed, Goldman?"

9

"Neither, sir. The name's Goldman but the mind is free."

"Free of what, Goldman?" Sterling stood. "I'll have a look around."

Goldman took a notebook from the pack on the floor beside the desk and opened it to the page of the last entry. Below "Peaceful night, got four hours' sleep" he wrote, "June 11" in a shorthand he had invented—first, because keeping a diary was a violation of army security and, secondly, as a friendly challenge to the enemy intelligence officer who might, in spite of the provisions in Goldman's will, come into possession of Goldman's body. "June Eleven." That bastard Ahearn. He had foreseen trouble with Ahearn. Why had he not been able to prevent it? And how much had he foreseen?

Turning the pages of the notebook, he fixed on the date April 14. "Finally got the word to go. Pushed off at 0500. Resistance light. Sterling thinks enemy right flank smashed. Heavy fighting right and left. Center—us—quiet." Further along: "April 21. Our turn. Eleven casualties. Lieutenants Nicolai and Bergen killed. Promoted acting first sergeant."

The collection of heavy and inaccurate phrases did not contain the action; it cued it. "Pressed on. Air superiority beginning to tell. Looks like a rout. For the enemy." Another page: "Picturesque little village. Came through so fast the enemy didn't have time to burn it. Busted into big wooden building—schoolhouse?—and found five American nuns sitting in chairs against wall. Introduced themselves. Sister Agnes said three of them—herself, Sister Esther, and Sister Catherine—were registered nurses. They would be happy to help with our wounded. Bolton went in back and came out looking happy. Cold bastard. Said later, 'You know what's back there, Sarge? Cribs!' Only he didn't mean corncribs, he meant straight—or French—honey cribs. Told him to please keep information to himself. Bad enough for the rest of us, but the Catholics?" And: "Orders to pull back. Heavy fighting on our right. Lost contact with regiment. Looks like Pat's going around us." More notes: "Well, we finally got it. Two hours of mortar fire and a frontal assault in battalion strength. Put nuns in last available transportation and assigned Ahearn, a real Catholic, to drive south till he contacts regiment or runs out of gas. Down to twenty-one men, counting captain." And: "Worst is when you have to leave your wounded and then at night listen to Pat sticking them. One scream per man. Then silence." A week later: "Sister Catherine definitely carrying one. She hides it pretty well under her habit, but once in a while—when she moves or turns—you can see it is there. Sister Esther, the nuns' messenger or liaison man, is a real beauty. Why give it all to God? Only her hands—rough, creased, red. Like a bricklayer's."

Goldman riffled the pages in the notebook. There it was: "Ran into Ahearn with nuns. Truck broke down. Guess we're stuck with them. No sign of regiment." Then, several pages later: "A real strolling picnic. Sterling has sketchy map, and we're proceeding south. Offered to carry Sister Mary, but she insists on walking. Sister Agnes has everything organized. They do all the cooking and cleaning up, dig their own latrines, sew on buttons, stitch cuts. At night they rig an open-top tent with blankets and shelter halves. Offered to stand guard at night but without carrying weapons. Offer declined by Sterling, who used a little foxhole language. Ahearn shocked. Sisters didn't bat an eye. Got to keep an eye on Ahearn. He doesn't want to believe what he sees. Sisters try to keep it from him. Cheery as hell. Talk about self-sufficient."

Another page: "Proceeding south. Have lost all contact with the enemy. We're in the eye of the hurricane. God's eye, Ahearn says. 'Where's that,' Koslow says, 'in a pig's ass?' The needle." Recalling Koslow's square Slavic face set in its usual expression of general discontent, Goldman decided that the man had no real antireligious convictions; he was a heckler, a type for which stand-up comedians had invented such lines as "The last time I saw a mouth like that it had a hook in it" and "Your mother doesn't work at the S.P.C.A., she lives there." And if Koslow died, Ahearn would be guilty of murder.

Goldman continued skimming over his uneven script. "Caught Sister Esther collecting the dirty laundry. Gave her hell but got nowhere. Later had a little talk with her. Only, it seems now,

I did the talking. Calls me Sam. She did say that there were twelve sisters originally but wouldn't say what happened to others." Further on: "Koslow claims Sister Roberta told him the others were killed. I suppose they'll all crack wide open one of these days. Right now you'd think nothing had happened to them, nothing at all. Iron women. Even Sister Mary. She follows the same routines as the others, including the dirty work, and the others let her. Therapy, I suppose. Or maybe something stronger, a way of life? Offered to carry Sister M. on a litter. Offer declined. Instead insists on carrying her share of supplies. And Sister Esther asked me to tell Sterling that they understood military problems came first and that they would obey any order, including an order to get lost, in line of duty, but that if they chose to pray instead of sleeping that was their business. Were they holding us up? If so, they would gladly proceed on their own. Were they jeopardizing the morale of the company? Then leave them. Etc., etc. Sister Esther explained that nuns have to pray so many hours a day and that if you miss one period of prayer you have to make it up before you sleep. She would rather pray than sleep, she said, and she would rather work than do either, because work, Sam, is the noblest form of prayer. I think maybe she wants to get her hooks into me and I think maybe I'm letting her. Back off, Goldman. When the water gets deep the deep get watered."

And later: "Pinned down for the last few days. Saw heavy enemy equipment on road going south. Lots of planes, mostly ours, but they don't seem to be doing much damage. Crossed road and entered forest. Road littered with vehicles. Ours. Some unburied dead. Ours. Sisters wanted to bury dead, Sterling against it. Had to break off finally. Contact with enemy, who lobbed mortar shells at us but didn't pursue. Lukatz, Jones, and Uppman killed. Stokow and Strinsky died the next day. Buried them. Passed farmers out in fields. They stare at us, we stare at them. Waylaid by villagers with sick and wounded children. Nuns attended them while we stood and sweated blood. Ask for information, you get a shrug."

Hearing a knock on the inner door, Goldman put the notebook in his pack and said, "Come," expecting Sister Agnes. He wasn't too startled, however, to see Sister Esther.

"The Captain busy, Sam?"

"I'll call him."

"Please don't. It's not that important."

"Grab a chair."

Sister Esther opened her workbag and sat sewing on a fatigue jacket (Bolton's?) while Goldman, trying not to look at her hands, lit a cigarette. The freshness and beauty of the framed face and the splendor of the body, which the tropical habit as much promoted as concealed, testified to a loving God; her hands, raw and creased, to a vindictive one.

"It's so quiet, Sam."

"You miss the shooting, Sister?"

"Shooting? Killing?"

"I've gotten very lonely for the sound of shooting lately."

"Of all people, I'd think you were the least bloodthirsty, Sam."

"Yes, but I was hired to kill, Sister, not to run an escort service. I feel I'm not giving my employer his money's worth."

"You make a very nice escort, Sam. Very polite, very considerate, and very, very strong."

"You thinking of Ahearn's head?"

"You could have killed him, Sam. You didn't."

"I wish I had. Listen, that's not a shocker, Sister, that's the simple truth. Because if Koslow dies—"

"He will, Sam."

"You can smell it, Sister? Death?"

"Sometimes. I've been working in hospitals since I was sixteen. All departments. The operating room, the incurables, the mentally afflicted, the mentally retarded, the children's ward—death and I are old friends, Sam."

"The son of a bitch is no friend of mine, Sister."

"This particular son is a particular friend of mine, Sam. So please don't malign him."

In a minute, Goldman decided, he'd be trying to tell her dirty stories, to pretend to himself that he could ignore or bypass the

13

religious habit, the symbol of a total commitment to a strange and paradoxical way of life, to get at the person under it. And this, he knew, he could never do. Certainly these nuns were women. Certainly they were enormously capable of affection, and, the important thing, enormously responsive to suffering. Goldman knew that a twenty-four-hour watch had been set up beside Koslow and Petroni, and that only physical force or death could break it. But you could not mistake the skill and compassion of the nun-nurse for the tenderness of the woman. Because when you did, under stress or pain or despair, you were told, directly or indirectly, graciously but with a touch of iron, to remove your lines of communication or suffer them to be cut.

To sweeten the situation there was that stigmatic business of rape, outrageous because these were American women unavailable to the ordinary soldier, incomprehensible because they were also (in Ahearn's fine phrase) the brides of Christ. Till this evening discussion of these matters was forbidden, by silent but general consent. Now Koslow and Ahearn had broken this agreement and at the same time had removed themselves from the pressure of having to act on this shocking betrayal of company faith. Leaving such experts as Sam Goldman to act on it.

"Why don't you grab yourself some sleep?" Goldman asked, not really wanting to get rid of her, only to put her aside temporarily. Like a difficult book.

"I'd be better off with something to do."

"Then scrub down the joint. Again. Every time I look at those chopped-beef hands of yours—this is religion?"

"Why must you be so personal, Sam?"

"Let's put it a different way. What kind of complex do you have that makes you want to wallow in filth?"

"At present, Sam, we have an abundance of filth. It would be nice to have more saints on this earth, but what we need now is more janitors. Would you tell the Captain—at your leisure—that Sister Agnes would like to speak to him, please?"

"You came out to do the probing, that it, Sister? Take my military temperature?"

"Yes. You have a decision to make, one that we must know before we make ours."

"Not yet, Sister. Get some sleep."

"That poor boy."

"So that's what's on your mind?"

"You can't keep him locked up in the cellar like that, Sam. It's inhuman."

"Listen, Sister, Ahearn's an animal. Like you. Only he's dangerous. He's reverted. He's not a pack mule, he's a tiger."

"Surely you're not going to leave him unattended."

"He's attended. Goldman's boy."

"The least I could do is empty his bucket."

"Bucket. You know the law, Sister. Any one of you tries to make contact with the prisoner and we lock you up. I, personally, will lock you up. I, Sam Goldman."

"I just don't believe that, Sam."

"After what's happened to you do you still have faith in human nature?"

"I have faith in God, Sam. Which makes it a joy to have faith in human nature."

"Knock it off, Sister. You're corrupting me."

"I think it's you who are corrupting us, Sam. Good night."

Taking the blue-shielded flashlight from the desk—Sterling and Corporal Plinnett each had one—he blew out the candle and crossed the hall into the library. The bell tower could be reached by a door from the chapel and also by a door from the library, an arrangement that enabled Plinnett to relieve the guard in the tower without passing through the nuns' side of the monastery. Goldman could have quartered the nuns in the monks' cells, with access to the kitchen and the refectory, but he felt they ought to have free use of the chapel, where they could conduct their devotions unobserved.

He had an image of Sister Esther praying in one of the big wooden pews, her face lifted and exposed like a child's to the altar. Her eyes were shut. She prayed for the God she carried inside her, the seed not of the Holy Ghost but of Cain, the brutal hunter-brother of the elected farmer, jealous, sullen, enduring, whose blood-gift God had rejected. Shaken by his unnerving fantasy, Goldman pushed through the door at the corner of the library and walked down the hall to the circular stair leading to the bell tower. His low whistle answered, he climbed the steps and said to the dark shape standing with its back to one of the elongated slits in the masonry of the tower, "Kincaid?"

"Schofield, Sarge. How's everything below?"

"Neutral, Danny. See anything? Any sign of Lewis?"

"Haven't seen him, Sarge."

"Who can?"

Schofield, caught by the company joke, laughed. "That goddam Indian."

"The Invisible Man." Contact established. Goldman said, "What did you set up with Plinnett?"

"Well, you know how Lewis is, Sarge."

"Sure."

"The guy could walk right up to you and you'd never see him."

"Spit in your eye, Danny."

"So if I see anything I alert Plinnett, right?"

"Right. Only don't look too hard; you might see everything— including things that aren't there."

Going down the stairs, Goldman wondered whether Washington held the enemy in such contempt that it deliberately sent the boys to do the fighting and kept the men in reserve, ostensibly to do the thinking. Of the eight enlisted men, only Goldman and Bolton were old enough to vote. Schofield was just starting to shave.

Outside, in the courtyard, Goldman talked with Plinnett, and then circled the monastery to check for light leaks. He could hear the sounds of heavy guns beyond the hills to the west, a steady ground-rumble and, occasionally, as treble over bass, the higher-pitched lighter weapons. Closer. After a whimsical leave of absence the war had decided to return. Pat wanted a few more heads to add to his grisly collection. Kill the American aggressor, that is, the male American aggressor. As for his women—well, they *were* women. To Pat. Goldman remembered a dry, brittle lecture delivered by his history professor at Columbia: "The Russians in their sweep across eastern and central Europe in the closing months of World War II were like sexual locusts, devouring every woman and female adolescent in their path. This is not an indictment; this is an historical footnote to an interesting and decisive military campaign. Rape is the most direct approach to the intermingling of cultures. And by no means the nastiest."

Challenged softly, Goldman responded, "Shindig," recognizing, as he approached the graveyard, Bolton's lean silhouette. "Aren't you lonely out here, Bolton?"

"I've got lots of company, Sergeant."

"Where?"

"You're standing on it."

Shuddering with fear and repugnance, Goldman stepped quickly back to look for the snake. In the inadequate moonlight he saw only the roughened earth and small stones, and the two crosses near a single dwarf tree. "You scared the shit out of me, Bolton."

"You think it was a snake, Sarge? You really afraid of these stupid cobras?"

"You're goddam right I am."

"You ever hear of anyone being bitten by them?"

"No, but that doesn't make me feel any friendlier toward them. We don't have a snake kit with us."

"Notice the way they strike? They don't really strike; they fall forward." Bolton put up his right arm and let it fall slowly toward Goldman. "Like this. I like snakes. Used to keep a couple of copperheads in the cellar back home. Connecticut. You used to go to Yale, didn't you?"

"Columbia. Only two years, Bolton."

"And you dropped out to come here? Not a very bright thing to do, Goldman."

"I dropped out, but not to come here. Any sign of Lewis?"

"You don't find that hillbilly, Sergeant; he finds you."

Lewis, a mountaineer from Arkansas, was famous in the peninsula for his two- and three-day trips behind the enemy lines. Known

17

as the Invisible Man, he could move so silently and adroitly he could not be detected by ear and, once in position, could occupy so little space behind or under such simple cover that the brain refused to honor the eye's data.

"Look at this." Bolton dug the toe of his boot into the loose earth, revealing, as Goldman stooped, a piece of dark cloth. "You wanted to know where the monks were, Goldman. Right here. Well, at least Pat isn't queer, is he?"

"I guess not."

Goldman stared toward the southern end of the valley. Lewis had been gone since 1900 hours. It was now, on the luminous dial of his wrist watch, 2400. Lewis could make, in that mountaineer's lope, six or seven miles an hour. He had been told not to go farther than ten miles. And Lewis possessed a built-in pedometer as well as a splendid survival kit. Had Pat closed the ring?

"I had a dream about you last night, Sergeant."

"You really must be hard up, Bolton."

"Not that kind. I dreamed I had you up against a wall at the end of a long rifle barrel with my finger on the trigger."

"How big a hole did you blow in me?"

"I woke up. Now what do you think that dream meant?"

"You hate your father, Bolton. You want to kill him and sleep with your mother."

"I left home permanently when I was sixteen. After leaving it four or five times since I was twelve. What I can't figure is why I woke up."

"Never point a gun at a man unless you intend killing him, Bolton."

"You don't have to hate a man to kill him, Goldman. All you have to do is decide he's in your way. Like Ahearn."

"How is he in your way?"

"He's holding us back, isn't he? Like those nuns."

"Why not kill them, too?"

"I will. When you order me to. Look, Sergeant, you're not going to leave them to Pat, are you?"

"At long last a spark of decency, Bolton? Twinge of conscience?"

18

"Koslow dead yet?"

"Not yet. One thing, Bolton, don't get trigger-happy out here and start spraying the bushes. Anything you see or hear report to Plinnett."

"Give my love to Sister Esther."

"Sure thing."

Bolton, watching Goldman's back, wondered if he had touched him, put a finger on the man's sore spot. Every man, even the toughest, had a sore spot. Touch it and you become, for better or for worse, the man's master. Of the men in the company, including Sterling, only Goldman offered a challenging objective. The rest, Bolton thought, would do to pass the time. Goldman, touched, would really respond.

CHAPTER III

GOLDMAN, ASLEEP AT THE DESK, his head on his arms, awoke to see Lewis in the act of lighting the candle. According to his watch it was 0210.

"You made it, I see."

"I forgot the password, Sergeant, damned if I didn't. So I had to sneak in."

"You crazy bastard."

Goldman went out to rouse Sterling, who was sleeping in the library. Within minutes they had spread the one map in the company on the desk.

"How far did you go?" Sterling asked.

"I estimate about twelve miles, sir."

"Due south?"

"Due south."

"That would take you roughly here." Sterling tapped the map. "See anything?"

"Not a goddam thing, sir."

"You must have seen something."

"There's a road here—gravel—about seven, eight miles out, sir. It runs northeast-southwest. But there was nothing on it. I hung around about an hour but nothing came down it. Or up it, either."

"Well, that's simple enough, Goldman. Pat's coming down on either side of us. At a point—chosen by him—say, here—he closes the gap and hopes he has at least a division in his pocket. He certainly expects more than us. Of course, not controlling the air—thank God—Pat doesn't know exactly how big his bag's going to be. Our problem is to beat him to the point where he intends choking us off. All right, Lewis, thanks. If you had any brains I'd offer you another stripe."

"Pfc. is all I want, sir. Poor fucking corporal."

"Get some sleep."

"And let Plinnett know you're back," Goldman said.

"Wait a minute. You mean you—" Sterling waved Lewis away. "The hell with it. Jesus Christ, what kind of security have you got out there, Goldman? Bunk off, Lewis."

Sterling paced up and down the room, roughly between the Virgin and her crucified Son, his handsome face a brittle, corrugated pastry in the candlelight. Revelation-time, Goldman thought. He could see it coming. At a time like this a man had nothing to fall back on except his autobiography. "You know what a social Christian is, Goldman?"

"I can guess."

"You're looking at one."

"Yes, sir."

"I'm not only a social Christian, I'm a social drinker. As is my wife. We live in Greenwich, Connecticut, with our three beautiful and totally useless children, and climb, climb, climb. Up the social ladder, Goldman, up the golden assholes of people who serve absolutely nothing except themselves and would call the police if

Joseph and Mary asked to sleep in their stables. Something about liability. Set fire to the hay."

"If there's a ladder, Captain, someone has to climb it."

"In a few years I'd have been making thirty thousand per annum, Goldman. With more to come. That's what, in my ambition and stupidity, I gave up to get here. And when I think that you and I may share the same democratic grave—"

"But with you as senior partner, Captain."

"Exactly. Sterling and Goldman, a closed corporation." Sterling began to laugh, the laugh of a man no longer able to suppress a monstrous indignation directed toward whatever malignant forces had personal charge, at this moment, of his private situation. Sympathetic to this indignation, but also entertained by the mechanics of its expression, Goldman studied the map.

"Ambition, Goldman. Snobbery. Or snottery. A snob's at least a recognizable type. What am I? Princeton, New York, Greenwich. Advertising. Rising young account executive. You know what I did, Goldman? Now listen, don't miss a word of this. It'll cut you to the heart. If you've got a heart."

"A small one, Captain, but it's there."

"I married young, Goldman, off the campus, had my compulsory three offspring, and then, as part of my scheme to dig myself into the local establishment, joined this very select regiment, one that dated back to 1784. As a private, of course. You should have attended our regimental balls. That was the Army? But then some bright bureaucrat in Washington decided the country needed this regiment over here. You follow me?"

"That's out of my league, sir."

"But not out of your class. How old are you, Goldman?"

"Twenty-two."

"That's a real talent—youth. Well, most of our officers were either overage or overwhelmed, and so disqualified themselves from active service. The honor of the regiment, Goldman. And there were others who couldn't pass the physical. Bad backs, bad knees, night blindness, short pricks—you do follow me?"

"Yes, sir."

"On the roster, the regiment could muster fifteen hundred men. Actually, it mustered about three hundred. The cream off the top. Do you know how many of us finally made it, Goldman? About two platoons. The honor of the regiment. Among these outstanding few, Joseph Hays Sterling the Third. You're not required to laugh, Goldman, but if you'd care to snicker—"

"You made it, Captain. Two bars."

"You know how I made it?"

"The same way I made first sergeant."

"The goddess attrition, who rewards all survivors. But your permanent rank is Pfc. Mine is private." Sterling laughed again, as if to run a test on his sense of humor. "I tell you, Goldman, if I crack up—and I probably will—it won't be from lack of amusement. But what about you, Goldman? Or are you carrying your secrets to the grave?"

"Nothing much, Captain. My mother wanted me to be a dentist, and I couldn't see it. In Queens."

"A dentist."

"Teeth."

"Samuel Goldman, D.D.S. What does your mother call you, Sammy?"

"Sam."

"Sam. I knew a Marcus Goldman. Partner in Folkstone, Haveridge and Goldman. Any relation?"

"Not so far as I know, sir."

"There's also a Goldman in Perse, Temple, Goldman and Trench. Anything there? Brokers."

"Nothing."

"Just who in hell are you connected with, Goldman? Besides your mother."

"Nobody, sir. The woods are full of unconnected Goldmans."

"Actually, what worries me is my job. I didn't get a speech and a loving cup for joining up, Goldman. This is time out. Another year out here and my star'll be hitched to a garbage truck. Absent thee from felicity a while, Sam, and felicity will send you the standard 'Dear John' letter on engraved stationery and packaged in a scented envelope. Absent thee from thy job and the same thing happens—without the scent. Only there are more eligible women than there are eligible jobs. A sad truth, Sam, but an important one." Sterling yawned and stretched. "Well, let's get some sleep. Anything new with the religious?"

"They want to know whether we're pulling out in the morning."

"So do I."

Snuffing out the candle after Sterling had returned to the library, Goldman sacked out on the floor by the desk. He awoke at 0320, checking the time on his wrist watch. He lay listening to the sounds in the cellar, not loud in the dark room but steady and irritating, the human voice braying one of the ancient hymns to human distress. Taking flashlight and candle (he looked at his gun for perhaps ten seconds before laying it on the desk), he tapped at the door to the infirmary and nuns' quarters. Sister Esther opened it.

"I'll see about Ahearn, Sister."

"You're not going to hurt him, are you, Sam?"

"No blessed gun. Now ask him if he's going to hurt me."

Passing the refectory, he looked in at Koslow and Petroni, lying on improvised cots, and at Sister Roberta, sitting on a stool between the two beds, her shadow, projected by the light of the shielded candle, swaying on the semidark refectory wall, like a projection of Koslow's soul, detained briefly on the wall by the unsteady and shrinking candle. Yawning and shuddering, he opened the cellar door, stumbling on the rough wooden steps as he went down. On his left ranged the casks and presses the monks had used to make and store wine. On his right, in a bin probably used for the storage of grain, Ahearn. The bin was made of heavy wooden slats with an air space between them, its door, which swung out, of eight-inch planks.

As Goldman set the candle and the lighted flashlight on the cement floor outside the bin, Ahearn, as if cued by this action, screamed, "God damn them. May God damn them to eternal hell-fire—"

"Ahearn? Ahearn?"

"Whores—whores—whores—"

"Shut up, Ahearn. Ahearn?"

The door shook suddenly as Ahearn's body hit it, and Goldman, appalled by the intensity of a force he could not see but could imagine hurtling toward him, a human projectile, backed away from the door and jerked the hunting knife from its sheath on his belt. Goldman had no intention of being destroyed by the man he could have killed in line of duty but hadn't, one he might yet have to kill in line of duty. Had Ahearn no gratitude? How was it in Abraham's bosom—any softer? How was it in Sister Esther's—any thornier? Raising the knife, he drove it into one of the treads on the stairs. If he had to, he would use it—but only if he had to.

Moving the flashlight and the candle back and to his right, giving himself footroom, Goldman unknotted the heavy chain that passed through the two small holes Plinnett, a carpenter's apprentice back home, had made in door and jamb, and swung the door out and away from him. Ahearn, still screaming, came at him, and Goldman, checking Ahearn's charge with a straight left, hit him as hard as he could in the belly with his right hand. Slow him up, cut him down, and, as a last gesture, reach the knife on the stairs. He felt Ahearn's fingers clawing at his face, the whole hot screaming entity of the man engaged in the blood-embraces of a colossal anger. Feeling as much repulsion as fear, Goldman chopped at Ahearn's belly with both hands, driving him, step by step, back into the storage bin and against the far wall, where, switching his attack to the head, Goldman dropped him. Ahearn no longer screamed; he whimpered. With his legs spread apart flat on the floor and his shoulder blades against the wall he looked like a naughty doll, spanked and slapped into a corner by its indignant little mother.

"Now listen, Ahearn—no more screaming. You hear me? If I have to, I'll kill you. That plain enough?"

Come, let us reason together. Goldman looked into Ahearn's bucket (only a quarter full; at least the man had some control), shook his canteen to make certain he had water, and left him, again securing the door with the chain. For a time Goldman stood trying to see into the darkness of the storage bin through the slats. Maybe he ought to finish the bastard off with the knife then and there. Mercy killing. He could feel Ahearn's ribs and gut-muscles on his hands, as if his knuckles were hung with splinters and ribbons. Enough. Unchaining the door, he picked up the candle and set it just inside the bin. "Go ahead, burn yourself to death. Fry. Take the rest of us with you. Maybe—like me—you're afraid of the dark."

Goldman stumbled on the knife going up the cellar stairs, a lapse of memory that chilled him. Maybe he was using up the equipment in his survival kit faster than he could replace it. Sister Esther met him in the hall with the news that Koslow had died.

"One less to carry." He stared at Sister Esther. "Well, what did you expect, Sister, a medical miracle?"

"We'll prepare him for burial."

"Pre— Listen, Sister, just wrap him in a blanket and I'll send a couple of men in to lug him out."

"It won't take long, Sam."

"You understand we want to bury him now, Sister."

"In the darkness?"

"If we stay here another day, Sister, we won't want to attract Pat's attention by conducting a burial service at high noon. Maybe we could fire a couple of volleys over his grave. Jesus Christ, Sister, use your skull."

"Sam, Jesus Christ is my God."

"What's your heaven, a slit-trench? Just tap on the door when you have Koslow ready. How's Sister Mary?"

"Much better, thank you."

"Good. Then we can pull out any time, right? You can strap up Petroni, can't you?"

"It'll be very hard on him, Sam. His back—you didn't hurt that poor boy, did you?"

"In his condition? No. I didn't hurt him."

Sister Roberta appeared at the door of the refectory, her pale bony face belittled by large, dark, fiercely expressive eyes, eyes difficult to look into for any length of time. Goldman had already noted that of the five nuns she had been the least social, talking little (though none of them except Sister Esther, their liaison, talked much), effacing herself wherever possible, often screened by a protective wall of habits. When they wanted to—and this happened many times during the long, slow retreat south—the five nuns could withdraw from the company, no matter what the situation, with an absoluteness that shut out communication except for a single thin channel for necessary orders and directions.

"Can't you do something to quiet that poor man, Sergeant?" Sister Roberta asked.

"He is quiet, Sister."

"Now, yes. But it upsets Sister Mary to hear him—screaming."

"He upsets all of us, Sister." Sister Esther spoke gently as she moved toward Sister Roberta. "I'll help with Koslow."

"Can't he be given a sedative, Sergeant?"

"You know we have none, Sister. Only a little morphine. And I think we'd better save that for Private Petroni." Sister Esther, as she spoke, pulled unobtrusively at Sister Roberta's sleeve.

"Cursing God, threatening to kill us, calling—"

Sister Esther, who had swung directly in front of Sister Roberta, forced her, without physical contact, back through the refectory door. "I'll let you know when we have Private Koslow ready, Sergeant."

A crack, Goldman thought, as he came back to his desk in the visitors' room; a small one, but definite, and unless Sister Esther and Sister Agnes patch it up—

"Now what?" Sterling, lighting a cigarette, was briefly visible, sitting on a library table, as Goldman entered the reception room, flashlight in hand.

"Koslow's dead. I thought we'd bury him before daylight, Captain. If that's all right with you."

"That's marvelous with me, Sam. Only what the hell do we do with Ahearn?"

26

"Turn him loose, after we leave?"

"Give him to Pat? I'm not going to put a gun in his hand, Sergeant. He'd be better off if we shot him."

"After a proper trial, of course."

"We'll try him, Sam. Drumhead court-martial. Two minutes flat, with witnesses sworn and the case summed up by both sides. I thought I heard him acting up."

"He wants to kill the religious with his bare hands."

"So he's turned against them."

"I reasoned with him."

"He respects a gun? Maybe he's not as far gone as we think."

"I went in there with my bare hands, Captain. He may be in fogville but he's entitled to a fair shake."

"You're a tough son of a bitch, Goldman, you know that? A quality I admire. But the order of the day is prudence, and that order, by God, will be obeyed. Prudence, Goldman."

"Yes, sir."

Now why did I have to say that, Goldman wondered as he went out into the courtyard to get a burial detail ready for Koslow.

Maybe I'm trying a little too hard to qualify. Like Ahearn.

CHAPTER IV

KOSLOW WAS BURIED AT 0415 in the monks' graveyard, given a small wooden cross and a short funeral service spoken by Sister Agnes and Sister Esther. Goldman marked out the grave himself in a corner away from where he had been standing talking to Bolton. After the services, Sterling asked Sister Agnes and Sister Esther to come to the reception room for a short conference.

"Goldman tells me Sister Mary and Petroni can be moved. Is that right?"

"We'd prefer not to move them," Sister Agnes said, "but we will if we must." She was a short woman, round in face and figure, troubled by sunburn. Sister Esther's face, the oval not hidden by the tight cowl, tanned smoothly, evenly, and not too darkly. Sister Agnes's face was a rough map with pink squares, brown patches, and gray boundary lines. Now and then she pressed her lips tightly together or moistened them quickly, if she thought herself unobserved, with her tongue.

Sterling told the two sisters what Lewis had found due south and added his view of the enemy's probable action. "We have to face it. Our luck has been fantastic. It won't hold because it can't. Pat's main push may be on either side of us, but you can bet your—bottom dollar—that he's coming up behind us. I think —unless something occurs to change our plans—we ought to travel by day. We make better time, have less chance of anyone getting hurt."

Having had three weeks' experience with these strange, hard-working, committed, often obdurate, and pettifogging women, Sterling spelled it out for them. Knowing their fantastic practicality, he asked for an inventory of their possessions. "And I want an honest count. Those bags you carry—leave them. One blanket apiece. All medical supplies and surgical instruments to be retained—" Sterling went down the list, not forgetting toilet paper. A first-rate performance, Goldman thought—realistic, firm, convincing, brief.

"The only course is to pull out," Sterling concluded. "We'll aim for 1000 hours."

"And Private Ahearn, Captain?" Sister Agnes asked.

"Ahearn is a military problem, Sister."

"You can't ask us to condone murder."

Sterling leaned toward Sister Agnes as if to make certain he was not the victim of a clever illusion. "Do you condone the murder of Koslow, Sister?"

"Private Ahearn was not in full possession of his mind when

he assaulted Private Koslow, Captain. He can't legally be held responsible for his actions."

"He can't?"

"We must pray that he recovers sufficiently to confess his fault and do penance for it. Morally, one must always be held ultimately responsible, even for actions performed against the will, in defiance of the will, or in the absence of the will. Ethically, there is no middle ground."

"There isn't?"

"We've worked with such cases often, Captain. We find that they usually yield to patience, kindness, and understanding."

Sterling was not prepared to yield to patience, quite apart from kindness or understanding.

"Ahearn's a mad dog, Sister. He's killed one man—a valuable man. He gets treated like a mad dog."

Sister Agnes nodded to Sister Esther.

"He's a very religious boy, Captain," Sister Esther said. "If we could talk to him I'm sure we could persuade him that we view what happened to us as a test of our courage and sincerity. God's attention is not given to everyone in so pure and intense a form. We pray to be worthy of it."

"You pray to be worthy."

"There is this difficulty, Captain," Sister Esther continued. "You have no real understanding of our position; we have little sympathy for yours. Yet, for the present, we must maintain sufficient agreement to operate efficiently for the good of all. May we talk to Private Ahearn?"

"No," Sterling said. "No, Sisters—and this is an order—you keep away from Ahearn."

"I don't understand your objections, Captain," Sister Esther said, having moved from a military zone to a moral one.

"Tell her, Sergeant."

"He's turned against you, Sister. You go near him and he'll kill you."

"And your evidence for that belief, Sergeant?" Sister Esther asked.

"Ahearn's own words, Sister, straight from his foaming mouth."

The two nuns were silent. Sister Esther finally spoke for both.

"Then good night, Captain, Sergeant."

In the morning, after a few hours of wild and perishable dreams, Goldman told Plinnett of the plan to pull out at 1000 hours and asked about ammo.

"Fifteen hundred rounds of thirty-caliber," Plinnett said, "near as I can figure. Maybe twenty grenades."

"We're about as dangerous as a swarm of bees. Rations?"

"All we can carry."

At 0700 the sun had lighted the hills to the west but had not yet touched the monastery. The unshaven part of the morning, Goldman thought, with something of the night's dewy hairiness in it. The sounds of the guns were louder. As Goldman stood in the courtyard, six jets, moving northwest, appeared briefly above the southern end of the valley. To the east he thought he heard the slower-moving, air-hammering prop planes. More jets, flying low, came from the southeast, bringing what might be, perhaps ten miles distant, sounds of a major bombing run.

"Close," Plinnett said. "Think they might spot us, Sam?"

"They might. If they do they can send an eggbeater."

Goldman went inside the monastery to wake Sterling, thinking how pleasant it would be to have a couple of helicopters to crawl into. That would solve the problem of the nuns. And of Ahearn. Tie him and toss him in, one bundle for the heavy-security mental ward. Later in the morning, Goldman spoke briefly with Sister Agnes, who said that Petroni had been asking for him. In the refectory, Sister Roberta, who was sitting with Petroni, motioned Goldman to a corner of the room.

"Private Petroni's asleep," she said. "Are we leaving this morning, Sergeant?"

"Got to, Sister. This is no place to hide."

"Even though it might hurt Private Petroni to move him?"

"Sister Agnes agreed to move him. She's in charge, isn't she?"

"In point of service she is our eldest, yes."

30

She's cracking, Goldman thought—and smiled to conceal a strong feeling of contempt. His gauge was Sister Esther. "I'll send someone to give you a hand with Petroni."

"That won't be necessary, Sergeant." The extraordinary eyes were a dark velour, brushed against the grain. They held Goldman in an unbreakable grip. "Yes, I'm afraid, Sergeant."

"Who isn't, Sister?"

"But do you have any idea of what I'm afraid of?" The next words were delivered so gently, as in an aside to an invisible audience, that he could detect neither contempt nor anger in them, certainly not bravado. "I think not, Sergeant."

He could say only, "Maybe I don't, Sister. Maybe I don't want to."

CHAPTER V

At 0900 Goldman went into the reception room to report to Sterling. The bombing to the southeast continued, the planes making their low-level runs and pulling up to fly sometimes over the valley, sometimes to either side of it, before turning for the flight back to the airfield. Sterling, usually well groomed, had neither washed nor shaved, indicating possibly that his priorities had shifted.

After reporting on the state of the company Goldman said, "I had Francisco and Kincaid spell out the word 'help' on the ground outside the courtyard wall. One of the pilots might see it and send in a chopper."

"You had what, Sergeant?"

"The word 'help.' We spelled it out on the ground. With sticks and stones and a can of white paint we found in the toolshed."

31

"Correctly, I trust."

"I wouldn't want my life to hang on an error in spelling, Captain."

Sterling tapped a paper on the desk with a stubby pencil. "I think we ought to keep some kind of record of what's happening here. In view of what may come later."

"Yes, sir."

"I don't mean to imply that you haven't been keeping the company roster up to date, Goldman. Or that it isn't accurate or complete—"

"It isn't, sir."

"Under the circumstances I wouldn't expect it to be." Sterling lit a cigarette. "Well, now we come to Ahearn. If we can take him with us—if he'll behave himself—do you think he will, Sam?"

"I thought we'd settled all this, Captain."

"So did I. Till I started thinking about it. From a military point of view. Can you handle Ahearn?"

"You mean if we take him with us?"

"Yes."

"If it was just the company—if we didn't have those women— sure. Why not?"

"You don't like to sit in judgment on your fellow man."

"I will if I have to, Captain."

"How did Ahearn look this morning?"

"Quiet."

"Dangerously quiet? In your opinion, Sam?"

"Just quiet."

"Just quiet. Sleeping volcano."

"The situation is this, Captain: once we start out with him, we can't use a gun on him if he acts up. Might draw a crowd. So someone will have to use a knife."

"You don't have to spell it out for me, Sam."

"In full view of the religious. Have you consulted them?"

"Not this morning, no. Should I have?"

"You think I'm shoving a little too hard, Captain?"

"Let's take it a step further. You're second-in-command here,

Sam. Should I—in your judgment—show marked incompetence—and it must be marked—you have my permission to relieve me."

"Supposing my judgment doesn't coincide with yours, Captain?"

"That's what makes the situation interesting enough for your attention, Sergeant. And for mine." Sterling tapped the paper on the desk. "To the best of my recollection—and I know very little about military regulations—not being a military man—I'm authorized to take emergency measures—of whatever degree—to maintain discipline in this company. What I don't know is how far I can go. Legally, according to regulations. Of course, if we were back with the regiment we could turn Ahearn over to the M.P.'s and let him stand trial. At a general court-martial. But we're not back with the regiment."

"You thinking of an investigation, Captain?"

"If I order Ahearn shot there'll be a hell of an investigation. Which might lead to a trial."

"Who'd know, Captain?"

"We're going to have to make out some kind of report on Ahearn, Sam. You just don't shoot a man and forget to include him. What's on your mind?"

"It could be staged."

"So that's how my rotten soul appears to you, is it? Because you think I shrink from killing a man in cold blood, after killing any number of them in hot blood, you imagine I'm asking you to provide me with a way out. Well, I'm not, Goldman. If necessary, I'll try, sentence, and execute Ahearn myself—in full view of the company and our habitual guests."

"I know that, sir. But let's divide the honors. You sentence and I'll shoot. If necessary."

"That's the key phrase, Sam—'if necessary.' My intuition warns me that to play soft with Ahearn is to invite things to go hard with us. I agree with you. The sensible thing is to go down into that cellar and shoot Ahearn in self-defense. Only I can't. Do you wish to overrule me?"

Goldman wondered whether that question concealed a cry for help or a challenge. And conceded quickly that he didn't know and that it wasn't important that he should know. Best to leave such irrelevant speculations to the birds. They'd convert them, with exactitude and no pain.

"Then let's try Ahearn, Captain. Give him a fair shake. You preside, I'll prosecute, and Plinnett can defend. You make notes on the trial, and after I write it up we'll both sign it. We might have Plinnett sign it, too. Only—"

"What?"

"Plinnett's third-in-command. It might be better to have one of the other men defend Ahearn."

"Who? Look, Sam, when this report goes to the Judge Advocate General's Office—if it gets that far—I want it to read like a real trial, not something rigged for our convenience."

"We'll get Bolton to defend Ahearn, Captain."

"Why not Lewis? He's pretty shrewd."

"Bolton's one smart bastard. Besides, he hates authority. He'll do."

"You know the men better than I do, Sam. Well, let's summon Sister Agnes and let her in on the good news. Lay down the law."

"Supposing she doesn't want to leave, Captain?"

"Good God, Sam, I've been kicking that idea around for hours. Have you a suggestion?"

"Maybe we better talk to Sister Esther. She has a better idea of what the score is. A Westchester County girl, Captain, right down the New Haven Railroad from you."

"That's interesting. Larchmont?"

"Rye."

"Buddy-buddy, Sam?"

"She asked me a few questions, Captain, so I asked her a few."

"She asked you a few, you asked her— Get her."

Goldman knocked at the inner door, which opened, after a moment, on Sister Esther. "The Captain'd like to talk to you, Sister. If you have the time."

"Wouldn't you prefer talking to Sister Agnes, Captain?"

"You'll do." Sterling motioned Sister Esther to a position in front of the desk. "Now, Sister, are you ready to leave?"

"Ten minutes, Captain?"

34

Sterling stared at Sister Esther, then leaned back in the chair. "No sweat, then."

"And Private Ahearn, Captain?"

"Ahearn is a military problem and will be dealt with on a military basis."

"If Private Ahearn stays, Captain, we stay."

"The hell you do," Goldman said.

"Will you call us when you're ready to leave, Captain?"

"Just a minute, Sister. It's a little late for you to retreat behind that convenient religious wall of yours. You're out in the open, Sister, with the rest of us."

"I beg your pardon, Captain. You're right, of course."

"Let's make it clear, Sister. I'm perfectly willing to consult with you as to a course of action, listen to your suggestions, bend to your whims. But when I give an order, Sister, I expect you and your sisters to obey that order. Not that I'm any wiser, but I bear the responsibility."

"Sister Agnes will give me my orders, Captain."

"That's better, Sister. Now you're back in character. But let me remind you that when we found you— When was it, Sam?"

"Roughly three weeks ago."

"Roughly three weeks. Three years, to be exact. Three hundred bleeding years. You were in sad shape, Sister. Physically."

"Spiritually as well, Captain."

"Something was said about there being twelve of you originally."

"There were."

"What shape are they in, Sister?"

"For us, Captain, death is the golden door to eternity."

"How golden is the door just this side of death? Let's not get too romantic, Sister. I can't believe you want to go through that again. Not if you have an out. Which I'm offering you."

"I pray next time to resist, Captain."

"Resist? What the hell is this? Resist?"

"Let it go, Captain," Goldman said. "They've got rules against getting too personal."

"I don't want to discuss this with you, Captain, but you force me to."

"He doesn't force you to do anything, Sister. Now bugger off. Go empty Petroni's bucket."

"Can't you realize that I'm guilty of so heinous a sin that it's doubtful whether I can be given absolution? Don't you know what it means to me to be shut off, even for a moment, from God? And stretch that moment, Captain, till it snaps into eternity . . ."

And there it was, Goldman thought, in its raw and lethal state, the soul on its voyage to an ultimate and infinite ground interrupted by the accident of life. Goldman had enough knowledge of the major religions to know that while the Catholics cherished their filthy, mutilated, simple-minded saints, bags of rotting organs, and eyeless sockets, they did not often advertise them out of the Faith. You saw, as he now saw over Sterling's head, the naked Jew nailed to his cross, the blood, the wound in the side, but how often, unless you attended the Catholic Church, did you see that? And when you did see it, abruptly, brutally, what could you do except turn from it?

"I've taken some pretty good beatings in my time, Sister," Sterling said, "but you really rout me."

"Perhaps you should have left us where you found us, Captain."

"How the hell could we have done a thing like that, Sister?" Goldman demanded. He felt he had to defend Sterling against an attack from which he knew he himself had no defense. By entrusting Goldman with a short biographical sketch, one which offered a wry and perhaps untrue analysis of his emotional states, Sterling had made a most attractive bid for Goldman's loyalty, one Goldman found impossible to reject. The trustee of a man's virtues is no post of honor, but the keeper of his sins— "If we could have gotten you on that chopper before Pat busted us—but we didn't—"

"The wounded had priority, Sam."

"Go ahead, make yourself a case. But don't plead it to me."

"I think the death of Private Koslow—so horrible, so unnecessary—"

Sterling grunted. "Koslow would have gotten it one way or

36

another, Sister. Ahearn's in his second year, and the worst he's gotten so far is what Goldman gave him. We're all due. Christ, we're overdue." Sterling shoved himself away from the desk and stood, quite visibly releasing tension in motion. "Resist. Just don't bring that up again, Sister, no matter what the provocation."

"Does that disturb you, Captain?"

"Self-flagellation, Sister. That's the name for it."

"Knock it off, Captain," Goldman said.

"That's it, isn't it, Sister? Accuse yourself of all kinds of filth and then lay on with the cat-o'-nine-tails?"

"Have you studied anatomy, Captain?"

"That's enough of that. You're not aiming for salvation, Sister, you're looking for thrills. Compared to you, Ahearn's a five-year-old. Temper tantrums and wet pants. You're dangerous. You ought to be locked up. With Ahearn. You'd really cream when he came at you with the one fixed idea of stamping you into the pavement, wouldn't you? The blood of the martyrs. I don't think so."

"If you don't like what I suggest, Captain, remember that you don't have to live with it."

"Don't—live—" Sterling leaned over the desk and spoke quietly and with—to Goldman—an enormous, an eerie, conviction. "I live with it, Sister. Twenty-four hours a day. So does Goldman, and Lewis, Plinnett. Ahearn couldn't live with it—so he blew."

"What does that get us, Captain?"

"Don't protect me from myself, Sam. Please."

"In a few days—maybe hours—we'll be out of this. Why press it?"

"Go ahead, Sam, shoot me. Then you can shoot Ahearn."

"I think what I'll do, I'll shoot myself. Listen, Captain, what Sister Esther's trying to tell you—and maybe you already know and maybe you don't—is that this isn't a simple case of rape."

"All right, Sister, you had a bad time. The enemy abused as well as raped you. Oriental style. It's horrible, but it happened. A screaming nightmare. I agree. A violation on two counts, secular and religious. In your place I'd be like Ahearn. Or worse. A moaning vegetable. But not you, Sister. You're strong, maybe too strong.

But don't give me this damned-for-all-eternity speech. It doesn't fit. And, more important, it gets in my way. As commander of this screwed-up expedition. It impedes me in the lawful performance of my duty. Suffer, Sister, if you must, but don't crucify yourself. That's too ambitious and has a bad effect on the company morale."

"You poor man," Sister Esther said.

Sterling sat heavily in the chair behind the desk. "Don't tell me anything more, Sister. I'd be obliged to you if you didn't."

CHAPTER VI

GOLDMAN DID NOT HEAR MASTERS calling from the bell tower; he heard Bolton, who had come into the entrance hall on the double, say, "Masters wants you up in the tower, Sarge. He thinks he's spotted something."

"Get Lewis in here, Bolton. I'll be up in the tower." He waited till Bolton went before saying, "You want to take a look, Captain?"

"Oh hell, yes," Sterling said. "I wouldn't like to fall too far behind the times. You'd better wait here, Sister. We may have news for you."

Sister Esther took a stocking, a darning egg, needle and thread from a pocket in the white habit and sat at the desk, her smooth expressionless face ("religious deadpan," Goldman called it) in provocative contrast to the crude-looking but skillful hands. You could see in the oval framed by the cowl that the mind was at prayer; the hands—raucous, sensual, humorous—were on the town. When she sensed Bolton in the entrance hall she said, "I have your jacket for you, Theodore."

"I'd appreciate it if you'd call me Bolton, Sister."

"But Theodore means God's gift, Bolton."

"Not in English, it doesn't. In English it means guys chasing you down the block yelling 'Yoo-hoo, yoo-hoo, Theodore!' But you wouldn't know about that, Sister."

"Perhaps not."

Bolton leaned against the wall just inside the reception room, where he could see both the library and the front door. The helmet appeared too bulky for his small, sleek, temple-sunken head. "You a doctor, Sister?"

"Just a nurse, Bolton. But I've had training in obstetrics. Midwifery, medieval as that sounds."

"You could deliver Sister Mary if you had to?" The hands, Bolton noticed, stopped moving briefly, then took up their action smoothly.

"Yes, I could. If there were no major complications."

"The reason I asked, Sister, is if we run into Pat any one of us might find himself in charge of this fouled-up unit. So we have to know what we can do, right?"

"I should think so, yes."

"That's not to say I expect Sterling, Goldman, and Plinnett to get theirs any time soon, but it never hurts to look ahead. You take Sterling, Sister. He's not a soldier, he never will be. It's Goldman runs this show."

"You dislike Captain Sterling, Bolton?"

"Me? I don't dislike anybody, Sister. You underestimate me if you think I waste time and energy feeling for people. All I want to do with a person is to know him."

"In the sense that knowledge is power?"

"When you know a person, Sister, you've got him in your pocket."

"Do you have me in your pocket, Bolton?"

"You're not human, Sister."

Sister Esther laughed, a small laugh, controlled but natural, and Bolton, having missed badly, said, "You're getting pretty chummy with Goldman, aren't you?"

"I like Sam. I also like you, Bolton."

39

"But I thought you weren't supposed to like anybody."

"What exactly are you probing for, Bolton?"

"How do you know so much about people, Sister?"

"How do you know I know so much about people?"

"Because you don't waste your time saying, 'You're an odd one, Bolton, what makes you the way you are?' You see what I am and you take it for granted."

"Your poor mother."

Bolton laughed. "If you were a man I'd be afraid of you. Like this Joe I was shooting craps with back at the base. I switched dice on him and he caught me. So I jumped him. That's the way to get the edge. Don't heat the guy up with an argument. Jump him while he's cold and he'll usually fold up. Only this Joe didn't fold. He decked me and just took his money and the loaded dice and walked away. Slow. Easy. I could have stuck a knife into him. Cut him up a little. But I didn't. I learned something from him."

"Not to cheat at dice?"

"I don't cheat, Sister. I just give myself an edge."

"With loaded dice?"

"This deal you got, Sister. You don't think the dice weren't loaded against you?"

"God wills, Bolton. We accept."

"Is that the way you felt when it happened to you?"

Sister Esther looked directly at Bolton, smiling. "To know what is, Bolton, is to know all there can be."

"Sure. How about a cigarette?"

"No, thank you."

"You sure threw a hook into Ahearn. You know you've already cost us at least six men. Seven."

"Cause of death—religious complications."

"Come on, Sister, what about those cribs in the back of that schoolhouse?"

"Our sleeping stalls?"

"Cribs, Sister."

"Yes."

40

"You don't like that word 'cribs,' do you, Sister? You know what it means?"

"The pig knows better than you, Bolton, the nature of a sty."

Up in the tower Sterling, having adjusted the binoculars, said to Masters, a tough but not too bright B.A.R. man, "Where?"

"Right where we came in, sir," Masters said. "Under those trees." He pointed to Goldman's observation post of the evening before.

"What?"

"Something moved, sir. I couldn't identify it, just something moved."

"Take a look, Sam."

Goldman took the glasses from Sterling, adjusted them, and moved them slowly over the entrance to the valley. In the glasses he could see the thin line of trees clearly and under them the stony ground that sloped gradually away to nothingness. For Pat it was no longer a matter of pursuit, but of search, of smashing strong-points and cleaning out pockets of resistance he had bypassed in his dash south. By avoiding the main roads and taking to higher ground Sterling and Goldman had not so much eluded Pat as selected a route he wasn't, at the moment, interested in. Undoubtedly, thousands of men, in small groups, were strung out like bubbles along the main stream of the attack, moving slowly and crookedly south, some perhaps without food and ammunition, carrying, where possible, their wounded; others well equipped but avoiding contact with Pat, now moving, now digging in, not knowing which of the farmers and villagers who watched their harmless migration so stolidly and incuriously would radio their position to Pat or suddenly come at them with grenades and automatic weapons.

Some men, Goldman knew, were being picked up by helicopters. Others were being used as bait by Pat to bring the helicopters within range of small-arms fire. They had passed several of the big birds smashed on the ground with their dead strapped inside them, and they had waved to several in the air but had gotten no response. Goldman assumed that the Army could not afford to risk

41

these valuable carriers in picking up stragglers when it had such priority missions to fly as reconnaissance and the evacuation of the wounded, but he could also (right from his guts) wish for one just large enough to transport his five nuns (and he would gladly include Sister Esther) forever out of his sight. For they reminded him, flatly, that he could not fight his own battle, plan his own survival, plot his own moves, die his own death, go quietly to his own hell. He had lost his unity as an individual, his value as a soldier, not because they were totally dependent on him, but because he was partially and unwillingly dependent on them. They had come like guests to the house where he served. After accepting his services with no show of gratitude and little thanks, they would leave. One is not obliged to a servant, one is obliged to one's host, and his host, in the house where he served, was a god he did not believe in. Fantastic? Of course.

"I don't see anything, Captain, but that doesn't say Pat isn't there."

"You wanted me?" Lewis asked from the top of the stairs.

Goldman, suppressing a twitch, heard Sterling's carbine bang against the masonry of the tower.

"Christ," Sterling said.

"Ten years' growth," Masters said. "You goddam Indian."

"Take the binocs," Goldman said. "Right where we came into the valley."

Lewis, after a quick look through the glasses, shrugged and said that if Pat was there he'd be coming. "You want me to, I'll go out and take a look, Sarge."

"The hell with it," Sterling said. "If Pat was in force he'd come. If it's a patrol we can take care of it."

"He can't see us anyway," Goldman said. "Not so long as we stay inside the courtyard. And when we pull out he won't be able to see us—if we keep directly behind the monastery—till we reach the southern end of the valley. Keep your eye peeled, Bob."

"I could sure relieve your mind in a hurry, Sarge," Lewis said.

"Not today, thanks." Sterling motioned to the stairs. "Let's get organized, Goldman."

42

Goldman was filling his canteen from the well in the courtyard when the plane, a jet, veered from its course to the east to fly directly over the monastery. By the time Goldman spotted it the plane was several miles out over the hills to the west making its turn south. Back to the officers' club with its air-conditioned bar and well-ventilated women, Scotch poured over ice cubes, cold beer, steaks, clean beds—Goldman smiled, recognizing that he had been mousetrapped by the man-on-the-ground's familiar gripe against the man-in-the-air. Maybe the plane, despite its swift passage across the valley, had seen the word "help" spelled out on the ground with branches, chunks of wood, rocks, glass, and pieces of cloth, the whole splashed with a can of white paint. Goldman's whimsey. As he watched, the plane turned and came down the length of the valley in a long sloping glide, towing like an invisible target its sound pattern of ruffled air.

Plinnett, who had slept most of the morning, came to the well to wash his face, saying that, by God, now, Sam, he spotted us, don't tell me he didn't.

"I think he did, Al. Maybe we ought to stay here for a couple of hours. What do you think?"

"How far are we going to get in a couple of hours?"

"Masters thought he saw something where we came in to the valley."

Plinnett shrugged. "We'll keep going till we're busted and that's it. And if you ask me, Sam, that won't be long. We taking Ahearn with us?"

"You want to make that decision for us, Al?"

"Hell, yes. He fucked Koslow and I don't give a goddam whether Koslow asked for it or not; you don't kill a man because you can't put up with his language."

"How do the others feel about it?"

"They feel the way I do, Sam."

"I ought to have seen this coming."

"How? You know the way out of this army, Sam. Feet first. I won't have to pay any undertaker's fees, just rev up a bulldozer." Plinnett yawned. "But—what the hell—the funniest thing—the last letter I got from my mother—Dear Alfred, Bobby's most grateful for your assistance, et cetera et cetera, but he needs extra money for a microscope. You know something, Sam? Did I ever tell you this?"

"Not that I remember, Al."

"I'm putting my older brother through medical school. On my salary."

"I'll be goddamned."

"Isn't that a pistol? Well, you know, not really, not the whole thing, but I'm helping."

"You fond of your brother, Al?"

"You out of your mind, Sam? He's a bigger pain in the ass than my other brother and, shit, he's the original pain. No, but he has a chance to make it, Sam, and if I can help, fine. He's supposed to pay me back, but I'll never see it. I asked this medic back at the base hospital how long it takes to be a surgeon. And he said twelve years, at least twelve. So what happens when I get back to the States? I'm a good mechanic—wood, engines, anything. Plumbing? Sure, I can plumb. Dear Alfred—and I'll bet the bastard won't even take care of my kids free of charge."

"That's pretty funny, Al."

"The funniest. Dear Alfred. My own mother, screwing me blind. Well, I got to get some breakfast. How's Sister Roberta?"

"Fine. Probably a touch of the trots. Our problem is Sister Mary."

"I'll carry her myself, Sam, that's no sweat. Anything else?"

"Keep an eye on Bolton, will you?"

"A pleasure. Care to tell me why?"

"He's not going to panic, Al, I don't mean that."

"The needle? I wish he'd give it to me, Sam. I'd bust him."

On his way back to the reception room Goldman spoke to Francisco, Kincaid, Schofield, and the others, sitting or lying in the sun against the courtyard wall, packs and rifles within easy reach, bored, sleepy, sunk within themselves, the reptilian torpor of the enlisted man between appointments, whether friendly or inimical. The talk with Plinnett had cheered him, steadied him. He did not need a consensus, but he could use a vote of confidence.

44

Hearing a much louder noise than the after-whistle of a jet or the bombing run beyond the hills to the east, Goldman looked up to see an American prop plane, the bomb slung under its fuselage, crossing the valley on the southeast-northwest diagonal. Missed his target, Goldman thought, or his release mechanism didn't work, or he prefers coming in at the back door. As he watched, fascinated by the slowness of the plane—it couldn't be making more than a hundred and fifty miles an hour—he saw it begin a leisurely clumsy turn out over the hills to the west, a turn that if extended would not bring him back on the southeast-northwest diagonal but on a direct south-north approach, the long axis of the valley. What the hell is he up to, Goldman thought. Is he in trouble or on Stupid Street? For it was clear now that the plane, banked in its turn, if it did not straighten out, would make an almost complete circle. Which would bring it directly over the southern entrance of the valley. Did the pilot intend dropping his bomb on the monastery? And why not?

"Down," he shouted to Francisco, who had gotten up to get a better look at the plane. "Get down—" And Goldman dived for the protection of the broad steps where they jutted out from the front of the monastery wall. When he heard the sound of the plane diminish and rise in pitch he ran to Francisco, who now lay on his back, his left arm almost ripped from his body by a bullet from one of the plane's fifty-caliber machine guns. Where was the bomb?

"He's had it," Plinnett said. "Tell the nuns the bastard's coming back."

"Get out behind the wall, Al. It's your best chance."

Goldman ran into the monastery, bumping into Sterling.

"Ours?" Sterling asked.

"Get the nuns in the cellar, Captain. He's got a bomb. I'll see if I can stop him."

Goldman ran through the library and climbed the circular stair to the bell tower, shouting for Masters.

"I'm all right," Masters said. "Jesus."

"We'll see if we can get him coming back." Goldman knelt at one of the slits on the north side of the tower. He could poke the barrel of the gun through the slit but not his arms, and though he could see the north end of the valley clearly, he had, more or less, tunnel vision.

"We got a prayer," Masters said.

"Just spray and pray, Bob. When you see the dust spurt from the ground, duck. You'll have time."

But the plane, coming at an angle to Goldman's restricted field of fire, was on and over them, giving Goldman and Masters time enough only to jerk their guns from the slits and flatten out. The bomb, probably a five-hundred-pounder, hit the ground some distance from the monastery and skipped into the base of the northern wall, a section of which rose at an angle and smashed against the building. The blast itself shook the stone building, cracking the mortar between stones, but did not cave in the walls. The top of the tower was blown off over Goldman's and Masters's heads, the bell flying in a strict mathematical arc (these slide-rule engineers) to land mouth down over Koslow's grave, the two of them, bronze tongue to jelly, in a profound and static communication.

Leaving a dazed and superficially bleeding Masters, Goldman stumbled down the stairs and took a short cut through the chapel to the nuns' quarters. A pillar of dust rose from the choir beyond the rood screen, lighted and activated by the sun shining through the glassless windows behind the altar. Broken and pulverized glass and stone, intact candles and wooden splinters, torn missals and pieces of cloth lay in the choir stalls and on the inlaid floor of the sanctuary, but the central images—the crucified Christ behind the rood screen, the Virgin in her niche on the gospel side of the nave, the patron saint—had not been damaged, an effect promulgating a hard core of the Church, impervious to accident and time, around which could be collected the temporal and the impermanent, the crutches of worship as well as the forms and the symbols, the clay of man but not his soul.

Seeing no one, Goldman went into the refectory, where Sister Roberta knelt beside Petroni's cot, on the north side, Goldman observed.

"All right?" Goldman asked.

Petroni, clearly in pain, held Sister Roberta's left hand tightly to his chest. "Ours, Sarge?"

"Sure."

"Good. Pat's bad enough as he is, but if he's going to get an air force—"

"I'll have Sister Esther give you morphine," Sister Roberta said.

"Save it." Petroni smiled. "For my old age. Thanks, Sister."

"If you'll let go of my hand I'll bring you a glass of water."

"No sweat, Sister." Petroni watched Sister Roberta glide from the room. "He didn't get Ahearn, did he, Sarge?"

"I doubt it, Angelo."

"Tough. Now you'll have to get him. Anybody else?"

"Francisco. I don't know about the others. I was up in the tower with Masters."

"When are we pulling out?"

"Pretty soon, Angelo. Do you think you can stand it?"

"Get off my ass, Sarge."

"You're the star, Angelo. If you stay, the sisters stay."

"From here that price don't look so good."

Hearing movement in the rooms around him, voices outside the building, Goldman lit a cigarette as deliberately as he could and put it to Petroni's lips.

"Thanks, Sarge. Well, you got work to do. Only—"

Sister Roberta re-entered the refectory with a cup of water. "Sister Esther will give you the morphine, Angelo. Then you can rest."

"I hope so. I'll see you later, Sarge. Later?"

"Right."

As Goldman expected, Sterling had not been able to persuade the other nuns to go to the cellar, perhaps, considering the limited time between the two attacks, a good thing. They had knelt on the north side of Sister Mary's cot, steadying both the cot and the patient.

"I checked at the cellar door," Sterling said as he and Goldman went into the courtyard. "Too goddam bad we couldn't have put

47

Ahearn up there." He pointed to the jagged gap in the north wall. "Like Humpty Dumpty."

Plinnett reported that he had sent Kincaid and Schofield to dig Francisco's grave. "Bled to death, sir. We couldn't stop it. Shit, like he had a pump in him."

"You'd better relieve Masters in the tower," Goldman said.

Plinnett looked up at the beheaded tower. "If that goddam barber'd taken a little more off the top I could've made sergeant."

"Not in my lifetime," Sterling said. "Tell Bolton I want to see him."

After a brief aimless inspection of the courtyard Sterling and Goldman went into the reception room. The naked figure of Jesus still hung on his cross; the Virgin Mother, however, appeared to have risen on tiptoe, as if leaning toward her son. Her head, the nose broken off, lay on the tiles at Goldman's feet. Picking it up, Goldman saw that the pin holding the head to the hollow body had snapped.

"Lost her head," Goldman said. "Not dependable in the clutch." He placed the head at the base of the pedestal, which, he saw now, was bolted to the floor. "Like Ahearn."

Bolton came to the reception-room door and half saluted, half waved. "Captain requested my presence, Sarge."

"You ever defended a human being, Bolton?" Goldman asked.

"From what?"

"A charge of murder," Sterling said.

"I don't want any part of that, sir."

"Do you believe Ahearn's entitled to a fair shake, Bolton?"

"Why ask me, Captain?"

"A real shithouse lawyer." Goldman looked at the door to the nuns' quarters. "We don't have much time, Bolton."

"If I'm the best Ahearn can get, he doesn't need me."

"Let's get Plinnett, Sam."

"Maybe you don't understand what we're driving at, Bolton. We want someone to plead Ahearn innocent."

"I respectfully request, sir, that I be released from performing this duty."

48

"Noted," Goldman said. "You're not volunteering."

"Ahearn's crazy, Captain, out of his bastard mind. This your idea, Goldman? You want to torture the poor guy? Stick pins in him? If you don't want to take him with us give him his gun and one clip and let him go. I'll volunteer to stay behind to see he doesn't shoot anybody in the back."

"Shall we take him up on that, Captain?"

"That's one solution, yes."

"I'll let you get two or three miles ahead and then I'll catch up."

"With Ahearn holding a gun on you?"

"I'll hide the clip, Sarge. Where he can find it. Later."

"And after Ahearn finds the clip he plays Santa Claus. Gives the sisters one bullet apiece. In the teeth. Or maybe he goes after them barehanded. The way he did with Koslow."

"You're not going to leave those nuns, Goldman. Not Sister Esther anyway."

"What can I do, Bolton? If Ahearn stays, they stay."

"You can't solve it, Goldman. So you shove it off on me."

"I shoved it, Bolton. And you took it."

Bolton laughed. "You sure did, Sarge. You're a real iceman, you son of a bitch."

"We can't have that, Bolton," Sterling said.

"What I mean is, he's my idol, Captain. Ahearn, he believes in that headless horsewoman over there. Me, I believe in the Sarge here. Now if he'll just take me out of his pocket I'll be happy to defend Ahearn."

CHAPTER VII

WHEN SISTER ESTHER LET GOLDMAN into the nuns' side of the monastery she said that Petroni had refused morphine and wanted his rifle. "He's in such pain, Sam. I don't think he's rational."

"How much more morphine do we have, Sister?"

"Four ampoules."

"Does he know this?"

"I think he does, Sam. The sick are great readers of the current situation. They're rarely fooled."

"You didn't say dying."

"He should be placed in a cast. Immobilized. Till we can get him to a hospital—"

"From your experience, Sister, do you think we could take Ahearn with us? He'd have to be quiet, obey orders. We couldn't let him have a gun."

"You'll have to, Sam."

"I've come up against this before, Sister. You see things one way, we see them another."

"Of course."

"Between us nobody is safe. You get them in the long run, we get them in the short. Let's make a deal. I'll try to see it your way if you'll try to see it mine. Agreed?"

"No, Sam."

"The ground you stand on is sacred, Sister. So you don't give an inch of it. Very good. But one last stupid question. A man, even the cruddiest, is entitled to a fair shake. Don't you think we're trying to give Ahearn a fair shake? Well, don't you?"

"You'd make a wonderful priest, Sam. You'd be such a comfort, such a joy—"

"Priest?" It was as if, out on patrol, approaching the enemy lines, a giant searchlight had been switched on, catching him with one foot off the ground, freezing him in a sitting-duck pose that Pat, that eminent sculptor, would change with just a touch of fifty-caliber pressure into a dead-duck attitude. Saul, Saul, why persecutest thou me? Turn in your circumcision, Goldman, we're sending you to the Apostles' Candidate School. "I'd better see to Petroni, Sister. Unless you want me to hear your confession."

"Self-mockery, Sam, is the most sinister form of prayer. Will you remember that, please?"

"Of course."

Going into the refectory, he asked Sister Roberta to leave him alone with Petroni.

"Please assure him we have plenty of morphine," Sister Roberta said.

"He told me that," Petroni said. "And I won't talk much, either, Sister. Be assured."

"Thank you."

Goldman sat on the stool by Petroni's cot and lit a cigarette, drawing at it, then holding it for Petroni.

"I'm a Catholic, Sarge. That's the hell of it."

"They take it, Angelo. Why can't you?"

"Listen, Ahearn didn't bust Koslow because he's a Catholic; he busted him because he couldn't take Koslow's needle. That isn't what bothers me."

"No?"

"I'm not all that helpless, Sarge. Look, I can move my legs. It hurts a little, but I can move them. It's only when I try to sit up."

"I think Sister Esther's planning to fix you a walking cast, Angelo. But what's the difference? We can carry you. What do you weigh, coming out of the shower, one thirty?"

"I always was a runt. Mentally, I'm no giant, either. Look, Sarge, move me out of here, will you? Out in the open. That shed in the courtyard. The tool shed. Just give me a bucket. I'll be all right, I'm not sick."

"What are you driving at, Angelo?"

"I don't like all this attention, Sarge. What am I, a crip?"

51

"Feeling sorry for yourself, Angelo?"

"You're goddam right I am. I'd rather go to hell with Koslow than meet St. Peter with—him. The son of a bitch. He's no Catholic, Goldman. Neither am I, when you come right down to it. It's the women in the family. My father used to spit on the porch whenever the priest left the house after a visit. 'Whenever I see a priest,' he'd say, 'I hear the devil walking.' He believed in the devil and he believed in God, but he didn't believe in priests."

"How about nuns?"

"He'd say give God the cripples and the plain ones. Every girl ought to have a husband. Let those that can't find a man sleep with God. Move me, will you?"

"What's this about wanting your rifle, Angelo?"

"Hm?"

"Sister Esther said you wanted your rifle."

"Sure. My canteen, too. And my pack. What the hell, you think I'm thinking of committing?"

"Not me, Angelo."

"That M-1, that's my old lady. That's jerk-off stuff. She's a cold bitch, not too many curves, but I like sleeping with her. Goddam it, Sarge, they tell you I'm slipping my pier? Well, don't jump to conclusions. It's just that I can't breathe in here. Too close—"

The isolation syndrome. Goldman had felt this himself, on leave, or detached from his outfit for special training. He had seen it, too, visiting his men in hospitals and saying good-bye to transfers and to those lucky few leaving the peninsula, as much in a man who had served his time as in medical washouts and hardship cases. What was happening out there? You lay and listened to it, apart, separated, and knew you had been handed the short straw. You couldn't wait to get out. And when you got out the slamming door was both the cleaver that severed the bloody stump of your inness and the hot iron that cauterized it.

"Hang on for a while," Goldman said. "We'll settle Ahearn and then we'll pull out."

Petroni shut his eyes. "You start moving me and I start screaming, and then what are you going to do, kiss my ass?"

"Take the shot, Angelo. The good needle."

"I'm always in to my friends, Sarge."

Goldman stood. "With your disability payments, Angelo, you can buy up Staten Island. I'll see you."

After he left Petroni he said to Sister Agnes and Sister Esther (and no goddamned argument) that he intended bringing up Ahearn and that he wanted the nuns to shut the doors to the hallway and stay out of sight. "You can understand that, can't you?" he said to a point between the two nuns. "We don't want to excite him. Unnecessarily." They had marvelous control of their facial muscles but they could not control the dilation and contraction of their pupils. Except that they could lower lids and lashes, and he could not, without excessive embarrassment, stare at them. A firm look and look away. Besides, he needed more light. How was it, despite the insufficiency of cowl and veil, that even in strong sunlight their faces were always partially in shadow?

"Leave Private Ahearn with us, Sergeant," Sister Agnes said. "We can take care of him."

"Your offer, duly noted, will be reported to the Captain, and given every consideration. Now please clear the hall." Goldman stared first at one, then at the other. "Don't push me, Sisters. I'll revert. Like Ahearn."

"Sam—"

"No Sam, just Sergeant Goldbrick." Sensing their indecision, he moved closer to Sister Esther, as if to engage her in private conversation. As he expected, she fell back a step. "Now you, Sister?" He turned toward Sister Agnes. Talking to them, chiding them, he forced them into the room where Sister Catherine, the tallest and gauntest of the nuns, sat with Sister Mary. After shutting them in he closed the door to the refectory and went into the cellar to bring up Ahearn. Slinging his gun over his left shoulder, he undid the chain and called to Ahearn. "Upstairs, Ahearn. The Captain wants to see you." He expected no trouble, feeling after the interview in the hall the momentum of success, and Ahearn, walking jerkily ahead of him, gave none.

Goldman did not particularly like Ahearn, nor did he feel,

pitting Ahearn against the departed Koslow, the instantaneous sympathy he would have felt—or ought to have felt—for a man in Ahearn's spot. Why? Ahearn had joined the company two weeks before the launching of the great attack from the seaport at the southeastern end of the peninsula. A Pious Peter and a loner, he had been assigned to Goldman's platoon as an ordinary rifleman. Outside of a tendency to freeze when ambushed or fired on from cover, he performed well enough. And he survived, an important talent, particularly during the offensive north, when Pat, alternately running and standing, bit off his harriers in small but telling chunks. Ahearn's piety in a company of agnostics, social Christians, and unlabeled believers drew the usual acidulous comments, the least of which was grandstanding, but in no way affected the efficiency of the unit. The prayer book, the scapulars, the rosary, the kneeling devotions, could be recognized as a man's crutches or lifeline and so honored, provided that Ahearn, unlike the tailless fox, didn't insist that everyone else adopt his condition. Then, too, why drive God—or any superpill—out of your corner when—who knew?—He might be able, all else failing, to pull you through this serious attack of mortality? God could take your personal skepticism, but an affirmative and outspoken mockery? Besides, having been bitten by a cobra, with no antitoxin available, would you refuse a native remedy for snakebite?

Ahearn had not been with Bolton and Plinnett, Goldman remembered, when they kicked open that schoolhouse door, expecting resistance, and found the five nuns sitting in a line along the wall to their left. Goldman, coming behind Plinnett to lend him the support of his automatic weapon, paused and stared (should he have removed his helmet?) before pointing to the door to the left of the blackboard, at an angle from the big desk on its dais, and telling Bolton to check it out. The nuns stood. "I'm Sister Agnes," one of them said. "On my left, Sister Esther, Sister Mary, Sister Catherine, Sister Roberta. Sister Esther, Sister Catherine, and I are registered nurses, Sergeant. We would be happy to help with your wounded." "What I want to know, Sister, is where Pat is. You

54

alone?" "We believe so, yes." "All right. Just stay here for the time being. If you hear shooting, hit the floor."

Outside the schoolhouse Bolton said, "You know what's back there, Sarge? Cribs!" "Please keep that information to yourself, Bolton. It's bad enough for us, but think of the Catholics." Ahearn and Petroni. Later, as Sterling questioned the nuns, Ahearn had come in to help set up the company switchboard. "Meadowlark to Firefly—Meadowlark to Firefly. Secured objective. No sign of Pat. Please advise. Will do. Over." Their orders were to secure the village and stay put. Baker and Dog Companies were moving up to dig in on their flanks. Colonel advised ammunition and supplies forwarded when available. The local picture, Sterling said later to Goldman, stank of success. Division, all the way back there, smelled a trap. The regiment, extended roughly over a mile front, could expect a counterattack. Division, engaged on its flanks, could spare only a single battalion in support. The regiment was to hold till position became untenable and then fall slowly back on supporting battalion. "In other words, Goldman," Sterling said, "Pat has us in classic position number one and is about to unsling his tool. I've requested transportation for the nuns. Should be here in the morning." None came, though the company did receive, at 0900 the next morning, two thousand rounds of thirty-caliber ammunition, a hundred grenades, two boxes of bazooka shells, forty rounds of eighty-one-millimeter mortar shells, for which they had no launcher, and two boxes of fifty-caliber bullets, for which they had no machine gun. And any number of boxes of C and K rations. Furnish your own water.

Seeing Ahearn's astonishment at the sight of the nuns (not that he remained unastonished himself), Goldman talked to him later outside the schoolhouse, giving Ahearn the poop without too much of the crust. "They're foreign missionaries," Goldman said. "Missionaries. They had a small hospital about eighty miles to the southeast. Pat's been using them to take care of his wounded. They're nurses, you know. We'll get them back to the regiment in the morning." "When were they captured?" "Not too long ago. They look a little thin but otherwise fine. Their home convent's in northern California. They run a hospital there, too." "They're probably Ursulines." "They didn't say, Jack." "You can tell by their headdresses." Ahearn said that he had attended a boarding school run by nuns of the Order of St. Vincent and that—and that— The words dribbled out of his mouth and lay, quite visibly, in spots of mucus on his lower lip. He's copping out, Goldman decided, on a cheap plea of—whatever it is—God-killing? Mother violation? But Ahearn had not copped out, not then or at any time during the three weeks' trek south. Beyond a moment of wanting to kill every organism in sight, beginning with Goldman, he had shown admirable control and disinterest.

Or had he? Obviously not. Except that Goldman, as close as he was to the men in the company, hadn't seen it, didn't know, couldn't observe for himself. Command. He moved in a circle of light, the law-giver; the men watched him from the semidarkness of the commanded, at the perimeter of light. They saw what he himself could be only half aware of; he saw what they wanted him to see. Even his intervention was solicited. Should he cry?

CHAPTER VIII

AHEARN SAT QUIETLY IN THE dark heavy chair near the headless statue of the Virgin, which, in the detachment of mind from senses, he may not have noticed. Sterling sat at the desk, flanked on the left by Bolton, who stood holding his rifle in his right hand, the barrel slanting toward the floor, and on his right by Goldman, who stood, feet apart, arms folded, staring at Ahearn. Corporal Plinnett leaned against the wall near the doorway, inside the room, but obviously taking no part in its ceremonies.

"Let's have no misunderstandings," Sterling said. "As commanding officer of this company I take full responsibility for assembling this court—if we can call it that—and for whatever happens while it's in session. You all know what we're faced with. Technically, we're trying a man for murder. I will act as judge, Sergeant Goldman as prosecutor, Private First Class Bolton as counsel for the defense. Should I, as presiding judge, find this man guilty as charged, I will pass appropriate sentence and adjourn the court. A very simple procedure. Except that after sentence, what?" Sterling turned to Plinnett. "You understand what we're trying to do here, Corporal?"

"No, sir. Not exactly, sir."

"Not exactly. Tell him, Sergeant."

"Ahearn is under arrest, Al. For clobbering Koslow."

"I can see that, Sam."

"If we can—no matter what the Captain's verdict—we take him back with us and turn him over to the M.P.'s. If we're still alive we'll have to testify at his court-martial. Ahearn will be represented by an officer appointed by the court to defend him. Someone with a legal background, if he can be gotten. But no dimwit."

"You understand that, Plinnett?"

"Yes, sir."

"Proceed, Sergeant."

"But we may not be able to get Ahearn back to the regiment. He might—for security's sake—have to be dealt with here and now. So what we want is a kind of guideline on how to treat him. Plain enough?"

"If you ask me, Sam, this shit is for the birds."

"By God now," Sterling said. "We have a declaration. I didn't think you'd stick your neck out that far, Plinnett. Bucking for another stripe?" Plinnett shrugged. "You came out, looked around, decided you didn't like the air, and ducked back in again. What do you call home, Plinnett, a hole in the ground?"

"I respectfully suggest that the Captain has no right to accuse me of minding my own business, sir."

"Have I the right to shoot you, Plinnett?"

"Only for extreme dereliction of duty, sir, and only under circumstances that would clearly endanger the safety of the company. Like I'd go berserk under attack and start shooting my own men." Plinnett's face returned from the blankness of memorization to the vividness of participation.

"Killing your own men, Plinnett. Wouldn't I have to wait till you actually shot someone before ordering you shot?"

"That's up to you, sir. You're in command here."

"I beg of you, Plinnett, to remember I have five nuns in there who very clearly point out how limited my command is. Surely you can see that, Plinnett."

"Yes, sir."

"Then take it a step further, Plinnett. Do you want to see these nuns brought safely back to the regiment?"

"Yes, sir. I do."

"Dead or alive?"

"You can't—" Plinnett looked at Goldman, a clear call for help in relieving an officer of his command, perhaps only the first suggestion that he should be relieved of his command.

"Are you questioning my competence, Plinnett?" A shrug. "You have the right, Plinnett."

"In a pig's ass, I do. Sorry, sir. I respectfully request—"

"Get the hell out of here, Plinnett. Or no, no. You're third-in-command here, in the chain of command. Share the responsibility. Now, Sergeant, state the case against Ahearn."

"Murder, sir. We've got ten, fifteen people who saw Ahearn clobber Koslow."

"Self-defense," Bolton said.

Sterling twisted in the chair to stare at Bolton as if not quite attuned to this voice from his left. "Go ahead, Bolton."

"Ahearn's a good Catholic, sir. You all saw him with his beads and his prayer book. And those things he wears around his neck."

"Scapulars," Sterling said.

58

"Finding these women, these nuns, the way they were was a hell of a jolt. It shook me up. And you, sir. And Goldman. And you know Goldman doesn't shake up that easily."

"The way they were isn't very exact, Bolton," Goldman said.

"Ahearn knew, Sarge. He could see it in Sister Mary."

"Maybe he didn't. He wouldn't want to see it unless someone called it to his attention."

"Koslow. Otherwise why did Ahearn clobber him?"

"Supposing we ask Ahearn," Sterling said.

"You can't force him to testify against himself," Bolton said.

"I'll be goddamned."

"You want me to defend him, Sarge. Well, I'm defending him."

"Unexpectedly ably, Bolton," Sterling said. "Is this procedure all right with you, Plinnett?"

"You're handling it, Captain."

"A dissent at this point in the proceedings might look very good on the record, Plinnett. As you can see, I'm taking a few notes. Which I might ask you to initial."

"If we don't get moving there won't be any record, sir."

"There I agree. Bolton?"

"As I say, this business shook us up, but what do you think it did to Ahearn here? Raised by nuns, taught by nuns. The three R's. And the fourth R, religion. The brides of Christ, he called them. That right, Plinnett?"

Plinnett smiled, thinking what he thought but not yet ready to express it. In a company where humor sprang from the recollection of old jokes and common experiences, where bigger pratfalls produced bigger laughs, Plinnett passed for a wit. Like most humorists, however, he had a real sense of his situation at any given time and a silver-plated regard for his dignity. Pride, Goldman thought, watching him, not a pride that forced him into violent actions in defense of his interests and beliefs but one that compelled him to do the job a little better than it had been done, a little better than it could be done. Next to Lewis, who could behead a chicken at three hundred yards, the best shot in the company, Plinnett often volunteered for missions where he could demonstrate his skill with

59

a rifle, and also, Goldman thought, his reliance on it. Yet under this pride, perhaps the base of it, Goldman remembered, a hard-rock integrity that would not permit him to cheat you, either at cards or under fire.

Satisfied by his quick assessment of Plinnett, Goldman turned his attention to Bolton. In the action to come, the question of survival had to be asked beforehand, and if Sterling and Goldman opted for nonsurvival the five nuns would have their leader in Plinnett. Furthermore, he could handle Bolton, an important consideration.

"Koslow's a good head, Captain," Bolton said. "Was. If you went out with him you'd know he wouldn't panic or shoot you in the back or steal your last clean pair of socks. But you heard him, both of you. We all did. The needle. At first so sharp and so gentle Ahearn didn't realize it was the needle. I know something about touching people. Koslow was a master. He set up Ahearn here little by little and then one day, when he figured the mark was ready, he let him have it. Socked it to him, Captain. The jagged oar. And Ahearn did what you and I and Goldman would do. Went after Koslow. And he got him. Busted him up. Made himself a little Polack sausage. With his hands. No steel, just the mitts. And I say Ahearn was right. I mean more than right, justified. I liked Koslow, but this time he stepped out of bounds. Crossed over where no man has a right to cross. Outside the law. Self-defense, Captain. A man that wouldn't defend what Ahearn was defending—you'd call it his honor, I'd call it his difference—that man is no man. And any law that doesn't recognize a man's right to defend his difference—the thing that makes him himself and nobody else—isn't worth keeping. I say Ahearn acted in self-defense—just as if Koslow'd come after him with a gun or a knife. And if Ahearn hadn't acted he'd be admitting he hasn't anything to defend. That's it, Captain. That's the best I can do for Ahearn—or for anyone. It's what I'd like somebody to say for me—if I was in Ahearn's spot."

Goldman wanted to jump in on Bolton's argument (Jesus, you thought you knew a man and then you knew you didn't), but decided to let the silence hang—till it collapsed on Sterling like a tent, suffocating him. He's let it go too far, Goldman thought, allowed it to cool off, permitted the devil's advocate to insert the evidence against the candidate for beatification (Koslow) into the record. O villain, villain— As Sister Esther had said, in one of her little talks, the job of the devil's advocate (what was the term, Promoter of the Faith?) wasn't to praise the projected martyr or saint but to vilify him, to plead the devil's claim to the person, not God's. Goldman had a glimpse, abrupt and incomplete but searingly intense, of the kind of open furnace these nuns inhabited, where comfort and safety destroyed the soul, where slave labor and danger purified it. And could, in excess, also destroy it. Reason only fogged the lenses through which you viewed such things; faith began but could not complete comprehension.

Sterling, clearly recognizing the necessity for a rebuttal to Bolton's plea but also discounting it before it could be offered, made a little ceremony of lighting a cigarette—cupping his hands around the match, drawing a great draft of smoke into his lungs. "Well, Sergeant?"

"The charge is murder," Goldman said. "Mental cruelty may be good grounds for divorce but it's no justification for homicide."

"I could have mentioned temporary insanity," Bolton said. "That's probably what Ahearn's lawyer would plead. At the court-martial. Look at him, Captain. Would you say Ahearn is in his right mind?"

"He's got to be, Bolton." Sterling leaned back in his chair, as if backing away from the awful reality of the hulk across the room. "That's the hell of it."

"Why don't you push it further?" Goldman said. "Take a hypothetical case. A man is convicted of a crime he didn't commit—a murder—and sent to prison. While in prison he accidentally—or on purpose—kills a guard. Then his innocence is established. Someone else—usually an ex-convict—confesses to the murder. What do you do with the man in prison?"

"Sam—Sam—"

"Would Ahearn have killed Koslow if it hadn't been for those nuns in there? Did he hire out when he took the oath of service as an escort to a religious group? You know goddam well he didn't, Captain."

"Don't overstep yourself, Goldman."

"We went too far with it, Captain. You and I—we overstepped ourselves. That's the hell of it, nothing else. We should have shot the bastard out of hand. I should have killed him when he grabbed Koslow. Now we can't."

"All right, we'll turn him loose. Bolton's idea—"

"Jesus Christ," Plinnett said.

"That will cost you your stripes, Plinnett."

"How about Goldman, Captain? You going to break him? Or do you figure you can't make it without him?"

Sterling looked steadily at Plinnett, seeing him, adjusting himself perhaps to a newer reality. "I beg your pardon, Corporal. You have a right to disagree—under the rules of this inquiry. You earned those stripes. Please keep them."

"I didn't mean—" Plinnett looked at Goldman.

"Now you realize it, Al. We're operating according to their rules, not ours. They don't want us to shoot a man, we don't shoot him. Not that I want to, either, but I don't like this power taken away from me. Hobbles a man. Handcuffs him."

"Look, Sarge—" Plinnett paused, aware of the staggering complexity and imbecility of the idea he was trying to express. Like a man walking around a strange object he had volunteered to lift, in search of a handle. "Look, he can't hold us up—no one man has the—" It isn't evil that corrupts a man, but knowledge of the possibility of good, of the intervention of a higher force as a stable, indestructible element capable of changing a person's character or situation while itself remaining totally resistant to change. No man had the right to endanger others, especially one under restraint for the commission of that most human of crimes, an unnecessary, a sporting kill. From its airless crypt, Goldman thought, the dead hand of God was laid on Plinnett's shoulder, the smell of its rotten fingers rising through the nostrils to stupefy the brain, the god of the white birds across the hall in yet another criminal revival—the odor of sanctity, decay.

62

"He seems pretty quiet," Sterling said. "What do you think, Sam?"

"If I were in my right mind, Captain, I'd say shoot him."

"Plinnett?"

"I'll go along with Goldman."

"Not me," Bolton said. "I've got a stake in Ahearn. I defended him."

"The thing is, Bolton," Goldman said, "those nuns in there aren't going to abandon Ahearn. Not alive. Our only hope of getting them out of here is to take Ahearn along with us. Or maybe you're in favor of leaving the nuns."

"They'll come, Sarge. If we get tough with them."

"If you stay with Ahearn, Bolton, you either abandon these nuns to Pat or you—" It was Goldman's turn to light a cigarette.

"A bullet in the back of the head?" Bolton considered this, possibly from a viewpoint strange to him, outside his dense and implacable self, as in his attempt to touch and maul the suffering core of Sister Esther, which he knew existed but which she refused to acknowledge. In a sense, humiliation by a pride greater than his own because it depended on (or dangled from) an outside agent. "Maybe I could do it and maybe I couldn't. But I'd have to know there'd be no investigation."

"In other words, you're crapping out," Goldman said.

"If I was, I wouldn't be telling you about it, Sarge."

Goldman dropped his cigarette and put his heel on it. The air in that icon-heavy, being-crowded, will-studded room had become thicker, moister, riper, with an underbase of T.N.T., burnt steel, and heated dust, a smell not of battle but of casualties, evacuation, and cleanup squads. To rest is to lose your edge, to fall apart, to disintegrate. In a little more than twelve hours, Goldman thought (and he could feel his guts arching like the back of a frightened cat), the company had been bitten and infected by that deadliest of military viruses, the fortress mentality. They should have by-passed the monastery, recognizing it not as a halfway house but as a tomb. Outside in the courtyard the remaining enlisted men, the tough fire-hardened core of the company, lay in the sun like civilians

63

on a beach, their mission suspended, their purpose dulled, their reactions no longer predictable; at least not predictable enough for intelligent planning, even such simple planning as would be needed for the march south, which had, for an objective, either contact with the regiment or hostilities with Pat.

The plane, for example. The pilot, even under the necessity of carrying out a secondary mission on his own after having aborted the planned one, would never have machine-gunned or bombed them in the open, not with the time he had for identifying and selecting a secondary target, not flying freely with no expectation of effective fire from the ground. From the air the monastery probably looked like an ideal post for army or corps headquarters. Under questioning the pilot would remember that he had seen no vehicles moving in or out of the valley or parked in the courtyard outside the gates. And he would recall no particular activity except a single figure in green or black waving at him as he started to pull out of his long shallow dive to begin the slow bank for the return run. Undoubtedly the pilot, low on gas, unable to land with the bomb half released under the fuselage, had been just as bemused and enchanted by the monastery as Sterling and Goldman had been. The seduction of refuge—for the company a realignment of its snarled personal relations, for the pilot the safety of his plane and compensation for an aborted mission. And the pilot in the debriefing room, under the cool prodding of nonflying intelligence officers, and Goldman in the monastery, under the sting of reason, would share the same dismal disenchantment.

"The hell with it," Goldman said, unsure of the nature of his consignment but powerfully relieved by its dispatch. "Let's see how far gone Ahearn is."

"Let him alone, Sarge," Bolton said. "He's out of it. All we have to decide is what to do with him."

Goldman crossed to Ahearn. "Ahearn? Now listen, Jack, we're pulling out and you're coming with us, understand? No sweat, no crap." More roughly than he intended, Goldman touched Ahearn's arm, and Ahearn, reacting with an unexpected and irresistible quickness, sprang out of the chair to grapple with him. Bolton's hand jerked the barrel of his rifle up, his index finger closing against the trigger. Goldman appeared to consummate his embrace of Ahearn with one convulsive lunge and muscle-locked quiver before sliding slowly down Ahearn's body to the floor. The barrel of Bolton's rifle issuing its smell of gunpowder was like a profane thurible being swung, in benediction, over the prostrate Goldman.

Sterling rose slowly and leaned across the desk, staring at Ahearn, who had backed toward the statue of the Virgin, then at Goldman. In falling, Goldman had turned his body away from Ahearn's feet, so that he lay now on his back, arms at his sides, legs slightly apart. His eyes were shut, though not squeezed shut. It was apparent that the heart, if not stopped, had been greatly arrested, the bullet having entered the back under the shoulder blade at perhaps an angle of thirty degrees and torn through the heart to exit from the bloody hole near the right breast pocket of the fatigue jacket, and so missing Ahearn. How could it have happened? Ahearn, jostled from his stupor by Goldman's hand on his arm, had come suddenly and powerfully to his feet, and Bolton, the rifle held under his right arm, finger on trigger—after all, it had been established that Ahearn was dangerous—had jerked the barrel of the rifle up and fired, a purely reflex action, perfect in its simplicity and execution. That was it, wasn't it?

"It was an accident," Bolton said. And his voice was not that of a bell, but of the wooden clapper used at the Masses during Lent. "You saw it, Captain. Plinnett?"

Sister Esther came into the room quietly and crossed to kneel by Goldman. With one hand on his pulse she used the other to push back his eyelids so that she might stare, in a profound and ungrieving fixity, at his dilated pupils.

"How badly—how badly—is he hurt?" Sterling asked.

"He's dying," Sister Esther said. "Clinically, he's dead."

"Come on, come on, come on, come—" Sterling stooped to pull at her arm. "Get your instruments. We'll probably need blood. His blood type's on his dog tags." Sterling pulled Sister Esther to her feet and screamed at her. "Go get your goddamned instruments. Get Sister Agnes—get—you're nurses, aren't you? What do you want? You want to sterilize—boil some water, Plinnett, boil—"

"He's dead, Captain."

"No. Not till you people have done what you can for him. Give me a hand, Plinnett. We'll put him up on the desk. We'll—"

But it was clear to Sterling, kneeling beside Goldman, very clear, that no amount of medical aid, in quantity or quality, would help the big sergeant. Stretched out on the floor he was enormous, extending from the headless Virgin, before which Ahearn now crouched, to Sister Esther's feet, a distance so incomprehensible that the eye, marbled by finity, veined and hooded by mortality, could not begin to measure it, a distance that accelerated from the familiar inch to the mile to the parsec—

"One shot," Bolton said. "One—"

"Birds of death," Sterling said. "How many more of us before you're finished? You want us all? What's your limit, ten? A hundred? A thousand?" He became aware of his hand on Goldman's wrist, of the heavy lifeless flesh pressed against his palm. Standing, he said, "All right, Plinnett. Get a couple of men. Lewis, Francisco—"

"Not Francisco, Captain."

"Schofield then. Anyone. And you, Bolton." Sterling pointed to the crouching Ahearn. "He's yours. You earned him. Take him. We're leaving, Sister. Nothing to hold us back now, is there?"

"Captain—"

"That's two litter cases—Petroni and Sister Mary. We'll have one of the men fill your canteens at the well—" Sterling put a hand on the desk, not so much to steady himself as to feel his way back to the old order. They had closed off both ends, now they were coming at him through the middle. "Get moving, Sister. Maybe if we do something—"

"We can't leave, Captain. Sister Mary—" Sister Esther's hands sketched the medical situation briefly in the air. "It will be a difficult birth, Captain. The shock of the bombing—" Sister Esther obviously hoped Sterling would need no further explanation, seeing

66

immediately that he would. "To save the child, Captain, we may have to—destroy the mother."

Sterling hit her across the face with his open hand, knocking her against the door, a gesture of obliteration. Neither one of them heard the helicopter coming toward the monastery from the southern end of the valley, nor could they see Lewis, who, unlike Francisco, could divine (or smell) the scope of the machine's mission, waving a suspicious and highly reluctant pilot and crew into an immediate landing. But like a bird scared off its glide to its nest by an intrusive ornithologist, the helicopter skittered up and to the west in a flutter of blades, assaulting the indignant air, and Lewis, hand-shielding his eyes from the blast of its departure, yelled to Plinnett to get Sister Esther out of the monastery and courtyard as a final lure. The sergeants manning the two machine guns in the open side doors of the jittery bird might have seen the armed man in the topped tower or the rifles of the men in the courtyard and demanded a more cautious approach, or the pilot, who knew the vulnerability of his thin-skinned craft to small-arms fire, might have decided to pull up and talk things over. True, in his approach he had not drawn fire, but in the peninsula, as he well knew, against a tricky and resourceful enemy, caution first, boldness later.

Inside the reception room of the monastery Sterling said, "You let—you let—" but even as he tried to phrase this terminal barbarism, to give it verbal form, to make the magic phrase that would serve now as a cranial opiate and later as a mode of forgiveness, he saw, as Goldman had seen, the infernal floor on which Sister Esther stood and felt, through his open mouth, through the receptive grid of his skin, the terms that defined the equilibrium of the soul and the alternatives that it must choose from.

You may spit safely, even necessarily, in the face of God and only clarify and emphasize His generosity, but in the presence of His alter ego, the Prince of Darkness, you must invoke the image of His suffering and thereby underline and accept your nothingness. Sterling could realize, even in shock, that he had lost not so much direction as momentum. Abandoning the reception room and, in a sense, the remnants of his company and the five nuns, he walked out into the courtyard, where he became aware, imperceptibly and incompletely, of the reluctant helicopter. As he watched it, accepting its presence, recognizing its mission, he wished bitterly that it would crash or that he could order it shot down. He had never felt such hate for the enemy. But then, he did not know the enemy, would never know him, did not care to know him. He knew his countrymen, though. Great God, how he knew them.

The Church

CHAPTER IX

ONE MAY NOT SUSPECT the Holy Father of intrigue or manipulation, Ottavio Cardinal Bellini reminded himself, but one may properly wonder whether, from the huge masses of processed information which he receives in the chair of fallibility, he can always select the winning option. The flat dry voice, the desiccated hands, the coolly terraced face revealed very little of the intellect that operated, at all times, at heights few had climbed and in atmospheres chillier than most. One could not say his Holiness lacked warmth; one could say only that he did not radiate warmth. But then, can a man elected to personify the Church as Christ's Vicar be asked to heat it?

Now talking, selecting just those words that would express precisely what he wanted done (and would convey possibly what he expected Ottavio Cardinal Bellini to do), his Holiness released, consciously or not, a most delicate and perishable anxiety, perhaps a saintly anxiety, well grounded in the spirit but in the corridors of the flesh a passenger pigeon.

"Were it a simple question of violation," his Holiness said, "the affair of these five poor nursing sisters could be relegated to the mercies of prayer."

"As it is, Holiness, we must depend on the mercies of the flesh."

"Your Eminence is perhaps less disturbed by the agonies of these nuns than we are."

"I'm more disturbed by their frustrations, Holiness."

"You see it as an administrative matter."

"In a word, yes. Your Holiness in calling this affair to my attention must remember that there are other departments of the Church better equipped to dole out sympathy than mine is."

"You have always had a bitter way of jumping at the truth, Ottavio, as if you intended strangling it—" The remembrance of

71

a strong boyhood friendship, of youthful studies shared, and of an honest respect for differing but undeniable talents had apparently moved (or checked) the saintly Pope, throwing him back from the universal to the provincial, from all peaks to his local street, a supposition that might well push the gullible into thinking that he was either a genuinely simple man (despite his half-dozen earned academic degrees and wide diplomatic experience) or the artfullest of dodgers. Ottavio Cardinal Bellini knew his man too well to split him between such stale alternatives. And he had, further, a breath-takingly naïve belief in the chair the man occupied, a chair in which an aging cardinal, through a series of ballots cast by electors as corrupt and divisive in such matters as any lay parliament, became the true successor to St. Peter, the original Bishop of Rome and the rock on which Christ founded His temporal dynasty. What more fertile soil for the lily of Rome than the rich guts of the College of Cardinals? For that was the only miracle—the production of a few critical and imperishable ashes from the combustible materials of flesh and bone.

"But you must not transform our rightful concern for these suppurating children into a suspicion of their spiritual integrity."

No, of course not. "I shall, with your Holiness's consent, conduct a discreet but thorough and, needless to say, sympathetic investigation of these nuns' ordeal. Twelve nuns were captured by the pagan, five survived his—activities. We cannot deny the other seven the possibility of martyrdom."

"Nor can we afford the ambiguities of an international scandal."

"But, Holiness, these women are American citizens first, and only secondly the faithful daughters of the Church."

"We have been reliably informed—through our delegation in Washington—that no action will be taken by the State Department in either the political or the civil zone."

"Is the rape of a nun no longer news, your Holiness? Are we to suppose that newspaper correspondents of such secular countries as England, Scandinavia, Australia, and the United States of America itself will suppress, voluntarily, a scandal of this order? By the ghost of Daguerre, no photographs?"

"Fortunately, none." The Pope might have been Hamlet palpating Yorick's skull. "Your famous collection of the illustrated sins of mankind must remain incomplete, Ottavio."

"I do not bait your Holiness's anxiety; I share it. At its most critical level. But as Prefect of the Sacred Congregation of Rites I must hold to an iron dissent. If we are to accept the martyrdom of seven, we may have to establish and accept the degradation of five. Holiness, there is no other course."

The Pope stood, bringing the Cardinal to his feet, a piece of business noted and filed by the observant Cardinal, who had to use a cane to support a bad foot. Gout. Not the disease to draw the sympathies of an ascetic Pope.

"We specifically forbid you to conduct an inquisition, Eminence. We are truly grieved by the unique sufferings of these poor sisters and wish only to support and comfort them in the bitter hours of their enforced debasement. We see them exalted in their trial, not cast into darkness by it. If we must choose between serving the letter of truth and its spirit, we emphatically select the latter. As you most certainly shall, Eminence."

"Of course, Holiness."

In preventing the Cardinal from bowing himself too humbly from his presence his Holiness tapped him briskly on the shoulder, a reassurance as well as a warning, and a salute from one old campaigner to another. His Eminence Ottavio Cardinal Bellini, the wriest of sentimentalists, welcomed the little tap as he might welcome another cope of barbed chains or a biretta with an inner lining of thorns, but he drew from it also the implication that while hands were certainly being wrung they were even more certainly being washed.

At home in his palace, a walled villa on the outskirts of Rome, Ottavio Cardinal Bellini rang for his at-home secretary, Monsignor Luigi Cinotti, and asked for the Alpha file, a list of the bright young dynamic foreign priests imported by the Vatican from the various countries of the world, given special training, assigned posts in this department or that, and, whether retained in Rome or sent back home, watched for those signs of boldness and intransigence that often mark the coming man. For the Church, having forbidden its clergy to reseed itself, could not suffer from the plague of nepotism, only from the chronic itch of preferment. From the Cardinal's study, really a suite (a canny cardinal never left himself too far from a bathroom), French doors opened onto a terrace with a southeastern exposure. From the terrace a flight of broad shallow steps inclined to a small garden, nothing distinctive, simply a place to walk.

Although the Cardinal sometimes received his more eminent guests on his front porch, he more often received them at the rear entrance of his salon, which could be reached by car from the street and which, while not grand, at least offered the comfort of a small piazza defended by only three shallow steps. For the great double doors at the front of the palace could be penetrated only after a climb of thirty-seven steps, useful for the cooling off of hot monsignors and delegations from Milan and America but a death march for his peers.

Sitting in his study in the late afternoon with the Alpha list before him, having checked the evening appointments with Monsignor Cinotti, the Cardinal exiled the interview with the Holy Father from his mind and considered the names on his list— Anderson, Aoyama (no, an Asian would not do), Becker, Cartin— he hesitated at Milanowski, then back to Laforge—yes, Kramer, Thomas Paul. Age thirty-seven. Born in Altoona, Pennsylvania. Local high school. All-state end. End? University of Notre Dame. Ah, football. Adjusting his reading glasses, the Cardinal skimmed the report for its relevancy to his needs. Fluent in five modern languages, Latin and Greek excellent. Studies in Bible, particularly the Old Testament. Excusable. We cannot let the Protestant scholars take complete possession of the Bible. Pastorates? Curacies in New Orleans and Albuquerque, New Mexico. Recommended for further studies in Rome by Michael Cardinal Brooker. Brooker, the famous American liberal. What would an American pope be like? Slap his cardinals on the back and offer them cigars and whiskey. Poker in the Vatican. Touch football with orphans in Vatican gardens. No, really. An excellent man, Brooker. Progressive, social reform, impatient of ceremony. Recommended Kramer. Another big athletic American? Returning to the report, the Cardinal saw that Kramer had suffered a deep concussion at the end of his sophomore year, relieving him permanently of any value to the Notre Dame coaching staff. Interesting. Entered seminary the following fall. Monsignor Thomas Paul Kramer.

With a foreigner, specifically an American, as a backup man, the Cardinal selected five more names from the Alpha list, and during the next week, by devious and sometimes indelicate methods, eliminated them. Laforge? A scholar. Lots of platinum, no steel. Schreiber? All steel. Anderson? A brilliant neurotic and, in Ottavio Cardinal Bellini's opinion, a coming alcoholic. The Frenchman Cartin? A corkscrew Jesuit who would pull many a cork from bottles no longer on the Church's shelf. The Cardinal had not ruled out the Italians, he had suspended them, on the grounds that few Italians under fifty knew anything of the female psyche. They pinched without feeling, they talked without probing, and, without using their excellent noses, divided women into sheep on the one hand and goats on the other. The Cardinal liked, appreciated, and courted beautiful, cultured, witty women, but only in his salon or theirs. In more than fifty years no woman had put her hand on the Cardinal's heavy crotch, although a few, despite the glowing red light, had managed the knee, and none would. He was not a womanizer; his sin was gluttony.

And Kramer? What was his weakness? Women, alcohol, gambling, food, homosexuality, hysteria? Was he a toady, a bully, an esthete, a bird watcher, a gossip, an old woman? Well, apart from body and soul, a man consisted of two things—his work and the opinions of his colleagues and superiors. The Cardinal could ignore the opinions of Kramer's superiors just as he could omit soliciting the opinions of Kramer's colleagues. But the man's work —that was the man himself, naked and unswerving. The Cardinal read several reports Kramer had made on the martyring of certain Belgian priests and nuns by certain savages in the Congo. The reports were routine, that is, of a level of excellence expected of men marked for preferment by the Church. At the end of one report Kramer had written, "There is in those who seek to help others a consistent disregard for duly established authority, whether that authority be secular or religious. This disregard for authority does not seem to consist of simple disobedience—or even of complex or unconscious disobedience—but of an overpowering need to goad leaders and superiors to punitive action by a most provocative and outrageous self-centeredness. Sometimes this self-centeredness leads to the sublime. More often it hurls its possessor toward the pit." Was Kramer describing himself? And, if so, to what degree? Time, the Cardinal decided, for an interview.

The Cardinal could not have said, when he received Kramer in his study two weeks after the interview with the Pope, why he had known Kramer would refuse sherry, tobacco in any form, and take only lemon in his tea. Tall, gaunt, strong-jawed, with thick wavy hair and the bluest of blue eyes, Kramer, in the Cardinal's opinion, looked more like a Bible-thumper than a burly intellectual. A cross-burner? With an impatience that surprised him the Cardinal asked Kramer what he had learned from his researches into the African atrocities. "Beyond the lesson that no foreigner is safe in the vortex of a country's nationalism."

"Every victim of murder must co-operate with his killer, your Eminence."

"Seduce him, Monsignor?"

"At least place himself within the killer's reach, Eminence."

"You're saying that every missionary is a potential martyr. That's as mechanical and as unilluminating as saying that every test pilot of an airplane is a potential suicide."

"I may make a mortal enemy in Italy, Eminence, and to protect myself fly to the United States of America or Australia. Far from putting myself beyond my enemy's reach, I would only be signaling his attention and, worse, hardening his purpose."

"Simply by running away?"

"Flight from an enemy, if only a potential enemy, grants the right of pursuit. From a physical right it is only a short step to a moral right. My back, Eminence, becomes a mirror in which my enemy recognizes his obligation to kill. My face, however, grants no such right."

"You frighten me, Monsignor."

For a moment Kramer appeared very unsure of himself, showing a distress based on something deeper than a superior's rebuke or disapproval or a crushing recognition that he had, from arrogance or ignorance, overstepped himself. He looks like a girl, the Cardinal decided, who, in straining to please, produces an indelicate noise. A not very modern girl, the Cardinal reminded himself, or one convent-trained and not yet adapted to a world where girls may make noises like motorcycles without blushing for them. As a result of Kramer's reaction, the Cardinal, a formidable but sensitive man, found himself in the unwelcome position of having to appease a person he intended attacking and of being forced to concede territory he had resolved to defend to the last tricky adverb. His petulance was such that he dismissed Kramer abruptly, and his remorse (and self-regret) was such that the next morning he appointed Kramer to investigate the affair of the five nuns with the sour reminder that his Holiness kept the affair not on the papal sleeve but close to the papal heart. He then sent Kramer a letter of conditions:

(1) Since evil is, it cannot be assumed. The obvious is not to be taken for granted.

(2) There were twelve nuns in the group captured by the pagan. The deaths of seven must not be held against the lives of five.

(3) The innocence or guilt of those who participated in the assaults on these nuns cannot be established either by the Vatican or an American court. This is the province of the pagan authorities.

(4) Racial prejudice may be abhorrent to the civilized person; it is unknown to God.

(5) A fact is worth its weight in gold, a supposition in blood.

(6) If a person is to be held accountable for his beliefs, how shall the Church escape censure for her judgments?

(7) To investigate this affair at this time is an error, a necessary error, but an error. Be sure, therefore, that such stains and smudges as you may uncover are produced by the object of handling and not by the handler. Remember, you enter this affair with unclean hands.

77

On a separate page the Cardinal appended a list of the survivors of the military company that had escorted the five nuns to safety.

> Captain Joseph Hays Sterling III, Fox Company, Second Battalion,
>   ——th Regiment.
> Corporal Alfred S. Plinnett, same.
> Private Roosevelt Hull Lewis, same.

He ordered Monsignor Cinotti to give Kramer photostated copies of the documents and masses of information in the nuns' file, same to be treated as confidential and returned *in toto* after the investigation. He wrote letters to the following: The Very Reverend Mother Magdalene, Superior General of the Order of the Sisters of St. Luke, whose home convent was situated near Pescara, on the Adriatic Sea; the Supreme Allied Commander of NATO; the Apostolic Delegate in Washington, D.C. After that, Ottavio Cardinal Bellini, a skeptic in all matters worldly and in many unworldly, but a firm believer in God and a powerful defender of his Church as the best of all fallible systems and even in error the hope of mankind, went into his private chapel to pray. The Cardinal did not let his infirm legs and gross and indecent torso weaken his posture in the presence of God. He knelt, to be sure on a corrugated cushion into which his knees bit firmly, upright, his back straight, his elbows unsupported by pew or railing. Like a dozing horse he locked himself into this position and began the slow process of emptying mind and body so that the Divine Presence, always invoked and ever resisted, might press into and overthrow the mercenaries of his palace guard and for a time, moment or eternity, repossess what had been taken from it.

God willed; the Cardinal interpreted.

CHAPTER X

AFTER MAKING A THOROUGH STUDY of the nuns' files and feeling that he needed both more information and a clearer indication, if not order, as to how he was to proceed, Kramer tried to arrange another meeting with the Cardinal, only to be told by Monsignor Cinotti that the Cardinal had flown to Milan to appear at the dedication of yet another automobile plant and that he (Kramer) should come to the Cardinal's residence (no, not his offices) to pick up his Vatican diplomatic passport, an unspecified sum of money, letters of introduction to papal legates in various sections of the world, and a report from the Very Reverend Mother Magdalene on the present state and condition of the five American nuns.

"But are there," Kramer asked, when he saw Cinotti, "no further instructions?"

"Monsignor, you have his Eminence's confidence. Do you need his rules of procedure?" Cinotti, who wore his master's hat in the Cardinal's absence, though not in the presence of his master's peers, gave Kramer a pouch containing the promised materials and said that the Cardinal expected a weekly report, and perhaps later, depending on the nature of Kramer's investigation, a daily report. "I received word this morning that Captain Sterling is in Paris on his way to America."

"America."

"There are planes to America."

"No doubt, no doubt."

"There are also planes to Paris."

"But if Captain Sterling is leaving Paris, Monsignor—" Kramer felt a slight shock, as if Cinotti had abruptly taken off his mask and shown him, at his feet, the great curved profile of the world, the temptation not of the promise of power but of the gift of power. He hoped Cinotti would not notice his vertigo or, failing that, ascribe it to doubt, a humble assessment of his worthiness, and a bleak recognition of its poor quality.

"I should think the commanding general of NATO would be delighted to co-operate with his Eminence in a matter of great importance to the Church and of little inconvenience to the general's staff."

"Yes, thank you."

"Shall I arrange to have Captain Sterling await your presence, Monsignor?"

"Yes. Would you also call the airport, Monsignor? I can be ready in two hours."

A different, not necessarily lesser, man would have enjoyed a few days in Paris—also Stockholm, London, Oslo, Prague, and New York. To Kramer, however, the luminous city was a platform for action surrounded by approaches which could be used for either study or sleep, conveyor belts of differing speeds and comfort. Having no business in the shops and restaurants—and having seen the museums and churches on an earlier visit—he settled himself in a room at the papal legate's residence and prepared an agenda for the interview with Sterling. He could have followed Sterling to New York; he preferred to see him in Paris, in transit, in uniform, on the wing. He did not know his man, but he would know him. He said to the priest who acted as his secretary, "I'd like a bottle of good bourbon and a pack of American cigarettes. When Captain Sterling arrives keep him waiting fifteen minutes and then show him in."

When Kramer acknowledged that he did not know his man he was warning himself not to let an intuitive dislike of Sterling, in advance of meeting him, change what had been planned as a dry and impartial search for facts into a personal attack. He realized this when he saw Sterling, by appointment, at five in the afternoon on the day following his arrival in Paris. For what he saw was what he had been raised to abhor—the boss's son. Kramer of the coal fields of Pennsylvania against the absentee owner of the Princeton–New York circuit. The habit of rigorous self-examination forced him to acknowledge his intuitive dislike, but it also made him guard against it. After introducing himself and seating Sterling, with an offer of bourbon and cigarettes (declined), Kramer said, "Good of you to grant me this interview, Captain."

"I'm here, Monsignor, because a certain very important general ordered me here. And for no other reason."

"My office made a request, Captain. I'm distressed—may I say indignant?—that it came through to you as an order. I have no power to detain you unnecessarily and no desire to." Obviously Sterling had been drinking, Kramer decided, but he was neither drunk nor slow to react.

"Just what is it you wanted to see me about, Monsignor? I'm not a Catholic. And I have no recollection of having expressed a wish to be converted."

"I represent a department of the Church called the Sacred Congregation of Rites, Captain. I have been assigned by the head of this department, a Cardinal Bellini in Rome, to investigate certain events in which you participated and of which you may fairly be expected to have valuable knowledge. I would greatly appreciate—"

"What events, Monsignor?"

"Need you ask, Captain? I might add that the fate of these five poor sisters causes his Holiness much anxiety."

"So that's it." Sterling lit one of his own cigarettes, as if, having been given the answer to a question that had been puzzling (and perhaps depressing) him, he now felt obliged, despite anxieties to come, to express a genuine gratification. Watching him, Kramer wondered, with concealed distaste, what the man had expected.

"A simple account of those three critical weeks would be very helpful, Captain."

"To whom? Your church? Just who are you, Monsignor? And spare me the titles and the bureaucratic claptrap."

"Would you understand me if I said inquisitor?"

"Earlier you used the word 'investigate.' "

Kramer smiled. "A much better word, Captain."

"You're not, I take it, intending to investigate me."

81

"Of course not. Actually, I'm asking only for your help."

"I must be undergoing considerable mental depreciation." Sterling tapped his head. "Significant loss of marbles."

"Surely the sufferings of these five nuns don't leave you unmoved, Captain."

Sterling stood. "As you say, Monsignor, you have no power to detain me—"

"No. But I ask you to consider the enormity of the situation the Church is faced with and the consequences of leaving it unresolved. No, please, Captain. I am no one. In the hierarchy of the Church I'm at the level of a law clerk. Yet it is at such a level that this investigation must begin. In my hands, as clumsy and as weak as they are, may lie the future employment of these nuns. And not only physical employment, but spiritual. An awesome responsibility, Captain, one I hope—and pray—you will help me bear."

"But why, Monsignor, any investigation? What in God's name can these women be guilty of?"

"You may not know, Captain, that there were twelve nuns in that convent when the enemy seized it. Seven preferred to die rather than submit to their captors. We cannot refuse these seven who died so violently—and perhaps nobly—the courtesy of an inquiry."

"The dead have a right to be represented—" Sterling broke off abruptly and turned to pace the room. As he did so, he saw the crucifix on the wall, a small icon, silver, chaste, no blood. Turning from the crucifix as from a road block, he encountered, face to face, a statue of the Virgin, an insignificant Virgin, no taller than a child's doll. He walked then to the desk and poured himself a drink of Kramer's bourbon. "Christ, will it ever stop? After the poor bloody infantryman secures the territory in comes the Judge Advocate General's Office. A man has no guarantees."

"He has the guarantee of his self, Captain. And of his God."

"But what guarantee does the man who judges him have, Monsignor? The law, a code, a rule book. In my case, the Articles of War. In your case—what?"

"Canon law."

"A book, Monsignor."

82

"If you like, yes. But the Articles of War, as you well know, judge only physical acts and reward or punish them physically. The Church's powers are purely spiritual, her sanctions or censures only what one who is in error would wish to inflict on himself, her penalties—well, how does one penalize the sinful? By laying on them the burden of repentance, which is the means to salvation. Promotion, Captain, not persecution."

"The death penalty can serve the same purpose as your censures, Monsignor. And, if we're to believe the chaplains in our death cells, often does. And please don't say, 'But not always.' "

"You believe then, Captain, from your observations, that these nuns have been greatly wronged."

"I would say in anyone's opinion."

"You would then have to believe that they neither solicited, however unconsciously, these repeated assaults on their bodies, nor at any time, however unconsciously, participated in them, nor at any time gave, however unconsciously, partial, incomplete, or reluctant consent to these assaults."

"Now I know what these flying saucers are. The souls of the damned broken out of hell and come back to—" Sterling hit himself on the forehead with the heel of his hand, as if to rouse himself from a kind of empathic hypnosis induced not so much by the timbre of Kramer's voice as by its intensity. The well-known domination of the open mind by the closed mind—or, no, the centered mind, which throws against the flabby defenses of doubt and irresolution the armored column of all or nothing, forcing the defender to believe that resolution and implacability, irrespective of their ethical bases, have a moral value of their own. For how do you fall, through an irresistible power or a lack of firmness? Were you pushed or did you collapse? Is the author of your debasement iron or are you slush? And just a minute—are you sure you're being attacked? Or is this another of your whining attempts to cede responsibility for yourself to another? And if you are being attacked—come now, friend—isn't it because you have decayed to the extent that you must either welcome a corrective force (how blond the conqueror) or accept a new beginning in

83

the belly of the vulture? For who are the true expendables? Think. No, no, no, no—of course you've got it, the useless.

"Would you like another drink, Captain?"

"Why not?" Sterling sat in the chair he had sprung from so quickly (stripped for argument), appearing much heavier, soggier, having put on weight by the act of sitting. He again saw Goldman, who might have achieved his freedom for the purpose of relinquishing his life, lying on the tile floor before the headless Virgin, he heard Sister Esther's cool declaration of death, and he felt her flesh in the palm of his hand as he slapped her against the door. Precisely what had happened? Or forget the precisely— in the main what had happened? "Where are they now? These nuns."

"In a convent in Italy, Captain."

"Are they well?"

"Four, yes. One died in childbirth."

"Yes, Sister Mary."

"Sister Catherine, Captain."

"Sister Catherine?"

"A most difficult and exacting labor. For the sake of the child—"

"And Sister Esther?"

"The healthy mother of a very fine boy."

Sterling accepted the drink Kramer offered him and drank it, declining Kramer's gesture toward the bottle with a lift of the hand. "I know you don't believe in abortion, Monsignor—and let me say I don't believe in free and open abortion myself— therapeutic, yes, but not just— But what do you mean by 'the sake of the child'?"

"I obviously do not mean what you're thinking, Captain."

"Get the kid out and to hell with the mother."

"Why not in all cases of childbirth a Caesarean section? This would spare the baby the arduous and often traumatic trip through the pelvic basin and vaginal canal and relieve the mother of hours of painful and punishing labor by subjecting her instead to a major abdominal operation. With its abundant and by no means petty risks. We give priority to the child, yes, Captain, but only

84

that priority the mother herself, as she conceives, is willing to grant it. Let me assure you, Captain, three of the top obstetricians in Italy were assigned to these nuns. The Sacred Congregation of Religious has set aside special funds for their care and for the care of the children. And all over the world nuns in the affiliated houses of the Sisters of St. Luke are rejoicing that one more of their number rests safely in the arms of her sacred Bridegroom. For Sister Catherine made a most conscious, deliberate, and sanctified end, an end any Christian of any sect might envy."

"There's the answer to your investigation, Monsignor. In what she told her confessor. Only you can't get that information, can you?"

"Please don't joke about the seal of the confessional, Captain. To some priests it's a cross of lead. But you asked about Sister Esther in particular. Perhaps you knew her better than the others. And believe me, Captain, I suggest only a social relationship."

"I didn't know her at all, Monsignor. Goldman—Sergeant Goldman—" Sterling sighed, baffled by what he could remember but not co-ordinate, baffled possibly by the always unpredictable and altogether inadequate acts of memory, so vivid, so provocative, so incomplete.

"Goldman?"

"My—the company's first sergeant. So now they're mothers, are they? Well, science hasn't yet proved that the female of Homo sapiens can be impregnated by an animal."

"Racial prejudice may be abhorrent to the civilized person, Captain; it is unknown to God."

"Along with a real interest in human affairs." Sterling stood, an act that might have astonished him. "Air's a little thick in here."

"Perhaps tomorrow morning—"

"The hell with it. You can call the Army if you like, Monsignor, but definitely the hell with it."

"That I won't do, Captain. But I thought perhaps we might cover, briefly, some of the details of your retreat south."

"Ask Lewis—Plinnett. Three men, Monsignor, out of a hundred

85

and thirty-one. One time when the captain did not go down with his goddam ship. Didn't get much sleep last night. On the town."

"My secretary will show you to a bathroom, Captain. Thank you. Shall I convey your regards to Sister Esther?"

"I don't think she'd welcome any personal attentions, Monsignor. None of them would. I—" Sterling left the room, a man wholly in the service of his stomach.

Sitting at the desk, Kramer took a pencil and made a diagram of the interview—exposition, development, denouement. Exposition, incomplete; development, negligible; denouement, delayed, to come. Why give the interview either the significance of a diagram or the order of a design when its stamp was so obviously that of the wild horse, Kramer with a silk lariat in pursuit of a cantering Sterling, who, in motion or at pause, remained unropable. That conceit that he would know Sterling. His first error. Information, facts. Only he had no facts except possibly that any man with any intelligence or experience was at all times his own variable. Was it inexperience or stupidity—or self-indulgence—that had made him play neither the man nor the schedule, but a program of his own? And if so, what program?

His secretary knocked at the open door, holding a spool of magnetic tape. "Shall I transcribe this, Monsignor?"

"Please, Father. In Italian. Three copies."

"Will the Captain be back?"

"I think not, Father. Apparently, the ordeal was a little much for him."

"Judging from his appearance as he left the building, Monsignor, I would say his ordeal is just beginning."

"As is mine, Father. Pray for me?"

CHAPTER XI

BEFORE HE RETURNED TO ROME Kramer airmailed a copy of the transcribed interview with Sterling to Cardinal Bellini, enclosing only a brief covering note conceding the inadequacy (he did not write failure) of his interrogative methods and suggesting that he be given, if possible, a clearer, perhaps a more direct, viewpoint from which to work. He knew that he risked a massive rebuke for his effrontery in questioning a superior's directive, no matter how vague or perplexing, and he knew also (this he knew) that to plead too strongly his own lack of merit would be to charge that powerful and oblique intelligence with having made either a frivolous appointment or a dull one. The Cardinal might welcome an impudence offered with sufficient wit and sparkle (beyond Kramer); he would certainly not welcome vulgarity. There was the possibility, too, that the Cardinal (with an assist from Cinotti) had decided to let the bright young American priest impale himself on the horns of a lethal issue, a bull from the endless visions of the Apocalypse, thus blunting its weapons for the immediate future. The second article from the Cardinal's seven-point schema ran like a scarlet river through Kramer's mind —"The deaths of seven must not be held against the lives of five."

How far should he go? Or, rather, how should he prevent the investigation from carrying him beyond limits the Cardinal had not even suggested? And why had the Sacred Congregation of Religious, which had exclusive jurisdiction over the discipline and privileges of nuns, permitted the entry of the Sacred Congregation of Rites, which had jurisdiction only in the field of beatification and canonization? Perhaps the investigation had been set up to declare, formally, the seven murdered nuns martyrs. Why then had he not been told this?

Back in Rome the following afternoon after a rough flight from Paris, Kramer called Cinotti, who said that the Cardinal was confined to his bed with a bad cold but would see him tomorrow, say at five? "Bring the nuns' file," Cinotti said. "You should know that Captain Sterling was picked up by the Parisian police at four o'clock this morning and turned over to the military authorities. Drunk and disorderly. Suspected of having picketed the papal legate's residence carrying a sign reading 'The hell with Rome.' His Eminence has been informed."

Climbing the thirty-seven steps to his Eminence's portico at ten minutes to five the following afternoon, Kramer was almost overpowered by a shocking urge to laugh. Not smile or chuckle or grimace or titter, but to laugh. He could see, he could really see, an indignant but probably solemn Sterling staggering along the gutter carrying his homemade sign and perhaps shouting its collegiate text to an empty street. So Sterling had something of the clown in him. Difficult people, clowns. Rational, of course, perhaps too rational. Often startling insights into themselves. Powerful compulsions to surface and act out their conflicts. In a distinctive and sometimes very artful pantomime. They could hurt themselves and also hurt others. You mock me, sir. No, by this hand.

The Cardinal did not lie or recline on his great four-poster bed; he sat on it in a kind of legless chair, his elbows comfortably supported on its padded arms. A low table stood over his lap. On it papers and pens, pamphlets, several books, and a wine glass into which Cinotti poured a vintage, clearly, sherry. Cinotti's typewriter stood on a table near the windows. On the far side of the bed from Kramer a tape recorder. His Eminence motioned Kramer not to advance too far into the room, a gesture that did not include an invitation to sit.

"You say this"—touching several bound sheets of paper—"was transcribed from a tape recording, Monsignor?"

"Yes, Eminence. The tape, by my instructions, has been erased."

"Did you request this recording? Or was it suggested to you by our brothers in Paris?"

"I was told a tape recorder and microphone were available, Eminence. I made the decision to use them."

"I suggest you start training your memory, Kramer. Such equipment will hardly be available at the convent in Pescara."

"I wanted your Eminence to have an unedited report of this interview."

"Why?"

"Because, Eminence, appointing the editor does not always give one the option of auditioning the man."

Cinotti, who had been moving quietly about, bowed and left the room, possibly on a signal from the Cardinal, possibly on his own. Though the room was powerfully baroque, the few pictures hanging on two walls, Kramer noticed, were nineteenth-century landscapes, a Corot possibly, a view of Venice, and—Catullus's Verona?

"If tact is the most graceful form of timidity, Monsignor, you have courage. But then, if I'd wanted a tactful man I'd have appointed one. What was your purpose in seeing Sterling?"

"I thought a factual account of these critical three weeks might be invaluable, Eminence."

"You didn't see him simply because Cinotti persuaded you he was there?"

"No—" Kramer moved his legs apart, digging into the carpet. "Yes."

The Cardinal's heavy Semitic face, extended by a pouch under the chin and a hairline halfway up his gray skull, expressed, to Kramer, a certain pleasantness, not quite satisfaction, not quite good humor. "Having blooded yourself on Captain Sterling, you possibly feel better prepared to attack the nuns."

"I do, Eminence."

"Attack."

"Interrogate."

"You have drained the pools of arrogance to fill the reservoirs of charity."

"May I ask this question, Eminence? If the seven nuns who pre-

ferred death to violation are true martyrs, would it necessarily follow that the five who accepted violation are filth?"

The Cardinal's great fist came down on the table. "You—Protestant. No, be quiet." The Cardinal took a tissue from a box on the
bed and prepared to sneeze into it. After a series of massive shudders, one movement building on the other, he produced not the
expected blast but a nasal whisper, delicate as a sigh. "Well, Monsignor? Have you any more such bridges to burn?"

Kramer waited for the second sneeze and said he felt the investigation must have a center, a focus. "Otherwise, Eminence, why
an investigation at all? Accept the seven nuns as exemplary keepers
of the Faith and permit the five survivors—four, now—to live out
their lives peacefully and productively within their Order."

"You don't see that you could simply take the testimony of these
nuns—without asking too many questions—and recommend that
no further action is indicated. Or do you think this, Monsignor,
is the voice of Satan?"

"I think your Eminence is far better qualified—" Kramer dug a
little deeper into the carpet.

"You want specific orders, Monsignor. So does anyone. But I
have none to give you. Only a request—at best, plaintive; at worst,
wistful—from the Holy Father. And permission from my brother
in the Congregation of Religious—at best, exasperated; at worst,
choleric—to examine these nuns for possible—" The Cardinal gestured with both hands, as if releasing a balloon filled with helium,
having held it not by the string but by its skin. "It has occurred
to you that we have jurisdiction in only one aspect of this case."

Kramer came up on his toes. "May I ask your Eminence a direct
question?"

"I have had enough direct questions, Monsignor, particularly
from a man who seems unwilling to ask them of himself. But I
can tell you this—we are not looking for saints; we are looking for
causes."

Before leaving for Pescara Kramer went to see his good friend
Monsignor Licciardi, who worked in the offices of the Congregation of Religious. Licciardi, whose family had donated him to the

Church (a third son and not, from his bony frame and bad eyes, a good breeder), said that no one he knew personally was an expert in canon law, "except people like Scanfort and Bardelli, and they're too high up for ordinary questions and ordinary people, but I can give you a rundown on forms and simple procedures, if that's what you want."

"How is a cause for beatification started, Arturo?"

"Beatification? You're on the way up, Tom."

"You'll have to take it on trust, Arturo."

"Those nuns of the Order of St. Luke?"

"Tell me, what does his Eminence Cardinal Anareani wear next to his skin? I'm told leopardskin drawers."

"Rome is not a place for secrets, Tom. Beatification. So soon?"

"The word is otherwise, then."

"No. The word is no one wishes to volunteer for this assignment in good health or bad." Licciardi shook his head. "So Bellini wants an American. The language barrier, I suppose."

Kramer laughed. "All right, Arturo. I was scared to begin with; now I'm frozen with horror."

"Better than being fired with joy, Tom." Licciardi got up and closed his office door. "By the way, the Council has a warm one. Some Mexican priest who shot and killed his common-law wife and three children and shot and didn't kill himself. But that's simple. He will suffer life imprisonment or less at the hands of the government and degradation at the hands of the Church. Degradation includes deposition, the perpetual privation of ecclesiastical dress, and the reduction of the cleric to the lay state. And if you don't think that's enough, he also loses his pension. The canons may be dusty, Tom, but they still fire."

"Monsignor, I came to you because as a priest my soul needs a good blasting. Not a sweeping, but a blasting. I also came to you as a man who has one foot on ice and the other in outer space. I'd hoped you'd act as a kind of unofficial confessor. Or confidant?"

"This is your second trip to this ecclesiastical swamp, isn't it?"

"Yes."

"We've known each other less than a year, haven't we?"

"Roughly, yes."

"You don't have any really intimate friends, do you, Tom?"

"I can't say I'm too unpopular, Arturo. Although I think I'm referred to now and then as 'that athletic American.'"

"And your field is the Old Testament?"

"It was. Lately, I've been getting quite a taste of politics and administration."

"Obviously. The Church doesn't see you as a scholar. But then, it has no objections to a well-rounded man. Now, I'm not going to forecast your future in the Church, but a man isn't called twice to Rome for further studies out of simple Italian curiosity. Who is your patron in the United States?"

"Cardinal Brooker."

"The American agnostic."

"Excuse me, Arturo. Cynicism, yes. Vilification, no."

"You speak Italian fluently, Tom, yes, but you don't know the Roman language. That is, the language of the town. I speak English fluently. True. But if I were in New York or Los Angeles I'm certain that even among not particularly intelligent or sophisticated people who were making every effort not to speak their local dialect I would miss half of what was said. Hear the note clearly but not the overtones. Tom, my family has been contributing sons and daughters to the Church for eight hundred years. Cardinals are as familiar to our homes and dinner tables as the robin is to an American lawn. I've known them as men, as administrators, and as priests. Few of them are saints, many of them are good businessmen, none of them are less than granite in defense of the Church. How they stand with God, only God knows. The Curia is an essentially conservative institution. What was done yesterday will be done tomorrow. I don't see the Curia as a launching pad for innovations. That isn't its job. Its job is to hold and hold again and to hold yet once more. Change will come, yes, but it will come in a direct and orderly line and not around these craggy old men, through them and, if necessary, over them."

92

"What you're saying is that I'm that old standard, the naïve American."

"Classification is for filing clerks. And I'm not a filing clerk. What I say is, Tom, that you could suffer massive defeat and perhaps gain a mass of patience. And this, possibly, is what Bellini may have in mind for you. Please don't ask me to read his cards. He has a hundred decks in the air at any one time and a hundred more on the table." Licciardi sat back in his chair and lit a cigarette, American, filter. "You doubt yourself, Tom, that's all."

"I happen to think that's a great deal."

"Then you have that inside you, some secret and inalienable passion, that you don't want exposed. Are you a prophet? Fascination with the Old Testament, the Lutheran heresy."

"That's too easy, Arturo."

"Are you engaged, and does she use contraceptives?"

"This is the talk of your town, Arturo?"

"It would be all right if you were secretly engaged, but you must not connive with her in the use of gadgets. Would you think, to look at me, that I have a flaming libido?"

"I *am* naïve."

"In part. But what would I be in New York? Or Washington? But this is in keeping with nature. You probably could have almost any woman you wanted, and that satisfies you. I could have almost none, and that dissatisfies me. I've faced my weakness, and in a few more years I shall have it conquered. Without having once, Tom, given into it."

"I applaud you. With both hands. I don't know my weakness and shall probably never know when I've given in to it. Pride, yes, anger, envy—but those are the easy sins, the petty currency of the confessional."

"Is it power, Tom? The inability to take it, when offered, is very bad, especially when accompanied by an excessive emotional reaction. An upset stomach would almost certainly prove that you're suppressing a powerful desire to run amok among the faithful with a hockey stick. In your fantasies, when you were younger, did you ever see yourself as the world's greatest surgeon?"

Kramer laughed. "I certainly did, Arturo."

"So did I, so did I. Very good. Let me ask you this—do you believe in the devil?"

"I believe in evil, yes. Though if you asked me to define evil—"

"Is that your doubt?"

"Possibly."

"Or do you believe that evil can be created?"

"Not by man, no."

"And what would you call the begetting of children?"

"Reproduction."

"And is your God a loving God?"

"There has been too much talk of love and not enough of justice, Arturo. That's to spare ourselves the trouble of moving from a position where we're all in harmony to one where we're not."

"That may mean you're capable of administering justice and not of dispensing love."

"Love cannot be dispensed, Arturo, any more than the earth's atmosphere can be dispensed. It is there."

"It is indeed. But you asked about beatification."

"You actually had a case recently, didn't you?"

"Not I, no. Anyway, the procedure is this: a person begins to act strangely, miraculous cures are attributed to him, a cult springs up around him, the more gullible believe he's a saint. The local bishop, disturbed by these scandalous procedures, investigates. If he doesn't think he can put a stop to them without causing a serious breach in his parishioners' faith, he sends a Pontius Pilate letter to Rome. A washing of hands. Just who acts on the letter and how, I don't know. But if the Holy Father—and I suppose any number of his counselors—decide to proceed, the matter is turned over to the Congregation of Rites, and the reigning cardinal, now Bellini, appoints, one, a postulator to plead the cause of God, and, two, a promoter to plead the cause of the devil."

"The bishop's letter needn't be a Pontius Pilate letter, though."

"Bishops don't convert that easily, Tom. Not when they know the temper of Rome. Which is, that we have more saints than we have room on the calendar. I'm not denying that there are saints on this earth, Tom. There have always been saints, there will always be, by the infinite grace of God, saints, but I'd hate to be the man who proposed one for official investigation by Cardinal Bellini."

"Thank you."

"When, as a child, you ran for comfort to your mother, Tom, you probably always got it. But what happened when you ran for comfort to your father?"

"You've been a great help, Arturo."

"Whether I know it or not. The cliché of the confessional. This time, indirect."

Kramer laughed. "I wanted a blasting, Arturo. You gave me one. Thanks."

"Old friend, I may call on you sometime."

"I'm no expert on women, Arturo."

"That is your first denial, Tom. 'Before the cock crows twice—' Interesting play on words, isn't it?"

Shocked, Kramer withdrew, pursued by a jet of smoke from Licciardi's cigarette. He did not know—and would never know—that the day before Cardinal Bellini's doctors had confined him to his bed (the Cardinal's great throne in absence of his desk) the Holy Father had detained Bellini after a meeting on the concurrent crises of defecting priests and nuns clamoring for a share of the world outside their convents and asked him, with his customary gentleness, how it went with these nuns.

"I have appointed an examiner, Holiness," the Cardinal said, "with fairly limited powers to probe and recommend. An American. Monsignor Thomas Paul Kramer."

"A gentle man, Ottavio? A sympathetic man?"

"An impressionable man, Holiness. Who, in the long run, may be more valuable than one inclined, to his detriment, to pity."

"You insist on this line, Eminence?"

"Holiness, there is no other." The Cardinal, heavily invested

95

with the germs of this world, staggered to retain his balance, and the saintly Pope, quickly seizing his arm, guided him to a couch and sat him there.

"Patience, Ottavio. The world, apparently, has you by the throat."

"So I may be released in God, Holiness, the world may take its will. But this Kramer—" The Cardinal turned his face away so as not to cough directly at the Pope.

"Lie back, Ottavio. You're ill."

"Only physically, I trust. But may I explain to your Holiness why I appointed Kramer?"

"I would have preferred a gentler man."

"I know, Holiness. But I detect in this affair—by intuition, of course—not the hairy paw of Satan, but the pulse of God. And whoever has the temerity to take the Divine Pulse must have fingers of asbestos, not of silk."

CHAPTER XII

DR. MARIO Q. POLI, a first-rate obstetrician and known to be a staunch lay son of the Church, finished his examination of Sister Esther and immediately left the small windowless room the convent had ceded him as a surgery for the postoperative care and treatment of his religious patients. Sister Luisa, the necessary chaperone, followed him into a larger room which the doctor used as an office. It contained, besides a desk and couch, a filing cabinet, two bookcases stocked with drugs and medicines, and a big white four-wheeled cart carrying surgical and diagnostic instruments and medical supplies, rolls of bandages and tape, tongue depressors, scissors.

"You can take this stuff back to the hospital," Poli said. "I'm through here."

"The Reverend Mother Magdalene would like to know when the child of the Lord can be weaned, Doctor," Sister Luisa said.

"Sister Esther's child, Sister."

"The Lord's child."

"It came from her belly, didn't it, Sister? I removed it myself. And, as you may have observed, a nice little Caesarean section."

"When, Doctor?"

"I'd say any time. But let the pediatrician decide. I'm going back to Rome. This time to stay. Would you convey all that to the Reverend Mother, Sister?"

"And your report, Doctor?"

"I'm writing it now. As for that scar on Sister Esther's abdomen, you can explain it to the doctor who examines her in the future as—uh—the result of an operation for a large abdominal tumor. Benign. I'll make a record of it."

Poli thrust his head and shoulders a little farther over the desk as he wrote. When first consulted by the Church in the person of his Eminence Giorgio Cardinal Andreani of the Sacred Congregation of Religious, he had reacted with a schoolboy vehemence that later astonished him. An orphan raised by a married aunt, schooled in the Church, educated by the Church, his medical studies subsidized by the Church, Poli acknowledged his debt, openly and submissively, and paid it, both in money and in services to the charitable hospitals and institutions run by the Church. He could afford it. But this business of five pregnant nuns—and one, Sister Mary, with complete blockage of the cervix by the placenta, not partial, whole. He prided himself on that one. As for Sister Catherine—Poli did not like to think about it; a butcher could have done as good a job. With Sister Roberta, however—Poli was used to charity patients who could pop them out like peas—but to put Sister Roberta up into the stirrups for a routine vaginal and find

97

himself looking at a three-inch patch of the baby's skull—and no spotting, no labor pains—poor woman, poor sister—those great vacant eyes. No, not vacant, filled with an immense absence of God. Where had He gone? To the alienists with her. He had done his job. Now let the psychiatrists take over.

Aware of Sister Esther standing silently at his left, he said to Sister Luisa, "Tell her that she is released, Sister. She's fine. No special instructions."

Without waiting for a translation Sister Esther bowed and left the room, Sister Luisa, after a brief nod, following her. If they think I'm such a disgusting creature, Poli thought, why did they accept my services? After his first shock he had wanted to defrock them temporarily and put them in a nursing home as lay patients. Overruled. "We have plenty of room, Doctor. We'll convert an unused section of the infirmary into a maternity wing. They need," Reverend Mother Magdalene had said, her great ugly face thrust out of her cowl like that of a gargoyle splitting its stone coif, "the protection and comfort of their Order." So be it. "Now as to an anesthetist, Mother—" "We shall of course dispense with the services of an anesthetist." Oh hell, yes, Mother. "Perhaps you believe that since the fathers of these—uh—poppets are not large physical models the problem of delivery will be, in all cases, a simple one." "I am a nurse, Doctor. I have worked in the maternity divisions of several hospitals. I know the pains of giving birth, even though I have never felt them. But it is the choice of these nuns that they be delivered without deep anesthesia." "But with the possibility of protracted labor, to overlook for a moment the possibility of complications—granted, granted, the child comes first —still, under certain conditions, as you well know, Reverend Mother, the life of the child as well as that of the mother can be endangered." "I cannot go against the wishes of these brave sisters, Doctor. Nor, I think, can you."

Holy Mother, the barbarities of the good, the pious, the devout. His job was to relieve suffering, not inflict flagellation. "No, no, Mother, I cannot undertake to deliver these nuns without the guarantee of at least a stand-by anesthetic chosen by me and a person—if you will, a nursing sister—who has the skill to administer it. Do you have such a person?" "I myself, Doctor, have had some practice in administering anesthetics." And Poli, biting down on his teeth, thought, How are you with the tongs, Mother, the hot slivers, the nutcracker? "You know," he said aloud, "I have a set of ethics I'm sworn to uphold. Vows, Mother. A death in the delivery room must be promptly and accurately reported—" "This is the conscious and deliberate choice of these nuns. They wish to deliver naturally without the interference of drugs or gases."

There it was. And if he resigned the case, another doctor, perhaps less skilled, less committed (and now Poli was wholly committed), would be called, and if— Except that the babies would be born whether anyone medically qualified attended them or not. "You know, Reverend Mother, that his Eminence Cardinal Andreani wishes these nuns to be given every—" "I cannot overrule them in this matter, Doctor." "Well, we will start them on special exercises. I myself am no expert on natural childbirth, but I shall acquaint myself with the literature on the subject." But only Sister Roberta, who had been sick in body as well as in mind, had delivered without assistance from the pharmacologist or the gas tanks. On one point of behavior he had had his way. The mothers, of course, were not to see their babies. Better that way. Out and forgotten. Except the little Caesarean, Mario—Poli had named him himself—this one, he said, goes to his mother's breasts. The pediatrician, a first-generation professional man, agreed with him. But then it had meant a formal march to the nursery, a pardon-me-Sister, a taking up of the baby, a grave march to the bedside, a presenting of the baby. He had put Mario to the teat himself, and the face of the nun-mother as she suckled her child— What all you women should do, Poli said to the Reverend Mother and the attending sisters, is get down on your knees. Shocking, of course. A bad scene. But the mother had not heard or minded—or—her face was over the child—

A mistake? A wet nurse might have been procured—except that he couldn't have entrusted little Mario, a truly beautiful child, to the great dark sweaty spigots of a peasant-cow, not even after de-lousing, blood tests, smears, douches, and shaving. I, Poli thought, watching the blind frantic mouth close over the delicately guided nipple (how beautifully she does that), am the human element, the grease of history, yes, but also, on occasion, the sand in the gear box. Aware that he posed to himself, a beneficent, germless Poli strutting for an irascible, vilely mortal one, he felt that as a physician he acted from the great chair of Hippocrates the healer, who also had his deposit of faith.

Odd, though, that with the exception of Sister Catherine, who had (he swore it) the pelvis of a twelve-year-old boy, little Mario should have given him the most trouble. Why should he have been so reluctant to leave the nest? Poli had done everything except jump on the mother's belly—massaged, kneaded, pressed, pushed, squeezed, hammered—the little leech. He had let it go as long as he dared, longer than he should have, while the mother, refusing relief from pain, bit through one after another of the cloth, leather, and rubber bullets he devised for her. Barbaric. He under-stood that she needed to suffer, to cleanse herself of the dark bodies of her assaulters and, more important, to atone for the in-visible fault that underlay this too-visible cancer. Unlike the others, this Sister Esther, with her splendid body and work-bitten hands, the only flaw in the lustrous scheme of her flesh, had an awareness that surpassed the tittering shame of Sister Agnes, the bovine acceptance of Sister Mary, the schoolgirl humility of Sister Catherine (he had not been in on her final confession, of course).

Pride? Perhaps. But finally he had picked up the knife, and said, leaning above the slowly collapsing face, "It's over, Sister. I'm going in. I'm not thinking of you, I'm thinking of the child." And to the Reverend Mother Magdalene, a better nurse than he had expected, "I can do a real Caesarean, if you like. Posthumous?" Even after that crude joke he had received only a tacit assent, nothing verbal, no gesture, just that blank shell the long-oppressed turns to the oppressor, the biggest nothing the human being is capable of—so. Well, he had given Sister Esther her cross. With his scalpel. And she would bear it, on her belly, the rest of her natural life.

Poli lit a cigarette, blowing the smoke at his report, toasting it, obscuring it. How was it that you could never carry out an order (or execute a commission) without, in one way or another, exceeding it? The chain of command sometimes got its human links twisted. Surely this dark comedy, with its stubborn, opinionated, bitterly committed actors, who were short on taking direction and long on improvisation, was not what Cardinal Andreani had intended. Except that the Cardinal in Rome commanded not only from too great a distance, where each linear mile showed a loss of power, but from too great a spiritual height. What he transmitted (the proper term) had to be received by equipment inferior to its assignment and worked out by people unaccustomed to tempering action with the cold fires of ideological subtleties. And where reception had proved to be excellent (*vide* the Reverend Mother Magdalene) there was the interposition of such volatile elements as Poli, Mario Q., which forced reaction in excess of intent and certainly in excess of directive.

Furthermore, he could not talk about it. Except to Cardinal Andreani. And then only briefly. And only once. He could not even confide it to his diary. And certainly not to his colleagues. Maybe he could talk it over, quietly, with God.

CHAPTER XIII

WHEN SISTER ESTHER WENT TO the nursery for Mario's two o'clock feeding a week after Dr. Poli had dismissed her, she saw Sister Luisa dismantling Mario's crib. Made of a particularly heavy dark wood, a chore to handle, it had been lent to the convent by the local contessa, a charitable woman and a rich one. Between them, the contessa and the convent owned most of the arable land in the district, thus indirectly owning the various families that worked the land and only a little more indirectly the merchants in the fishing village and decaying port that lay on the beach at the foot of the uplands like a discarded piece of costume jewelry.

Seeing Sister Esther, Sister Luisa nodded at the crib, and the two of them, working without speaking, finished the dismantling and carried the pieces—the heavy carved headboard, the smaller footboard, the one fixed side, the sliding side, together with mattress and spring—out onto the front portico, where they would be picked up by the convent driver, in the convent pickup truck, and taken to the contessa's villa. After which Sister Luisa said, "You will report immediately to the Superior General's office." "And my son, Sister?" "The Lord's son, Sister." "It would be indelicate of me to ask to have a breast-pump delivered to the infirmary, Sister. I wonder if one of my beloved sisters will have the charity to do so for me." Sister Esther's Italian, which she had been studying and practicing for four months, did not quite convey her intent, but a look at Sister Luisa's dark flat face suggested that the words themselves had carried and been received.

Little crosses, Sister Esther decided, are very hard to bear, especially the cross of Sister Luisa, who usually had the assignment, the very necessary assignment, of course, of chaperoning Sister Esther's physical examinations by the handsome Roman obstetrician Poli. Sister Luisa had also attended at the birth of Mario and very probably had observed, with an obsidian eye, Sister Esther's shameful try—not for heroism, dear God, but for composure—in the delivery room. After all, there was the example of Sister Roberta, who had not, the sisters said, made a sound, not a whimper or a moan, not even, the sisters said, a sigh. And this with no hint of sedation, not even, the sisters said, a purloined aspirin. But dear God, the pains. They had broken her finally, shrunk her to a child. Or, worse, enlarged her to one of those supermodern women who could not have her teeth cleaned without four hypos of Novocain. And Sister Luisa, of the blood of the original Latins, the hill people, had observed all and forgiven her nothing, particularly the special diet prescribed by Dr. Poli to maintain and enrich her flow of milk.

Decidedly, little crosses are hard to bear. Or, as one of the local proverbs went, the larger the tongue, the smaller the wagon. Or the larger she became as a woman, the smaller she became as a nun, where ideally the opposite should have been the norm. The more you bear, the stronger you become. And only the doctor, Poli—and perhaps the Reverend Mother Magdalene—understood that to serve God as a nun she had first to serve Him as a woman. If she carried the Lord's child, she carried the Lord's intent. One could not serve Him in one capacity without necessarily starving Him in another, though ideally she should have served Him absolutely in both. But how could she, when the doctor insisted she eat and rest for the child, and even the sisters, powerful in disapproval and quick with charges of singularity, permitted no haughty deviations from pregnancy's schedule on the grounds that it would be more evil to go against nature than to indulge her? Add one more fault to the many she had incurred, that of forcing others to envy her.

From where she stood on the portico Sister Esther could see through the open iron gates the ancient olive grove which a contemporary of Jesus must have tended. Below the grove, plains of wheat and barley newly plowed and planted, and, below them, the road descending to the sea. The flagstones she stood on were a twentieth-century addition to the convent; the doors behind her, though not all the carved panels, were fifteenth-century. The walls and the stones in the courtyard were the same age but had been set in different centuries, the earliest in the fifteenth, the latest in the twentieth. She was thirty-four and had been sixteen years a nun, that is, novice and nun, but she had been a woman for twenty-one years. She recognized that last statistic with an intellectual nod, an interior bow, because nothing in her training as a nun and nothing in her love for Jesus had prepared her for this moment in this place. Her breasts, supported by a maternity bra, the nipples shielded by sterile cotton pads, ached for the relief of her son, the little enchanter whose unseeing greed and raucous selfishness had amused and enslaved the driest of her sisters. As a nun she approved the Reverend Mother's decision to remove Mario from the convent and place him—he would receive—she did not doubt—but as a woman she resented, she deeply resented— she could see herself confessing her fault to her sisters, hear the inflectionless voice from which all emotion had been squeezed— why had Doctor Poli, whom she respected, insisted that she nurse her little Mario? And why a name, which individualized the child, instead of "he" or "it"? Medically, perhaps Poli was right, just as now the Reverend Mother was right, but had they considered that she stood between them like a she-animal charged with their contending purposes and conditioned by their wills? A stubborn animal, too, not because she opposed her will to her superior and to the religious routines of her Order, but because, necessarily, she opposed her body. She could not starve Mario to feed her soul no matter what the cost in religious futures. But now? Poli had dismissed her. She would feel the flesh draw and pucker along the scar on her abdomen for some time to come, psychic adhesions to replace the physical, until she learned to accept the scar as an incident in her medical history. Like an operation for gall bladder or appendicitis. Sister Luisa had had an appendectomy; one of the little Italian novices, so achingly beautiful that even the girl-hardened Mother of Novices smiled when she rebuked her, had undergone extensive tests for the unknown disease (leukemia?) that would in a few months or a year kill her. How did her ordeal differ from theirs, especially since she had survived it?

Sister Esther smiled, thinking that in a few weeks or months she would be able to pass Sister Agnes or Sister Mary in any convent hall without the minutest hint of a secret alliance or a brief uncommunicated referral to an experience unavailable to their sisters. Again the yielding to the temptation to consider herself unique. She would overcome such temptations, but when? And as she looked at the dismantled crib she understood flatly that the proposed when, the great fiction of the past year and a half, had become the active now. As eager as she had been to come to this necessary point, the place where she could re-enter the magnificent cycle of her religious life, she felt that not enough had been demanded of her, that she had simply accepted and endured on the physical level, that the great springing insight that should make her ordeal (or beating, rather) meaningful had not been revealed to her. Possibly in her present condition the mind could not free itself of the massive, earth-oriented, maternal flesh long enough for the kind of sustained spiritual drive needed for such insights. Ah, but how long would this present condition last? Or, rather, how long would she continue to use it as a cover for lethargy, petulance, rudeness, discourtesy, rebellion, all the little indulgences the small nature grants itself in defiance of God, superiors, and vows? Perhaps she should no longer think of subduing the flesh, at best a monstrous cavil, but of mortifying it. Not the tongue, but the whip.

Passing through the arch that led to the anteroom outside the Superior General's office and seeing no one sitting on the hard wooden benches, she had the impression, without any outer stimulus, of having left a warmer atmosphere for a chillier, of having been thrust brutally through the sticky membrane separating the spiritual time zone from the physical. After a moment of adjustment she realized that what she felt was the return of the nun's extraordinary perception of mental and material data, a faculty very highly developed in some, in others little more than a total use of the existing five senses. Sister Esther thought that she belonged to neither group, but she could, on occasion, know (or have knowledge of) things or events not easily traced to standard means of reception. Since the Order of the Sisters of St. Luke was not a contemplative order, that is, one given over primarily to a monastic life in cloister, it discouraged and, when necessary, refused mystics and natural contemplatives. Though the Order observed the seven canonical hours and enforced the reading of the breviary, it placed its trust in labor, skilled and unskilled, believing that no higher service could be offered to God than the care and healing of the sick, the teaching and training of the ignorant and the unenlightened, and the relief and comfort of the poor.

This sense of perception, then, was hardly the property of the mystic, who more often shut out the senses than expanded them, but a training of unused intellectual powers—in a word, courtesy, a fierce and unyielding attention to the needs of others so that these needs might be foreseen and tended without undue fuss and without straining the charity of the recipient. You foresaw and anticipated so that you might act wisely and effectively. Your gravest fault was the effort the sick or the dying, or simply one in want, might have to make to request services you should have offered before the lack of them became critical. But this perception, your most valuable tool in nursing and teaching, was also the finest of your aids in self-diagnosis and the scalpel with which you did those self-exploratory operations for spiritual cancers, the odious malignancies that were like living sepulchers for the soul, a stain to your sisters, and to the lidless eye of God an ultimate grievance.

Feeling that she had been granted a favor she had often prayed for during the last long months, Sister Esther knocked on the door of the Superior General's office and entered, advancing six paces into the room and kneeling to make her obeisance. Then something black and hard (Satan's hand?) rose up and smashed her in the face. The floor, of course. Why should she try to make something grand out of a simple act of fainting?

When she became conscious again she lay without moving till she had thoroughly re-entered the sphere of the office. Rejecting as firmly as she could the dark claims of panic, the highest of the Satanic calls for abdication, she raised herself on her knees and tried to focus her eyes on the face above the huge desk at the long end of the room. It was as if the face hung from a pendulum that swung toward and away from her, toward and away— She put her hands to her breasts and felt the damp cloth over the nipples, feeling also a slight contraction of the uterus. At least her body functioned, whatever the condition of her mind.

"And how are you today, my child?" The Reverend Mother Magdalene's voice came to her so firmly and with such benevolent disinterest that she felt as if she had been picked up and set firmly in place. Like a wobbling child.

"Very well, Reverend Mother."

"But not well enough yet to resume your normal schedule?"

"I should like to try, Reverend Mother. Now that—" She felt, as she had felt for some months, that gush of self-pity, irresistible and unexpected, burst through the floor of the intellect and short its circuits. One could only endure; it would subside. "Now that my son—the Lord's son—"

"Naturally, you find it difficult to let him go, my child."

"Naturally, Reverend Mother. Supernaturally, no."

"Don't be too harsh on yourself, my child. Being a nurse—I believe you specialized in obstetrics and pediatrics—"

"I did, Reverend Mother."

"Then you know the enormous physiological changes conception, parturition, and lactation work in the female animal. And with these, of course, psychological changes. You are as much controlled by these changes as you would be by malaria or a hallucinatory drug." The Reverend Mother Magdalene, like a clerk in a courtroom, continued with the reading of the case. "You should know—without having to be told—that your passion for our beloved Saviour must be turned now and then to less exalted objects. Love, Sister, like our Saviour's cloak, is a seamless garment. If its sleeve touches the divine, its hem sweeps the floor. Undoubtedly, it distresses you, as you reach toward God, to find your spiritual arm weighted with soiled diapers and bibs."

"It does, Reverend Mother."

"Then remember that while your attention may wander, for good and sufficient reason, His does not. And let me assure you, Sister, few of us in the long history of our Order have been asked to endure His attention in so pure and so intense a form. I cannot say, had we here been so honored, that we would have borne such a cross with exemplary grace or sanctity."

"When God chooses the strong to carry His cross He honors them. When He chooses the weak He censures them. You see, Reverend Mother, the depth of my fall."

"You have been granted a temporary pardon, my child. The Church does not wish to add to your sins by demanding you take complete responsibility for thoughts you clearly, for good and sufficient reason, cannot control. However, I must warn you. Your period of amnesty has now ended. We must think of your future."

"And Mario's future, Reverend Mother? I confess my fault in asking for him and I assure you this will be the last time I will ask."

The Reverend Mother Magdalene observed a half-minute of silence, whether in prayer, rebuke, or composition, Sister Esther could not say. The twenty-fourth Superior General in the history of the Order of the Sisters of St. Luke, she exuded a spiritual militancy that had been the pride of the Order's founder, that powerful, peppery, most unsaintly but greatly sanctified woman who had condemned the slaughter, pillage, and rapine of her time in these words—"Who wounds my sister, my brother, my servant, my slave, and my dog wounds me." Shocked by the neglect by her peers of the impressed peasant-soldier, she left her father's quarters in the tower of his fortress-castle to set up a dispensary for the common soldier in the stables (most of the horses had been eaten by the castle's defenders during the latest siege by papal troops). Knowing nothing of nursing, she bandaged wounds, cleaned bodies, lanced boils, carried slops, comforted the dying, and, little by little, heckling doctors and midwives, faith healers and herbalists, instructed herself in medicine. Though considered mad, the fifteenth century's device for dismissing those too strong and willful to cope with, and threatened with excommunication for exceeding her station both as woman and as daughter and for cohabiting with her inferiors (she slept in a cubicle she had made herself from planking, barrel staves, horse blankets, and straw), this unconquerable, valiant, and resourceful woman attracted a following of women, young and old, high and low, and set up on her father's estates the first hospital of her Order.

To prevent scandal and to circumvent the many natural enemies she made from her father's peers, allies, and supporters, she sought the protection of the Church and herself journeyed to Rome to receive from Pope Sixtus IV a papal charter freeing her hospital-convent both from secular powers and from the jurisdiction of the local bishop. She drew up the ground plan for the cloister, a model for all later houses of the chapter—the hospital and chapel in the north wing, in the center offices and living quarters, and in the south wing the school and service areas (kitchen, bakery, sewing rooms). The chapel, she felt, ought to be associated with the hospital. When she died she was buried under the choir of the chapel, a good three meters from the altar. After burial, there was found in her papers a clear directive that she be interred, with proper rites, under the surgery, "where I may perhaps be cleansed by the blood of those unfortunate enough to require the services of our surgeons." She did not think much of, it seemed, fifteenth-century doctors. The uniform she prescribed for her nurse-nuns was a coarse woolen gown to be worn over a shift "of a material tender enough to the skin so that the nurse need not be distracted in the care of the sick by a constant urge to scratch, squirm, wriggle, or dance." A wimple, a white bib, a leather belt, and a rosary hung from the left hip completed the habit. A six-teenth-century Superior General added a pectoral cross, an optional item not often worn by nursing sisters on duty.

"The color of this sacking," the founder wrote, in a journal still preserved at the convent, "should be dyed a deep dark blue, blue being the color of our beloved physician, St. Luke." She jotted down little notes of instruction, presumably to those less practical than herself. "The head need not be shaved except when infected with lice or other bodily parasites, nor need the hair be cut shorter than the length of the first joint of the thumb." On cleanliness: "The hands should be washed when sufficiently soiled and the nails cut close. The feet should be bathed at least twice a week and the webs between the toes thoroughly cleansed. The toes then should be artificially articulated by hand." The soldier's pre-occupation with feet. "Also the nails should never be cut in such a manner as to permit them to grow into the flesh." She also wrote the phrase that dominated and enriched the Order. "I am nearest God when I am privileged to touch, with a healing hand,

His violated image on this earth." Before she died she had over-seen the building and staffing of three hospital-convents in Italy, and on her deathbed said simply, "I dream of Africa."

Sharing the Superior General's silence, Sister Esther could appreciate and enjoy—more than that, rest against—the powerful moral force of this gaunt aging woman, the mother-spider at the center of her international web, prepared at any moment to rush to its remotest corner in repair or replacement of its silken cables. No less militant and progressive than her predecessors, she had fought, schemed, plotted, and contrived to get her nursing sisters out of the convent and into the homes, apartments, and caves of the poor and sick. "We must not only cure our suffering patients," she had said, "we must remove the conditions that cause them to suffer." Forbidden by an outraged Cardinal Andreani (my beloved enemy) to set up a visiting-nurse program, she nevertheless contrived, through the device of an outpatients' clinic and the co-operation of her needy clients, to promote a counterprogram that violated the Cardinal's edict only in spirit. Since the sisters did their own shopping, driving the convent's station wagon themselves, they could, in town or en route, be called to help out in cases of necessity where no other aid was immediately available. Along with a medical kit the station wagon carried a kit of another kind, one containing soaps, scrub brushes, mops, and disinfectants.

It was this Superior General, Sister Esther reminded herself, who had scandalized Catholic Italy by proposing that the most gifted of her nursing nuns be permitted to take degrees in medicine, sociology, and law. A nun a practicing M.D.? Only the Pope himself saved the Superior General from the piping-hot Andreani, who proposed to lay on the Order the ban of the cloister, all nuns to withdraw forever behind the convent's walls and henceforth be seen, except *in extremis,* by no person, not even the nun's confessor and the papal inspector. Peace, Eminence. But his Eminence, far from being appeased by a placatory letter and by distant acts of contrition, demanded her appearance in Rome, where, as the unspoken story went, she had done an extraordinary retreat of three months, locked in a cell containing a watering can, a bucket, and a dozen loaves of coarse black bread. A pretty story, one fit for the convent's archives, and, probably, considering the anger of a prince, only exaggerated or falsified by the process of selection and condensation. This, then, was the presence to which Sister Esther kneeled, one which aspired to a corona not of light but of fire.

"If you were prepared to give your life for this child," the Superior General said, "you cannot protest too warmly against the added burden of nursing it. For I know it is a burden. A cross of love, the hardest of all crosses to bear. Attachment. Do you think unkindly of me for having cut this strangling cord so abruptly?"

"Yes, I do, Reverend Mother. But I also honor you for it."

"You must know that while Dr. Poli decided—on medical grounds alone—that you breast-feed the child, you could not have done so without my consent?"

"The child must be protected."

"Yes. Now it is up to you, Sister, to prove that our confidence in your spiritual strength and integrity was well taken. As for the child, he will be given every advantage to which a ward of the Church is entitled—a decent home, affection, religious instruction, an education suited to his intellectual level—does this satisfy you, my child?"

"Yes, Reverend Mother."

"Now as to your own spiritual state, my child, how do you stand?"

"Like the clumsiest and the most frightened novice ever to enter a cloister, Reverend Mother."

"You may think that an honest answer, my child, and it may well be. But it is a sophisticated honesty encrusted with very lively experiences and riddled with pride." The Superior General's face, a hawk on its height, appeared to stoop suddenly for the rodent in the grass. "You single yourself out for more of God's attention than one person deserves. Or can successfully withstand, Sister. Remember, when one draws God's attention one also draws His fire. But let's turn for the moment to more practical matters. You and your sisters will be sent back to the United States of America, to your mother house, to reinvest yourself in the spiritual life. What happens to you then is no concern of ours."

"Thank you, Reverend Mother. You know my fear of being— dismissed from the Order."

"But this is something you yourself must decide, my child. I can't speak for your superiors in the States, but I can say with all confidence that those who truly will to serve God shall always be permitted to serve Him."

"You know I have only one desire, Reverend Mother: to offer my experiences—I don't say ordeal—to the glory of God. Quietly, anonymously. A life of penance through service to others. If God so wishes, in the Far East."

"You wish to go back there, my child?"

"More than anything. If it is God's will and the order of my superiors."

"And you believe you can see your experiences as a simple test of faith and nothing further?"

"I do, Reverend Mother, I must."

"You believe you can serve within the framework of our Order and let no single stain of pride or uniqueness become visible to your sisters?"

"I ask only sufficient time to regain control of my body."

"And you believe you can regain sufficient control without the uses of a superior humility or excessive mortification?"

"I do, Reverend Mother."

"That will be your thorn, my child, to suppress a feeling of uniqueness without this effort—at any time—becoming either an offense or a rebuke to those who have less vivid personal histories."

"It would be a great help to me, Reverend Mother, if I could return to work."

"The hospital?"

"Anything, Reverend Mother. Gardening, painting, carpentry— do you need a hand in the fields?"

"We shall see, my child. But at the moment heavy labor is out

112

of the question. Much as I concede its therapeutic value." The Superior General smoothed a paper on her desk, an action that effectively silenced Sister Esther. "I have something to say to you now, my child, that greatly troubles me. For several reasons. But first let me remind you that I have not been privy to your secret thoughts. Nor have I solicited your confidence in hope of lessening or alleviating your sufferings. I regret this, but only because like most of us I rejoice at the opportunity to serve, however badly and with whatever poor results. In all truth, my child, there was nothing I could do beyond seeing that you were reasonably comfortable, had adequate medical care, and were offered sufficient spiritual sustenance. Your case, my child, no matter how little I may like it, is not for me to decide."

"My case alone, Reverend Mother? Or that of all of us?"

"You are frightened, my child?"

"I had hoped—I had hoped—"

"You may continue to do so, my child." The Superior General clasped her hands and settled them on the papers on her desk. "What I have to tell you is this: the Office of the Sacred Congregation of Rites wishes to examine you and your sisters."

"I shall be glad to tell the representative of so exalted an office everything in my power to reveal, Reverend Mother." Dear God, she must not, she must not feel such petty resentment, such defensive indignation. Like a child being told to wipe the lipstick off her face. "I welcome, I truly welcome—" Turn the toes outward to prevent slippage sideways, lean back till you feel the pull of the major thigh muscles, breathe deeply through the mouth, hold the diaphragm extended, exhale slowly through the mouth—the excess intake of oxygen will affect the balance, but only temporarily.

The Reverend Mother Magdalene stood, waiting perhaps till she had calmed herself, that peculiar self-rocking action that may have been a search for the lost rhythms of childhood, and then walked slowly toward her. Stooping, she took Sister Esther's hands in hers and raised her, an embrace, yes, material, certainly, but also the touch of the nurse who knows the value of physical contact.

"If you chose violation instead of death, my child, you cannot object to an examination of your motives in so doing. The Church is wiser—and kinder—than you realize. Alone you can never make the journey into the depths of your soul that is necessary for a free and joyous return to the religious life. For the others this should not be difficult. But for you, Sister—" The Reverend Mother Magdalene made the sign of the cross on Sister Esther's forehead with her thumb. "For you, Sister, it will not be easy."

CHAPTER XIV

UNABLE ANY LONGER TO LOOK directly at the nun kneeling on the floor of the Superior General's office, Kramer got up from the desk and turned to the bookshelves perhaps six feet behind his chair. A life of St. Teresa, naturally. *The Legend of St. Joan.* An edition of the works of Meister Eckhart. Ruysbroeck, de Sales. *The Catholic Encyclopedia.* It had been said of him, at the seminary in Ohio, that he owned a nose for damnation. The first task of the seminary teaching staff was to make an atheist of the new pupil. "Tell me, Kramer, do you believe in God?" And God help you if, as he had done, you said yes. Had anyone ever answered no?

Turning to Sister Roberta, he said, "This basketball court, Sister. Could it be reached directly from the basement?" Again the attempt to speak, again that whisper he could hear only if he did not approach her. "Yes? You and your sisters were in the basement. Twelve of you. Is that right?" Again the pantomime with the lips, the whisper that was perhaps the sinister reduction of the gale blowing through her mind. Well, he had seen her, observed her, questioned her briefly. "Thank you, Sister."

And before she stood she made the sign of the cross. Against him? Did she suffer? Who alive didn't? But how alive could she be? "Remember, you enter this affair with unclean hands." In Catholic America the Jesuits had kept Satan alive; in Italy it was the people who would not let him die. At the desk Kramer, who had now, in the third day of the investigation, talked with all four nuns, studied his notes.

The safe thing would be to continue the interrogation as he had begun it, simply to record the stories of the four nuns, prompt them when necessary but not guide or lead them, write an extensive commentary, and deliver the package to Cardinal Bellini. On the surface a very straightforward, plausible, and attractive plan of action, one the reasonable and temperate man might well be expected to make, a plan that would serve all parties—the nuns, the Church, himself. And who, Kramer thought, would serve God? What God?

He stood again in the office at the seminary while little Father Gerlain, a kobold from the basement under the chapel, barked at him, "What God, Kramer?" "The God of our Fathers—" The unfortunate answer shattered him. He was an imbecile being heckled by a wise old child— "What God? Damn it, Kramer, don't you even know your catechism? Well?" "Sir, I—" "Sir?" This seemed to finish Father Gerlain. "Football players, nances, and intellectuals, that's what we're getting, Kramer. Have you ever had a homosexual experience?" Prepared for that question by the psychiatric examination, Kramer said, "No, Father." "But you've been approached by homosexuals, surely? Well, haven't you?" "Not that I know of, Father." "Not that you— Would you know a homosexual when you saw one?" "Some types, yes, Father." "Types. You've studied the subject." "Briefly, Father." "And alcohol?" "Once in a while a little beer, Father." "But not very often. Have you ever had a heterosexual experience?" "Yes, Father." "But she did all the work." Kramer realized that Father Gerlain was looking at his hands, which were now fists, very large ones. "What are you sore about, Kramer? You were thinking of hitting me, weren't you?" "No, Father." "The first healthy idea he's had and he lies about it."

Father Gerlain made a circuit of Kramer, seeing him from all arcs. "Listen, Kramer, we've had it here with Pious Peters, phony mystics, eager beavers, and virgins. Polluting the sheets isn't a crime here. So don't try to cover up. As a matter of fact, you're expected to have a wet dream at least once a month. That is, during your first year here. Masturbation is out. Forget it. In my judgment you'll need plenty of physical exercise. We'll see that you get it. What do you think are your principal impediments to vows? Don't think about it, just answer." "Women, Father." "Qualify that." "I don't know, Father. The idea of women, I'd say. Physical—" Kramer shrugged. "I hope you're right, boy. We need men. When the priest mounts the altar you should hear his balls clank—"

Kramer, who had thought to repress his experiences in the coal towns of Pennsylvania, now decided to use them as points of reference. Slowly, at first angrily, he began to understand that though the Church wanted priests, good ones, it did not want him. He saw, one by one, his classmates pack up and leave, some saying, "I came here to strengthen my faith in God, not to lose it"; others, "I know when I'm not wanted"; a few said nothing, leaving in a semihypnotic condition, profoundly astonished, profoundly shaken, profoundly grieved. Kramer persisted. By the end of his first year at the seminary he had lost his faith in God— or, rather, he had lost contact with God. Stubbornly, he routined himself in the forms and customs of prayer and worship just as he had routined himself in the motions and reflexes of the split end in football. Dirty work, hard work, grace would come in the game itself, if after six or seven years of fundamentals his teachers permitted him to play it.

"Do you know how much it costs the Church to educate and train a priest?" Father Gerlain would say. "About three thousand dollars a year. What about your parents, Kramer? Can't they contribute?" He was given a six-week vacation in July and August. "Get as far away from the Church as you can," Father Gerlain said. "Live it up." Kramer went home, stayed three days, and then went to Pittsburgh, where he got a temporary job on a construction gang. When he returned to the seminary he handed Father Gerlain an envelope containing three hundred dollars in cash. "A bribe," the old priest said. "I shall have to report this to Monsignor Morris. Your first major offense. Beyond the daily stupidities we expect of first- and second-year men." The seminary kept the money, but it was clear to Kramer that he was a marked man. So, he found later, in the cynicism and bleakness of his third year, were the others. Harrigan, Listel, Pilcher, O'Malley, Burns, Cherly—the seminary broke them, deliberately, slowly, logically, and then put them together again. The seminary hit not at their weaknesses, as Kramer had been taught to do in the coal fields and on the gridiron, but at their strengths. The greater your candle power the bigger your field of darkness. You faced a most ingenious and dishonest obstacle course, one in which the hurdle was moved while you were astride it.

As his confessor said at the end of Kramer's third year when Kramer asked about the possibility of a year's leave of absence, "You took a little longer to get around to this than we expected, Kramer. But the answer is no." "I'll walk out then, Father. Pack up and leave." "Why? Can you tell me? And don't give me the easy answers, give me the real ones." "There has to be a reason why I'm here, Father. I don't have one. I'm not using or marking time, I'm killing it." "You want to be a priest, Kramer. Isn't that good enough for you?" "Does the seminary want me to be a priest, Father?" "No." "What does the seminary want, Father?" "It wants you to decide what you want, Kramer. I'll tell you what we don't want here—problem people. Congenital soreheads. Self-pitiers. Listen, it isn't what we demand of you, it's what you demand of yourself." "I'm giving everything I've got, Father. Isn't that enough?" "I'd advise you to reorient your thinking, Kramer. In football you don't give up because the man playing against you is tough, fast, intelligent, and resourceful, do you? Tell me, when you played football what was your object?" "To win, Father." "You don't think you can beat us, Kramer? Why not?" "I wasn't aware that I was playing against you, Father." "But you are now. We're not so tough, Kramer. We can be taken. But keep on the alert. And don't play the same type of game against us week after week. When we shift our defenses vary your attack. When we change the rules adapt yourself to them. Certain fundamentals never change, no matter what the circumstances, but our interpretation of these fundamentals can change. And will. Your goal is ordination. We give ground slowly, but we've never yet been able to stop a really determined opponent. I admit that this is a very sophomoric analogy, but it might help to clear your thinking. Which is also very sophomoric." "Is God my enemy, Father?" "No, but His representatives often are. Mainly, because people like you have such an exalted and bilious opinion of the uniform, you're annihilated when you see a man's head above the collar. Surely you've noticed that our emphasis here is on character, not piety. Because, Kramer, it's the secular priest's character, not his piety, that's going to make a success of his pastorate. Look at Moses. A most sinful man. But he brought his people out of Egypt and up to the border of the Promised Land. And if you reject Moses, look at Christ. I don't mean the Christ of the pretty pictures and nursery stories, I mean the great hairy brute that drove the money-changers out of the temple, the hot-tempered colossus who said, 'I come not to bring peace but a sword.' And I mean the egocentric lad who told his mother to mind her own business. In other words the Christ who didn't stop at the entrance to the elevator shaft but went down into the bowels of the earth with your father. Do you know Him, Kramer?" "I dream of Him, Father." "Then what else do you need?"

"What else?" Kramer pressed the button on the desk and said to the nun who opened the door into the waiting room, "Sister Esther, please." He studied his notes for perhaps five minutes before looking up at the nun kneeling where Sister Roberta had knelt. No, he had not been mistaken. He felt, as he had felt at her first interview, the tension of a man hunting not the unknown but the unforeseeable. The other three would undoubtedly surprise and astonish, would this one confound him? A feeling, yes, but one should trust the animal senses, the early-warning system, of the body. She impressed him. More than that, she offended him. And he could smell her. The female, the great warm hairy cleft of her— Ah, but when he had cause enough to interrogate her sharply why goad himself with such medieval prods?

"There were twelve nuns in the group captured by the enemy, Sister. What happened to the other seven?"

"They resisted our captors, Monsignor, and were immediately killed."

"Immediately?"

"Yes, Monsignor."

"Resisted. With force? Guns, perhaps?"

"They refused to—" Her hands moved in a gesture of such grace and power that Kramer had the sensation of being physically pushed away from a scene at which he was not recorder and advocate but a vulgar spectator.

"I don't think we need be so coy, Sister, in discussing this, granted, extraordinary event. What did they reject?"

"Our captors' request that they submit to them physically."

"For what purpose, Sister?"

"Sexual intercourse."

"You weren't simply taken and raped, then. You were asked to consent to intercourse."

"Yes, Monsignor."

"The core of the apple, Sister. Seven of your sisters preferred death to violation. Five preferred violation. Why?"

"I don't think I can give you a proper answer to that question, Monsignor. Not at this time. Perhaps later—"

"You what, Sister? I beg your pardon. You know why I'm here. You know the importance of this investigation. You've had more than a year to think this thing through. Yet you say you cannot give me a proper answer." Kramer stood and crossed to her. "You evil bitch, you stink of abominations that gag me when I'm forced to report them to my superiors. You, a bride of Christ, smell before the august presence of my office of the black sweat of the men who repeatedly enjoyed your body and of the sour milk of your animal breasts—yet—"

Sister Esther, on her elbows, face to the floor, said, "Forgive me—forgive me—"

"Forgive? I forgive? Am I your God, Sister? Are you so much in love with the male principle that you grovel at my feet and ask me to forgive you? Perhaps you suggest something else."

"No, no—"

"The Reverend Mother Magdalene has told me of this strange, perverted, obscene pride of your, this unnatural coddling of your sins—as if these demanded constant care and loving attention lest they fade before the eye of God. Do you fear that by doing penance you will lose His attention? And the attention and interest of your superiors?"

"I have tried—I have tried—"

"Perhaps you hope for God's mark on your forehead so that wherever you go, among what peoples and nations, this mark will set you apart as one eternally condemned and therefore under God's protection. A great honor, Sister. Shall we fire the iron and burn your shame in the flesh of your face? Or shall we permit the evil core to burn through to the surface till we see in the smoldering, decaying skin the true map of your soul?" Kramer returned to the desk. "Get up, Sister. If you have a handkerchief, use it. If you can, pray. Examine yourself. I will, of course, want to see you again."

"May I confess myself, Monsignor?"

"Before you do, ask yourself what further mockery you wish to inflict on the Church by trying to confess to sins you either are not aware of or are deliberately withholding from yourself, your confessor, and your God. Pray for guidance, Sister, and accept it."

Feeling that he now had committed himself wholly to the investigation, a move the Cardinal might think dangerous but must not be permitted to believe unnecessary or gratuitous, Kramer rang for Sister Agnes and subjected her to the same brutal grilling. He needed a control.

"You realize the necessity of this investigation, Sister."

"Yes, Monsignor."

"And welcome it."

"I will do what I can to help, Monsignor."

"Willingly, Sister. Joyously."

"Willingly."

"But not joyously. A dark business, one for which eternal night is light enough. I accept your attitude, Sister, but hope for your encouragement. Without your ardent assistance I face a very discouraging prospect."

"Your will is mine, Monsignor."

"And the devil's will, Sister? Whose will is his? Signor Satan, well known for his great charm and fine intellect. Often portrayed by our poets as an inimitable seducer and lover of women. In easier days, when we had more faith than science, believed to be the whore's patron, the hero of the Black Mass, the phallus. Surely, in this romantic disguise, you have known him a little?"

"As you say, Monsignor, I—have known him."

"And enjoyed him, Sister? Of course you have. The irrepressible flesh. I also enjoy pleasures of the flesh. Some pleasures."

"Before God, Monsignor—" Sister Agnes's gesture had neither grace nor power. To Kramer it expressed the fatty bathos of a particularly crafty and insensitive crone, a false judgment, he knew, but overwhelming.

"Your flesh is not irrepressible, Sister? You do not, occasionally, enjoy a fine spring morning? You are not, now and then, distracted from your spiritual austerities by the song of a bird? Your eye has never been delighted by a great painting nor your ear bewitched by a splendid lyric? I envy you." Sickened by his derivative sarcasms, he saw, nevertheless, that he had roused her.

"I confess that I find it hard to understand you, Monsignor."

"You confess that you find it hard to put up with my sneering at you, Sister. As you should. Few of us are large enough of soul to forgive our mockers."

"You have not offended me, Monsignor."

"You bear up well under mockery, Sister, but how will you do when stoned by the truth? Yes, we can confess freely what we're not guilty of, even die gaily under false accusations, but we cannot stand the minutest exposure of the true ground of the soul. When I suggested that you enjoyed sexual intercourse with the enemies of our country—this despite a very powerful vow of chastity—you recoiled but didn't collapse. Why is this?"

"I can say only that I regret, deeply regret, not having chosen death, Monsignor."

"From the safety of the present, Sister, you can say anything. One further question—during these lustful embraces did you console yourself by wearing—between your breasts—the cross, the sacred figure of our crucified Redeemer?"

Sister Agnes did not faint; she dropped slowly back on her heels and then slid sideways, supported by first one hand, then the other. Kramer waited, watching the downturned face for signs of emotion.

"Get up," Kramer said. "No, stand. Listen, Sister, what I believe or the Church believes is in your case secondary to what you believe. What I have tried to do is bring into your consciousness extremes of behavior you might have trouble bringing in yourself. Do you understand?"

"Yes, Monsignor."

"Good. Now I want you to write me a brief history of your capture and treatment by the enemy, your experiences with the company of soldiers that rescued you, and a simple account of your life here. It need not be long and it certainly doesn't have to be literature. Twenty or thirty pages will do. I'll see that you have sufficient time for this project. What I want is your story, your viewpoint, your ideas. Be simple, be clear, be accurate. And don't try to put down what you can't recall or didn't witness. Say that you don't remember or weren't there."

After dismissing Sister Agnes, Kramer, feeling a real need for exercise, went for a walk in the hills above the convent. Except for the ancient buildings—the convent itself, the stone-and-plaster barns, the cottages—he might have been in Nebraska or certain sections of Austria, but not in Pennsylvania, not in the coal towns, where the rocky inner lining of the earth, stripped of its vital coal, lay heaped in great barren tumuluses along the railroad tracks and above and beyond the plants and the towns. For his father, apprenticed to the mines as a boy, the sun shone, when it shone, only on Sundays, the Christian Sabbath. Therefore, his father was not a Christian, but a sun worshiper. Kramer's confessor had been wrong. Christ had not entered the elevator with his father. He had been interred at Ellis Island.

And himself? He needed a pastorate, not necessarily a slum church and not, certainly, a rich one, but a church that served a large industrial district, with its mixtures of lower-income groups, white-collar workers, and minorities, one to which, through prayer and enlightening labor, he might bring the true Christ, the God-Man, the forgotten Christ who destroyed to create, who tapped his neighbor's chest not to percuss his heart but to awaken his soul, the fisherman, the prophet, the preacher. He needed—to lose weight, for one thing. He had played football at one ninety-five. Now he weighed two twenty, perhaps two twenty-five. How much had Christ weighed?

CHAPTER XV

THE NEXT MORNING KRAMER said an early Mass and returned to his apartment in the guest wing of the convent, where Sister Luisa brought him a breakfast of cereal, eggs, bacon, toast, coffee, and orange juice.

After breakfast he sat at the window and smoked one of the

cigarettes he had bought for Captain Sterling, something he had never done before, a new action, vaguely necessary, like, for instance, that second glass of wine with last night's dinner in town. He had not finished the wine, nor, this morning, did he finish the cigarette. Between breakfast and lunch he worked on his notes and wrote the first pages of his report to Cardinal Bellini. What he thought of the case, his findings and recommendations, would come later, in a separate commentary, a few pages, brief and airless, an agenda for the inescapable interview with Cardinal Bellini, who probably had already ground the mirror in which he would show Kramer himself, in effect make Kramer judge himself and proceed on that judgment toward an indefinite future.

Future? The heresy of individualism, that particular horror for which Joan of Arc burned and for which Galileo, in an ecstasy of ironic renunciation, oiled and bent the hinge. Who makes the future unmakes the past. Who spies on God, whether with Joan of Arc's paranoia or Galileo's brain, shows that the Church's institutionalism has gotten the better of its ministry, that the intuitive shepherd has been replaced by the rational wolf. But, Kramer thought, the star of individualism is anarchy, a most potent error, a death-star leading its followers, however wise, to the pit. From which few rise. No, the Church had not convicted Galileo of saying that the earth moved (what had this to do with the core of faith?), but of exposing a future into which he assumed the Church could never lead him. Enough, enough. Prayer was more productive than thought, and work finer than either.

In the Superior General's office Kramer put his notes on the desk, arranged his pencils, damned the stained-glass windows at his back, switched on a lamp, switched it off, summoned the Reverend Mother Magdalene. He asked her, abruptly, what plans she had for Sister Roberta. "I can only report to his Eminence Cardinal Bellini that she needs psychiatric care."

"I shall, of course, report to his Eminence that she does not."

"What would you say she needs, Reverend Mother?"

"Work, Monsignor. In our hospitals, orphanages, homes for the aged. Perhaps in our mental institutions. Believe me, Monsignor, she will make an excellent nurse. She is already training in our hospital and has shown great aptitude for caring for and comforting the aged and the incurables. This is the therapy she needs. I'll say more—if she is subjected to psychiatric programs she will be lost forever."

"Strong words."

"I mean them, Monsignor."

"And your plans for the other three?"

The Reverend Mother Magdalene, a splendidly disciplined nun, did not indulge herself in meaningful pauses or dramatic hesitations. No, it was as if she were listening to the unspoken part of his question, that part audible to her even though not yet consciously entertained by him. "Soon—I should say within a very short time—all four nuns will be sent back to their mother house in California."

"Do you think this is the best course, Reverend Mother?" He was improvising, using time he had just been told, abruptly, he did not have.

"This is not for me to decide, Monsignor."

No, of course not. And as he moved the papers on the desk, in imitation of a man making a decision, he wondered why instead of being depressed by her news he should feel elated. "Would you agree with me, Reverend Mother, that since I've now been told I have a limited time for this investigation I should not waste it on routine examinations of all four nuns but, rather—" he leaned across the desk to stare directly at her—"but, rather, concentrate it on one?"

"And which one would that be, Monsignor?"

"Sister Esther."

After a moment she said, "I realize that for the purposes of your investigation, Monsignor, you must appear as the deputy of the Adversary. Whose claims may be refuted but not denied. But the shepherd's first duty is to his flock, even when the wolf is Mother Church."

Kramer nodded and sat at the desk. He need not press further for her approval of his projected course of action, nor need he force her to acknowledge that he had it. "I'll see Sister Esther then, Reverend Mother."

"May I add that the Order of the Sisters of St. Luke in America has its own superior general, Monsignor, and its own cardinal-protector?"

"But as international head of the Order—"

"The American chapters are quite independent of us."

"And their cardinal-protector?"

"Cardinal Brooker."

Brooker. "You probably know—or do you?—that Cardinal Brooker arranged for me to study in Rome and that I expect to be incardinated into his archdiocese when I return to America."

"I had hoped that you would have some influence with Cardinal Brooker, Monsignor. I needn't say that the sufferings of these children have entered into my bones."

"I shall be writing Cardinal Brooker very soon, Reverend Mother. As you know, the office of cardinal-protector is often treated as another honorary title, fine in print but in practice something to be left to filing clerks. However, in the hands of an able man willing to oppose the dictates of the Curia—when he believes them excessive— And don't forget that California is not only an ocean away from Rome but a continent away. A word from Cardinal Brooker to the Holy Father should, I believe, be enough to counteract any unrealistic program imposed on these nuns by, say, Cardinal Andreani or others who deal in generalities and not in specifics." Had he made himself clear? Apparently, from her silence, he had. "Now as to Sister Esther—"

The Superior General went to the bookcase, selected a book, opened it and read aloud this passage:

> What though the field be lost?
> All is not lost; the unconquerable will . . .
> And courage never to submit or yield;
> And what is else not to be overcome . . .

Shutting the book, she returned it to the shelf. "This is Satan talking, Monsignor, the Satan who was also the most luminous of the archangels. Lucifer. Hardly the words of a small nature. Certainly not the boast of a reclining one."

After she left, Kramer, annoyed by having had to make a deal with her but pleased that he had gotten her approval to question Sister Esther in depth (this would help should Bellini challenge his methods of investigation), reread his notes quickly, particularly those passages condensing and interpreting the testimony of Sister Agnes. He could not risk a mistake, however inspired, with so little time available. He was astonished (yes, astonished) at Cardinal Andreani's willingness to return the nuns to America, though he admitted he could not know Andreani's mind or the circumstances that compelled that powerful and stubborn Cardinal's order. The obvious reason for the order was a perfectly natural wish to remove the nuns from the jurisdiction of Cardinal Bellini's Congregation of Rites. Or, not remove the nuns entirely, since this could not be done, simply make further investigation more difficult. Well, while Rome juggled, he could work. He had the approval of the Superior General, whose perceptions he could rely on. Why wait?

When Sister Esther entered the room and kneeled she appeared, to Kramer, to exist spatially but across an air bridge of time, a figure in a small fifteenth-century painting, startlingly present but unapproachable.

"Please," he said, placing a chair for her some three or four paces from the desk. Going to the bookcase, he took the copy of Milton's *Paradise Lost* and read the passage the Superior General had quoted. "A powerful statement of defiance, Sister. Do you know it?"

"I recognize it, yes, Monsignor."

"A conscious statement of defiance. Taken out of context, a magnificent statement of defiance. 'What though the field be lost?' Is that your position, Sister?"

"Nothing can be lost, Monsignor, that you refuse to give up."

"Nothing spiritual, perhaps. But you can refuse to lose an arm and still be forced to give it up to the surgeon."

"Of course."

Kramer crossed to the desk and took several papers from his

briefcase. "I have here a report, a very favorable report, of your mission in the Far East, Sister. The number of converts you made among the natives, the success of your clinic and hospital, your highly productive farms, your teaching programs—an outstanding job. In addition you apparently inspired in a great many natives who knew of your accomplishments only by hearsay an immense affection, respect, reverence."

"For God, I hope, Monsignor."

"And for yourselves, Sister. What respect would a person, particularly an uneducated person, have for God if he had none for you? I don't see in this case a cult of personalities; I see a courageous and imaginative evangelism based on very practical methods and sustained on a highly selfless level. Bishop Key in his report to his Eminence stresses the word 'selfless.' I'm sure that if he had felt that you were singling yourself out for more attention than the God you served he would have sent you the appropriate reprimand and placed a curb on your activities. So far as I know, he did not."

"Without Bishop Key's support, understanding, and sympathy we could have done very little, Monsignor."

"Have you thought what this might mean to the godless rebels who tried to overthrow the lawful government in that peninsula and install a pagan police state?"

"They will learn to tolerate us, Monsignor. And we shall teach them to love us."

"Brava, Sister. Well and smugly said. If you feel you need to coach yourself by mouthing such dubious propaganda for your glorious Order, please do. Anything to hold you together long enough to answer the important questions a patient and much-suffering Church thinks it imperative to ask."

"I suppose we have no place in their order, Monsignor. Yet."

"But some day you will."

"With the help of God, we pray so, Monsignor."

Kramer looked at the sheet of paper headed by the word "questions." "Tell me, why did you and your sisters permit yourselves to be caught by the invaders? You must have had some warning of an impending attack."

128

"We were in charge of a hospital with many critically ill and wounded patients, Monsignor."

"Before the attack, Sister, you could have had no wounded patients."

"There were always rumors, Monsignor, reports of attacks that never took place, fictional aggressions, many of them, we believed, circulated by the rebels. A war of nerves."

"You received no warnings at all from either the American army of occupation or our ambassador or his staff?"

"Yes, but we—" Sister Esther gestured, letting the movement of her hands describe the childishness and incredibility of such warnings, letting Kramer see that while she and her sisters had been amused, touched, and perhaps genuinely embarrassed by such devotional concern they could hardly be expected to act on it.

"You felt that it was your duty to remain at your post despite the warnings of our government's accredited representatives and your own knowledge of the pagan's character and aims?"

"We believed that the rebels would respect the neutrality of our nursing diplomas if not the habits of our vocation."

"Such joyous innocence, Sister, might be interpreted in some quarters as arrogance."

"We can hide from an enemy, Monsignor; we cannot hide from God. We were proud, yes, but for the sake of those who depended on us we dared not show fear."

"And these dependents?"

"Some were converts to Christianity, some were not. We found we couldn't simply go into the villages and preach, Monsignor, even if that were our mission. We lured the people by offering free medical care and entertainment. We had an old projector that we cranked by hand and some very old two-reel comedies and Laurel and Hardy movies. We also had radios and mechanical record players. Later, when we had electricity—"

"I can't believe that these natives were living in the Stone Age, Sister."

"There's the difficulty, Monsignor. And the reason for our mission. The people in the coastal areas, in the capital and larger cities, were quite civilized. Many had been converted to Catholicism. More of them had been converted to nineteenth-century capitalism. They considered themselves quite superior to the farmers in the rice-growing delta and even more superior to the tribes back in the hills. It was those tribes we wanted to reach."

It was as if, Kramer thought, she had detached herself from a *tableau vivant* depicting the suffering of the five sisters after the assault to come forward and speak for herself. "How long were you in the peninsula, Sister?"

"Seven years, Monsignor. Sister Catherine and I came out together."

"Had you had any contact at all with the natives who were later to become your enemies?"

"Only indirectly, Monsignor. In a civil war it is a matter of ideologies and not of physical appearance."

Kramer smiled. "Very well put. And even though you weren't sure of the loyalty of the people you served you refused to abandon them."

"We loved them, Monsignor. We wished to serve them. In danger as well as in safety."

"You humble me, Sister. For the sake of a handful of scrubby natives whose Christianity probably went no deeper than the lips, you risked violation of your vows. What heroism."

"We could never assume that, Monsignor."

"No. But there's a point here I wish to clarify. After seven years in the peninsula—and none of your sisters were there fewer than five—you couldn't have been totally ignorant of the methods and aims of your enemies. Did it occur to you that you were a prime target for assault? That the enemy, shrewd and practical as he is, might wish to do something more than simply capture or kill you and destroy your convent and hospital?"

"It did not, Monsignor."

"No? You felt that the enemy was improvising, that he had no real plans for your disposal, that when he captured your convent and hospital he found himself encumbered by the presence of twelve white nuns and no idea of what to do with them."

"I—"

"According to your own testimony, Sister, the captain of the detachment—or commanding officer—spoke excellent English. As did the political—shall we say commissar?—who accompanied him. I suggest these sophisticated gentlemen knew exactly who you were and exactly what to do with you." Kramer paused, assessing her silence. "Look at me, Sister."

"Yes, Monsignor?"

"Did your superior, Mother Benedict, have any plans for evacuating the area in event of an attack?"

"She said, more than once, that the presence of American troops in the peninsula endangered our neutrality, Monsignor. She did not say that the troops shouldn't be there; she said only that if fighting broke out involving the American troops we, being Americans, might not be able to preserve our status as noncombatants. She did not fear this; she mentioned it as something to keep in mind."

"Could Bishop Key have ordered your evacuation, Sister?"

"I believe he could have, Monsignor. But he was in the Philippine Islands at the time and only returned to the peninsula three days before the attack."

"The fact is that you and your sisters remained at your post despite several clear warnings from the Army and representatives of our State Department, and your attitude suggests that you would have obeyed a direct order from Bishop Key to evacuate the area only after making every effort to evade it. And probably only after the order could not be obeyed. Is this a reasonable construction of your state of mind at the time, Sister?"

"Yes."

"In law there is the phrase 'attractive nuisance.' Have you heard it?"

"No, Monsignor."

"The sense of it is that you can place an object or objects on your own property of such overwhelming attraction or aggravation that persons, such as children and adolescents, may be lured to it against all rules of conscience and propriety. And you, Sister, in

131

case of damage either to this object or to its destroyers, are liable."

"But, Monsignor, you cannot vow to serve God without reservation and at the same time calculate the advantages of becoming an 'attractive nuisance.' "

"You miss the point, Sister. Or, rather, from pride—" Kramer tapped the desk—"from pride, Sister, you argue the point."

"I don't understand you, Monsignor."

"How can you, when your energies are directed solely to countering and refuting me?"

Sister Esther looked at her hands, as if these, the autonomous tools of her body, contained that most striking and irrefutable of wisdoms, accomplishment. What had she to do with the aged priests who conducted the Church's ceremonies and protected and reinforced its traditions, who, hawk-headed and lion-footed, patrolled the bloody stones of the Vatican to seize and destroy the errors and heresies of seven continents, who locked the book of Christ in a lead-shielded vault to prevent its irradiation by the still-potent flashes of its Hero? Her business was labor, fertile but anonymous. Others destroyed; she builded. Inexorably, because she and others builded through a most loving and compassionate Son, inspired by the most brilliant and vital of all spirits, the speed of construction would exceed that of destruction, the hand that pulled down would become, through patience, understanding, and love, the hand that put up.

Before she could put this into words, Kramer dismissed her, saying that he would see her at two o'clock that afternoon.

CHAPTER XVI

"OBEDIENCE," FATHER GERLAIN HAD SAID, in Kramer's fifth year at the seminary, "is the boldest of the acts of the human will. Only when you think of it as a positive step toward perfection, an eager, an aggressive step, can you begin to understand its true meaning."

Obedience. A direct order from your superior must be carried out—provided it entails a reasonable and appropriate response. However, neither the pastor nor the bishop could order you to drive a nail through your hand as a test of faith or to climb to the top girders of a bridge in the hope of bringing you nearer to God. He could inflict on you silence, house arrest, and devotional programs to curb a militant and restless spirit, and he could forbid you to take part in an interfaith discussion, to speak on the radio, to appear on television, to be photographed with a movie star, to publish an article or book, to hobnob with longshoremen, to conduct Bible classes, to leave your parish, to visit your dying father in California (he might be more lenient in the case of your All-American mother), and he could add to your restrictions many more prohibitions, great, small, or mediocre.

Obedience. But only small spirits succumbed to its iron rule and only insufficient spirits broke away from it. Obedience. This was his preparation—this and an hour of prayer—for his session with Sister Esther that afternoon.

"How was the enemy's behavior toward your patients after he seized the convent? Those he might have considered unfit to build a new society."

"The critically ill and wounded were either put to death or permitted to die. The others were subjected to interrogation. We were not allowed to know what happened to them."

"Obviously the enemy, models of self-control, let you see and hear what they wanted you to see and hear, and nothing else. Did this occur to you?"

"No, Monsignor."

"You realize that I'm offering you, with a great deal of patience and tact, a reasonable explanation of your defection."

"An offer, Monsignor, that I reject. Without reservation."

Kramer slapped the desk and got up to look again at the book-case, a move, he reflected, that was becoming habitual. "You are determined to suffer."

"For my faults, yes, Monsignor."

"And for no one else's?" Kramer turned to her. "You refuse the mantle of Christ."

"As would anyone sensible of his unworthiness."

"But no one insensible of or to his unworthiness would put on the mantle."

"What is it you wish to know, Monsignor?"

"You may go, Sister. When I wish to see you I will summon you."

Her stubbornness infuriated him. Could she not see where it would take her? He decided to let her wait, impose on her the ghostly and unslippable yoke of his office. And then, since he found this occult transfer released energies for purposes he could not con-done (wicked fantasies and daydreams soaked in scarlet), he sum-moned her the next evening. "Now, Sister, after you surrendered the convent—as you should have—you were taken to a—basketball court?"

"To the basement of the hospital, Monsignor."

"Out of sight of your native charges."

"Yes."

"You and your sisters were the only Occidentals at the convent at the time of attack?"

"Father Sills was visiting a village at the southern end of our district—we had one main village and five or six small ones—and farm settlements; and Dr. Girard and Dr. Guy were—elsewhere."

"You had no resident doctor?"

"We drew from a pool of doctors at the big rubber plantations to

134

the east of us, Monsignor. We had the promise of a resident from the States, but he never came. Actually, we could offer excellent medical service, especially in the fields of pediatrics, obstetrics, and postoperative care."

"This only reinforces my opinion that you were a prize package for the enemy, Sister, a showcase position. But that's been established. The important thing, though, is what happened in that basement."

"We were asked—told—to remove our habits, Monsignor."

"When you were taken to the basement you had no idea that this was what the enemy had in mind?"

"None, Monsignor. None at all."

"You didn't know at the time that this was part of a major attack?"

"What does one know at a time like that, Monsignor? Except that the land and the people you love will never be the same for you again and that the things you built will either be destroyed or come into the possession of other, perhaps less skillful, less tender, hands."

"The barbarian, Sister, is always our successor. And what happens to the vow of poverty when a nun claims for herself the work of her hands?"

"I do not know, Monsignor. Truly, I do not know."

Repelled by an honesty he applauded but could not recognize officially (actually, as he admitted later, he had lost control of the interview), Kramer said, "We'll continue this in the morning, Sister."

In the morning he restated his position. "I am not your prosecutor or your judge, Sister, I am your historian. I'm not preparing a case or taking evidence, I'm recording a narrative, one that may be placed in the Vatican's files, after a routine reading, and never be officially taken out again. Source material for scholars. A curiosity, nothing more."

Sister Esther nodded, as if convinced not of the truth of his statement but of its necessity.

"Now—" Kramer shuffled his notes—"you were in the basement and had been told to remove your habits. What then?"

"Mother Benedict refused, Monsignor. When told a second time she again refused. She said that she released us from—that each of us would have to make her own decision—each according to her conscience—"

"Do you think she did this because she knew she couldn't command your obedience or because she wanted you to understand that violation was a choice of a lesser evil, not a most grievous sin?"

"I have thought about this, Monsignor. Mother Benedict was a magnificent nun and a magnificent woman."

"And she chose to die rather than submit."

"Yes."

"Did she know—was she sure—that these were the only choices, death or violation?"

"I can tell you only what happened, Monsignor. I cannot tell you as positively what did not. After her refusal we were taken from the basement into the basketball court—it was a gift from the U.S. Army."

"There were American troops in the area, Sister?"

"A few, Monsignor. One day a sergeant and a dozen men drove up to the hospital and asked if we'd like a basketball court. They said the Army had received a shipment of several thousand basketballs. And baskets and backboards. The sergeant's expression was, 'They're coming out of our ears.' We built the court in one day, Monsignor. It was our most popular attraction."

As he listened Kramer wrote in his notebook, "A sense of horror. Why do I feel it? Basketball." Prattle. Perhaps that was it. The survivors of concentration camps passing over the incineration of corpses to recall the warmth of the ovens. A cold winter, friends. Perhaps.

"What did you play, Sister, a zone defense? Or man to man?"

"It was a place of special significance to us, Monsignor. We made many conversions there, more than in the chapel. As for our doubts about choices—these were very quickly and efficiently resolved. When Mother Benedict again refused the order to remove her habit she was stabbed—bayoneted—as were Sister Veronica, Sister Ursula, Sister Stanislaus, Sister Joseph. These were the older nuns, Monsignor."

"A question I would have had to ask eventually, Sister."

"We seven survivors were then forced back into the basement. Sister Roberta collapsed. She is, as you know, not yet thirty. Sister Dolores and Sister Thomasina—I don't know, Monsignor, whether they refused to obey the officer's order or could not. They, too, were led out and killed. We heard them praying—"

"Seven refused, Sister, five consented."

"Perhaps 'acquiesce' is a better word, Monsignor."

"Because it is more accurate or a better umbrella?"

"Monsignor, I have tried to remember—every word, every thought, every act—the tone, the setting—yet I cannot say, truthfully, what the degree of consent was. I can tell you this: months later, when we were given back our habits, we were all astonished—and ashamed—that there were only a few tears in the cloth. If we are to accept the truth of our habits we must accept the truth of our consent. Yet I have no recollection of consent. Only of a—yielding—yes, the thing to come because it had to come."

"Physical cowardice, Sister. The wilting of the flesh before the finality of disintegration. Or a reluctance to accept a death that might appear heroic to some and suicidal to others."

"I cannot say that we feared death, Monsignor. It may be that we shrank from the means of death. There was the delay, Monsignor, between the threat and the act—and a contempt for the flesh and its values—"

"Can you be sure?"

"It was not I those soldiers took, Monsignor, but my body."

"I would agree, Sister, if this were a simple case of rape."

"Do you believe that we are whores, Monsignor?"

"What do you believe, Sister?"

"Have any of my sisters told you that the officer in charge of us, after that first day, collected money from the many soldiers who visited us?"

"Sister—"

137

"Does this disturb you, Monsignor? That we were used for profit as well as for pleasure?"

Kramer got up and walked the length of the room, to the door leading to the anteroom. "How do you know this?"

"One of the officers, a major, I believe, made it a point now and then to tell us what we had earned for his people, Monsignor."

"Did this officer also visit you, Sister?"

"No. He said he did not consort with women of our type."

Kramer came back to the desk and took up his pencil. "Let's get on with it, Sister. The narrative."

"We were kept in the basement of the hospital for two months— we made calendars on the walls of our cells."

"Cells?"

"Smaller rooms in the basement, Monsignor. We used them for sewing, for teaching the smaller children, for storage. There would be days when we saw no one except the soldiers who brought us food and water. There would be other days when fresh troops coming down from the north— We offered to nurse their wounded. They said they had no wounded. But we used to hear them in the hospital at night. I'm sure they were short of drugs—" She looked at Kramer, seeing him, not seeing him. "But you know most of this, Monsignor."

"Go on, Sister."

"After two months we were put into the backs of trucks and driven north, more than a hundred miles. The rains started. Between the rains the American fighters and bombers with their gifts of napalm, fragmentation, and phosphorus bombs. The rebels shrugged off the bombs, but the fifty-caliber machine guns that fired slugs as big as a man's thumb terrified them. Sometimes we traveled no more than five or six miles a day. There were gasoline dumps buried in the fields and alongside the roads. Often we walked. We drank the water in the ditches. Our rations were a half-pound of rice a day and what vegetables and edible plants we could find in the fields when we stopped to sleep. We were afraid of dysentery and typhoid. And a special disease that is like a mild form of plague. After ten days we reached a range of hills and began

138

to climb. We had to leave the trucks because the roads weren't safe. Five days later—I think five—or six—we came to a camp on a plateau. There were barracks and gun emplacements, a mess hall, an auditorium. We were taken to a corral surrounded by a barbed-wire fence. In it, lying in the mud, were what looked like coffins, a dozen of them. Except that the ends, both ends, were covered by heavy wire screens instead of wood. We lived in these boxes for—it's hard to say—two and a half to three months. Twice a day we were let out to use a trench which we dug ourselves. We were forbidden to talk."

"How big were these boxes, Sister?"

"I should say six feet long, eighteen to twenty inches wide and—a blessing, Monsignor—high enough for us to turn in. It was a world of cold, silence, and restriction."

"Still, a corner of this earth."

"Only the brief daily contact with our guards kept us human, Monsignor."

"And your faith, Sister?"

"To be alone with God, Monsignor, is a test few persons can pass with honors. But to be alone, knowing that He is all there is—" Sister Esther smiled. "It's a good thing, Monsignor, that the Church stands between God and us. It's a place where God is tempered—or reduced—to the human being's ability to receive Him. In concentrated form, in His purity, His totality, God, I found, is lethal."

"I should think a certain amount of despair and loss of faith would be a wholly normal reaction, Sister."

"In such isolation, Monsignor, you lose the power to verbalize. The will softens and looses its grip on the centers of being. The body registers sensations the mind cannot monitor. You have no singularity; you have only gross responses. Any medical doctor or psychologist will give you the symptoms, Monsignor."

"But you are not any patient, Sister."

"Any conceit I may have had that my vocation, training, and long period of spiritual routining—even acquisition of grace—equipped me to endure pain and attrition better than someone not so well favored—no, Monsignor, we of the cloth are no more ready for a test of faith than we are for a test of character."

"You forget the seven who died, Sister. But go on."

"After roughly three months we were taken from the boxes and put in barracks. We had difficulty walking, keeping our balance. Sister Mary suffered from edema and nausea, and the march to the barracks, a distance of perhaps two hundred yards, took more than an hour. The guards permitted us to help each other, to massage cramps from suddenly activated muscles and to rest while a fainting sister was revived and pulled to her feet. We entered, finally, one end of a long wooden building, and lay on cots separated by wooden partitions a little higher than our heads, a little lower than our knees. Across the room from the partitions there was a single toilet bowl and a basin with a single tap. Just beyond the last partition a plank wall with a plank door. There was no stove, but the cots had two blankets each. There were four sizable windows in each of the side walls, without shades or curtains, and one light bulb hanging from the rafters in the center of the room.

"We were left to ourselves for eight days—even the guards came into the room only occasionally—we were forbidden to talk—and then the interrogations began. We never knew when they'd take place—morning, noon, midnight—or which of us would be called. A guard would come in and take one of us into a small windowless room at the other end of the building—we occupied about a third of it—and seat us at a table. Sometimes we would sit there for an hour before the interrogators arrived. Several times we were taken back to our room without being interrogated. We would be questioned for two, three, often four or five hours by officers working in teams. We were required to sit without moving, with a light in our eyes, but we were never physically hurt. If we nodded or slumped the guard would tap us with the butt of his gun, lightly, never hard enough to bruise or break the skin."

"What did your interrogators wish to know, Sister?"

"They wanted to know about troops, troop movements, munitions, self-propelled weapons, regimental numbers, insignia, troop morale, signaling equipment. They believed—or so they said—that

140

we had stayed—or been left behind—to act as spies. They said that even if we had no instructions to spy we were capable of giving information to the imperialists." Sister Esther, who had been talking in a rapid singsong (patter song), snapped her head back, a motion to check drowsiness or the action of memory which induces the body to reassign itself, partially, to the repugnance now felt for it. "To the Americans." Kramer nodded, letting her decide whether to explain or to continue. "We told them that we were a religious order dedicated to serving the spiritual and material needs of Christian and non-Christian alike and that we were also nurses whose code demanded that we treat the sick and wounded regardless of creed or ideology. They couldn't believe—or pretended not to believe—that any woman would willingly take vows of chastity and poverty. They understood a vow of obedience."

"You were not subjected to torture, Sister?"

"No, Monsignor. Threatened with torture, shouted at, bullied, pleaded with, charmed, coaxed, but not tortured. We said we could tell them nothing of military matters because we knew nothing. Of military matters. I think—after four or five weeks—they believed us. At least the interrogations stopped. A few days passed, quietly. We began to hope that—nothing else would be demanded of us. But the camp began to fill up with troops— In the basement of the hospital we could at least think we were being punished for not having the courage to resist. At the camp, after those intervening months—this time, Monsignor, we tried to resist but this time we were not given a choice between death and violation."

"You talk as if all this had happened to someone else, Sister."

"Because when I talk about it now, Monsignor, I know that it happened to me."

He dismissed her then, partly because she had isolated herself in the recital of those astonishing months, partly because his mind had turned flaccid and incurious, bored with what had become a statistical and self-perpetuating outrage. Instead of variety there were only numbers. In place of the hard sharp moment, as beautiful as it was breath-taking, the dull psychiatric hour. He needed a rest. Did she?

Summoning Sister Esther the next morning, after a thorough study of her testimony, Kramer asked why the enemy, who had been following, apparently, a conscious program of attrition, had abruptly released them.

"I can't say, Monsignor. After a month or so in the barracks we were again moved north, and put in a schoolhouse in a village—I don't know the name of it—"

"Not important, Sister."

"No. Sometime later, a few weeks, the officer in charge of us gave us our habits and said that we could use the schoolroom—we were quartered in a room to the rear of it—but were not to leave the building. We dressed and went into the schoolroom—we heard firing, explosions, voices, American voices—there's a quality in the American voice I hadn't noticed—I suppose hearing it after so many months of Oriental recitative—"

"After eight months of captivity—was it eight?"

"Approximately, yes, Monsignor."

"You were suddenly freed. And you don't know why?"

"No."

"Were you at any time during these eight months subjected to what has been called brainwashing, Sister?"

"No, Monsignor."

"Would you recognize these techniques if they were applied to you, Sister?"

"I believe so."

"You show a decided sympathy for your captors. Is this accidental or incidental? Or an implanted suggestion or order?"

"It is our training as Christians, Monsignor."

"May I remind you, Sister—again—that this kind of pietistic garbage is not only unwholesome but dangerous?"

"We are taught to love our enemies, Monsignor."

Kramer began to clear the desk, slowly, deliberately, putting papers and notebooks into his briefcase, pocketing pencils and erasers, returning books to the bookshelf. "When you're ready to talk to me, Sister, see your Superior General and arrange an appointment."

The next afternoon he spoke with the Reverend Mother Magdalene, who said that she had received a letter from Cardinal Andreani ordering the immediate return of the four nuns to their mother house in California. "Two cabins have been reserved for them on a ship sailing from Naples in five days, Monsignor. You have this afternoon, tomorrow, and the day after to finish your interrogation. There is a telegraph office in Pescara if you wish to communicate with Cardinal Bellini."

"In that case I should like to see Sister Esther, Reverend Mother. Immediately."

That afternoon Kramer asked Sister Esther to tell him of the three-week retreat south with the company of American soldiers, Captain Sterling commanding. He let her talk, interrupting only to question details not covered by the stories of Sister Agnes and Sister Mary and to dig at incidents he sensed she suppressed or omitted. "As I understand it, Sister, you were particularly friendly with Sergeant Goldman."

"Captain Sterling commanded the company, Monsignor, but Sam—Sergeant Goldman ran it. Usually, when Sister Agnes wanted to speak to Captain Sterling or to make a request she asked me to clear it with Sergeant Goldman."

"You possess the social graces, Sister."

"I've had more experience dealing with people outside the Order, Monsignor. When I took a degree in psychology—at Berkeley—and when I studied for a year at Johns Hopkins—even a nun, Monsignor, can't completely isolate herself from total contact with her fellow students, teachers, visiting lecturers—perhaps I am by nature more worldly than Sister Agnes."

"Your Order believes in higher education."

"Many of our sisters have not only their bachelor's degrees, Monsignor, but their master's, and, in some cases, doctorates."

"For what purpose, Sister?"

"A tradition of the Order, Monsignor. To teach in one of our colleges a nun must have at least a master's or its equivalent."

"Tradition, Sister, is a particularly sinister form of corporate pride."

"For nuns only, Monsignor?"

Kramer smiled, not darkening his annoyance but lighting it. "What part of this self-confidence and self-reliance comes from your feeling of natural superiority, Sister, and what part from the security of your place in your Order? No, don't hesitate, just give me a quick estimate." Had he touched her? "Or do you think that question ill-bred?"

"I don't know how to answer you, Monsignor."

"A bit of a snob, Sister?" He watched the constriction of her hands, a struggle of pale squid in her lap. "Your father has a seat on the New York Stock Exchange, doesn't he, Sister? The big board?"

"Yes."

"And your mother? Wasn't she a Whipple? Very old Manhattan people?"

"I took a vow of poverty, Monsignor, and I've kept it."

"The Westlakes of Rye. Sister Agnes, your nominal superior after your capture, recognized this superiority when she delegated you to act as intermediary between nun and soldier, didn't she? Sister Agnes's father is a small truck farmer in California. She wouldn't feel she could talk easily with Ivy League types like Sterling and Goldman."

"No, no, Monsignor, Sister Agnes is very shy, very—"

"Your background has never caused little jealousies and misunderstandings, Sister? Well?"

"But this is the kind of petty social variance that every postulant and novice is familiar with, Monsignor."

"Variance?"

"Like a pronounced accent. Or two left feet. Or wit, excessive shyness, a tendency to tears or giggles. Believe me, it disappears into the anonymity of the life and the habit very quickly and is rarely, if ever, referred to again."

Although exultant (the proper word) at having agitated her, Kramer suppressed a strong and natural feeling of contempt, reminding himself that such easy defeats are too often the false con-

144

cessions the proud and the determined make to conceal and protect the true nature of their ambitions and failures.

"Interesting that from this background you should enter an organization whose vows are chastity, poverty, and obedience and whose work consists chiefly of tending the poor, the foreign, the incomprehensible. All of which are unwashed, infected, ignorant, crude, and characterless." Did she think because he had created this bad smell he saw no need to apologize for it? "Well?"

"I have no real wants, Monsignor. The people I serve do."

"More platitudes, Sister?"

"It's very hard, Monsignor, to answer such questions properly, especially since they are not very real."

"Let me ask you this, then." (Why had he forgotten to have a pitcher of water placed on the desk?) "What made you decide to become a nun? Did you suffer a revelation? Hear voices? Receive a call?"

"I had always wanted to be a nurse, Monsignor. Perhaps because I was so well off—materially—"

"In your position, Sister, I'd remember that toy traps are set for toy game."

"I'm sorry, Monsignor. I began to work as a volunteer in hospitals. When I was sixteen. The presence of God is very strong in hospitals, particularly at night."

"But why a nun and not just a nurse?"

"I became acquainted with some nursing sisters. In hospitals in Westchester. They—impressed me."

"Their skills, Sister?"

"Their attitude, Monsignor. To lay nurses nursing was a means to something else. Husbands, money, a career. To these nuns—" The hands expressed it, from the schoolgirl's admiration for a mysterious and awesome calling with its theater of song, procession, and Mass to the young adult's passion for God and the service of His creatures. The hands completed the spiritual circle no question could penetrate, from which no answer could be heard.

"Thank you, Sister." Kramer began to put his papers in his

briefcase. "If you have anything further to say you may confide it to your Superior General, who knows where to reach me."

Sister Esther stood. "But is this all, Monsignor?"

Ah, he had touched her, finally, by the simplest means. She could endure interrogation but not dismissal. "I don't understand you, Sister."

"I assumed—"

"What, Sister?"

"What is to happen now, Monsignor?"

"Do you wish to cross-examine me, Sister? Do you have some broad statement to make, some philosophical apology? For the record?"

"I know that I exceed my station, Monsignor, that you know better than I—"

Kramer tapped the desk, a teacher recalling a pupil from the irrelevance of personality, the frivolous and embarrassing cult of the private ego, where the I is put before the God in I. "Sister, it's unrealistic—I don't say irreverent—to demand to appear at every function in which your name, your name in Christ, appears. I suppose your next demand will be an audience with Cardinal Andreani and after that with the Holy Father himself."

"The wish to be present, to represent yourself, at all times and in all places, is too serious a temptation for mockery, Monsignor."

He smelled it then, the corruption of an individualism so intense that the infected body cannot be cured without radical treatment. Kramer said, "You made the point, Sister, that you tried to love the enemy in spite of his frequent assaults on you and your companions."

"That is the Christian approach, Monsignor."

"You're mistaken, Sister. The Christian approach is to love your enemy *because* he attacks you. To withhold your love from someone who treats you as a woman only *when* he does is to hold a knife at his spiritual throat. And at yours. For if you cannot love the sinner in his sinning, the violator in his violation, the golden moment, Sister, when he is himself, what possible good can your love do him

146

when he is in a state of quiescence or negative grace? God does not withhold his love from Satan. Shall you?"

"If you propose this priceless insight as the moral of your investigation, Monsignor, you have indeed had a frivolous chase."

Unbelievable. She dared? Well, that was a challenge he welcomed. "Whatever the results of my investigation, Sister, its purpose is hardly that of a salvage operation. I'm not here to help you recover your lost virginity or to restore you to that cloudy state of grace from which you fell into your present condition. No, such dubious articles have no place on my agenda. You mislead yourself if you think they do. Tell me, in your years as postulant, novice, and nun, were you much troubled by sexual desires?"

"Occasionally, yes, Monsignor. I am a woman."

"Did you know—even for a moment—ecstasy in the arms of your seducers?"

"No, no—"

"Few women enjoy being raped, Sister, but many become quite used to being made love to."

Sister Esther stepped forward to put a hand on the desk, perhaps only to reassure herself of its solidity. "Before God, Monsignor, I can say truthfully that I did not. I can't say, as truthfully, that I remained absolutely indifferent to such attentions. In the basement of the hospital I suffered physically from penetration. I don't defend myself, Monsignor, I tell you a fact. In my case an instrument—a knife or stick—had to be used to effect the initial entrance. I don't know which because I'm ashamed to say I lost consciousness for a time. Later—"

"Sister—"

"Please, Monsignor, please listen to me. Later, in the barracks farther north, I still suffered some pain and discomfort but nothing unendurable. That is, I found that I could—lessen the pain if I—didn't totally reject my partner. I couldn't stop the pain but I could ease it."

"What you're saying, Sister, is that during these sexual passages you actively co-operated with your partners."

147

"When the pain became so great, Monsignor, that I could no longer endure it—almost as great as labor pains—I did what I could to lessen it. I learned a very bitter lesson, Monsignor—no matter what my dedication to God, there are some things beyond my power to offer Him. He bore His cross with grace and sanctity. I dropped mine, Monsignor. I don't pretend to compete with our Saviour but I am—much ashamed that when I was offered the chance to follow Him I could take only those few short mean steps before falling."

"Yet, Sister—" Kramer took a sheaf of papers from his brief-case—"yet your superiors, both in your country and out of it, in their reports on your conduct and achievements—you know of course that these reports exist."

"Yes."

"Interesting that these reports rate you very highly in achievement—very, Sister—but express some doubts about your spiritual life. For example, those who supervised your work in the Far East—priest as well as nun—remark on your many conversions and the great reverence you inspired in the natives of your district. And beyond, Sister. Apparently, you have the human touch. And this even I am afraid to mock. You are a born missionary, Sister. Also, according to the various doctors you've worked with, you're a first-rate nurse. No, let me finish. You're an excellent teacher and a tireless worker. Your relations with those outside your Order are enormously satisfactory and very fruitful. You're obviously, in this area, material for leadership in your Order. But spiritually, Sister, there are distinct and practical reservations, principally concerning your inability to take orders. You go too far. In the good cause, yes, but beyond the limitations of the nun. No one suggests that you are deliberately disobedient, but almost everyone points out your tendency to pursue a course in your own way regardless of your superior's restraint and advice. A better fault than docility, Sister, but still a fault."

"That is my weakness, Monsignor, and I have tried—with God's and my superiors' help—to correct it. And I will correct it, I will—"

"A militant nature. Like Jacob you prefer to receive God as an opponent and not as a loving Father. Perhaps forgetting, Sister, that Jacob was Israel and you—California."

Sister Esther knelt before the desk, a move that dismayed Kramer but at the same time alerted him. "Monsignor, I have been proud, arrogant, rude, insolent, and thoughtless. I have been contemptuous of the disciplines of my superiors and unmindful of the needs of my peers—all these things. But I assure you that now I am only confused, afraid, deeply in need of guidance—"

"Get up, Sister. You demean yourself—"

"I am in that gray area of the soul where I await penitence without hoping to receive it. I have one desire—to resume my life as a nursing sister, to slip quietly and anonymously into the ranks, to work for my salvation through the salvation of others. I have been a bad nun, I have many grievous faults. I don't say that I will ever be a good nun, a model in achievement for others to pattern themselves on. Perhaps I can never fit the mold perfectly. But, Monsignor, I pray God that I may be permitted to try. I pray God I may be permitted to offer the poor gifts of my body and soul to the glory of His name. Though I fall short of perfection, Monsignor, I beg to serve Him by serving not His splendor but His mutilated image—the sick, the poor, the infected, the despised, the hated—yes, the evil—to tend this image when it is so defaced and impersonalized as to be unrecognizable by others. I know this is a great deal to ask. And I do not ask it, I pray for it."

"Sister—"

"I admit, Monsignor, that I rebel against the smooth, comfortable, unroughened life even when such a life is useful and sanctified. I want no comforts, no coddling, no easements, no exceptions, no safety. Occasional praise is sweet to me, yes, but is not the Mother of God herself pleased now and then with our hymns to her glory? I want and need tools, yes, for the sake of the needy, but possessions, no. I could return to my former life—if God so wills, I must—but I don't think even He Who knows our secret wishes and often so sweetly thwarts them for our own good will condemn me to that."

Magnificent. He had thought her beaten. Now she threatened to overwhelm him. "My child—"

"Monsignor, for the love of God, help me."

"You presume to ask that?"

"I ask everything, Monsignor. Without your intercession I am lost."

Kramer crossed himself. "You are already lost, Sister."

CHAPTER XVII

IN THE SECOND WEEK OF ADVENT, that glorious yet anxious season when all Christendom awaits the coming of Christ, Ottavio Cardinal Bellini, leaving a small meeting of a dozen of his peers and the Holy Father, observed (without catharsis) that Giorgio Cardinal Andreani, Prefect of the Congregation of Religious, had come up quietly on his left and hung there, as if wanting a quiet word but unwilling to coerce a sick man. To Cardinal Bellini, who during a long summer and fall had (under doctor's orders) lost fifteen pounds, this was the solicitude of the harpooner who has his whale under the gun but waits a quieter sea. Bellini would not be provoked by his colleague's muttered charge of interference into the affair of the assaulted nuns, nor would he plead the anxiety of the Holy Father for the investigation of this affair or publicize Bishop Key's disclosure that a group of natives in the Far East had replaced the cult of the Virgin Mother with the quasi-worship of the figure of a standing nun holding a basketball in a pair of roughened, oversized hands. He stood his ground. At least for a time.

For the present he had Andreani on his left and could think of nothing beyond the purest banalities—what's new with the Americans, or Brooker wants to put a chapter of Dominican monks in orbit and call it the Monastery in the Stars—with which to challenge the man. Furthermore, since it is common knowledge (and what a cross that is, folk wisdom) that a man on a starvation diet becomes moody and irascible (actually, Bellini felt younger and stronger)— But Andreani had spoken to him, and Bellini, not hearing the words for the music in Andreani's *basso cantante*, said, "Hm, I suppose."

"Three copies," Andreani said. "One for the Holy Father, one for my files, and one for you."

"Where is it then? My copy."

Andreani extended a letter. "Here."

Bellini read the letter at home after a light lunch and a short nap, sitting on the terrace enjoying the icy Roman air he knew would bring Andreani his annual cold and to others among his colleagues gifts of chills and fever, aching muscles, coughs, and inflamed sinuses. Nothing like a Roman winter to remind old men of their mortality. He could not say that he had expected such a letter, nor could he say that it astonished or shocked him. It did, however, demand that he act. It did not demand that he act quickly, impulsively, greatly, nor did it demand that he act positively. According to the letter—it came from Cardinal Brooker—Sister Esther had requested to be released from her vows, and after due consideration the request had been granted—by Cardinal Brooker— and this information had been forwarded to Cardinal Andreani. A routine matter conducted routinely and needing, probably, only a routine reaction. Possibly Andreani had informed his Holiness, possibly not. Because of the Holy Father's interest in the ordeal of these nuns the odds were that he had been informed. Bellini took two weeks to think about the letter before saying to Cinotti, "Please ask the Reverend Mother Magdalene when I shall have the pleasure of seeing her in Rome. And you might give Monsignor Kramer, who is most anxious to return to the United States, hope of doing so very soon. After you give him copies of the letters from

Bishop Key in the Far East, particularly the letter in which Bishop Key describes the idol that was placed in the basketball court. As an athlete Kramer may find the symbolism stimulating."

After Epiphany, in the quiet of the pre-Lenten season, Bellini, whose social life had been restricted by his doctors and who for that reason had been dunned with invitations he could not accept (his observation), made an appearance at a charity ball given by a papal count and sponsored, benevolently, by Cardinal Andreani. The money raised would be used to found schools and asylums in the Far East for the benefit of the many Catholic widows and orphans donated to the economy and the Church by the recent war there. Watching the dancing in the ballroom from the mezzanine, after the raffling off of small objects of art and personal effects given by the guests, Andreani said to Bellini, "Your Eminence honors this assembly by his unexpected presence."

"His Eminence also enriches his doctors by his unexpected appearance."

"You've lost more weight, Ottavio."

"Possibly the result of having read the letter from your fabulous American colleague Brooker."

"Nevertheless, Ottavio, that poor woman nags at his Holiness's charity. It's as if he saw something in her we—pardon the reference to Rome's optometrists—do not."

Bellini watched the dancers, particularly the younger set, which seemed to be mocking, vigorously, the mating dances of extinct birds. Where was the amber sweat of his yesteryears? "In our position, Giorgio, the best way to face a scandal of this order is to treat it as you would, at a formal ceremony, a restless child."

"Till a doctor—in this case his Holiness—decides that the child's restlessness isn't due to hunger but to a burst appendix."

"May I believe you didn't think a rigorous investigation of this affair necessary, Giorgio? Whether by my office or your own?"

Andreani, long and lean, blew on his glasses and rubbed them with a silicon-coated paper. A towering scholar whose work on the origins of the Church was much consulted and quoted, he was also an ardent antifeminist—or, rather, a devoted opponent of feminist movements, arguing that the Holy Mother, the perfection of femininity, had had neither the vote nor money of her own.

"As for your investigation, Ottavio, it was begun at the instigation of his Holiness and concluded with my consent."

This, Bellini thought, was like saying you did what you had to do and when it was done I put my seal to it. "You understand, Giorgio, that the investigation was preventive and not vindictive. The information we have now can be used effectively to crush any future romanticism in this affair. For example, a proposal of beatification."

"Neither you nor I will see that."

"No, but our successors might. In two hundred years."

"The Church is a predictable entity. Our successors are not."

"May I offer you Monsignor Kramer's report?"

"Kramer?"

"An American lent me by Cardinal Brooker."

Though Andreani knew this—and certainly by now knew Kramer—he apparently wanted to use the American as a base either for attack or for negotiation, a move foreseen by Bellini but not yet given importance, too much importance.

"And Kramer's report, Ottavio? Does it satisfy you?"

"Wholly. A brilliant piece of work, Giorgio. Actually, a little too brilliant. What I wanted—and expected to get—was an extension and elaboration of your own interrogation. A recital of events. At best, history; at worst, journalism. When his Holiness defined this affair as something more than a simple case of assault and rape, he widened the field of the investigation. Yet I still hoped—and so indicated to Kramer, and I chose my man carefully—to confine—" Andreani, he observed, had withdrawn his attention. Below him the great ballroom vibrated with the stamp of flesh and the visceral rhythms of contemporary popular music, of the masses, for the masses. Annoyed by Andreani's inattention, he said, "What do you propose to do about Sister Esther?" in a tone that suggested, "Have we no more important business at hand than the sensibilities of a defecting nun?"

"His Holiness is greatly shocked by Sister Esther's impulsive action," Andreani said.

"Was it impulsive?"

"I quote."

"I see three possible courses of action, Giorgio, since his Holiness obviously wants action. Find her and persuade her to return to the Order—it's well within his Holiness's power to grant this dispensation; find her and make an effort to keep her in the Faith—ridiculous—is the Church to kneel to her?—or excommunicate her, as a schismatic."

Andreani stood. "I must mingle, Ottavio. As for your three courses of action, I would choose the second."

Satisfied that Andreani would leave Sister Esther to him, Bellini rested his case. Several days later Cinotti read a brief note from the Reverend Mother Magdalene, which said she would be in Rome at the beginning of the Lenten season and would await his Eminence's pleasure. Bellini sent a cablegram to Sister Esther's mother superior in California and received by airmail an account of Sister Esther's talks with both superiors and confessor (in the latter case where not covered by the seal of the confessional, of course) and estimates of Sister Esther's state of mind and soul, together with assurances that no one at the convent knew where she was. A second cablegram to Cardinal Brooker ("My dear Brother in Christ") brought a formal letter containing a brief résumé of the case and its solution and the reminder that "Of course the records of this procedure have been forwarded to his Eminence Cardinal Andreani for his files."

For his files. The independence of these Americans. Had they set up a separate Congregation of Autonomous Ecclesiastical States which recognized the Curia as a Roman House of Lords and the Papal Father himself as a gelded prince first only in the primacy and age of his title? It chilled him to realize that this was the scream of an old man on the rack of time. The complaint of the red hat—to seat himself on a throne that looked backward. And he saw himself facing not what time proposed but what it had dispensed with. He said to Cinotti, "Have I a luncheon appointment for the twelfth of February?"

"The delegation from Milan, Eminence. To counteract the Communists."

"I'll need an appetizer. The Reverend Mother Magdalene—followed by Monsignor Kramer."

"Both, Eminence?"

"The Communists will expect pig—we'll serve them venison. As for Monsignor Kramer—wire Cardinal Brooker that I'm sending him home. No, write him a letter and stamp it with my signature."

Ah, it isn't the chains of office that bind a man, it's the threads. Later in the week Bellini was summoned to the Pope's study, to discuss, he assumed, the situation in the Far East. Andreani was there, along with Roberto Cardinal Lamattina, Prefect of the Congregation for the Propagation of Faith, the man directly responsible for the work of missionaries and the spread and maintenance of missions. After a brief prayer, a reminder that without the fire of the Holy Spirit the clay nods, the Pope gestured to Lamattina, who said, "As your Holiness knows, the group of American nuns of the Order of the Sisters of St. Luke that now staffs the convent hospital in the Far East has suffered some embarrassment from, you might say, a legacy of faith left them by their violated predecessors. At first they assumed that the statue carved by the natives and set up in the—in a basketball court was a memorial to their beloved sisters. After considerable tactful maneuvering they managed to persuade the natives that the statue should be placed over the graves of their martyred sisters."

"Is it there now?" Bellini asked.

"Yes. But the nuns noticed that the reverence given the statue was, in their opinion, excessive. They notified their confessor, Father Sills, who in turn alerted Bishop Key. He has investigated. He reports that there is a strong and widespread belief that the nun represented by the statue will come back to the peninsula to liberate the mountain people from their oppressors in the coastal plains and to give them great health and many strong children. Simple wishes based on their historical situation."

"The nun, I suppose, is Sister Esther," Andreani said.

"The native name—or title—is roughly translated as 'The sainted lady of the wonderful hands.' "

"They're worse than Africans," Bellini said. "The Neolithic period, I should say, characterized by the domestication of ruminant animals and primitive hoes. Which is their principal deity, thunder?"

"Our heavenly Father, I thought," the Pope said.

"No, Holiness. Under a patina of Christianity the worship of the female as earth-mother."

"I disagree," Lamattina said. "She holds not a child, but a basketball."

"A symbol of the earth?"

"But, Ottavio," Andreani said, "at the stage of culture you assign them the earth is flat."

"Does Bishop Key wish the Congregation of Rites to make an official investigation?" Bellini asked.

"No." Lamattina looked at a letter, presumably from Key. "He seems to think the emotion is one of love, not reverence. True, the statue is that of a superior being, but you will notice, in Rome at least, some thousands of statues of superior beings, all of which birds and children honor and no one worships."

"I say burn the statue and smash the cult," Bellini said. "The woman no longer professes the Faith. Should we honor a defecting nun?"

"I assume then you have jurisdiction," Lamattina said.

"The one thing I wish to avoid, Eminence, is a jurisdictional wrangle. I have never believed the quarrels of old men advanced the cause of the Church or promoted public trust in the wisdom of the Curia."

"You choose to be tart, Eminence," the Pope said. "No, I'll have no jurisdictional squabbling. Since you handled the interrogation of these poor women, I propose that you follow it up."

"Agreed," Andreani said quickly. Lamattina nodded, as from an elevation. Bellini's problem.

"But how, Holiness? For what purpose?"

156

"If she did return to the peninsula—" The Pope shrugged.

"She must not," Lamattina said. "As either lay or religious. No, I strongly oppose such an unwise move. Without her, the cult of worship—if that's what it should be—and I agree with Key that it isn't—without her—"

"We don't know what the woman will do," Bellini said. "She can't return as a nun, obviously, unless his Holiness so wishes. As for going back as a nurse, a word from our delegate in Washington to the State Department—"

"No, no," the Pope said.

"A lesser evil, Holiness."

"A point, Holiness," Andreani said. "How else could she operate outside the Church except as a schismatic, a deviationist, the leader of a cult? Whether she wished it or not, some such role would be forced on her by the devotion of her followers."

"I think we overrate the danger," Bellini said.

"I disagree," Lamattina said. "The power of the Faith, its strength, is in its purity, its refusal to bend to the expedient to promote a temporary rapprochement with a backward people."

"You're forgetting the concession God made to a backward world in the form of His beloved Son," Andreani said.

"Shall we leave it to you, Ottavio?" the Pope said.

"Of course, Holiness."

On the twelfth of February, with the delegation from Milan already gathered and quartered in the great salon on the ground floor of the villa, Bellini received the Reverend Mother Magdalene in his study on the floor above. Regretting that he had written her and feeling that her prompt response to his invitation could not be justified by her reports on the state of the nuns who had been entrusted to her care, he decided to give her the appropriate fifteen minutes and at least sixty per cent of his attention. Also, she had two brothers in the shipping business and a cousin in the Foreign Office, negligible attributes but not to be overlooked or slighted. "The children are well, Reverend Mother?" he asked, after seating her (or permitting her to seat herself) intimately by the fireplace.

"I have personally visited the four of them, your Eminence. They are very well placed."

"And healthy?"

"Very, your Eminence."

"We grieve for the death of Sister Catherine. And for the child."

"A difficult birth, Eminence."

"The will of God, Reverend Mother, the will of God. I assume you've heard from—or of—your charges since they left for America?"

"My responsibility in this affair ended with their departure, your Eminence."

"Is not their mother house an affiliate of yours?"

"They are a separate chapter quite independent of us."

"America, apparently, keeps declaring its independence."

"I cannot say that this is a good thing, your Eminence."

"No." Impressed by the unswerving ugliness of that medieval face, he added, "But then, in America we can look forward to our first female cardinal. Though I'm told that in nature only the male sings."

"Perhaps because he alone wears the red hat, Eminence."

Delighted with her reply, remembering that Andreani had had his troubles with her, he said, "Your report stressed—certain difficulties. But of course you faced an extraordinary situation. I understand that Dr. Poli, an excellent man—he delivered two of my grandnieces—wanted these nuns placed in a private sanitarium, as laity. You opposed this suggestion."

"Strongly, your Eminence. The only place for them in their ordeal was the sanctuary of their Order. I think to have separated them immediately—in their condition—from the familiar embrace of the cloister would have done them great psychological harm. No, the one tenable ground for such an unwise move could only have been medical. And Dr. Poli conceded that our medical facilities and staff were excellent. Besides, do we know how these poor sisters might have reacted to such a worldly environment, with its immense material distractions and influences?"

"Your intuition tells you that these nuns have all made excellent adjustments to the purely spiritual life?" As she hesitated he added, "I have received only banalities from America. I believe they speak of suicide as the last positive act of a disorganized personality to integrate itself with a greater reality."

"I have great hopes for Sister Roberta, Eminence—if she is permitted to follow the program we laid out for her here in Italy. Sister Agnes and Sister Mary are quite docile and wish only to slip back into the ranks."

"And Sister Esther?"

"Only a great act of will can save her, your Eminence. And I'm not sure she is prepared to make it."

"Inside the Church."

"I cannot say."

"I trust your intuition, Reverend Mother."

After a moment the Reverend Mother Magdalene said, "One way or another, Eminence, she is for the fire. Whether she will be consumed by this fire—or tempered by it—I do not know."

After she left, Bellini sat turning the pages of Kramer's report until Cinotti announced its author.

"Where did you put the delegation from Milan?"

"In the drawing room, Eminence."

"And how many steps must my visitor climb to reach my unworthy portico?"

"Thirty-seven, Eminence."

"And did Monsignor Kramer climb those thirty-seven steps?"

"I believe he did."

"Would you kindly inform Monsignor Kramer that I am a strong advocate of wholesome exercise and that it would please me very much if he descended those thirty-seven steps and climbed them again?" Cinotti bowed. "On his knees. And place the delegation from Milan in a good position to overlook this tactical exercise."

Bellini seated himself at his desk and began to reread Kramer's report, an attitude that did not encourage Kramer, when that young man entered the study, either to make instant conversation or to approach too closely the Cardinal's field of attention. Kramer's knees, accustomed to prayer, ached from prolonged and unnatural contact with the Cardinal's stones. Had this been Bellini's idea or Cinotti's?

"Have you a good nose, Monsignor?"

Kramer, his mind touching all points on an expanding circle of indecision, said, "Your Eminence is angry with me—" and recoiled in advance of the Cardinal's reply.

"You speak as if you were my mistress." (It could have been worse.) "A few days ago I received word from America, this unutterable land, that Sister Esther has been released from her vows. Well?"

"I—"

"Can you guess why, Monsignor?"

"I would have to—know the circumstances—"

"Perhaps the Church, having taught her a profession, wishes to send her into the world to practice it. Had you any foreknowledge of her intention?"

"*Her* intention, Eminence?"

"That astonishes you."

"I'm certain that to go out was the last thing she wanted, Eminence, the one thing she feared might be forced on her by her superiors."

"Have you any idea why this was permitted, Monsignor? Like so many naïve Europeans I find myself unable to follow the sophisticated American mind."

"Perhaps, Eminence, her superiors decided, on good evidence, that she was unfitted for the rigors and disciplines of monastic life."

"Monastic, yes. But there are nuns who serve as well as pray. One would think, Monsignor, that such an able pair of hands dedicated to the service of God would be so enormously useful to the Church and mankind that some extra effort would be made to nurture and develop her spiritual life. Do you find this too romantic?"

"But if the question was one of excessive pride, Eminence, a stubborn and most appalling refusal to submit her will to the Church or to those delegated by the Church to oversee and to guide her spiritual life—"

"And what would the charges be? Simple or even multiple disobedience calls for discipline, not dismissal. Yet all I have is a plain statement—from Cardinal Brooker's office—that Sister Esther asked to be released from her vows and that my distinguished brother in America, after due and weighty deliberation, granted her request. Till I receive further details of this extraordinary business I can think only that either our American colleagues have suffered another of their periodical ascensions into the intellectual ether or that you, Monsignor, in the course of your investigation, so disposed Sister Esther that she decided she was unfit for the charitable offices of the nun."

"I did what I thought necessary, Eminence. Others may plead the cause of these poor nuns; I could not. Your Eminence knows the dangers of false pity."

"How is it then that in your report to me there is no mention of spiritual disorders grave enough to lead Sister Esther to this unnatural step?"

"My instructions, as I conceived them, Eminence, were to investigate first for evidence of sexual collaboration. I found none. Secondly, for sexual toleration beyond the limits necessary to sustain mental and physical balance. I found none. Thirdly, for conscious or unconscious provocation above and beyond the province of the nun's vows. I found none. And fourthly, for evidence of a false and misleading exultation of the spirit based on pseudo martyrdom, that is, excessive welcoming of suffering and great pride in being selected to suffer. This I found, Eminence, in Sister Esther, and so reported."

"Perhaps too dryly and unpoetically to attract my attention." Bellini paused as if to intimate to Kramer that he would pass this explanation, but only with reservations. "Now, Monsignor, let me press a point you perhaps are insufficiently aware of. His Holiness, being a great humanitarian, a man of all the people, has, despite his enormous responsibilities, taken a great interest in the ordeal of these nuns. You know this."

"Yes, Eminence."

"Is it possible, Monsignor, that his Holiness, from his great spiritual height, has seen something in this case that we dwarfs have not? Is there in his compassion a thread of anxiety? Who are four violated nuns against the impending damnation of billions and a faltering and medieval Church?"

Kramer bowed, the only answer.

"I asked earlier about your nose, Monsignor. In your sessions with these sweet sisters did you smell nothing beyond mortified flesh?"

"Only what I reported, Eminence."

"Not, however faint, the odor of sanctity?"

So that was it. "If his Holiness, with his extraordinary powers—"

"Please, please, Monsignor, it is your nose we are concerned with. Perhaps you've never smelled the odor of sanctity. You haven't? But if you did you'd expect the subtlest and most exhilarating of perfumes."

"Certainly exhilarating, Eminence."

"Scented ammonia, perhaps? A thoroughly peppered rose? To give it piquancy? Not exactly. The odor of sanctity, Monsignor, is precisely the effluvium of a roadside slaughterhouse at the end of a long hot unsanitary day. It repels, it sickens, it suffocates, it stifles, it disgusts. The slightest trace of it burns in the nostrils."

"I assure your Eminence that when I questioned these nuns I did so against the possibility that their murdered sisters might well qualify for martyrdom and that the stench of rape and sexual assault might act as a cleansing agent, a purifier. I'm well aware that the great scandals of the Church are its saints, and that we must do everything we can to prevent or ignore their appearance. After all, Eminence, what is the difference between saintliness and heresy? Hindsight."

"I took great care to suppress that kind of cynicism till I was seventy, Monsignor. You are not yet forty. But we have a possibility to consider. What would you suggest?"

Obviously, timidity would not do. "I suggest first, Eminence, that while rape is a shocking insult to a nun it is hardly a guaran-

162

teed springboard to martyrdom. The blood of martyrs is not a stain; it is a flood. In the procession of saints would you have St. Catherine and her wheel followed by a nun waving a bloody clout?"

"Such talk isn't sacrilegious, Monsignor, it is only coarse. You don't shock me; you betray yourself."

"But it disposes of the issue of martyrdom, Eminence."

"And the seven murdered nuns. Are they so easily disposed of?"

"A choice of weapons, Eminence. They preferred the bayonet."

Bellini checked a nod of approval. If the investigation had not honed the young American's soul it had at least polished his wit. "There is still the imaginative and courageous Sister Esther."

"Eminence, the odor of sanctity is, at least initially, the product of hysteria. It is made in the noses of the naïve and the devout and floated abroad by the cynical and the ambitious. For one thing, we have no evidence of miracles. Who has benefited from Sister Esther's enthusiasm for suffering?"

"You overlook the future."

"I rely on the future. Eminence, miracles happen only when faith in the next world exceeds a belief in this one."

"And the statue, Monsignor?"

"A visual aid for the promotion of the Faith. It can be dispensed with when the primitive intelligence has been sufficiently instructed to differentiate between idolatry and worship. No, Eminence, if Sister Esther is to reappear as an evangelist surrounded by a magnetic field of sanctity, she will need a theater in which to create and to sustain the proper sensation. Where is she to find it? Who is to say she will search for it? Where are we to locate a sufficiently ignorant and naïve audience large enough to attract her and cohesive enough to follow her?"

"Questions I would like very much to have answered, Monsignor. Are you prepared to seek these answers?"

"I had hoped, Eminence, that my part in this ulcerous affair had ended."

Bellini smiled, certain that he had his man. "We will arrange an investigative tour of certain primitive areas in America, Monsignor, beginning with the convent in California. With traveling and living expenses kept to a minimum in case you are tempted by the unparalleled lures of American society. You will avoid the main streets, which are, I've been told, paved with gold, and travel the side streets, which are paved, much more practically, with the skulls of the poor and the bones of those martyred by the automobile. You will report yourself quietly to my brother in America, Cardinal Brooker, explaining your mission, and you will talk particularly to ex-Sister Esther's ex-Mother Superior. You will be prudent, humble, alert, pleasant, and irreproachable. If you do your job well we will give you a week in Las Vegas, the desert paradise of the new Canaanites. I'll expect regular reports. After you have found Sister Esther you will cable—or phone—whichever is quicker or most convenient—and follow up this message with a detailed narrative of Sister Esther's fleshly and spiritual life. Does this please you?"

"I beg your Eminence's indulgence, but I plead, one, that I have no talent for espionage, however high-minded, and, two, that I am too close to this case to see it objectively."

Bellini slapped the desk. "We have inquired about the condition of your nose, Monsignor. What is, after your humble climb to my study, the condition of your knees?"

Kramer knelt. "Nevertheless, Eminence, I am not the man for this mission."

"We believe you are."

"But how, among almost two hundred million people, am I to find this woman?"

"He gives his consent but withholds his obedience. You will find her, Monsignor, because you are looking for her. I don't believe, from what you have reported, that she will accept assistance from her parents. Nor will she, directly, from us."

"And after I've found her, Eminence?"

"When I want comfort, Monsignor, aside from reassurance, I often turn to very unlikely sources. To atheists, for example. One such, who is also a great physicist, said, 'We live in a world where anything can happen but only certain things persist.' And after you absorb that splendid piece of thinking remember Socrates'

'The unexamined life is not worth living.'" Bellini stood. "I have an important luncheon for which I am already late. But if you will give me a hand down the back staircase I may be able to slip into my chapel unobserved. Whatever my sins, Monsignor, I retain a very simple faith in my Creator."

"May I join you in prayer, Eminence?"

"I'd be honored."

City of Angels

CHAPTER XVIII

A MIRACLE? NO, ONLY A MAN in a helicopter talking into a bullhorn, but to Sterling, driving the Freeway at sixty miles an hour and being tailgated by a green station wagon, the voice of God. "Dash o-o-something-three—you are too close to the car ahead of you. Repeat—you are—too close—to the—car ahead of you." The tower of Los Angeles's City Hall, Sterling's beacon, swung into the center of the Buick's hood, and Sterling, having had enough of the Freeway, pushed up the arm of his signal light and took the first exit, never mind which. As he said to Dolan in the bar of the Hotel Yardman, from which he could see Pershing Square, one of the wonders of downtown Los Angeles, "Goddam it, Bob, it's worth your life."

"Well, Elaine Brant isn't, the delinquent bitch. What are you drinking?"

"Is she still there?"

"Room three seventeen. Knock and walk in." Dolan signaled to the waitress. "She went up with two stud types but they came down a half hour ago. At two thirty-three. So she's either up there alone or she's—" Dolan tapped the glass partition that separated the lobby of the hotel from the bar. "There's the desk and there're the elevators. I've got her staked out. Like a goddamned F.B.I. agent."

"Well, let's go upstairs and put the cuffs on her."

"Funny to you, Joe, but I've been watching this kid since ten o'clock last night."

"You can see her better from in bed, Bob."

Dolan, a name and a face in Letty Peebles's Micaltor Productions, Inc. (a title derived from the names of her three adopted children, Michael, Calvin, and Victoria, each married now and living, on

169

the average, twenty-five hundred miles away from their foster mother), said that he would rather get in bed with a male cobra, provided its fangs weren't drawn. "This is Letty's fun streak showing, Joe. She doesn't really care about this bitch, she's making her puppets dance."

"Thanks."

"At least you're public relations, Joe. I'm office boy number two and headed for the out-basket. What'll you have?"

"Vodka Martini on the rocks. If I have time."

"You have time. The vixen is winded and gone to ground. A week in Frisco takes a lot out of a girl. It's a thirty-second wonder she didn't go to Las Vegas. Or Hawaii."

Vital figures: Elaine Brant, 37–26–36, auburn hair, brown eyes, *Playboy* calendar girl, age twenty-two, supporting player in one of Letty's TV serials, "The Hatbox" (story of models), unmarried ("I guess I'm not very lucky in love"), considered for lead in next year's ace program (sensational in pilot film), A.W.O.L. from Micaltor Productions, Inc. ("I don't know anything about money, I just know I'm not getting enough of it"), thought to be on alcohol, pills, and sex.

"Have you talked to her at all, Bob?"

"Briefly. She has a basic vocabulary of six words—well, you know her, Joe."

"Not very well." Sterling drank half of his Martini. "You think I can just go up there and grab her?"

"Protocol. She's not going to give herself up to just anyone. You'll do, though, because you're here." Dolan yawned. "I've got to get some sleep, but I'm afraid to drop off in downtown Los Angeles. I'm scared to death I'll wake up here. Good luck."

"How about the stud types?"

"They were walking low, Joe. This kid's a meat-eater. Unless they went out to get the rest of the squad."

After Dolan left, Sterling finished his drink, thought of having another, decided reluctantly that it might be better to keep his nerves alive for the Freeway, and went up to Room 317, from the outside a door in a hotel hallway. Color of chocolate drop set in color of cough drop. Dirty amber. He knocked, listened, knocked again, turned the knob. He said, "Open up, Elaine, or I'll call the police." Elaine the fair, Elaine the lovable, Elaine the lily— "Joe Sterling, Elaine. I'll take you home. No questions." Ah, the immemorial murmur, the creak of the immortal bedspring, the thump of bare feet. The door opened. My God, strange woman in her slip. What gigantic salesman lay on the bed beyond to rise and clobber him?

"Skip," the woman said. "Or I'll break your back." And shut the door on Sterling's foot. He shouldered it open, forcing her deeper into the room.

"Now, now, now," he said to the naked girl lying on the bed.

"I think someone's trying to rape me," Elaine said.

"What are you on now?"

"Just straight Scotch. Pour me some."

The woman hit him in the groin with the flat heel of a shoe, and Sterling, clutching himself, pointed out that the extremes of jealousy didn't necessarily include castration.

"Get out," the woman said.

"Don't muscle me, honey. Besides, those two stud types are in the lobby. Think you can handle them?"

"Go wait in the lobby. I'll bring her down in fifteen minutes."

"There's an interesting statistic. No deal."

"Enough's enough," Elaine said. "What's your name anyway? And who invited you in here?" Sterling poured Scotch from a bottle on the bureau into a dirty glass and handed it to her. "I must be out of my fucking mind." She got off the bed and picked up a skirt. "Well, now, will you look at this. Oleg Cassini. Imagine a gold-plated trot like you working a joint like this. I must be out of my fucking mind." Taking the woman's arm, Elaine drew her into the bathroom and shut the door. Sterling took a drink from the bottle, another, and sat in a straight chair by the big double window that opened on an air shaft and offered a view of an identical window. Assignation alley. Faced with the impossibility of love, sex became a throwaway. If a man's past consisted of what had happened to him, did it also consist of what he had done to

171

himself? He could put a plank across the shaft from sill to sill but would he, if the lure were great enough, cross it? And what the lure?

Elaine jerked open the bathroom door and strode into the room, shouting over her shoulder, "All you can do is make me nervous. Where's the bottle?" After the woman left, probably to continue the search for what, when found, could never be enough, Elaine said, "What do women see in other women, Joe?"

"Another woman. Put your goddam clothes on."

"Not interested."

Sterling looked at her, from toe to crown. "Physically, I don't think I've ever seen anything more perfect, Elaine."

"Look, Uncle Joe, you're studding half the women in this god-damned town."

"That's no distinction. Now put your clothes on."

Elaine began to dress. "I didn't go to Mass on Sunday."

"We can stop by a church on the way home."

"That one on Olvera Street. I want to buy a candle."

"Not to take with you."

"Don't say that, Joe, please."

Shocked by the intensity of her reaction, Sterling said, "Sorry, I'm losing touch. No perspective. What happened in Frisco?"

"That's why I missed Mass. I picked up this Italian—I don't know—contractor—construction worker—that was Saturday night. Listen, Joe, that man—" Elaine began to laugh. "You won't believe this—from two in the morning till about seven. Then he woke me up about ten and kept me at it till about one. I was never so sick of one man in my life. God, look in my purse. Have I any money?"

Sterling searched her purse. "Eight cents. I'll buy the candle."

"Well, I only had about a thousand to begin with. Then I wrote a check—two checks—bouncing Betty—maybe you'd better call Frisco."

"I'll take care of it. Anything else?"

"I didn't make the papers, did I?"

172

"Nope. Did you wear a wig?"

"Shit, I had three to begin with. Two, three suitcases. My ring." She held out her hand. "Gone with the guinea. Or maybe those motorcycle jockeys took it. Let's get out of here, Joe. They're coming back. With the rest of the troops."

Sterling took her home, a small apartment in Westwood Hills, neat, quiet, with no assumption of grandeur and no clue to rebellion. Living room, bedroom, bath. Neighbors—lawyers, doctors, teachers. Neither a tiger's cage nor a platform for circuses and exhibitions.

"Phone?"

"What are you going to tell Letty?"

"What did you cost her?"

"Two days' shooting."

"Can you be on the set tomorrow?"

"That depends on how she asks me, Joe. You can see that, can't you? I'm going to take a bath."

"Want me to wash your back?"

"Wash my feet?"

"All over."

He phoned Letty at the studio and was told that she had left for the day. Getting her at home, he started to tell her, in a style she liked, that he had found Elaine and that— "In person," Letty said. And cut the connection. The bottle of Scotch he had brought from the hotel stood on the table between the windows, beside a vase filled with blue flowers, that is, desiccation in the form of once-blue flowers that smelled, as he approached them, of—swamp water. In the peninsula. Bolton with his belly ripped open by a mortar fragment and the two sergeants who had given up their places in the helicopter to Petroni and the five nuns— Ah, Petroni —cut his throat at the base hospital when he understood, from what the doctors and nurses told him—or did not tell him—that he very probably— And the two foolish and intransigent sergeants, birds grounded by the complexes of combat and slaughtered in an alien element. One of the sergeants had cried, not because he

173

expected to die (he knew he would, of course), but because he could not die in the air or strapped into the seat of his lethal butterfly.

Pride. Just as the American pilot who had dropped his medicinal pellet on the monastery would, on being told of his mistake, blush for an inefficient performance, for an aborted prime mission, and for a poorly constructed and clumsy secondary mission. Stupidity, the only sin. He found a glass and poured himself some Scotch. A light beverage, pale in color, a belly-warmer taken neat, but not the drink for the peninsula. Lewis, the lanky imperishable mountaineer. No patrol was any match for Lewis. He would stalk it and pick off the enemy one by one, beginning with the officer or noncom. One bullet, one man. The long rifle. He knew the exact distance at which automatic weapons became ineffective. Obtuse or dedicated company officers operating by the book could send him into ambush but they could not kill him. He—the craving for excellence, one of the great psychic hungers. An empty belly demanded food. What in a man forced him to dream of excellence, whether his own or someone else's? A detestation of self, a hatred of a system, isolation by type (ethnic, physical, political, religious), yes, but was this all? Perhaps only a need for a superior type, royalty, Plato's absolutes, God.

Hearing Elaine calling, he went into the bathroom, where she lay in a pond of soapy and scented water, and after taking off his jacket, tie, and shirt began to wash her with a fluffy pink cloth. He began with her face and neck, using Q-tips to clean her ears. He scrubbed her hands and nails with a short stiff brush, which he also used to burnish her elbows. As he rubbed her back firmly he noticed the absence of the two white bands of flesh, narrow below the shoulder blades, broader across the rump. Not a sun lover. She winced as he pushed the soft cloth through the anal cleft and brought it between her thighs. He did not probe her but patted and pressed the vulva. Cupping her right buttock in his left hand, he soaped and cleaned her belly, screwed the cloth into her elliptical navel, rubbed her breasts lightly, being careful of her nipples. As she lay back in the tub he washed her legs, using the scrub brush on her knees, shins, and heels. He cleaned the white wrinkled flesh between her toes and brushed the soles of her feet. Letting out the water in the tub, he fitted the five-foot length of green hose on the faucet and rinsed her body, first with luke-warm water, then with cold. He then helped dry and wrap her in a thick terry-cloth robe. She leaned against him, shutting her eyes. Stooping, he picked her up and carried her into the bedroom and laid her on the bed. After he shut the Venetian blinds he dressed and left the apartment, making sure the press-lock on the door snapped behind him. Damnation. He had forgotten to wash her hair.

A relationship between two people had a built-in obsolescence. Like a washing machine. So there you were with your spin-dry working perfectly and her wet wash a mass of jangling gears. Ah, but you had used cold-rolled steel in your part of the design and she— He had walked down the steps of an airplane on Long Is-land like a proconsul returning to Rome after a successful governor-ship of an eastern province, and he had fallen up the steps of another airplane six months later to savor the award of a minor post among the barbarians on the West Coast of the United States, that of translator or human ferry. Was this flight west an ascent or a descent? Or, a better question, could it be understood in such outdated terms as up and down, across and back, good or bad? And how important was it that he understand at all?

Poor Virginia. And Joe Junior, and Lester and Millicent, the last with no memory of him, none at all. Had he rejected his wife in advance? His letters home, the diary of a bristling stranger. "You smell different," Virginia had said that first night home, before a shrieking Millicent, his offended daughter, had interrupted an awkward passage of love-making and crawled into her mother's bed. Yankee, go home. A week later he had been introduced, casu-ally, to Victor Winslow (Uncle Victor), and that night, as the house creaked of its uneasy despots, each with a plan of action against the intruder, had had to listen, at length, to something that did not need explaining but would have been monstrous without it. No, Winslow, an older man, separated from his wife, the last of his children in college, had not assumed the position of Virginia's lover, only that of appointed head of the Sterling household, a crown forced on him after repeated rejections. A pipe-smoker, by God, secretary of an old and honorable corporation that dealt in grain futures. Secretary now, and in time president. Presbyterian elder. Lover of chamber music and German lieder but not—yet—the lover of Virginia Sterling.

No, that honor had come to Sterling. *He* was his wife's lover, and Winslow, the true head of the household, the dignified and suffering husband. Hardly astonishing that Virginia Sterling, after a few bitter weeks of legal whoredom, should say, indirectly, with appropriate despair, that she could not do this to Winslow. Sterling, receptive to the niceties of her point and disgusted by the mechanics of a nonconjugal lust (what with the raging and inconsolable Millicent, they had often been forced into the bathroom and the closet and several times into the garage), had agreed. They did not completely sever all carnal connections, since Sterling, the irresistible invader, might yet snatch the crown from Winslow and after suitable alteration and cleaning wear it with grace and security. There was the problem of contraception. Naturally, Virginia, fixed spiritually on Winslow, could not have a child by her demon lover. No. But both Lester and Millicent, while planned, had arrived before the time set for them, a fine testimonial to the virility and endurance of his sperm and of the hustle and *esprit* of her egg.

Naturally it happened—and what could have stopped it?—the classic missed period, the ripest of domestic scenes. She had blamed herself, Virginia had, leaving Sterling the job of thinking himself out of an artificial hell he had built from the odds and ends of fictional passions operating in the most advanced and fantastic settings, and suddenly his Rosalind not to exit pursued by bear but to be eaten by it. And while she checked the calendar (surely he had invented this), counting backward on her fingers, he asked himself and a fair-minded god of personal relations if Winslow would accept the child, knowing it to be the product of obstinacy and reluctance, the two faces of honor. Ten days of waiting, which he endured mostly in New York, at his office and in a number of quiet bars where he could drink incognito before catching the eleven twenty-five local at Grand Central for Greenwich. Since his return he had lost his footing in local society, his neighbors and peers having subtly reoriented themselves to the Winslows, man and wife-to-be. They saw his period of military service for what it was, a three-year sentence to a chain gang in the deepest possible south for the crime of aspiring to a position his birth, breeding, and money did not entitle him to. Did he care? Yes, but not enough, not even when Virginia told him she had finally come around and having come around did not wish to risk her *status quo* till they had decided, between them, which way he would jump.

A few weeks later, at the end of the fifth month after his return, he spoke with his boss, Marshall Lipton, founder and owner of the advertising agency Sterling had once hoped to head (in time, of course).

"How am I doing, Marshall?" Sterling asked. A fighting question, in excess of his place but not of his predicament.

"Well enough, Joe," Lipton said. "I have no complaints. You were a little slow adjusting—what's your fix?"

"Personal mostly."

Lipton, a small man with a large handsome head, nodded as he reviewed, mentally, Sterling's file. "I've always been very fond of Virginia, Joe."

"I hope you still are, Marshall. I'd appreciate your good will toward her."

"Are you thinking of a divorce?"

"At least. After a suitable separation." Sterling spoke briefly of Winslow and of Winslow's fondness for the children and the children's fondness for him. "I'm absolutely nonbitter about this, Marshall. And Virginia, in my opinion, is an ace. I don't know how to say it, but there are no villains in this piece. It's the kind of thing the *Daily News* leaves to the New York *Times*."

"I'm glad to hear that, Joe. People insist on telling me about the private behavior of my employees and I keep telling them to go to hell, but what can I do?"

"Herewith my resignation, Marshall."

"If you were a genius I wouldn't accept it, Joe. And I'm very, very reluctant to accept it now. I respect your gesture because it has the sincerity of being impromptu. You didn't come to this office to resign, did you?"

"No. Furthermore, I had no idea you'd fire me."

"I don't intend to. I have a reputation for getting rid of people painlessly. Oddly enough" (Sterling was to remember that "oddly enough" later), "I've had a feeler for your services."

"The bartenders' union?"

"Letty Peebles."

"Who is—not the ancient movie star."

"The same. But she's also a big—and a very successful—producer for television. A difficult medium, Joe."

"Television commercials?"

"Public relations. I can only guess she wants a flack without a circus or burlesque background. Someone who shaves."

"Public relations."

"It's not so different from advertising, Joe. You see that."

"You think I ought to accept it, Marshall?"

Lipton sighed, ending with a whistle. "I never give advice, Joe, I point out opportunities. My wife calls me—not within outside earshot—a reluctant moralist. Unlike Alexander Pope."

"I don't have to decide tomorrow, do I?"

"How much time do you want? A year? Two?"

"Thanks, Marshall."

"You see, I have the problem of replacing you, Joe. Well, let's think about it."

Oddly enough—that phrase again—Virginia, once he said he would go, had not wanted him to go, foreseeing possibly the death of sex (and its powerful funeral), possibly her removal to the cool tents of middle age, where everything would be permitted her except another Sterling. Perhaps she had wanted Winslow as a replacement and had been appalled to realize she would have to

178

accept him as a substitute. Or perhaps the children had made the choice for her. It might be simply that in the race for death and disintegration he was miles ahead of her.

Leaving Elaine Brant (he would stop by to pick her up in the morning and drive her to the studio), Sterling, deciding that he had had enough of Letty Peebles, drove to the small house he rented in Laurel Canyon, his refuge from Beverly Hills and Universal City. He would cope with Letty tomorrow. In the meantime he could put his feet up on the railing of the back veranda and contemplate the wooden footbridge that during the rainy season shook to the thunder of a rampant creek. With a large bottle of vodka and a small bottle of vermouth (and the free use of his elbows) he could defend himself against the nightly attacks of the forces of darkness and decadence and, if necessary, mount a counterattack of his own, with Goldman and his grease-gun on his left flank and Sister Esther and God on his right. When the quart of vodka was half empty (or for that matter half full) he would go into the kitchen, put on his chef's apron and hat, and prepare dinner for one, tonight lamb chops, potatoes Sterling (onions, green peppers, garlic salt), and a modest green salad. After which he would hit the sack—before the sack hit him.

CHAPTER XIX

FROM THE WINDOW OF HIS OFFICE at one end of the ranch-type building housing Micaltor Productions, Inc., Sterling had a view of a street and a sound stage, not much of a view but enough. There were, he knew, eighteen sound stages on the lot, six of them leased to Micaltor Productions, Inc. What went on inside these six sound stages, the routine filming of scripts, did not concern him. What went on inside the people inside the sound stages did, particularly when what was inside leaked outside. He saw himself not as a molder of images or a creator of imaginary profiles, but as an interpreter for a group of illiterate and inarticulate talents to an often hostile (and always curious) press and public. Now and then, of course, he saw himself as a male nurse and janitor in a home for delinquent adults run by Letty Peebles. My day with Elaine Brant.

That particular day, at five in the afternoon, he was trying to persuade Colin Burgess, a free-lance writer of articles for large magazines, to do the right thing by Letty Peebles. "She's an extraordinary woman, Colin. If you're going to do the kind of profile that begins 'Letty Peebles is a perfectionist' forget it."

"I don't have to tell you what I'm going to do, Joe." Burgess, a tall, loosely constructed man putting on weight, pointed a finger. "You've forgotten to ask yourself the healing question: Who the hell am I?"

"You wrote one good book, Colin. Don't assume you can write another."

"When I need reassurance, Joe, I can go to any public library. Where do you go, to the men's can?"

"When I can locate it, yes."

Burgess laughed. "When I knew you in New York you didn't have a sense of humor. All right, what's your idea?"

"Did you know that Letty collected a hundred and fifty thousand dollars for Bishop Havemeyer's fund for orphans in the Far East?"

"Did she give it to him?"

"What do you know about her three adopted children?"

"You're joking."

"She has quite a private life."

"One you can't make public."

"Begin with her origins, if you like, Colin—how she was born in a theatrical trunk backstage while her father improvised till her mother could get back on stage, the famous screen test where she lost the top of her dress—and all the other lies and half-truths. Including the four husbands—two of which were men. But I can give you something better, the woman."

"With Letty's consent?"

"If you do a good job on her you won't need her consent."

"First, I'll have to see what you've got. Frankly, I wasn't considering doing a solo on Letty Peebles. But if you can persuade me she's real—"

Sterling left at six thirty to change into black tie and escort an actress to a function at the Ambassador Hotel. The next afternoon he again took the Freeway to City Hall, where he paid a fine for speeding, his second moving offense in six months. He did not count against himself—nor did the police—skidding off the road coming from Lake Arrowhead at four in the morning (another hatchet job for Letty Peebles) and ending right side up in a gully a hundred and fifty feet below the highway. He had hidden the bottle of vodka under a rock before climbing, on his hands and knees, to the place where he had gone through the railing, an exercise that, combined with the fear blowing through his body-mind like an interior gale, sobered him sufficiently to give a reasonable account of the accident to the San Bernardino police. He bought a new car and said nothing beyond "Got to get more exercise; my back's killing me." He also resumed writing the book on his experiences in the Far East, a project he had started under compulsion and wished to complete before he analyzed the compulsion. He tried to work on a schedule to prevent himself from believing he had given himself a deadline.

At Letty's insistence he went to her doctor for a physical. The doctor suggested a corset to support his back and asked if he had blacked out lately. "Well, when I slipped on the steps and hurt my back I also banged my head." "I mean alcohol." "Sometimes things get a little hazy, Doctor, but I don't pull a blank." The doctor then said, to Sterling at least, an astonishing thing. "Excessive drinking, Mr. Sterling, isn't necessarily a dangerous business —you can kill yourself just as effectively by overeating—but unless it's accompanied by a sense of celebration—" "Thanks. Should I take anything for my back?" "Aspirin. If you have anything else in your medicine cabinet get rid of it."

A sense of celebration. Later in the week Letty sent him north to the grape country to investigate reports of deteriorating relations between one of her TV units and the local townspeople. Behind this interesting hassle Sterling found a hysterical matron, fanatical to her bobby socks, who asserted that one actor in particular had insulted the minister of her church. It seemed, after due investigation, that the minister who preached the "foursquare gospel, brother, foursquare" had appeared at the location where the unit was shooting on a Saturday afternoon and declared that he intended conducting "God's filibuster" to prevent the unit from working on Sunday. He was supported by the matron and three other ladies of the church. While the director spoke to the minister, the actor walked up to the group, bottle in hand, and asked the minister to join him at his motel down the road—"a little gang-bang, Preach, invite your friends." As Sterling expected, the matron could not be mollified, the minister settled for a new roof on the church. Sterling explained it to the indignant actor: "You pay taxes to the government, you tithe to the church."

If he had not gotten drunk with the actor he might have started the drive to Los Angeles at ten in the morning instead of two in the afternoon and so might have missed seeing Sister Agnes sitting in the station wagon at the gas station he had chosen, not because he needed gas, but because he needed a six-pack of Seven-Up, a beverage that in his opinion mixed much better with vodka than any of the usual colas or fruit drinks. Pry the cap off with the special bottle opener he carried in the glove compartment of the car, pour out half the Seven-Up, fill with vodka, and recap. In the gents' room. Then drink it in the open while waiting for the attendant to change a ten-dollar bill. The station wagon was headed north, so that Sterling, glancing through the gas pumps, saw first the nun driving and then the nun sitting in the front seat beside her. Recognition was not only instantaneous but, if possible, retroactive.

He had known—yes, for more than a year—that the nuns' home

office lay in this section of California (the grape-bright land), and while working on his book had often thought of writing or calling the convent. Form a Purple Heart Club. Meet once a year in the nearest winery. Yet he had done nothing, perhaps from a feeling buried so deeply inside him that only the faintest pulses reached his recording centers (and then at random) that it would be done to him. Without the anxiety to know—how would Sister Agnes respond if he spoke to her? Had he the right to speak to her, to engage her in a shockingly public intimacy that might, so far as he knew, reopen a dialogue dangerous to them both? He had to think. And while he was thinking, the station wagon, having somewhere to go, moved off the apron in front of the gas pumps and onto the highway.

Then two things happened, not necessarily related or of any particular consequence: he became involved with Elaine Brant, and his wife, Virginia, from whom he was unofficially separated, wrote that she would be in Los Angeles for ten days come next Tuesday (the closing of her uncle's estate in Pasadena).

The relationship with Elaine Brant had, if not Letty's concurrence, her toleration. "We all went through it, Giuseppe; better you than an actor." Did this place him a cut above an actor or a cut below? Elaine put her car in the garage outside the house in Laurel Canyon and two suitcases in the closet of his bedroom. They slept in a double bed, a practice that made him reluctant to change the sheets (violation of the nest, a tearing down of the fruity walls of the womb). Uncle Joe, she called him, even when he plowed his nightly acre. She thought him sexually reticent, which might have pleased her; he thought her sexually nonselective, unable to choose for long those erogenous zones that might have developed the special closeness he believed necessary to spiritual release.

He saw, of course, the stupidity of demanding from a physical act responses impossible to it. A gymnast a little out of training, he need only climb her like a rope or a slightly oiled padded pole and discharge would follow. He took her to public parties, private parties, night spots, day spots, beaches, movies, and to Letty Peebles's summer place at Lake Arrowhead. Her narcissism, the one constant of her personality, baffled him. He talked it over one night with the writer, Colin Burgess, not because writers were more intelligent or more observant than their betters, but because they chewed a bitterer cud, an indestructible mass of childhood losses and the refusal of an adult world to put them on the big teat.

"Shortage of men," Burgess said. He pointed to the group of people standing around someone's pool. "When a man arrives here he's usually married. If he isn't, the competition for him is so terrific he can afford to be choosy. And he can marry anyone. A woman can't."

The simplicity of this argument staggered Sterling, especially since, like most Easterners, he had assumed that whenever Hollywood went Hollywood, it did so in violation of his laws instead of in obedience to its own. Having felt strongly that he did not belong, he became aware that he had arrived, a transfer from a sealed boxcar to an open grave. Aware that he paid less attention to her, an instinctual observation, Elaine accused him of being in love with himself, the only competition she could imagine. He cut down on his drinking to give her more of his attention and bought a sun lamp. Twice a week, at eight in the evening, he took Elaine to a classy gymnasium run by a former middleweight boxing champion who taught them to skip rope and gave Elaine lessons in how to protect herself from rapists and mashers and Sterling lessons on how to overcome such defenses. As a result, when he met Virginia at the airport in Glendale he had the masterful look of the mediocre, whose pleasures and passions are those of their milieu and not of their selves.

"You look wonderful, Joe," Virginia said.

"You've been hearing otherwise?"

He drove her to Pasadena, where she was to stay, took her to dinner, brought her home, and told her firmly that she looked tired. He sensed that she was in the Indian summer of their separation and might want to run through the grape arbor in her bare feet before the first frost, a vision connected in his mind with a visit to the cell of a capital offender the night before deportation or hanging. "How are the kids?" he asked for the third time.

"Mother came up from Florida to look after them."

"And how's your mother?"

"Not too well. She has bursitis in her left shoulder."

"And Winslow?"

Virginia shrugged. "You're not too glad to see me, are you, Joe?"

"I've built a scab over that sore and now—of course I'm glad to see you. Only—"

"Other commitments?"

"It's just that I have this girl—an actress, not a girl—it's part of my job—"

"Joe, you're not *living* with her?"

Suspicious of her excitement and of the wriggle on the chair that exposed most of her legs, as if she were stripping for combat, he said, "Well, it's only a temporary arrangement—Gin, she's had a bad time—you can't judge situations like this one from a Connecticut viewpoint—" Hilarious. He had *really* said it.

"Is she famous, Joe?"

"Not that famous, no."

He explained the situation the next day to Elaine—Virginia's late uncle's will, the terms of the divorce, the custody of the children, probable alimony, visiting rights. To his astonishment he saw the same excitement in Elaine that he had seen in Virginia.

"She wants a reconciliation, Uncle Joe. And I'm the girl that can give it to her."

"Now look here, Elaine—" Uncle Joe stating that life could be difficult when you didn't have someone to write it for you.

"What's her phone number?"

"I told her about you, Elaine."

"She doesn't care about that. My God, you've got to be stabbing someone, don't you?"

"That's a hair-raising remark, whether you recognize it or not."

"I'll bet you she's doing her hip exercises right now. If she isn't at the hairdresser's. The best thing's an open approach. We'll have dinner together. I'll wear an old dress—"

"Why don't you come as David Brinkley?"

"I'll move back to my apartment for the time being. And after dinner you can bring her back here. I'll change the sheets."

"Elaine, if we have dinner I'll take her back to Pasadena."

"Uncle Joe, you can't screw her in Pasadena. There's a city ordinance against that kind of thing."

"I don't intend—" He wondered whether realism was only the acquired characteristic that helps you take what would happen for granted.

As he held Virginia in his arms in the cold double bed, after a sincere effort to warm it, he felt as if the currents of his magnetic field had reversed themselves, as if from a body with a positive charge he had become a dark intaking force with a negative charge, antimatter which did not occupy space but time. He felt, not superior to the position of his body, but unrelated to it.

"It won't work, will it, Joe?"

"The only absolutes I had in the Far East were you and the job, Gin. I conducted my part of the war on those two fixtures."

"I'm ashamed."

"I wish I were."

Elaine did not move back to the house in Laurel Canyon after Virginia left—"I don't like to feel so dependent on any one person, Uncle Joe. Besides, it's time I took my religion seriously." Letty Peebles now demanded his time, particularly to act as Micaltor Productions' representative in the discussions with Sister Ann Girard in St. Louis, a nun who had survived important atrocities in Africa. Letty wanted to make a realistic film about Catholic missionaries in Africa, using Sister Ann's experiences there as a basis for the script. She also wanted Sister Ann to act as technical adviser for the picture, a project that her good friend Bishop Havemeyer approved but could not advance. In his report to Letty, Sterling said, "All I can get from Sister Ann is a commitment to keep the discussion open, Letty." "Not good enough, Giuseppe." "You don't need Sister Ann. The story of the atrocities in Africa appeared in all the newspapers. A good writer can whack you up a script without going personally to Sister Ann or anyone else." "I want Sister Ann's story." "I can give you a better one, Letty." He added quickly, "Anyone could. A little imagination—"

The following Sunday morning he woke up in one of Letty's guest rooms without remembering how he had gotten there. He remembered only that he had misbehaved—some arguments—he had talked with Bishop Havemeyer but what about? Too many people, too much booze—he had been all right, on his feet, drinking, yes, but quietly—Letty had probably—what was he guilty of? Nine thirty, according to his watch. Dressing quickly, he took two aspirin from a bottle in the bathroom and went downstairs. Seeing no one, hearing no one, he got in his car and drove home. He had, he admitted, a first-class hangover, the kind for which he must make plans—no booze, not even a bottle of beer, till five o'clock. Then three Martinis—make it four—dinner, and bed. He felt vulnerable, very vulnerable, open to attack, defenseless. He had suffered a loss of immunity, committed himself, but where? How? He would have to wait. Say nothing, act as if he had been totally responsible for what he could not remember, move from strength, avoid any hint of asking for information, make no concessions.

The following Saturday Letty, who had flown to New York the Monday after Sterling's occupation of one of her guest rooms (she had five), phoned from her home to ask him to bring her the mail and the contents of her in-basket. She received him on the patio that opened off one side of her cathedral living room. The striped bikini, short gold coat, and heeled sandals emphasized the thirty-year-old figure she had forced from a fifty-year-old body.

"On my way back from New York I stopped off briefly in St. Louis, Giuseppe. Sister Ann wouldn't talk to me, but her mother superior said that the deal for her story was off. Have you heard from Sister Ann?"

"Not yet, no. I'll probably get a letter Monday."

"I suppose you told Sister Ann I'm only a television producer now."

"I did. Emphatically."

"And that my naughty international period, for which I have been much publicized and abused, is like my ass, stunning but behind me."

"I also made a point of saying you'd converted to Catholicism several years ago and were steadfast in your faith."

"You make it sound as if I'd switched from oil to gas. You personally delivered Bishop Havemeyer's letter, didn't you?"

"Weeks ago, Letty."

"A truly magnificent story, Giuseppe, one I truly wanted to do. Heroic nuns and martyred priests but authentic. Nothing faked, all real. Did you foul up the deal, Giuseppe?"

"Obviously, I mishandled it. But not deliberately."

"Make me a vodka and tonic. And be sure yours is a double Martini."

"What the hell, Letty, you don't need Sister Ann. You don't—"

"Do I need you, Giuseppe?"

"Give me a definition of public relations."

"What I tell you to do is what you do, Giuseppe. You seem to be slacking off with Elaine Brant."

"Only in my private relations."

"I sent your apologies to Bishop Havemeyer for last Saturday's performance. I didn't think you'd remember."

"All right, Letty, I don't. And change needles. My ass is getting sore."

"The help is getting snotty."

"Do you want my resignation?"

"If I fired you, where would you go?"

"I could always marry you for your money, Letty. Here." He handed her a vodka and tonic, twist of lemon, and steadied a large Martini in his right hand by a cold act of will.

"You must have gotten an advance from your publisher, Giuseppe."

"I was brought up to ignore such noises."

188

"*Our Ladies of Delight or Is Sex a Habit?* Even Bishop Havemeyer was moved by this high-powered title."

"You're making that up."

"*You* made it up. If the book has what you say it has I'll pay
you a hundred thousand dollars for it. And give you two per cent
of the gross."

If his individuality, his person, his self, was only a contrivance
and encumbrance to him why should he object when others saw it
as a package, a marketable commodity to be bought, used, and discarded?

"I'm afraid I overstated the case, Letty. I don't have a book, I
have a memorandum."

"I'm sure you have. And now I'm offering you a chance to turn
that memorandum to your advantage. And you're balking, Giuseppe. Why? You yourself brought up the subject of these five violated nuns. For what purpose?"

"If I could answer that I'd give up drinking."

"Why did Sister Ann refuse to see me, Giuseppe? Was it because
you failed to sell me to her?"

"I tried."

"You failed to sell me because you couldn't. You don't know
me."

"I said you were one of the better producers in the field, mentioned the good programs you'd done, offered to run a tape of that
thing you did on the Mexican fruitpickers—"

Letty handed him a heavy silver mirror whose handle was a
small copy of Michelangelo's David. "Turn around, Giuseppe.
Now look at me in the mirror. Over your shoulder."

"I don't remember this scene, Letty. What's it from?"

"Be honest. Or, as they say, objective. Now what do you see?"

"Wouldn't you rather play post office or stink-finger?"

"What do you see?"

"I see—"

"An aging whore?"

"Letty—"

"An aging whore?"

"Christ, yes."

"A vulture got up like a flamingo?"

"Yes."

"A grotesque?"

"Yes."

Letty took the mirror, smashed the glass on the edge of a metallic table, and gave it back to him. "Now what do you see?"

"Splinters. The back of the mirror."

"An aging whore?"

"Letty—"

"An aging whore?"

"Yes."

"A vulture got up like a flamingo?"

"Yes."

"A grotesque?"

Sterling dropped the mirror. "Yes."

"And that's what Sister Ann saw when you took my loathsome image out of your little duffel bag and said, 'And now, Sister, behold the face above the hands in which we propose to place your heroic story.' "

"Letty—"

"We could take—we have taken—in our stride the worship of animals, pansies, illiterates, perverts, the mentally retarded, murderers, thieves, gangsters, whores, pimps, and now we ask you to trust yourself to this cracked bitch who promises to piss on you through the golden tube and insist, Sister, that in this stream you be born anew."

"You're right, Letty. I don't know you, I will never know you, I refuse to try."

"Who wants you to, Giuseppe? Not I. Do you know where these nuns are now?"

"No, I don't."

"Then your book really has no ending."

"Neither ending nor beginning."

"We'll talk with Father Serrano, Giuseppe, you and I. Or do you remember Father Serrano?"

"Vaguely, yes."

"You have no objections to visiting downtown Los Angeles, have you? Now that you know the way."

"If it's in line of duty, none."

"I'll go take my nap. Have I forgotten anything, Giuseppe?"

"Nothing important, no."

"Of course I have, Giuseppe." Letty took a small plastic vial from the pocket of her gold coat. "Putting you to bed last Saturday night—after the Bishop left—I found this in your pocket. Have you missed it?"

"Thanks. Thought I'd lost it."

"Bad heart? Diabetic?"

"In case of capture during the war. If you decided you couldn't take the interrogation just slip the little pill under your tongue."

"Then why do you carry it now, Captain?"

Sterling turned to the bar to refill his glass. "You know what it was like out there, Letty? The same as it is anywhere." When he turned with his drink he saw that he was alone. "The joint is full of absent women."

CHAPTER XX

THE INTERN IN THE AMBULANCE that picked her up on the southeastern corner of Main and Seventh Streets in downtown Los Angeles handled her for obvious concussion and possible internal injuries, and the resident who received her at the county hospital, noticing the cheap print dress and short hair, along with the rough hands and calloused knees, put her in a ward with other accident cases. No pocketbook, no shoes, no hat.

The police at the place of the accident were unable to collect any witnesses who had actually seen the car strike the unidentified woman. "Man, I didn't see anything," one young male wearing an orange-colored raincoat and purple beret said. "No hunner-stan," another said. A boy of twelve when questioned about the disappearance of the woman's pocketbook seemed to be in shock —till the policeman shined his flashlight in the boy's eyes. Not wanting to provoke this impromptu assembly of his peers, the policeman reminded the boy that curfew had rung three hours earlier and said to his partner, "Let's git."

Forty-one hours after the accident, after the woman had identified herself as Margaret Westlake, age thirty-five, unemployed, newly arrived from San Francisco, no address, no relatives, a Miss Shirley Quando came to visit her in the ward, introducing herself as a representative of a Catholic welfare agency. "We'd like to help you, Miss Westlake, get you a room, a job, that kind of thing. Mind if I smoke?"

"No, of course not."

"Down on your luck?"

"No."

"Radcliffe? Wellesley?"

"No."

"Look, Miss Westlake, you're obviously a cut above the usual cases I see in the course of a good day's work. I think so, the doctors think so, the nurses agree—now how about it? No? Okay then, what are your qualifications? Teacher, steno, secretary, research scientist, housewife?"

"Unskilled labor, Miss Quando."

"Miss Westlake, tell me to go away and I'll vanish into the cracks. Like dirty water. But the county relief people are going to be here, and before they let you become a public charge, a drain on the county's pocketbook—and that means money out of some low-grade politician's Sunday pants—they're going to do everything except fingerprint you. And the only reason they won't do that is that women generally don't have fingerprints on file. Now we already know a good deal about you—your blood type, physical characteristics, dental structure, et cetera. And we also know that, married or not, some mechanic did a beautiful Caesarean on you, the kind you don't often see on charity patients. Two things don't fit—the hands and those calluses on your knees."

"I'm astonished that so many people care."

"Honey, nobody *cares*. Better you were D.O.A. That way the body could be disposed of and the inquiry as to just who the hell you are and how you got here tossed into the files. Nobody *cares*, but once the machinery's set in motion, provided you're breathing, it's hard to stop. Why don't you throw in with us?"

"Thank you."

"Does that mean you will or you won't? Have the police been to see you?"

"Yes. This morning."

"Don't worry about it. They'll check the wanted and missing persons files, and if you don't show up in either that'll be the end of it. I take it you don't have a police record."

"No, I don't, Miss Quando."

"Good. Then supposing we put you to work, find you a place to live—what size are you, twelve?"

"I think—yes, twelve."

"I checked your dress, Miss Westlake. Twelve. Remember that. The shoes I couldn't check. Did you have a pocketbook?"

"Of course."

"How much was in it? Well, you had to report that to the police, didn't you?"

"A few dollars, Miss Quando."

"Westlake your real name?"

"Yes."

"Miss Westlake, I've had a great deal of experience interviewing people and I can usually tell very quickly—you didn't even blink."

"Miss Quando, I appreciate—"

"My ass, honey. But you see, you haven't thought this thing through. You want to be let alone to pursue—whatever it is you want to pursue—and the first thing you do you give your real name. It's not a common name. I don't know how many there are around because I didn't bother to check. Now you have a Social Security number, don't you?" Miss Quando stood. "I'm no Paula Pry, Miss Westlake. Father Serrano'll be in to see you this evening, and I'll be by tomorrow to check you out. If you want me to."

"Thank you. Oh—Miss Quando—what about the hospital bill?"

"You'll have to sign a statement that you can't pay—honey, it's not a pauper's oath."

"But I can pay, Miss Quando. I'll have to—go to the bank."

"Then I'll pay it and you pay me. Or maybe you'd rather let your husband know where you are and *he'll* pay it. Okay—talk it over with Father Serrano."

Precisely the thing she had not wanted to happen had happened, almost, she thought, the way she had planned it. She remembered, though, that she had left the world where Freudian psychology did not apply and entered the world where it did, an adaptation perfected in its first attempt. Looking about her in the ward, she saw an immensely fat woman, a thin one, an old one, an extensively bandaged one, a young one with a swollen face and a jaw from which, perhaps, a few teeth had been brutally extracted—in other words a diabetic, a case of chronic anemia, an alcoholic, a high-grade moron, and a tubercular multipara with a manic husband. A young doctor, probably an intern, entered the ward and looked at her chart. He looked at her chart but studied her.

"How do you feel, Miss Westlake?"

"A few bruises, Doctor."

"You didn't see the car?"

"It was screened by a truck. My fault entirely."

"I was riding the ambulance that picked you up. You don't remember me."

"No, Doctor. But thank you."

"You were really out then."

"For three hours, I'm told."

"No headaches, no seeing double, no dizziness?"

"Nothing, Doctor. Unless the X rays—"

"You're fine, Miss Westlake. And lucky. No complaints?"

"None, Doctor. So long as I can leave the hospital tomorrow."

194

"We're not sure that you should, Miss Westlake. For your own protection."

"But I can sign a release, can't I, Doctor? Absolving the hospital —can't I?"

"Yes—"

"Thank you, Doctor. I'll leave tomorrow, then."

With Miss Quando? Yes, but the man who grabbed her pocketbook and pushed her toward the car had also grabbed the bankbook Mother Vincent had given her just before she left the convent for Los Angeles. "As you know, the nun's dowry must be returned to her"—three hundred dollars in cash, twenty-four thousand seven hundred dollars deposited to the account of Margaret Westlake in a Los Angeles bank. Her father, relinquishing her to the arms of the cloister, had said coldly, "I can't stop you from doing this, Middy, but I'll see that you damn well don't accept charity." Twenty-five thousand dollars at four per cent interest— her father could easily have given more, he refused to give less. A nice calculation. The Order kept the interest, quite rightly, and under the rules returned the capital. The will she had made on entering the Order, a complex document in which she renounced all monies and possessions but kept title to future bequests, in the name of the Order, had also been returned to her.

In the Order the nun's habit furnished immediate and complete identification, on sight, and would procure for her, in any emergency, whatever monies or services she might need. No one questioned her, few listened to her name. Even those who disliked nuns, whom she annoyed by her appearance, who would accept and pass on any lubricous story of behavior in convent and monastery, would never question her identity. She was a nun, a member of a religious order, what more could be known about her? Look, see, and forget. But in the week she had been out in the world, the same world she had left sixteen years earlier, she saw that she could no longer be so easily identified and accepted. People became confused and angry when she dealt with them. The cheap dress and shoes placed her in one category, the voice and the carriage in another. Men approached her with ease and confidence and left her quickly, embarrassed or sarcastic. Apparently she no longer used the practices of small talk and indirection skillfully. She could not be placed satisfactorily. And money. Would she ever learn to spend it properly? Handled improperly, money, the exchange of money, became an act of arrogance, the most intolerable of insults, in fact an indecency. Obviously, she had offended Miss Shirley Quando just as she had offended (and puzzled) her doctors and nurses. She needed an identity. Or, if she could not make or acquire one, a biography. She would have to invent an imaginary life. She would have to live, if not deceptively, fraudulently, and she would have to so adapt or shape herself that even the most perceptive observer would accept her.

What should she do? The major choice of a profession, a religious profession, had made all minor choices irrelevant, even that of service. As a nun it did not matter whether she served as a nurse, a teacher, or a scrubwoman. All labor is acceptable to God, none is preferable, none has precedence. You loved and served God by loving and serving His children, and in your habit you could do things with a serenity and purpose no one questioned or disapproved. Some might not like your interfering in worldly affairs, but they could not logically argue against your dedication. Atheists could object to your formal routines, Protestants could think you medieval, people could avoid you, but none could prevent you from performing your duties, and all, really, respected your obvious singularity. Sacrifice. And now?

Had she erred in going out? Could she believe after a week outside the Order that she could serve God as diligently and as satisfactorily as she had served Him inside the Order? Even though she had served Him badly? She could never live comfortably, placidly, lazily. She would never marry. She doubted that she could accept or tolerate a sexual relationship. Children? A marriage of convenience, even if she could make one—of course, she might change, in time, adapt herself. In discarding the self-restraint of the nun what qualities or talents for relating herself to a worldly society might not appear? To commit herself now, while she still thought and acted like a nun, would be a mistake. But how long a period would she need to discover her new self, if one were there, or to make a new self, if one could be made? When she left the hospital tomorrow she could go back to the room on Spring Street (her rent was paid in advance) and from there she could go to the bank where her money was on deposit, identify herself, explain the loss of the bankbook, pay her hospital bill (or Miss Quando)—but first she had to identify herself. Mr. Doe, I am Margaret Westlake. Are you? Where are your credentials?

Her heartbeat had accelerated. Her hands were damp, as was her upper lip. She could not think simply and clearly. Could she think at all? Astonished, she observed herself feeling a new kind of fear, but fear of what? Of people? Of groups of people? Of places? Of her—and this stunned her—future? What did the word mean? And how could she preface the word "future" with the pronoun "her"? Her future? The phrase could occur to her obviously, but could she define it? Her future? You exceed yourself, Sister. Dear God, how could You have permitted me to commit such a stupid and dangerous error? At last, someone to blame. Naughty God, shameless Saviour, cynical Spirit, how could You have so ruthlessly and efficiently betrayed me even though I don't know who I am and have lied to the doctors and Miss Quando (why didn't I tell her about the room on Spring Street?) and am now well into the hairy arms of panic, whose symptoms I have often observed in others, and will they put me in the psychiatric division after I scream?

Whatever she had been as a nun, she was a very ordinary woman, as silly, vain, stupid, and hysterical as the next. And as afraid. How did she differ, say, from the fat woman in the next bed, a ruminant whose cud was cheap candy and pastries? Or the bandaged woman across from her whose problem was to keep her husband out of her bed. Or the old woman near the door. Granny, perhaps, to young jailbirds and prepuberty prostitutes. As part of her training she had had a year in a women's penal institution, a reformatory and not a prison but at all times a jail.

Wards of the court, that was the euphemism, female misdemeanors worked out in an institution run by the Sisters of St. Luke and assorted female attendants. She preferred, really, the demented, whom God Himself could visit only occasionally. And never for long. Her nursing diploma. Was it still in the room on Spring Street?

The kindness of Mother Vincent, who had indeed exceeded herself. My child, my child. She ached for the comfort of that formidable old woman. But Sister Esther no longer existed. The name itself had been removed from the files of the Order. Furthermore—and here was the unbearable touch—it would never be given to a postulant. There would never be another Sister Esther. It was a name of dishonor, a vanished, an unspeakable name. It would never be spoken again in any of the Order's houses in any part of the world. There was already a new Sister Catherine. There would be another Sister Agnes, another Sister Mary— That had been the cruelest of all questions—why do you, Sister, when the others, who have suffered also, choose to remain, wish to go out? The only reply: I am not worthy. Ah, but why?

In her talks with her confessor, Father French (a theologian, not a pastor), she had been forced to say finally that she could not repent what she could not verbalize. "A sin of pride or anger or sloth, Father, is confessed very easily, even eagerly. They are formal categories and very useful. Almost any fault can be relegated to these stock pigeonholes and filed. And your response is almost as automatic as my solicitation of that response." "Must you insult me, Sister?" "Thank you, Father, for seeing this. Yes, I must insult you. And the Church. And, I suppose, God. My true sin is being kept from me. I grant you, very probably by myself. Call it pride, that convenient category, and absolve with warning and appropriate penance." "You stand behind a curtain, Sister. A very thick, very strong curtain. That's clear at least. A membrane, perhaps a caul." "I know only that I can go through the list of recognizable faults and sins and never quite reach the one I'm guilty of." "That, of course, can be credited to pride. But we must be careful, Sister, of piling pride on pride—like a child playing with blocks. To say that you refuse to recognize a most obvious and grievous fault is to take the first exit from, granted, the very difficult way of truth. And, of course, truth is not, as many think, self-explanatory. Would you like to see a psychiatrist? Father Schelling in San Francisco has helped many religious clarify—I don't say solve—their difficulties. Now I certainly don't urge you to see Father Schelling simply to select a category in which to place your female troubles. If you have such troubles." "No, Father. Please." "If putting the blame on toilet-training or your early relationship with your father will help, why not try it?" "Pride, Father."

After several such talks Father French asked her to give him, as truthfully as she could, her sexual profile. "Begin with the externals. For example, masturbation." "I have never masturbated, Father, nor have I ever had an urge to." "Child, such heroic statements only confuse and distract us. Do you know the mechanics of female masturbation?" "I *am* a nurse, Father." "And I'm a man, Sister. In my eighth year I started a program of, you might say, reluctant masturbation. I found that climbing a metal pole—we had one in our cellar—gave me an intense and very agreeable sensation. Later, of course, along with other neighborhood hellions, I learned the obvious method of self-stimulation and self-release. A most grievous sin, Sister, one I had trouble confessing. But I noticed that not only the weak and the morally deficient—such as myself—were addicted to this ambiguous perversion, but also the strong." "I knew several girls who practiced masturbation. But as for me—" "Did you ever have a sexual experience as a child or an adolescent, Sister?" "When I first started going out with boys I had to let them kiss me good night and sometimes—fondle me. But I never went any further." "You might say, then, that you're not strongly sexed." "Oh, but I know I am, Father. How do I explain it? I have, I think, a very powerful urge to give myself to others, but not as a sexual object. That's very badly put. A sexual relationship can be a very beautiful and fulfilling thing. Between the right people. That sounds horrible, doesn't it? So snobbish, so—"

199

In later sessions with Father French she tried repeatedly—and unsuccessfully, she thought—to verbalize her position. Yes, she had responded strongly when a boy she liked had touched and squeezed her breasts and patted and stroked her buttocks, but she had pushed him away and had never again permitted such—"Not indecencies, Father. I wasn't insulted by the boy's approach. I thought it quite normal. But I did have a code of behavior—that's the wrong phrase—dear God, what *do* I mean?" "And your dreams, Sister. Did you have many markedly sexual dreams?" "Some, yes, Father, but the mechanics are very vague. I don't think I dreamed in vivid sexual images. I'm certain that I didn't. But even as a nun I still had sexual feelings, a wish to be physically loved, but just how was never very clear. Father, I am *not* a neuter." "And homosexual desires, Sister?" "No, Father. At home I never felt unloved or left out or repressed or stifled—and I loved and admired my two older brothers. And I adored my mother. And my father spoiled me. It hurt him terribly when I told him I wanted to become a nun. But till then—would this help, Father? Perhaps it was because I felt so wanted at home that I had to go where I was needed. I used to be terribly ashamed of being rich when so many others were so badly off. At sixteen I was probably a dedicated socialist."

It embarrassed her to discuss sexuality with Father French, principally because she felt he was trying to give her a mental basket into which she could put her shame and unease and so be officially relieved of them. She thought she knew (pride again) as much about such matters as he did and had a better insight into her psychic make-up. It occurred to her that Father French might be warning her against (or preparing her for) a brutal awakening, some unimaginable thug to rouse her from her enchanted sleep not with a kiss but with a club. Certainly it was unusual for a priest, even a special confessor, to talk so directly about sexual matters to a nun. Perhaps—but she had not said, yet, to anyone, that she wanted to renounce her vows, nor had she said it, really, to herself. No, Father French was not talking to her as to a woman;

he was making a case for the Vatican's files. Like Monsignor Kramer. But why she alone? Why not, say, Sister Agnes?

She moved in an atmosphere of depression, a spiritual stupor, one that sedated the intelligence it ought to have prodded. She could not pray. One prayed from strength, joyously. Work, the only relief. But Mother Vincent refused her demands for more and yet more work. She suggested a retreat, an ordeal Sister Esther said she could not endure. Then one evening, coming out of the chapel after a long day in the operating room of the hospital, she collapsed. She did not black out totally, just fell slowly, clumsily, to the tiled floor of the corridor, as if her bones had bent or cracked or come unjointed. After a week in the infirmary, in the black hole of herself, she said to Mother Vincent, "I'm going out, Mother." Mother Vincent said calmly that such a symptom had to appear sooner or later in cases of spiritual sickness and that now that it had appeared perhaps the processes of healing would begin. "I should think, Mother, you would be pleased to get rid of such a ridiculous impostor." "Have you spoken to Father French about going out, Sister?" "Not yet, no." "Then do, please. After which come to me. In the meantime, Sister, persist."

Persist. Time, that bogus physician everyone assigns to the wretched and the depressed. "This would be absolutely the wrong course for you, Sister," Father French said. "A denial of the validity of your ordeal." "But, Father, I'm more and more convinced that my so-called ordeal was in fact highly invalid. It has the wrong touch of bravura. Would you like to buy a postcard with a picture of a violated nun?" "Hysteria, Sister." "Of course. The one real element. Father, a person must function. That's a natural law, and if he can't function in one environment he must find another." "You think like a man, Sister, but you feel like a woman." So gravely said, this powerful cliché destroyed Sister Esther. She did become hysterical. And at the beginning of her monthly period she suffered, for the first time since adolescence, from menstrual cramps, a clinical finding that gave her a pre-Christian feeling of having forgotten to perform an act of propitiation to the unknown God. She recognized that her individuality was slowly being reduced to a type. She would become, in time, a category. And finally a statistic.

So she went out. Mother Vincent could have refused to see her after Cardinal Brooker's office granted her petition for release. Except, of course, for the formalities of severance from the Order. But she did not. She said, "Yours is a most unusual situation, Margaret" (how it hurt not to be called Sister or my child) "and for that reason alone I feel I must talk to you. Since you so wish." "I couldn't ask you this before, Mother, but would I have been permitted to go back to the Far East if I had stayed?" "No." "Or to Africa or South America?" "You ask for a frankness painful to both of us, Margaret. Let me say this: your going out is a mistake but not an error. If you had stayed in you would not have made a mistake but committed an error. I can see now that in these last weeks I've underestimated the enormity of the attacks on your pride. You would never have been content to serve as a nurse in a domestic convent, not after such strenuous and exciting events, but what other therapy could we have offered you? The first requirement for the nun, Margaret, is a firm and joyous spiritual state. A nun is not a soldier, a crusader, a revisionist, or a rebel. She may do magnificent things, but she must do them quietly, within the bounds of her vows. Why choose the life of humility if you don't wish to lead it?" "It is the Church, Mother, that made me a woman, not I." "Then you are a woman, Margaret, and should choose, as you did, to live as one." "I don't like to be accused of nymphomania, Mother." Mother Vincent stared at her, perhaps in astonishment, perhaps in shock. "My poor child, don't you realize what your ordeal has done to you?" "But why should it have done anything at all, Mother? And why only to me? Why should I have been singled out for so much of the Church's attention? Are my reactions unique? Why should I be questioned endlessly on the one subject, sex, that is the most irrelevant point in the whole business?"

Mother Vincent touched her pectoral cross, the foundation of her calling. "I do not know the whole story, Margaret, nor do I wish to know it. But it's clear to me, after months of observation and face-to-face discussion, that your attitude and reactions puzzle and dismay the Church. She wishes to know what causes this nonacceptance of your situation. Sister Roberta's reaction is a disappointment and a cause for grief but it is perfectly understandable. As you may know, her work with the demented is first-rate. She can't leave the hospital grounds, but within them she leads a most useful and productive life. And a most spiritual one. Sister Agnes has resumed teaching and appears to be well adjusted to her situation. Sister Mary is strong and well and has found an inner peace much to be commended. But you, Margaret, you alone of the four have achieved nothing. Yet of the four you might have been reasonably expected to—I can say this now, Margaret—have achieved something of magnificence. Your sin, child, is a simple one. You have destroyed yourself. Why? You say you do not know why. I know that I don't. Perhaps Father French may know, perhaps not." "Is that the Church's viewpoint, Mother? That I've destroyed myself?" "It would be very unreasonable of you to blame the Church for thinking so, Margaret. What can you hope to achieve outside the Church comparable to what you might have achieved in it? You know our plans to establish fully accredited nursing schools. You might well have been put in charge of this program. Have you thought of that?" "I was never an ambitious nun, Mother." "Precisely. Your pride is female, not religious. Of course, it is a shocking fault for a nun to wish to exalt herself, but it is understandable."

Mother Vincent stood, ending the interview, Sister Esther's last talk with a fellow nun. She extended a Manila envelope. "Your nursing diploma. In the name of Margaret Westlake. You may have need of it. As you know, we do not mourn those of us who choose to leave the Order. We forget them. Or, rather, obliterate them. Nevertheless, child, I shall pray for you. Technically, you have defaulted, but I believe—" Mother Vincent again touched the pectoral cross—"that God has other plans for you."

So she did not go out into the world unarmed or, with her dowry, unshielded, but she did go alone. Still, even this romantic predicament was hardly a cause for anxiety. She need only write her mother, and her father or brothers would take the first available plane to Los Angeles and fly her home. To Rye. Forget me, she had said. But they hadn't forgotten her, nor would they. Her mother's letters arrived at the mother house in California (she wrote four a year) and were forwarded overseas. Sister Esther's replies (she wrote once a year) were sent to California addressed to Mother Vincent. Inside the outer envelope was a smaller unsealed envelope addressed to Rye and stamped. Mother Vincent, if she chose, could read the letter before sealing it and forwarding it to Rye. A matter of honor? No, protocol. She would have to write to her mother—the appalling thing was the entanglements. Suddenly, you no longer live in a world where there are few hellos and good-byes, no gossip, no decisions to make about eating, sleeping, working, praying, studying, where your relationship with your neighbor does not have to be reviewed weekly or changed, where transportation appears when needed, where you may exist for years without dealing with money, where no one asks for your Social Security number or checks your credit rating, where there is neither theft nor assault, family arguments, children, clothes— she supposed she would need a new pair of stockings when she left the hospital—yes, and a new pocketbook—and she would have to get another bankbook—

Dear God, she did not even know how to cross a street properly —and who had told her about pocketbook snatchers, cashiers who gave you change for five dollars when you had paid with a ten-dollar bill, and the prices, the prices, the prices— No, much as she disliked doing it she would have to depend on Miss Quando. This decision made, she could postpone others till she became more experienced in dealing with people, more knowledgeable about things even children knew, more poised, less open to panic, and, she supposed, harder, craftier, subtler. She had chosen this environment, she would have to learn to live in it. Would she ever have to appear in public in a bathing suit? And what *did* her legs look like? Should she shave them? And her breasts—the brassière she had was a little tight. And it lifted, thrust up and out, instead of flattening. When she walked did she wiggle? Should she, really, use lipstick?

That evening, as Miss Quando had promised, Father Serrano came to see her. Usually, when she permitted herself to think of them as individuals, she disliked handsome priests, particularly secular priests. Having lived, worked, and studied for several years outside the convent, she had observed that they distracted women parishioners and often had the air of posing for a coin. Father Serrano, however, had that special stamp she would have recognized and admired anywhere, that of the missionary. The skin bleaches in time, the body regains its normal weight, the fevers subside, but that slightly malarial (or sometimes wholly malarial) look remains, a compound, on a purely organic basis, of strange bacteria in the colon and weird antibodies in the blood stream, and, on a spiritual basis, of having known, loved, and served the poor in a fierce and unyielding land. Of course, there were missionaries who looked like hangmen, bankers, and spinsters—and behaved like these types—but they could be regretted and, if not converted to their mission, dismissed or ignored.

"Miss Quando told me about you, Miss Westlake," Father Serrano said in a soft tenor voice. "I should like, if you'll permit me, to help you."

"Whether or not I'm a Catholic, Father?"

"There are hospital chaplains of all faiths, Miss Westlake. You have only to make a request. Shall I do it for you?"

"How did Miss Quando learn I was a Catholic, Father?" Her knees?

"As you returned to consciousness the nurse thought she heard you saying an Ave Maria. I don't want to press you, Miss Westlake, but if you are a Catholic and are in need—"

"Both, I'm afraid, Father."

"Your husband?"

"I have no husband, Father."

"Any relatives I can inform?"

"I'll do that. Later."

"Shirley—Miss Quando—suggested that you move in with her.

Till we can get you a suitable room of your own. Miss Westlake, this is *not* charity. Her roommate married last month, and Shirley is looking for a companion to replace her. The apartment has two bedrooms, you will pay half the expenses—a very sensible arrangement—may I call you Margaret?"

"I'll have to have a job—"

"Any nursing experience? You needn't have a diploma."

"That's a little too grand for me, Father."

"Can you type?"

"A little, yes." She looked at her hands lying on the blanket. "Do you have an opening for a waitress, Father?"

"A waitress?" Father Serrano appeared to be checking the evidence of his senses against the details of her meager biography. "Yes, many. But wouldn't you prefer a job as a receptionist or an office worker?"

"No, Father. I could work in a laundry or as a scrublady—scrubwoman."

"There's always a demand for waitresses, Margaret. And certainly it's a job for which you need very little experience. Yes, well, Shirley will check you out tomorrow morning." Father Serrano stood by the bed for a moment, not in interrogation or embarrassment but in contemplation. "Shirley says she'll need your shoe size. And stockings."

"I won't need stockings, Father."

"No, but you will need—do you have a large foot?"

"Seven D, Father."

"Is there anything you want now? Candy? Cigarettes?"

"Thank you, Father, no."

Entanglements. And if the shoes did not fit?

CHAPTER XXI

THE RESTAURANT OPENED AT SEVEN in the morning, closed at ten P.M. It consisted of two rooms connected by a large arch, in the one room a semicircular bar and booths, in the other tables, counter, and booths. The dining area and the bar each had a separate entrance. The first few months she worked the morning shift, from seven to two thirty, harder work and smaller tips. The starched violet-colored uniform buttoned down the front and was worn without a belt. Most of the girls, because of the heat or the male customers, did not wear a slip. Usually, on the morning shift, five girls worked the dining room, two worked the bar. On the evening shift, beginning at two thirty, three girls worked the dining room, two the bar. At six, depending on the manager's judgment, three or four girls, some from the morning shift, helped work the dining room.

Breakfast started at seven and ended at nine. From nine to eleven two of the girls were usually withdrawn from the tables and counter to fill sugar bowls and salt and pepper shakers, clean tables, change tablecloths, make coffee, help the pantryman arrange and set up salads, polish glasses, fold napkins, inspect and rub down the silver, check the flower bowls, type menus, change menus, and straighten up the ladies' room. After which they could go to the cloakroom for coffee and a cigarette. The cloakroom had separate lockers for pocketbooks and coats, a small lavatory, and a couch for aching backs and tired feet. Most of the waitresses, whose names were Ruthie, Billie, Nickie, Bobbie, Frankie, Milly, Georgie, and Nelly, had, besides the standard female complaints, a back problem and a foot problem. The foot problem necessitated only unfinished discussions on corns and arches. The back problem, however, led into techniques practiced by the ancient Chinese and Hindus for the comfort and ease of the female while under masculine assuagement. It did not occur to the girls to ask the old man for a night off (they knew better) but they felt they had a moral right to better working conditions and subtler handling.

Shirley Quando, whose apartment she shared, doubted both her sincerity and her wisdom in wanting to work in such a joint. "Look, honey, come with me in the welfare office. If you want a slice of life that's where you'll get it. The creeps are very numerous."

"But I like the restaurant."

"Honey, the Hotel Yardman is one of the biggest whorehouses in the world. For both kinds."

"They're very lonely people, Shirley."

"Lonely? God. I wouldn't expect Father Serrano to know much about that kind of thing—to him everybody's a potential saint—but you, now you ought to know that creeps are born with a mission to creep and they get a nasty complex if you try to change them. When you take the fangs out of a rattlesnake what happens to the poor thing? It goes into a decline."

Shirley herself, a stunning mixture of Mexican and Japanese, could have worked in the better districts to the west but she preferred downtown Los Angeles, an area bounded roughly by Figueroa and San Pedro Streets and Chavez Ravine and Watts. Having been graduated from Berkeley and done postgraduate work at the University of Minnesota, she was well qualified in sociology and social anthropology but diffident about being accepted outside what she called "my old neighborhood." Besides, she considered Father Serrano's mission, the lopsided old brick-and-shingle church and the warehouse he was slowly converting into a home or halfway house for delinquent girls (aged nine to nineteen), more important than a better job or social standing. As she said, "Here's a guy who's had it, honey. In Africa they really stamped him into the ground. That business in the Congo? He lay out in the jungle for three days with a broken leg and back, and why the ants or the snakes or the leopards didn't get him nobody except God knows."

After closing the welfare office on her clients at five o'clock and setting the burglar alarm Shirley went down to the mission to help out. She came to the restaurant in time to walk Margaret home, after Margaret had earned enough seniority to work the late shift and when she worked part of both shifts. "I'm safe in this lousy town, honey, but I don't think you are—yet." She urged Margaret to carry a nail file in her purse. "You can't depend on the police. The poor bastards have enough to do delivering babies and shaking down the local bookmakers and junkies." Shirley, despite her good looks, also had a man problem. "I live between two worlds, honey, the one where they want to screw me and the one where they want to spit on me."

After six weeks of sharing the apartment Shirley suggested that they double-date. "I know a salesman's been after me for months. Not a bad type. He has a friend. They *all* have friends. I'd feel safer if we double. At least till I can get a line on the salesman when he's selling himself instead of his haberdashery."

"I think I've had enough of men for a while, Shirley."

"Now, shall I ask her or shall I not? No, I don't think I will ask her, but I'd like to. How about a shot of sherry?"

"I'll get it."

"Stay, stay."

Shirley went into the kitchen for the sherry while Margaret, who had had her usual day, sat in the overstuffed chair by the radio console listening to, as it happened, Bruckner's Eighth. One of the pleasures of the outside world was its music, and not only the music itself but its abundance. When she went into the convent she left behind Beethoven, Brahms, Mozart. Now that she had come out she had found Bruckner, Mahler, Bartók, Stravinsky, and Copeland. And overstuffed chairs and comfortable beds and a glass of sherry and clothes and people, none of which, including the people, were either important or necessary. She had adjusted well, she thought, well enough, but what next? "They also serve who only stand and wait." But had Milton, that strangest of Puritan sensualists, stood and waited? She remembered Monsignor Kramer (also a Puritan sensualist?) quoting Satan's exhortation from *Paradise*

Lost. "What though the field be lost? All is not lost; the unconquerable will—" What had she said to him? Nothing really, nothing
that mattered, nothing of interest except to sterile churchmen looking for the devil under the nun's cot. The phallus. The male
principle. And the same stale, bloodless, dreary line from Father
French. My God, how I do long for Thee. My God, my God—but
how could she reach Him? Not by foot, certainly, not by rail or
wing or miraculous dolphin. How?

"How about it?" Shirley asked, giving her a glass of sherry.

"Double-dating?"

"That was the original question."

"You're not doing this to cheer me up, are you? Poor Margaret,
let's do something real vital and nasty for her."

To her astonishment Shirley laughed and clapped her hands.
"That's the first human thing I've heard you say, honey. In all
these glum weeks. It's a little derivative and not too original, but
it is human. Now go whole hog and say you'll double-date."

"If you like, yes."

Shirley jumped across the room as if to hug her but changed
the gesture (in mid-flight, as it were) to a formal putting out of
the hand to clinch the bargain. How could she explain to Shirley
that she saw nothing abnormal or disgusting in the other girl's
advances, which were never more than an occasional pat or an
affectionate hug, but that she doubted (and was repelled by) her
own responses? How could she say that except when tending patients or repressing hysterics or the demented that she had neither
touched nor had been touched in sixteen years? That she had not
shaken a person's hand, not even her mother's? No, the nun's
body closed in on itself and left nothing dangling or extended,
least of all the human hand. The fact that she had been used by
hundreds of men in the Far East and examined and delivered of a
child by Dr. Poli hardly bore on the intimacy of a personal relationship. Historic occasions elicit historic responses. Having raped
and strangled a young girl, the underage killer must go home to
his mother with nothing changed between them. She saw this
clearly, and more and more clearly. What had happened had hap-

pened but not yet to her. Even the gross and abrupt departure from the spiritual life could not be conceived of as a proper response to her (and mentally she put it in quotation marks) "ordeal." No, it moved her into position to make that response, it could not be the response itself. In the meantime—

The two salesmen who met them at the restaurant that Saturday night ("There will be a slight pause while they size you up," Shirley said) took them to a night club featuring a five-piece band and a vocalist, and then to a private club on Western Avenue that featured a piano player who played "mood" music ("For middle-aged types," Shirley said). In the ladies' room she added, "Well, now you know what your price is—ten bucks plus tips. I always thought I was a twenty-dollar girl, but maybe that's only on alternate Thursdays."

In introducing them Shirley had said, "This is Jack and this is Bob—Maggie." Bob, the older of the two, smooth and well-fleshed, graying, sat in the back of the car with her making small talk and asking polite questions, questions she soon realized would affect his behavior toward her. "I'm a Dartmouth man myself, Maggie, but I can see the value of small colleges. Funny, I said to Jack, look, pal, a waitress. Include me out." At this point he took her hand. "Shows how wrong a man can be. Hey, Jack, where shall we *take* these living dolls?" "Home," Shirley said. "Not Hollywood, for Christ sake—" squeezing her hand—"I'm sick of that fruity town. Clip joints. What I'd like to hear is some good jazz. How about you, Maggie?"

At the night club she sipped bourbon and water while the others drank double Scotches. She said that she didn't dance and Bob said he didn't either but how about it? He held her loosely at first, walking to the music, humming the tune, and then in turning her brought her closer to him. Clinically she checked her reactions: pulse, eight beats above normal; skin, cool despite the body heat issuing from the dancers; mouth, a little dry. What else? No excessive vaginal secretions, no tremors of pleasure along her back, a slight but tolerable distaste for the man's heavy warm breath, a slight but tolerable annoyance at his sweaty palm. At the table he put his arm across the back of her chair and his knee against hers. In telling her pale-blue but not filthy jokes he patted her thigh. She gauged her behavior by Shirley's. If Shirley enjoyed herself—and she seemed to be enjoying herself—she would permit advances short of the sexual act itself. Provided Shirley did. She was determined not to prejudice Shirley's affair with Jack by snobbish shows of disapproval, disgust, or superiority to anyone's juvenile exuberances. She had hurt Shirley; she would heal that hurt. Just before they left the night club Bob, quite skillfully and not at all crudely, kissed her on the mouth. "That's an advance payment on my admiration for you, Maggie." "It's not a very heavy mortgage, is it?" He kissed her again, quickly, before she could counter the move, and said, "You hear that, Jack? A doll with a sense of humor."

In the back of the car, driving toward the private club, Bob apparently thought his pleasure (or pretended pleasure) at her remark had scored heavily for him, entitling him, if not to bedroom, at least to house, privileges. At the club, after checking out the place, Shirley invited her to the ladies' room. "How do you like Jack?" she asked. "Very much, Shirley." Shirley smiled, perhaps in relief. "He's divorced, so I'm not cutting in. Though I must say he's not spending any money on me." "You don't really care for Hollywood, do you?" "God, no. I'm glad you like Jack." "I do. But I warn you I'm no judge of character." "Hm." "Enjoying yourself?" "I've got a problem, honey. He's going to want to split up." "Wonderful, Shirley. That means he's serious." "Maybe a little too serious. But what the hell—" Shirley stared at her in the mirror. "I'm thinking of putting out. Do you mind?" Was it too late to respond? She put her hand quickly on Shirley's and squeezed it. "Of course I don't mind, Shirley. But thank you for thinking I would." "You're the strange one, honey. Damned if I know what you think." Too late, but she had come closer.

Back at the table Jack ordered fresh drinks and said that he himself never drank anything except Scotch. "I'm a Scotch man myself. How about you, Maggie? You a Scotch girl? You look like the Scotch type. Kind of patrician and long-legged."

"I don't really care, Jack."

"She's sober, Bob."

"That's the way I like them, Jack."

"Sober, sober, sober. Sides, top, and bottom. What's your last name, Maggie?"

"Westlake." She glanced at Shirley, hoping for guidance. The situation had perhaps not really changed but shifted, as if from the mock coupling of the dance to the clutch and break of the wrestling mat with the possibility of a fall. But with which partner?

"That's not a name, that's a park. Westlake Park. How about it, Bob? You planning to park at Westlake?"

"Let's get out of here," Shirley said.

They waited at the entrance to the parking lot while the men went to get the car.

"No goddam attendant," Shirley said. "The price is five." Before she could say anything or think of anything to say, something banal which she did not have on her tongue if in her vocabulary, Shirley added, "Hurry them up, will you, honey? I'm cold."

As she approached the car she heard Jack say—how had he gotten so drunk so quickly?—"It's a deal, then. I'll fuck the nigger and then we'll swap." "Sure, but I'll drive."

She returned quietly to the entrance of the parking lot to say to Shirley that the men were coming and that she had some aspirin in her purse.

"What I need is a hypo, honey. Well, now for the big brush-off in the vestibule."

"It *is* very late, isn't it?"

As Bob parked the car in front of the apartment house, a three-story stucco building with sun-bathing privileges on the roof, Shirley said, "After three. I guess we'll have to say good night here, gents."

"We'll have a nightcap upstairs," Jack said. "I've got a bottle stashed in the trunk."

"The lush's friend," Bob said, getting out of the car.

"The hell with it, then." Shirley got out of the car and waited till Margaret joined her.

213

Jack took Shirley's arm. "Got a little present for you. Give it to you inside."

"He's a witty man," Bob said. "Sometimes I'm funny, but he's witty." He put his arm around Margaret. "Which floor?"

"I said good night." Shirley pushed Jack away from her, a motion strong enough to force him against the car. "Come on, Maggie."

"Situation's changed." Jack appeared soberer, much more purposeful, the male with the game in hand deciding to end it with a meat ax. "Had a little bad spell, Shirley honey, but I'm all right now." He approached Shirley, hand out. "Shake and make up. No, come on. Can't end on a wrong note, can we? Too much at stake."

Shirley took the offered hand. "Maybe some other night, Jack."

"Why not tonight, Quando? Right here. On the grass. Five bucks. Cash. You don't have to report it on your income tax. Or maybe for free, huh? You work for free?"

Bob's hand on her arm held her a little outside, as it were, the arena where the action took place. She observed, without entering, the quiet street where the only lights were a distant street lamp and the twenty-five-watt bulb in the vestibule of the apartment house, the lights and the two people on the sidewalk, the jocular male with his long list of vocal obscenities, the girl twisted in on herself crying easily but not loudly.

"A little dark meat," Jack said. "You have to develop a special taste for it. Like venison. Use the back seat, Bob, while I converse with Snowdrop here."

Margaret shook off Bob's hand and put her arm around Shirley. "I'll give you a piece of chalk, Jack, and you can write your message on the sidewalk. Good night."

"Another holdout. By God, Bob, we keep drawing these high-class types. From the bottom of the barrel. Remind me to work the sewers tomorrow. Might flush out a round-assed angel."

"Give it up, Jack," Bob said.

"For fifteen bucks and a smile I could have bought myself a sailor. From this delectable object I can't even get a hand job. Couple of goddamned Lesbians. I ought to kick in their teeth."

"Forget it, Jack. A fruit's a fruit and you're not going to change them."

"A few alterations, Bob. Loosen the bite."

Bob gripped Jack's arm firmly. "We've had worse nights, Jack."

"Two questions. When? And where?"

Upstairs in the apartment Shirley went into her bedroom and shut the door, an action that appeared to Margaret like that of an animal crawling into a hole. Shirley's remark, "I live between two worlds, honey," had seemed ridiculous at the time she made it. A girl with her looks, vitality, and brains—why should she stoop to the crude sexuality offered by people like Jack, the hunter whose trophies could only be one-night stands and half-rapes? Still, when was the search for love ever conducted without incident? And while she could think she had never met anyone like Jack (as if to excuse Shirley), she could also think that Private Bolton in the Far East had prepared her for him. Dear Sam. The recollection of the big powerful sergeant startled her. Had she been in love with him? Nuns did fall in love despite their vows and despite their genuine adhesion to the spiritual life. But scandals of this degree were, she believed, rare, a tick of the nun's eternal clock.

But she had liked Sam, yes. She had said, to Bolton, that she liked *him*. And she had said to Shirley that she liked Jack. In a way she did. And why shouldn't she like Jack? Why should Shirley have hooked him if she refused to land him? And before God which stood the higher, Shirley's default or Jack's disappointment? Ah, but you started with the quality of the person, since unless judgment took into account a person's character— Puzzled, confounded, deeply unsure of herself, she turned to the mirror on the wall above the mantel. She disliked mirrors, distrusted them, but where else at this moment could she turn? She expected no magical insight, since the mirror could give her only the exterior she presented it—what did she expect?

The smooth nun's face looked back at her, grave and unlined, the original clay in which neither man nor child had set his thumb. There were no frown lines on the forehead, no semicircular pits under the eyes, no jowls, no lines around the mouth, and no pouch under the chin. No gray showed in the dark-brown hair. The whites of the eyes were clear and unstreaked, the pupils dilated in adjustment to the one lighted lamp in the room. You could read what you liked in the eyes, but it would be what you chose to read and not what was there to read. The face had not functioned as a register of feeling and sensation in fifteen years. Even the nun's smile, she thought, the readiest of her expressions, had other sources besides secular pleasure.

Shirley slept till eleven, her usual Sunday practice, took a shower (she disliked taking baths), and refused Margaret's offer to cook breakfast for her. "I see you cleaned the joint again." "I didn't vacuum the living room because I didn't want to wake you." Shirley sat at the table in the kitchen and lit a cigarette as Margaret poured coffee. "Well, I asked for it," she said. "No, I begged for it. Went down on my hands and knees and whimpered like a dog." She laughed, seeing herself as licking the hand that struck her. "I ought to be grateful he didn't slug me. Well, no more double dates. How do *you* feel?" "A little tired, Shirley." "Maybe I ought to apologize to you, honey." "I can take care of myself, Shirley." "For making you feel what you're feeling now. About me?" "I'm in no position to offer you sympathy, Shirley." "Okay, we'll discuss it later. Anyway, I have to rush or I'll miss the last Mass. Why don't you come along with me?" "I can't, Shirley." "Some other time. I think I'll stay and help Father Serrano with those wildcats of his. Two of them got into an argument the other day. They nearly killed each other. Both of them, six, seven months pregnant. Probably by the same boy. Jealousy, honey. He did it to me more times than he did it to you. No, he didn't. He did. He didn't. That kind of thing. Females. And the worse the man is, the closer they stick to him. Once they get a fix on a guy, that's it. Till death or life imprisonment do them part. And they'll do anything in the world for him, anything. Even after the guy walks out on them and shacks up with another woman. They figure that once they deliver the baby and get themselves back into shape Daddy'll come home for another seven months. And according to the statistics compiled by leather-hearted people like me, Daddy does. See you."

At two Bob called. "I want to apologize for last night, Maggie. Shirley there?"

"No."

"Don't hang up on me, Maggie. I'm over at Jack's. He wanted to call Shirley but couldn't make it to the phone. I've seen some sick men in my time, but this joker can't even keep down aspirin. Look, I'll make it short. There's a couple of things I want to talk over with you. Urgent."

"You needn't, Bob. I'll tell Shirley Jack apologizes."

"Please do, Maggie. Jack'll call later—when he can get his head above his knees—I can't talk on the phone. Unless I'm selling something. Look, I'll pick you up at six and we'll have dinner. Any place you like. *You* tell *me*."

"Thank you, Bob, but I'd rather not." What could she say to him?

"Could I make sense by saying that what I want to talk about isn't personal, Maggie? No pitch, no bill of goods, no hands?"

"Not today, Bob."

"Well, let's see. I've got to be in Bakersfield by ten tomorrow—opening of new department store—then on the third—why not clean this up now, Maggie, while we have the chance?"

She agreed finally, because she could not hang up on him, to meet him in the lobby of the Hotel Yardman at six. Before she left the apartment at quarter of six she checked the wallet in her purse. Three one-dollar bills, seventy cents in change. Would it be dishonest of her to put the ten-dollar bill she had hidden in a box of Tampax into her stocking or bra? How many times had Shirley warned her against going out alone without money tucked away on her person where, presumably, neither mugger nor assaulter could get at it? Yet to go disenchanted, alert, and distrustful to someone who perhaps needed her sympathy and consideration would be to contaminate any possible communication, at whatever level, in advance. She decided not to take the ten-dollar bill.

"Let's not talk about last night," Bob said when he met her, "not till we have some food in us."

He took her to Pietro's, in south Los Angeles, a barnlike building on the outside but inside a nest of small dining areas separated by railings, hedges in green boxes, and lattices hung with artificial grapes. Loud-speakers in the walls pulsed with Italian folk songs, marches, and operatic arias, played principally by strings and accordions. After the harsh clubs of the night before, a change of pace, but to her a pleasant one.

"I wonder if I might have a Martini," Bob said. "Join me?"

"Just a glass of sherry, thank you."

"Usually, I mistrust women who don't wear make-up, Maggie, but you—well, why argue with nature?"

During dinner—spaghetti and meatballs for her, for him veal parmigiana—he said that he sold floor coverings—"anything that goes on a floor—rugs, linoleum, tile"—and that he had been assigned the Los Angeles territory only a few months ago—"after three grim years in Wichita. My wife hates the place. As a matter of fact, she went home to her mother. In Indianapolis. We've agreed on a separation."

"Is this the national panacea for a sick marriage, separation, Bob?"

"By God, now, Maggie, let me hear you talk. Beautiful, beautiful. Jack's case is different, though—national panacea, that's great, great. But Jack's going for a divorce. At present I'm only thinking of it. Otherwise, I wouldn't be here. With lovely you."

He drank two Martinis before dinner and with dinner half a bottle of Burgundy. With the coffee he ordered a brandy and an Upmann cigar. "Nice, huh?"

"Yes, very nice. Thank you."

"Would I be too inquisitive if I asked you where you're from, Maggie?"

"As you can see, Bob. I've led a very sheltered life."

"Teacher?"

"Yes."

"That fits. You know, Maggie, I could probably help you get a teacher's certificate to teach here, if that's what's holding you up. Through my company."

"Shirley can take care of that for me."

"A hell of a nice kid, Maggie. You see, I don't know Jack very well. Met him in the office, he offered to show me the town, I accepted—of course, he's a lot younger than I am. I'm forty-two and look it. Please, please, no comments. You're, I'd say—uh—twenty-seven, eight?"

"Thirty-five."

"Any proof, ma'am? Driver's license, Social Security card?"

"I see no reason to lie about my age, Bob."

"I don't think you'd lie about anything, Maggie. Well, I would. About some things." Bob drew on his cigar and blew the smoke at a bunch of artificial grapes. "Great things, these plastics. You know, Maggie, a man in Jack's position can get himself into a hell of a bind. You're married but you're not married. You go home and half the time the wife's not there. Out spending his money in some dismal tavern. And laying the bartender to settle the bill. Sorry, but that's the unvarnished truth. And then he meets a girl like Shirley. A peach. A dusky peach but a peach. And he's genuinely attracted to her, genuinely attracted—and, in time, even though he's never really been out with her except for coffee or a quick drink—more and more attracted. But he can't marry her, which I think is what he'd like to do, and he can't take her on the office picnic because that's, goddam it, the way it is. Not the way it ought to be—or the way he'd like it to be—but the way it is. Now I'm no psychiatrist, but he hates himself for what he's thinking, see? Does that strike you as far-fetched?"

"No."

"No. You'll never give a man an earache, will you, Maggie?"

"I don't have much of a fund of small talk, Bob."

"Much of a fund. You were married, weren't you?"

"In a sense, yes."

"No further questions. Only I can't see you playing around or guzzling booze or putting the rent on the ponies— I've got it! You can't cook."

"Only simple things, Bob."

"What I'm trying to say is last night was partly my fault, Maggie. We'd been drinking before we met you—I could see Jack was getting a little wild—and I was throwing a few out of bounds myself. But—delicate question—is Shirley colored? I say she isn't."

"Her mother was a full-blooded Mexican, her father a full-blooded Japanese."

"You're hitting me where it hurts, Maggie, and I like it. I wish I knew what went wrong. With Jack. And me. To leave neither guilty party out."

"Masculine disappointment, Bob?"

Bob laughed and reached across the table to pat but not take her hand. "I'm ashamed to admit it, Maggie, but I guess we were slumming. At least I was. A waitress. And if I thought all waitresses were tramps or worse, why was I looking for one? Permit me to crawl under the table to get my bearings."

"I don't think Shirley holds any grudges, Bob. And I know I don't."

"Thank you, Maggie. But I guess last night washes it up with Shirley. For Jack. For any decent relationship between them."

"That's up to Shirley and Jack, isn't it, Bob?"

"I've got to argue the point, Maggie. What Jack said might be forgivable but is it forgettable? To get to the heart of the matter."

"I respect—and like—Shirley too much to speak for her, Bob."

"By God, you're a woman, Maggie. I'd like to have my palm read because I know it'd be good news. Face to face, that's the only way to clear things up. Where shall we go? Movie? Dancing?"

"Just home, Bob."

"Shirley'll be there, won't she? Which is fine, fine. Give me a good chance to talk to her."

"I'm afraid I've misled you, Bob."

"Not a chance, Maggie."

"I agreed to go out with you last night because of Shirley. And only because of Shirley."

Bob smiled, apparently confident of his position. "How did Antony meet Cleopatra, in a cigar box?"

"I have very little interest in men, Bob. And none at all in a sexual relationship."

"May the Lord bless and keep you, Maggie. An honest woman

at last. A treasure. We'll get along. Order some more coffee, will you? I want to make a quick phone call. The evening's not dead yet. Be right back."

In one of the two phone booths near the entrance to the restaurant Bob dialed a number and hummed, on pitch and quite pleasantly, a Jerome Kern tune from *Showboat*. Jack answered the second ring.

"About time," he said. "Well?"

"Nothing here, boy. How about you?"

"That's too bad, Bobbo. That one I could go for myself."

"You certainly screwed yourself up with Miss Twilight, son. And that's quite a dish."

"I have two on the line here. Interested?"

"One question—will they put out?"

"Bob, will the stars shine?"

"Not in Los Angeles they won't. Well?"

"Be here in twenty minutes. Your number is ringing."

When he left the phone booth Bob patted his pockets, looked at the hat-check girl (he had worn neither hat nor coat), pointed to the entrance, and walked slowly out the door. Well-fed, his thirst slaked, the cigar drawing well, he got into his car and drove out of the parking lot, still humming, on pitch and quite pleasantly, the Jerome Kern tune from *Showboat*.

CHAPTER XXII

WHEN EMILIO PARRAGA, ONCE A TECHNICIAN at the county hospital
and now on relief, saw Margaret Westlake in the vestibule of the
apartment house he took a drink of port wine from the bottle in
the paper sack and spat between his feet. When he saw Father
Serrano behind her he got to his feet and leaned against the wall
at the head of the stairs.

"Good evening, Mr. Parraga," Margaret said, halfway up the
stairs.

"Miss Westlake."

"Good evening, Emilio," Father Serrano said.

"Good priests make good jokes," Parraga said. "Bad priests make
babies." He drank from the bottle in the paper sack. "So you
finally got her, Priest."

"Go to bed, Emilio."

"After seven daughters, Priest, getting into bed is like crawling
into my grave." Parraga bowed, not to the sacredness of Father
Serrano's office, but to its strength. Short, thick, heavy, he looked
like a peon in an Orozco mural, the one under the wheel. "Is she
happy, Priest? Is she treated well? Do you give her fresh towels and
soap every day?"

"I haven't seen Inez in two weeks, Emilio. You can always turn
to the police."

"You don't run to the firing squad to have your warts removed,
Priest. Is she well?"

"I haven't seen her, Emilio. Good night."

"In two months my first grandson will be born, Priest. Without
a father and without a name."

"He will have a name, Emilio."

"Serrano?"

"His father's name. Colby. Now go to bed, Emilio."

"It's been well said, Priest—to die isn't such a bad thing, but to be born—" Parraga walked steadily down the hall to one of the two apartments in the rear of the building.

Inside Margaret's and Shirley's apartment Father Serrano said, yes, he would stay long enough to have a cigarette and, if she liked, to talk over the evening.

"I'm glad you called me, Margaret. Thank you."

"It isn't possible to die of shame, is it, Father? Of self-disgust?"

Father Serrano smiled, the masculine response to the female predicament. "Shirley told me about last night, Margaret."

"I owe you ten dollars."

"I think I can collect it from your friend Bob—you haven't given me his last name."

"I didn't get it, Father."

"The name of his firm, then, or business address."

"Would you like some coffee, Father?"

"Yes, please."

As she put the water on to boil she could think, truthfully, that she had not called Father Serrano, she had called Shirley. At the mission. How could she know Shirley would be busy upstairs helping a hastily summoned doctor put a threatened abortion to bed? Dear God, the farther she removed herself from the Church the closer she spun toward its center. She, not Shirley, should be with the threatened abortion. She had mishandled the situation. She needn't have called anyone. But the waiter—that look, that expression, the eyes on her, and then moving indifferently away when she told him she didn't have enough money to pay the check. And in the manager's office—a little child shall lead them? Perhaps. But not in the particular world she lived and worked in. Still, she would learn. But in her own way, in her own style. If she led would she care whether others followed? Damn Father Serrano, damn—was she going to cry?

"Instant coffee," she said as she handed Father Serrano a cup.

"Would you rather I left, Margaret?"

"Am I that easily read, Father?"

"I make observations, Margaret, not judgments."

"Do you? If you take the trouble to look at it fairly you'll see that you don't." She stirred her coffee, feeling the backlash of her resentment. "A genuine hand-crafted remark, isn't it?"

"Are you fond of poetry, Margaret?"

"Not particularly, no. Music, yes."

"Do you know this?

> "Western wind, when wilt thou blow,
> The small rain down can rain?
> Christ, if my love were in my arms
> And I in my bed again!"

"I may have heard it years ago, Father, but I don't recognize it."

"Would you like me to pray with you?"

"I? For what, Father? Not the state of my soul, surely."

Father Serrano laughed. "You've bested me. On a theological question, too."

"Must one always have one's love in one's arms, Father?"

"There are spiritual arms, Margaret."

"Is this from the book of prayer or from the book of experience?"

"When I was ordained I wanted to be a religious priest. Circumstances—in this case the bishop to whom I was assigned—forced me to become a secular priest. In the seminary I learned that to sin is to go against nature, to fail in the good that belongs to any being according to its nature. It was very hard for me, as a pastor, to reduce this beautiful concept of sin to a condition my parishioners would understand. The nature of the warrior is to fight, that of the merchant to buy and sell, that of the baker to bake. Yet I had to say to my parishioners, 'If you tell a little lie you are guilty of a venial sin; if you tell a big one you are guilty of a mortal sin. Failure to attend Mass on Sunday without sufficient reason—or proper dispensation—is a mortal sin. You work Sundays? Very well, we'll switch you to Monday. If I can clear it with the Bishop. But now you know, my children, that to partake of Holy Communion without first celebrating the sacrament of Penance is a most grievous sin?' Now, after two years in this parish, I've found that the only true way to deal with the people I wish to serve—and love, Margaret—is to go back to the concept of sin taught me in the seminary. I insist on confession and Mass because a Church *in* this world must have rules and injunctions *of* this world—that's obvious—but I also insist that unless the Church leavens its purely secular sanctions with a quite hardheaded and reasonable charity it will fail both as a temporal institution and as a bridge to God." Father Serrano stood. "I'll send Shirley home as soon as I get to the mission. Do you know what one of my girls calls it? Doll's House. And she doesn't know her Ibsen either. Good night."

In seeing Father Serrano's point she rejected it. Out of knowledge, stubbornness. She felt she first had to touch bottom, the innermost, deepest rock of herself, admitting that when she did she probably would not recognize she had. She asked the manager of the restaurant to allow her to work part of the morning shift as well as the full evening shift. The next day, when she went to the locker room for coffee, Nickie, a short blonde whose husband worked as a bartender in one of the exotic all-purpose bars on Main Street, said she would like a word with her.

"Listen, kid" (Nickie was twenty-three), "this stuff has got to cease."

"But I'm not asking for overtime, Nickie."

"That's the hell of it. What do you think you're doing to the rest of us? You want to moonlight, go ahead. But not here."

"I'm sorry. I'll work only the one shift."

"Nothing personal, kid. You're not doing your homework, that's the trouble. I don't go out with customers myself, but a couple of gents have been asking me about you. In the future what'll I tell them? Not interested. Okay."

One night, as they walked home from the restaurant, Shirley asked if she'd like to take her own apartment. "That way you wouldn't have me and my lousy habits on your hands."

"Would you like me to move out, Shirley?"

"You pregnant, Maggie? I don't see how, but are you?"

"No."

"Just depressed."

"Badly."

"Well, the first thing you need is a job you can get your teeth into. There's an opening coming up in the office in a month or two—girl's getting married—of course, you have to have a college degree."

"But I don't have one, Shirley."

"I can get around that, honey. I've already talked to the supervisor. Qualified girls are hard to get. You can type, can't you?"

"Of course. But I'd rather stay where I am for the time being."

"A crusade, isn't it? Carry the fight to the heathen. Well, you lose, honey. Listen, if you want to do something intrepid help Father Serrano at the mission."

"I can't, Shirley."

"He's got a primapara with a bad case of hepatitis. She won't tell us how she picked it up. Not that she knows, but she could at least give the doctor a few clues. And the hospital got seven cases of it last month. We may wind up with a goddam epidemic. She hasn't any needle marks on her. You can't get it orally, can you?"

"One type—the milder type—yes."

"Milder. Well, can you give blood? What's your blood type, do you know?"

"O negative."

"Would you be willing to give a pint in an emergency?"

"I wish I could, Shirley."

"Why can't you, honey? Excuse me, no direct questions allowed."

"I've had malaria."

"Malaria. Where in God's name did you pick up malaria? How about amoebic dysentery? Have you had that?"

"Not amoebic, no."

"I'm treading. Army nurse? I know—you got yourself pregnant and the Army threw you out. The reason I'm being so nosy, I overheard some rich Hollywood whore asking Father Serrano about you. This may be a good time for you to move on. I can hide you— if you want me to. You said you had some money in the bank. Draw it out in cash and I'll keep it in the office safe for you. Then if you have to run you can run loaded."

"I'm not in any trouble, Shirley."

"People like you, honey, never are."

The next morning she wrote a letter to Mother Vincent explaining the loss of her bankbook and asking that she send a letter of identification—"I know now what I wish to do with the money, Mother." When she received Mother Vincent's letter instructing her to report to the manager of the bank she also received two letters from her own mother dated three months apart. After sending the money to Bishop Key in the Far East with a request that it be used to help her successors there, she opened and read the letters from home. The first letter reported, in her mother's restrained style, that her father had suffered a stroke, the second that he was recovering but that he would need "an intensive program of therapy." A stroke. How old was he? Sixty-five, sixty-six? Older? Younger? She tore up the letters and flushed them down the toilet. She had never permitted herself to reread her mother's letters. What was the point?

Then one night, walking home alone despite Shirley's warnings, she became aware of two men following her. This did not alarm her. She had often been openly accosted, pinched, propositioned. She felt she could take care of herself. As she turned into her street she looped the strap of her purse twice around her left wrist. They could have the money, if that was their purpose, but she would retain the documents and the keys. The two men, walking quickly, came abreast of her in front of the apartment house.

"We're giving a little party," one of them said. "Would you care to join us?"

"You can be guest of honor," the other said. "We'll furnish the booze."

"Thank you, but not tonight."

"You're a little tired."

"We'll make it a short party."

Parraga appeared to rise out of the earth like a local deity, a grass-god perhaps, protector of lawns and sprinklers.

"Are you in trouble, Miss Westlake?"

"Are you Miss Westlake's boy friend?" the first man asked.

"Her defender, *amigo*." Parraga held a paper sack in one hand, in the other, suddenly, a thing that had a long tongue of metal.

"Watch it, Bill. He's got a knife."

She walked between them to the door of the apartment house.

"Get behind him, Al."

Parraga laughed. "Get smart and get lost, *amigo*. During the big war I was a ranger with Merrill's Marauders."

"Hear him talk, Bill."

"You live here, Spick?"

"Apartment Two D. Pay me a visit soon."

"That I think we'll do, Spick. Come on, Al. He's just drunk enough not to give a shit."

Upstairs she thanked Parraga and invited him into the apartment.

"I don't like you, Miss Westlake. You and the priest. You wish to do good. Are you a Marxist?"

"I have no politics, Mr. Parraga."

"I have enough for two. I'll come in for one drink."

Shirley had told her about him—war hero, his training as a medical technician under the G.I. Bill of Rights, his Mexican wife, who spoke little English, a new daughter every fifteen months, the drinking. "Another washout," Shirley said. "I have a very select list—alcoholic doctors who perform abortions when reasonably sober and they don't have the shakes, alcoholic lawyers who cracked up at City Hall, younger sons the family pays to stay away from them, an old movie director on heroin, goofballs, and whatever else he can steal— Parraga could work but he won't. Two of his seven daughters died—one run over by a car; the other, one of those deaths-in-the-crib things. No strangulation marks, no diagnosable illness, no evidence of smothering, just dead in the morning. He no longer sleeps with his wife. She won't use contraceptives or permit him to, and he won't have another daughter. By the way, he's dangerous but too smart to get himself locked up. Before the war he was a strong-arm man for a very, very corrupt union leader. I wouldn't have too much to do with him if I were you."

228

Parraga sat in a straight chair drinking from the bottle in the paper bag, having refused a glass, deliberately, she thought.

"You wonder why I don't like priests," he said.

"Yes, I do."

"Do you like priests, Miss Westlake?"

"Some, yes."

"With Shirley Quando I know where I stand. She thinks I'm scum and tells me so. You also think I'm scum but you can't say so because if you did you're afraid you'd be accused of prejudice. And above all you don't want to be accused of prejudice, do you?"

"You think I'm patronizing you, Mr. Parraga. But this idea usually occurs only to those who are terrifically conscious of their inferiority."

"An idea worthy of a schoolgirl, Miss Westlake. I have very sound instincts. They tell me you're a coward and a fraud, Miss Westlake."

"You're quite right, Mr. Parraga."

"You see, I wanted to be a doctor, Miss Westlake. I only became a medical technician. A microscope man. Two things stopped me from becoming a doctor—money and my Marxist past. I confessed I was once a member of a Communist cell."

"That's quite a background, Mr. Parraga."

"You should meet my good friend Mr. Summers. He's a renegade priest hiding out from the Church. Father Serrano should also meet him. After he surrenders my pregnant daughter, Inez."

"But he doesn't have her, Mr. Parraga. Nor does he know where she is."

"And your authority for this?"

"Shirley Quando."

"The nice Protestant boy couldn't marry her, Miss Westlake; he could only make her his whore. I see his point."

"Shirley thinks he wants to marry her, Mr. Parraga."

"From Germany? Maybe it could be done by telegram. I myself will stand proxy for him." Parraga laughed. "I admire this generation. My wife and I were very strict with Inez. Very. What time did she have to meet this boy? None. Yet she became pregnant. But where? How? Maybe he mailed her his seed. In a vaginal gun. Insert carefully and press the trigger. Have you been married, Miss Westlake?"

"No."

"But you've had a man."

"Many."

"Naturally."

"But it's true, Mr. Parraga."

"I am not your prosecutor, Miss Westlake. Thank you for inviting me in. Once—a long time ago—I was my wife's lover. Now I am her guest, one who refuses to leave. A dead fish, Miss Westlake, for which she can't find the garbage can. Good night."

As Shirley said, when Margaret told her about Parraga, "Don't get too romantic about him, honey; there's thousands like him down here. But I do wish we could find his daughter."

CHAPTER XXIII

BISHOP HAVEMEYER SAT IN HIS STUDY contemplating without actually reading the two letters on his desk, the one from his good friend Letty Peebles, the other from Michael Cardinal Brooker. Letty Peebles wanted him to help Father Serrano, the Cardinal wanted the priest investigated. The Bishop, who had just been told by his doctor that he was in splendid physical shape—"for a man of sixty"—wondered what the doctor would have said if he could have put his stethoscope to the Bishop's mind and listened to its hyperactivity. The Bishop admired Father Serrano and supported his mission. In the drawer of his desk he had a check for thirty thousand dollars, a gift from Letty Peebles intended for Father

Serrano. Well, five thousand for the Bishop's private charities, twenty-five for Father Serrano's mission.

"Serrano's plunge into welfare work," the Cardinal had written, "may be not only necessary but admirable. However, there are certain legal questions that must be answered promptly and unequivocally if Serrano is to be permitted to continue his charitable activities." The Cardinal was right. For one thing, Father Serrano did not have title (nor did the Church) to the old warehouse he had requisitioned to house his wayward girls, nor did he have permission from the Building Department (ah, City Hall) to improve and reconvert said warehouse. Furthermore, a private and tactful approach to the people who owned the warehouse by a representative of the Cardinal revealed that the price of the building, which could have been bought a few months earlier for a very small sum, had quadrupled. In addition, the Fire Department, though sympathetic and helpful, had suggested, firmly, certain immediate improvements to the building that would cost a goodly sum of money without adding to the building's facilities for taking care of its guests. And the police, good friends of Father Serrano and happy to have the streets cleared of pregnant female prostitutes and tramps, nevertheless had to point out that some aspects of Father Serrano's program could be taken by alert and loving parents fond of good works and litigation as illegal detention of their daughters. And the medical profession, though anxious to contribute their services *pro Deo,* had to state, courteously, that under certain conditions, which hung from every wall, their malpractice insurance could well be voided. And to operate a nursing home (not to say hospital) you had to have a charter from the state and, so far as the Bishop knew, a dozen licenses of various kinds, insurance of other kinds, and certificates from everyone in sight and hearing.

As an adjunct to Father Serrano the Bishop had the Roman playboy and international favorite, Monsignor Thomas Paul Kramer, Brooker's rose-bearer and a coming man, twice sent to the Eternal City (as if once were not enough) and still incardinated to Ottavio Cardinal Bellini. Monsignor Kramer. The Bishop, with an assist from Cardinal Brooker, had just retired an aged monsignor.

What was he to do with a young one who carried the same honorary title and was not under his jurisdiction? He would see. Pressing the button on the intercom, a gift from Letty Peebles, he said to his secretary, "I'll see Monsignor Kramer now, Father." Six thirty on the tall clock by the door of the study, the Bishop noted as Kramer entered. He would not have time for a drink before dinner, a rule urged on him by his doctor, in the Bishop's opinion the only sensible advice the man had given him.

"How is Rome?" the Bishop asked, after seating Kramer in a chair that faced the windows behind his desk.

"Fatiguing, your Excellency."

"Are you traveling on official business for Cardinal Bellini, Monsignor, or simply paying your respects?" Nothing like the blunt end of the stick for these theatrical priests.

"I came to ask your permission to investigate a matter that falls under your jurisdiction, Excellency."

"Mine and not Cardinal Brooker's?"

"I am a political innocent. The matter is personally distasteful to me, but since at the moment I am incardinated to Cardinal Bellini—" Kramer spread his hands.

"And how is his Colossalness, Monsignor?"

"Physically, not very well, Excellency. Spiritually, much disturbed. He shares his Holiness's anxiety in the matter I have been ordered to investigate."

"Those are your credentials, then, a charter from the papal chair."

"I was not granted an audience with the Holy Father, Excellency, only with his Eminence."

"Well, what is this matter?" The Bishop decided against using an adjective, preferring to stress matter alone.

"It concerns a nun who after sixteen years in the convent has left it."

"Left it?"

"Renounced her vows, Excellency."

"Did she? Such matters don't come under my jurisdiction, Monsignor. Was permission to go out granted or did she simply pack up and leave?"

"Permission was granted, Excellency. By Cardinal Brooker." Kramer again used his hands, perhaps to indicate that he was conscious of racking the Bishop's sensibilities but could proceed in no other way. "She belongs—belonged—to the Order of the Sisters of St. Luke, a missionary and nursing order. Sister Esther, the defecting nun, was one of five survivors of a particularly grisly business in the Far East. She is now here in Los Angeles working as a waitress in a bar-restaurant. My orders are to give her any assistance I can without disclosing myself or the Church."

"The ordinary procedure—and the one I would favor—is to have nothing to do with these maladjusted women, Monsignor. Excommunication would seem the only course."

Kramer briefly told the Bishop Sister Esther's story. "To be sure, Excellency, she defected when her companions stayed, but I was told by Cardinal Bellini that his Holiness said—these are his words— 'The Church cannot abandon this poor child.' "

That at least, thought the Bishop, remembering the saintly Pope, could be accepted in its totality. Having also studied and worked in Rome, the Bishop knew some of the Roman cardinals well, others not so well. He knew Bellini, and while he respected the old Cardinal's intelligence, he thought him, in administrative problems, arrogant and heavy-handed. True, a man in Bellini's chair had to be tough. That power corrupts is a convenient cliché for the simple-minded and the weak, who must be given the sugar-tit of their superior's fallibility, but it does not fix the powerful in any pose for fruitful analysis. For apart from power itself are the works of power, which personal corruption often cannot taint or gut, a lesson the Bishop had been taught by Cardinal Brooker, who often used men to support a cause and rarely used a cause to support men. It would be a serious error, however, to suspect Bellini of intriguing against Brooker under a papal directive. And Brooker liked and trusted young Kramer. So for the moment softly, softly—

"I suppose you've checked this matter out with Cardinal Brooker, Monsignor."

"I have, Excellency."

"Then why come to me? Am I to furnish you money, clerical assistance, a staff, a chauffeured car?"

"This nun resides at present in Father Serrano's parish. I believe he helped her and is still helping her—though she isn't a member of his church. Or any church, so far as I know. Naturally, Excellency, since Father Serrano is under your jurisdiction—"

"You could have written me a letter, Monsignor, particularly since you've already seen his Eminence Cardinal Brooker."

"I think that would have been a stupendous mistake, Excellency."

"Yes."

"As for the money, Excellency, that's furnished by the Congregation of Rites. And I don't think I'll need assistance—beyond your good wishes."

"You have them, Monsignor. Also my sympathy. And this door is open, should you feel the need to enter."

"Thank you, Excellency." Kramer stood.

"One question, Monsignor. What is the Congregation of Rites' interest in this affair?"

"It was felt that a thorough investigation of those five—now four —nuns would prevent serious error later. Should there be any question of martyrdom or beatification for the seven who died."

"A very sensible procedure."

After Kramer left, the Bishop restudied the letter from Letty Peebles, conscious of the check for thirty thousand dollars, a gift, he felt now, he ought to send to Cardinal Brooker. The Bishop had converted Letty, as he had converted a number of Hollywood people, and while he thought her sincere in wanting admission to the Church and deserving of being admitted, he also thought her capable of using her new religion to further her purely secular interests. Just as a Jew, for example, uses his Jewishness to protect himself from the often unconscious prejudices of his Christian friends. The son of a Jewish father who had not practiced his religion and of a German Catholic mother, the Bishop had been baptized a Catholic and had attended only Catholic schools and colleges. He had not known his father was a Jew till his third year in seminary. No one had told him. "Your father's dead," his mother said. "What difference does it make?" Nevertheless, he had told his confessor at the seminary, and his confessor, smiling that smile, said, "And you intend using this to your advantage, don't you, Donald?" After which nothing more could be said. Nor could he, as he first thought, leave the seminary, nor, with a truly brilliant mind, finish too high in his class. But that was thirty-five years ago, under the seal of the confessional and his reticence.

That evening the Bishop sent for Father Serrano and, while assuring him of his support, conveyed the Cardinal's objections and suggested that Serrano abandon the warehouse and find other quarters. "Some old house with five or six bedrooms should do, Father. And don't rent or take it on charity, buy outright."

"I don't have the money, your Excellency."

"If you find the proper quarters the money will be made available. Though that church of yours could stand cleaning and painting. Too bad you don't have a wealthy parishioner or two."

"I—" Father Serrano lifted his shoulders, a funny-you-should-say-that gesture.

"Well?"

"I do have a promise of money, Excellency. From a man named Sterling who works for a woman named Letty Peebles. A television producer. I'm not sure—that is, I can't be sure—how much money they intend giving or really if they intend giving any at all. To put it briefly, Excellency, they are people out of my experience. I'm positive they expect, if they do give, something in return. But what this is, considering that I have nothing, baffles me."

"If you can't handle them, Father, send them to me."

"And the warehouse, Excellency?"

"I'm sorry, but you must give it up. How many girls have you there now?"

"Four at the moment."

"There's the Clark Home for Unwed Mothers, Father. I'll call Father Nielson in the morning and insist he take the girls off your hands."

"The Clark is full, Excellency. Overflowing."

"I'll have them put up a tent in the back yard— How can I say this to you, Father? I applaud what you're doing and will back you in anything further you wish to undertake. Within the limits of my power. But in this case, Father, I must obey orders. And so must you. And with no prejudice."

"With no prejudice, Excellency."

Margaret Westlake. What was Bellini afraid of—that someone might exploit her? A nasty scandal, a particularly hairy and brutal scandal. A waitress in a bar-restaurant? Alcoholic and degenerate priests were bad enough, but a whoring nun? And from what medieval archive, the Bishop wondered, did that pleasant idea come? Not, surely, his own shaken-up psyche. His memory, often the assassin of his dreams, offered him Robert Frost's lovely line "But the strong are saying nothing until they see"—for which he thanked both his memory and Mr. Robert Frost—till his memory, that chronic and incomplete assassin, presented him with what the strong were saying nothing about—"There may be little or much beyond the grave." The choice of little or much there certainly did not preclude the lot that was here or the people that had to make do with it.

The invitation to a dinner party at Letty Peebles's hilltop castle permitted the informal approach he had been planning. Sterling's drunken revelations gave him the information he wanted. All priests are familiar with, at the end of an evening, the "What's new in heaven, Padre?" gambit from people who have either had too much to drink or no spittoon lately for their bitter saliva, the cud of the petty man crowded by his inferior superiors or his astrological chart. Sterling, a vodka Martini man, had had too much to drink. He had also had, apparently, too much of Letty Peebles, a feeling common to many in the tight incestuous ball of entertainment. When first told of Letty's project to film the story of Sister Ann, the Bishop, never a leaper, had resisted it. But after several talks with Letty, a visit to her offices and sound stages, and a screening of one of her excellent documentaries, he decided to support the project. "But only," he said to Letty, "if Sister Ann has complete control of the script. And you have a religious technical adviser. I could recommend Father Serrano. He suffered in Africa himself and could use the money for his church."

That evening, sitting with Letty on her patio, the other guests having left, the Bishop asked about Sister Ann.

"Joe's handling it," Letty said. "Not too well—you see, Donald, it's a problem in personal relations. Sister Ann stiffens up like a big board when she sees me—she still thinks I'm an international whore—which I never was—well, maybe for a few days in France—it's unfair, but I understand Sister Ann's viewpoint and give in to it as gracefully as I can." Sterling, drink in hand, approached them, a motion, the Bishop noted, that might be called terrestrial tacking. "Sit down, Giuseppe. We were discussing Sister Ann."

"Forget her," Sterling said. "She's just too goddam ethereal for the likes of you."

"I want that story, Giuseppe."

"Do you, Excellency?"

"If well done it could be a striking and original film. A change from golf-playing priests and happy nuns."

"I could give you a better one."

"I think we'll have to put you on a diet of solids, Giuseppe."

"I was there, Letty, I saw it, I participated. *Our Ladies of Delight or Is Sex a Habit?* Been thinking about it, been writing a book about it. Joe Sterling and his ball-point pen." Apparently, Sterling had been thrown abruptly from a tentative sobriety into a condition of abject drunkenness. He held himself, seemingly by will alone, at an angle at least ten degrees from the vertical. The drink spilled from his glass. "It was a bitch, neighbors. Christ, that I should care. Who the hell am I to care? I ask that dubious question of all and sundry. How doth it rankle? Got a hyena in my guts. Chomp, chomp—squirt."

"What are you talking about, Giuseppe?"

"Whores, Peebles, a subject you should know something about.

237

Christ, there they were sitting against the wall in the schoolhouse like—as if—they had just finished class in catechism. Got that out, didn't I? And in the back of the schoolhouse—Bolton saw them— cribs. I've offended the Bishop."

"Prostitution does offend me, Mr. Sterling, as does any form of buying and selling the human body."

"But these were yours, Excellency, your own, the brides of Christ. And white. Though I'm not a man of many prejudices. And what did the Church do to them? Ask Monsignor Kramer, the young inquisitor."

"Were you in the Army at the time, Mr. Sterling?"

"Captain Sterling. All they did was cost me my company. Bunch of degenerates, but still someone's sons."

"You're making this up, aren't you, Giuseppe?"

"What kind of a perverted mind would make up a story like that, Letty? It happened. And I'm the one who's going to tell about it. Not just rape, fornication. Five of them, servicing the enemy. And none of them cracked. That's what threw the hook in me. Cool as frost about it—got to watch my tongue. Only I can't see it."

"That's an astonishing story, Mr. Sterling."

"But true." Sterling laughed. "Guess I'm drunk. Booze has gone to my head. Made the big trip. Mind if I wobble upstairs and lie down, Letty? Can't keep my goddam eyes open."

"I'll give you a hand, Giuseppe."

"Not right yet, Letty. This Sister Ann bit. That isn't what you're after, is it? Marshall Lipton, my ex-boss in New York, let the cat out of the bag when he said you'd been inquiring about me. Don't think I don't know, Peebles. Well, you can't have it. And anyway, where's your ending? Where's that little item, Peebles?"

"A little investigation ought to dig that up, Giuseppe. I should say a little *further* investigation. By very talented and nosy people. But all hush hush, Giuseppe. Top secret."

"Letty—"

"Top secret, Giuseppe. But I can say this—a certain ex-helicopter-pilot gave me my first clue—does that ring a bell?—and a little eavesdropping—in the right place—gave me my second. This isn't only a revelation, it's a warning. Because, Giuseppe, it isn't your liver I want, it's your balls. Now on your feet."

Astonishing, the Bishop thought as he left his study for his dining room, truly astonishing. But what could he do? Letty, obviously, was a far more complex and interesting person than he had thought. In assessing her he would probably do better to think in terms of reflexes rather than of character. Coil and recoil. And not necessarily in anger, in response, very possibly to the touch she herself had provoked. She wanted something from Father Serrano. Very well, let her pay for it. He would have the warehouse privately assessed and, if the price were too high, condemned. He was sure he could buy it for a reasonable figure. Letty could pay for both the building and its improvements and renovations. The Cardinal, properly approached, would approve. Father Serrano need not move or undertake the job of looking for a new building. In personally supervising these activities he would be in a position to watch Letty and keep an episcopal eye on Monsignor Kramer.

He wondered if Sterling was quite sane. With what he knew of the two, he could say, unfairly of course, that while Letty endangered others, Sterling endangered himself. But in endangering himself—a bag of snakes and a mixed one.

CHAPTER XXIV

FATHER SERRANO, KNEELING IN THE EMPTY CHURCH after returning from carrying the holy oils to a parishioner knifed in a street fight, meditated on Augustine's "There is no possible source of evil except good." Before he could get satisfactorily into this powerful idea his curate, Father Wills, came quietly to the semidark pew and whispered that Inez Parraga was in his study, would he come? Of course. He wondered, as he left the side door of the church and crossed the dark walk to the rectory, where she had been hiding these past few weeks. Who had taken her in? And for what purpose? When you existed on such sickening levels of poverty and joblessness as most of his parishioners you did not think of morality and other such irrelevancies, but of making do. He reminded himself he must be careful of her pride. Though it was nearly nine he had not yet had his dinner. Perhaps he could send Father Wills out for some sandwiches (he did not like to bother his housekeeper at this hour) and so induce Inez to eat with him. She would not, he knew, eat alone.

Seated with her in the study, he avoided looking at the thin tight dress that pointed up her big breasts and protruding belly (was she proud of them?) and looked instead at the black hair and heavy sensual face. Lipstick. How pathetic.

"Have you seen my father?" she asked.

"Yes. He's been asking for you, Inez."

"He'd love to kick me down the stairs, wouldn't he? Well?"

"He's very angry with you, Inez. And angry with himself. You understand how keenly he feels his failure."

"Sure. Anything that concerns himself."

"And your mother?"

"A cow, Father. He won't even sleep with her any more. I used to hear her begging him to make love to her. 'Screw me, please, Emilio, screw me, my darling.' It disgusts me."

Father Serrano smiled. "You're angry with me, Inez." Had he said the wrong thing?

"He's an animal, that's all. And she's worse. At least he does have some intelligence. She's plain stupid. Why should I be angry with you, Father? I'm here."

"Would you walk out on me if I said I'd written to Colby's commanding general in Germany?"

"Write. What good will it do? I'm seven and a half months gone and he's even goner." Inez laughed. "What kills me is I didn't

240

even have any fun. Five times, that's all, and look what I got. And then not even in a proper bed. Like two dogs."

"Colby wants to marry you, Inez."

"How do you think he got into me, Father? I'm not a whore. Well, I wasn't." She rubbed her hands together, the tough gutter attitude abruptly gone. "Excuse my foul mouth, Father. I'm scared." She began to cry softly. "I can't even find a place to sleep, Father. Unless I pay for it. Why are people so horrible?"

"My poor child—" Shocked, Father Serrano offered her a small box of tissues.

"Isn't that something, Father? At first I couldn't believe it. I don't expect charity, but last night I slept behind a billboard, the night before behind some garbage cans in an alley behind a restaurant." She laughed abruptly, switching moods. "The accommodations were lousy but the food was good."

"I know you're proud, Inez, but you must let me help you."

"The warehouse? My father patrols that like he had a beat there."

"Then here—at the rectory. We have room in the basement. I'm sorry I can't offer you the upper floor—"

"The priest and his girl friend. No thanks, Father. I'd rather jump out a window."

"You can't be reconciled to your father, Inez?"

"Oh, sure. Tonight. Right now. All I have to do is let him kick the hell out of me three times a day and I'm in. Only I want the baby, Father."

"Of course, child. Yes."

"And after he's born I don't give him away for adoption, either. I keep him."

The sins of the father for all to see. "I hope by that time you'll be married, Inez."

"What I did, Father, I did for what I thought was love. How can you hold out on someone who needs you? Excuse me, who says he needs you. Cries on your shoulder. Oh, I knew better. This is what kills me. I know all the holds and get sucked in by the oldest."

This shift to the banal neither embarrassed Serrano nor destroyed his belief in Inez's sincerity. How else could she express the gift of her body (no, the phrase held) except in words she thought meaningful to him? She would say in a moment may I have a cigarette, Father, and after he gave her one, from the pack he kept in his desk, she would smoke it in great swooping drafts, really, kids, on top, you know, of the blast. But under the pose were the realities of the billboard and the garbage cans, and under these the ache for the arms of her father. Fathers exist to console their daughters for the loss of themselves in the disguise of their daughters' lovers, and for little else, once the seed has been planted. How many walls, streets, bedrooms, kitchens, doctors' offices, cribs, fields, and other glamorous enclosures had he sat in to find this important truth?

"It is possible that Colby's commanding general will give him an emergency furlough, Inez. At least let's ask."

"Sure."

"We'll try, Inez. Now let me call Shirley—she always has a few rooms available—"

Sex. In all forms. Male and female, female and female, male and male. He couldn't escape it. Surely, the Creator, having endowed men with this miraculous charter for procreation, could do more than punish man for violations of that charter. Uplift him? Through His Church? That was the dream, yes, but what was the reality? Inez Parraga. The mangled body of the girl in the abortionist's office. The fetus wrapped in yesterday's newspaper and placed between the chicken bones and the fish. Fat priests in silk clericals, renegade bishops moving priests about like commanding generals their troops, perfunctory Masses perfunctorily performed for an audience of pious and ignorant women, money extorted from the poor through devices a professional fund-raiser would be sent to prison for—every time he saw a candle lit he prayed God for forgiveness. Not the indigent confessing the sins of their indigence, but he, the pastor, the working shepherd in the field, who slaughtered the missing lamb for his supper, who if he cried wolf honestly would be hanged by his indignant neighbors.

He exaggerated. Had it been any better in Africa? No, because there, no matter how hard he tried to reach the people he wanted to help, he always remained the observer. He had not been pulled in, engaged in earnest. The sacrifices he made were as distant and as formal as those of the errant Jews who had laid the ram on the altar and cut its throat for the appeasement of a wrathful and jealous Yahweh. But here—and he had his warehouse and the promise of living, as well as material assistance. And a sympathetic and working bishop. He diagnosed his trouble dispassionately—he was a lean priest in the process of becoming a fat one. He thought of Margaret Westlake. She would make a splendid assistant, would she not? He could pay her, and after the alterations were finished he could offer living quarters in the building rent-free, as well as kitchen privileges.

But before he could think of a proper way to approach her a Monsignor Kramer came to see him at the rectory, introducing himself as an observer from Rome. "Nothing important, Father. I am interested in one of your parishioners, a Margaret Westlake."

"She's in my parish, Monsignor, but not one of my parishioners."

"She should be, Father. She's a nun who renounced her vows."

In reply to this revelation, so abrupt, so casual, in such bad taste really, Father Serrano could say only, "Are you serious, Monsignor?"

Kramer lit a cigarette and paced the study, a man in tension. "I won't go into the whole sordid business, Father, but I can say this—I wish to help her. But how?"

"Does she want your help, Monsignor?"

"She's standing still, destroying herself, working in a job that's little better than prostitution. I propose to jolt her out of this—spiritual despair."

"A waitress's job is menial, Monsignor, but not necessarily degrading."

"I'm a political innocent, Father; are you a worldly one?"

"I know this parish better than you do, Monsignor."

"Do you? Have you lived as a working man among working

people? I did. For a month. In a cheap hotel. I toured all the bars and other places of entertainment—saw the sights, was solicited by both sexes, robbed of money, accosted by drunks, run in by the police—Father, I'm sure there are worse places than downtown Los Angeles—for example, Hollywood—but I hope to be spared sight and smell of them. There are public places here where you can't use the men's room without being—what's the word—grabbed? groped? Marijuana is passed openly from hand to hand, as are barbiturates and amphetamines. Heroin is used consistently. Sex—well, as you say, it's your parish."

"I believe Times Square and Harlem also offer much the same thrills, Monsignor. As do certain sections of New Orleans, Philadelphia, San Francisco, Chicago, and, I suppose, Bangor, Maine."

"I apologize for my naïveté. But the point is that Sister Esther —Margaret Westlake—chooses to work and live here, indistinguishable from her pink and scarlet sisters."

Kramer did not mention that Cardinal Brooker had available several interesting and important jobs, say, vicar-general or private secretary, that might, if he were freed of Cardinal Bellini's orders, be offered him. How many years of his priesthood was he to devote to spying on a defecting nun, one who had coolly and deliberately chosen to leave the spiritual life for a worldly—existence? Cardinal Bellini's answers to his reports dealt in ambiguities and snippets of old men's wisdom and bodily ills. Obedience. Not the reflexive obedience of the animal but the checking and subordination of man's highest and most angelic faculties. He had decided to act. Destruction, of any party, was better than stagnation.

"What are you asking me to do, Monsignor?"

"Think, man. You know the woman. And please not the my-dear-child approach. She needs blasting."

"Really, Monsignor—"

"Is she any better than the semicriminals she cohabits with? And this roommate of hers. Is she proper company?"

"There you're dead wrong. Shirley's a fine girl, a splendid girl. She has her faults, but she is neither immoral nor criminally inclined. No, Monsignor. This is her milieu, her climate, and she exists in it in dignity and ease. If you're to argue that she's not a virgin—well, that, Monsignor, is a part of the milieu. Only priests and the newly born are virgins here, and I speak with confidence only of the latter."

"You're certain that you don't need a change, Father?"

Serrano laughed. "I'm needed here, Monsignor. I can exist without love but I cannot exist without being needed. Have you thought of leaving her to God?"

"We do not know God's time, Father, we know only ours. And then only imperfectly. If you will, darkly. Will you help me?"

"I should like to know a little bit more about the case."

"Of course."

It had not been difficult to trace Sister Esther, particularly since she had delayed taking the money for her dowry from the bank. The difficult thing had been the decision to enter the milieu, to follow her on foot and not in comfort from the air, to be pushed and kicked by those who pushed and kicked her rather than observe and record these actions, to live as she lived. To withhold himself from a simple and reasonable action that might enable him to test the dark forces engaging her, provided he denied in advance any intention of commitment on a level of irrevocable actuality, would have been an act of a most appalling timidity. He must not only follow her, he must know her, as she was. Besides, how would Cardinal Bellini receive a report in which he could read that Kramer had not even bothered to dirty his hands?

He bought a cheap suit, jacket, a pair of slacks, a pair of shoes, two shirts, four pairs of socks, three pairs of shorts, a tie. He took his own razor, a Gillette he had bought at the seminary, a broken comb, two toothbrushes. At Woolworth's he paid seventy-nine cents for a plastic wallet. He rented a room without bath in a cheap hotel on Spring Street, paying a week's rent in advance. He ate in hole-in-the-wall diners, at lunch counters, at chili bars, soup kitchens. He suffered mild attacks of gastroenteritis, twenty-four-hour sieges of the trots, athlete's foot, and various prolonged itches. He kept a bottle of port in his room, replacing it as he emptied it or

245

had it stolen, usually gargling the stuff before spitting it out in the sink. He had a sink and a permanent towel. He took few baths. He made sure his fingernails were dirty and that his shirts stayed soiled. He used a soft pencil to darken and deepen the lines of his face, smudging the clean strokes with his finger. He forswore deodorants, brushed his teeth only before going to bed, slept in his shorts, decided against spraying his room, used olive oil on his hair, shaved twice a week.

As he had hoped, this demeaning program did just that, demeaned and depressed him. Twice, his wallet was stolen. Men offered him money not to perform on them but to permit them, preferably abjectly, to perform on him. That he should be a target for homosexuals shocked and humbled him. His height and obvious masculinity (though not his undeniably splendid head) excited and provoked them into approaches they clearly both feared to make and enjoyed retreating from, particularly if, as on occasion, his polite aversion escalated to anger.

He worked as a dishwasher, a busboy, a janitor, a counterman, a distributor of pamphlets. He visited skid row and saw what lay inside its shadows, the half-men whose damaged brains produced the visions of nirvana. Passing a street brawl, he was picked up and jailed for being drunk and disorderly. In night court, after seven hours in the drunk tank and fifteen in what looked like a men's dormitory with barred windows and steel grates and doors, he stood before a woman judge and heard himself asked how he pled to the charges, guilty or not guilty. "Guilty," he said, unaware that he had pitched his voice to carry to all corners of that great acoustic horror, a public courtroom. The judge, a horror herself, stared at him. She took no guff.

"Is this your first offense, Kramer?"

"It is, your Honor."

"A fine-looking young man like you picked up on a drunk and disorderly. What have you to say for yourself, Kramer?"

"Only that I'm guilty, your Honor."

"Twenty-five dollars or a day in jail."

The judge swiveled in her chair and showed him a profile cut from yellow feverwood.

"I'm usually lenient with first offenders, Kramer. And since you've already spent a day in jail I'll accept that as time served. Now git. But—do you hear me, Kramer?"

"I do, your Honor."

"But if I ever see that pretty face of yours in this courtroom again—" she swiveled abruptly front—"I'll put a special delivery stamp on it and mail it to the county jail."

Laughter. And loudest from the old faithfuls who came to the courtroom like Rebecca to the well. Sitting in the back of the room after his release, he watched them being led in, stood against the wall, and brought out for sentencing, not one who failed to carry in his own peculiar image the downturned face of God. Watching them, he could dismiss the misfortunes of his coal-town boyhood and adolescence as irrelevancies, bitter and bracing, but off-center. "In the great hand of God I stand"—the doctrine of freedom of the will, of choice, the brilliant arguments of the "great ox," shot up in his mind, burst into constellation, and burned out. You cannot pity what a man brings on himself, but you can stop yourself from taking public satisfaction in the demonstrable validity of the law of cause and effect. Love will break the chain, charity will recast it.

He smelled the urine, vomit, blood, saliva, tobacco, and alcohol on himself, the common odors of the drunk tank, and remembered that of the beds the man Jesus had slept in this was not the strangest. He mocked the Man Who had chosen with a whim but pleaded that he gained an insight and not a kingdom. In the drunk tank, with a floating population of thirty men and capacity for perhaps twenty, you could neither sit down nor lie down—except on the floor and the stopped-up toilet. And the floor was coated with a shifting film of semiliquid which could not be wholly water nor wholly excrescences from the discharging (not to say suppurating) human bodies grouping and regrouping on the white tile. Odd, the purity of the tile beneath its romantic coating. A man shifting position on the floor wiped the floor clean, as if the reflexive shudders of his agony expiated his fault. Not then the conscious pleading in the confessional, but the unerring postures of suffering.

"Supposing we do take action," Serrano said, after hearing Kramer's story. "What possible good could come from it?"

"What possible good could come from waiting, Father?"

"You're pressing this from a personal viewpoint, Monsignor. I distrust it."

"What viewpoint did Saul press his prosecution of the Christians from, Father? And from what viewpoint did Paul press the 'good news'? You notice that I don't mention the great inquisitors of history, because I don't think of myself as an inquisitor. I come as a friend, not a torturer."

"In disguise, then, Monsignor?"

Kramer turned abruptly and left the room, realizing that in the recognition of his target he had overshot it.

CHAPTER XXV

A FEW DAYS LATER Shirley told Father Serrano that Maggie had moved to a place of her own, a one-room apartment with kitchenette and bath near the Hotel Yardman. "I guess I got too nosy, Father. I never could mind my own business. Did you know she'd had malaria?"

"She's still working at the Yardman, though, isn't she?"

"So far as I know, Father." Shirley gave him Margaret's new address. "Phone in the hall. Maybe she's hiding out from her husband. She's had a child." Shirley sounded less resentful than baffled. "I'm getting to be an awful Paula Pry, Father. Can't you find me a husband?"

"You haven't been to confession recently, Shirley. Are you doing what you shouldn't?"

"This salesman who gave us a bad time—I told you about him, Father. Well, he kept calling, calling, calling—"

"Does he plan to marry you?"

"He thinks we ought to live together before we do anything serious, Father. Oh, we'll be engaged. I'm half inclined to take him up on it. Though I know it's wrong."

"Are you asking me in advance to condone this business, Shirley?"

"I've always been honest with you, Father. Now that Maggie's gone I can't stand to be alone in the place. I'm going to end up being one of my clients. Dear Miss Quando, please send me a check for a hundred dollars because if I don't get it he will leave me and then I'll have to go back to my husband who beats me and also four lousy children by his first wife and our ex-landlady. P.S., I'm a *good* Catholic. That's so I'll know she's not a good *Protestant.*"

What could he do? Busy supervising the alterations at the warehouse, visiting the hospital, the jail, and the courtroom, calling on his parishioners, sustaining the spirit with Masses and religious festivals, baptizing (and sometimes marrying), Father Serrano had little time for private counseling, particularly for one who did not, really, need it.

As part of his pastoral duties, he had to be nice to Letty Peebles, who paid the bills for the warehouse, and to her familiar, Joe Sterling. He did not understand Letty Peebles; he had stopped trying to. Let Bishop Havemeyer, her sponsor, have her. Sometimes, looking at her, he had the sensation of looking through her, past skin, past organ, bone, and back and into a void, a hole in the otherwise boisterous and biting air. Not that she was strange, he reminded himself, an exotic or a mutation, but that he had not invented (and possibly never would invent) a language or a set of signs with which to establish and maintain accurate communication. He blamed himself for his provincialism and backwater limitations.

But she did press him. And when she insisted on taking him to dinner after a long day of carpenters and plumbers at the warehouse and an evening with its tenants, he consented. "Let's try the Yardman," Letty said. "Giuseppe'll need his liquid rations—no point in traveling too far—"

Letty chose a table near the sidewalk windows, suggesting to the waitress that since the dining room closed at ten they ought to start drinking doubles. "Vodka tonic for me, vodka Martini for the help, and you, Father?"

"A glass of sherry, Margaret. How do you like your new place?"

"Good enough, Father. Would you order now, please?"

"Steak," Letty said. "Just a salad for me, fried potatoes and salad for the others. No dessert." She watched Margaret Westlake cross the dining room and enter the bar. "Striking girl, Father. Not one of yours, is she?"

"No."

"She doesn't look like the usual tramp. Did you notice her, Giuseppe?"

"Notice what? Haven't those girls of yours parents, Father?"

"Yes, Mr. Sterling. A mother who holds down two jobs and a faceless male who stays long enough to impregnate her and then moves on to perform a similar function elsewhere."

"You're talking about the underprivileged, Father."

"I'm talking about the defacing and brutalizing of God's image, Mr. Sterling, nothing else." To avoid talking shop Father Serrano asked about Letty's picture.

"That's been off for weeks, Father. Haven't you heard?"

"Well done it would have made a very interesting picture, Letty."

"Giuseppe gave me a better one, Father. It's about five heroic nuns in the Far East and a company of American soldiers. It seems that Giuseppe here commanded the company."

"Captain Sterling?"

"Letty's always dropping these little bombs, Father. Sometimes they go off, sometimes they don't."

"Can you imagine Giuseppe commanding anything that isn't drinkable, Father? Well, he did."

Simply to get along with Letty, to work efficiently with her, Father Serrano, like others, had had to learn how to cope with the unexpected, the bizarre, the fantastic. And he had learned, principally by making Letty a creature who lived with (and could not live without) the unexpected, the bizarre, the fantastic. She could disturb, yes, but not shock—irritate but not benumb—annoy but not flabbergast—how little he knew her. And to compound his unease, how little he knew Joe Sterling, whom he had dismissed as Letty's familiar. Or no, not dismissed, accepted. An even more shocking act of contempt. He became aware of Margaret setting the drinks on the table and heard Letty say, mistress of the house to servant, "We'll have one more round before we eat, Margaret."

"We close at ten, ma'am."

"We'll finish in good time, Margaret."

"I'll have a bottle of champagne," Sterling said to Letty. "With dinner."

"Make that Burgundy, Margaret. No one has champagne with steak, Giuseppe."

"Burgundy."

"Champagne, then. Only nothing too vintage. Just what's in stock."

Father Serrano sipped his sherry, having decided to wait out Letty. Besides, much as he might not like it, Margaret Westlake was Monsignor Kramer's business, not his. The dining room emptied quietly as they ate dinner, the waitresses changed the tablecloths at their stations and left, the jukebox in the bar sang its songs of loneliness and despair in a variety of voices and accents, the manager of the restaurant appeared to salute them and urge them not to hurry, the doors to the kitchen stayed closed, the lights in the booths were turned off, the sign outside the restaurant was blacked out, Margaret fastened a thick red quasi-velvet rope across the arch between dining room and bar, she presented the bill.

251

"Pay it, Giuseppe."

Sterling put three ten-dollar bills and a five on the brass salver without looking at the check and muttered, "Keep it." He had not once glanced at Margaret (so far as Father Serrano could observe), nor had he anticipated being either served by her or relieved of his glass or plate. Pouring the last of the champagne into his wineglass, he appeared to be functioning without the active use of the higher centers of consciousness. Alcohol, the first draft at noon, the last at midnight. Had Margaret recognized him? The light was not good, but sufficient, Father Serrano thought, for identification. Still, if Margaret *had* recognized Sterling, what, really, should he have expected her to do? Nothing at all.

And Letty. After arranging the scene and bringing her people together, there she sat, with cigarette and coffee, neither excessively expectant nor particularly alert. What had she intended? And why had she wanted him, Father Serrano, present? As a catalyst? An observer? An umpire? When he heard Parraga, who had come in from the bar, say, "You, Priest, where is Inez?" Father Serrano rubbed his forehead with the hand he had raised to cross himself and stood to face the man. This, surely, could not be laid to Letty.

"Your daughter is well taken care of, Emilio. If you wish to see her—"

"You send her home to me, Priest."

"I've heard from Colby's commanding general, Emilio. He is sympathetic to an emergency furlough."

"From Germany?"

"A three-day pass would do."

"Since there's no necessity for a honeymoon, Priest, yes." Parraga took a switchblade from his pocket and released the spring. "Where is she, Priest?"

"He's got a knife," Letty said, as if reporting a spectacle not visible to the others.

"Let me walk you home, Mr. Parraga," Margaret said.

"And afterward, Miss Westlake?"

"Westlake?" Sterling, perhaps alerted by the steel blade, the

252

familiar metal of the peninsula, stared at Margaret Westlake but could not associate, seemingly, the waitress in the violet-colored uniform with the image evoked by the blade.

"Will you marry Inez, Priest? Under your fine bed? Her dowry is in her belly."

Parraga, Father Serrano thought, though clearly drunk, was not indulging himself. He had a mission, possibly in his mind a sacred one. "I'll do what I can for Inez, Emilio. We must wait till we hear from Colby's commanding officer."

"But you promise no miracles, Priest. Your religion is full of miracles. Dead miracles and dead fish. We'll see how the can opener works. Maybe you, too, are full of dead miracles and dead fish."

As Parraga moved toward Father Serrano, Margaret, with a quick one-handed motion, spun a chair at his feet. Stumbling and falling over the chair, Parraga dropped the knife, which Margaret delicately possessed, not in true ownership, but as if checking a valuable article for a customer vulnerable to loss or theft.

"Move away from him," Sterling said. He stood with one hand on the back of his chair, in command of the field. "I can handle this maniac."

"He intends no violence, Captain. Please don't touch him."

"He's a mad dog, Sister. You don't coddle mad—" Christ, that bloody, snake-infested, Pat-crawling peninsula— Ahearn?

"Shall we shoot him, Captain?"

"You don't coddle—" Ahearn? No, just a drunken Mexican who now stood holding his left wrist—not death, but a sprain. Not a lethal giant in fatigues down whose body slid a dying Goldman, but a shiny toad—in pain.

"He means no harm, Captain. His daughter has stolen his pride, and he believes he can recover it only by taking ours." Margaret (Sterling remembered those hands) retracted the blade of the knife and put the knife in her pocket. "I'll return this to you tomorrow, Mr. Parraga."

"Yes," Parraga said. "When I'm sober."

"May God forgive me." She took the knife from the pocket,

253

sprang the blade, and offered the knife, handle first, to Parraga. "Your property, Mr. Parraga."

Parraga, in possession of the knife, put the point of it to Margaret's throat. "Fear, Señora. You feel it?"

"Of course."

"A lie. You feel no fear, Señora. Something else, yes, but not fear." Parraga turned quickly and offered the knife to Sterling, who had moved, thus in a real sense disarming him. "This is not the weapon for Señora Westlake. No." He took a crucifix on a chain from his pocket, his left arm held across his body like a broken wing, and turning back to Margaret, thrust the cross toward her lips. "Do you know this sign, Señora? Will you kiss God's wounds?"

"I don't believe in the power of your symbols, Mr. Parraga, but I respect your veneration of them."

"A symbol. Yes, you're right. A dead man on a stick. So—" He dropped the crucifix on the floor between them. "If you won't kiss your dead God wipe your feet on Him."

As she knelt to pick up the crucifix, Parraga turned and walked into the bar, stepping quite steadily over the red rope.

"Ugly thing, isn't it?" Letty asked. She dropped the knife she had taken from Sterling onto the table, where it looked like a piece of cutlery instead of an unsheathed weapon. "These Latins. So melodramatic and undependable, Father. He tries to kill you because you won't give him his daughter and then switches his attention to Sister—excuse me, Miss Westlake."

Father Serrano, lifting Margaret, said, "I'm going after Parraga, Letty. Would you come with me?"

"I can't leave Giuseppe, Father. He needs me—Mother Peebles—" She shivered slightly, then laughed, deferring to the slender priest, but only this time and only because it pleased her, really, to indulge this abruptly petulant and demanding innocent. "All right, Father. Tomorrow at nine, Giuseppe."

She led the way, of course, permitting Father Serrano to unclasp the rope for her exit. Sterling sat at the table playing with the knife, poking the blade into the tablecloth and lifting the cloth to let it fall in wrinkles on the table top, so that after a time it resembled a topographical map with light chains of hills and darker shadows. Raising the knife by the handle, squeezing it between thumb and forefinger, Sterling let it drop to the table. The point of the blade pierced the cloth but did not bite deeply enough in the table top to hold the body of steel and hilt upright.

"If at first you don't succeed," Sterling said, "give up."

"Did you give up, Captain?"

"That was a situation I could do something about, Sister. The last such situation, obviously." Sterling realigned the knife with a forefinger so that the blade pointed toward the arch leading to the bar. "You remember Bolton, Sister? The enlisted man who killed Goldman."

"Enlisted man."

"I'm not the snot I was, Sister, but I'm not everyone's paradise pill either. Bolton's dead. Grenade got him." Sterling sang, "John Bolton's body lies a-moldering in the grave, John Bolton's body lies a— Well, before John Bolton became a body he said to me— this is what the legal profession calls a dying declaration— 'She touched me, Captain. They can't kill me, I'm already dead.' Despite which definitive statement, he died. On the sleeve of my fatigue jacket, 'She touched me.' You also touched Sam Goldman, didn't you?"

"The gentlest person I've known."

"For me the toughest. So we don't have quite the same memories of that long bloody corrupt retreat south, do we?"

"Dear Sam."

"Were you in love with him, Sister?"

"I loved him, yes, but I was not *in* love with him."

"Nothing carnal."

"Where does love stop and carnality begin, Captain?"

"Would that I knew, Sister, would that I knew." Sterling looked directly at her for the first time that evening. "So they busted you out of the service. Was that pretty-boy Kramer's doing?"

"I went out of my own free will, Captain."

"After they told you you'd have to cut yourself in half to stay.

What did the Church give you, ten dollars and a secondhand suit? To go with the short haircut."

"Are you correlating my misfortunes with yours, Captain? To make yours bigger, of course." She stood erect, holding the crucifix. "If so, you must accept my word that the Church, far from booting me out of the Order, did everything she could to keep me in it."

"Why?"

"Because, Captain, the Church, whatever the deficiencies of her servants, did not fail me; I failed the Church."

"A real she-wolf, aren't you, Sister? 'She touched me.' That was your gift, Sister, not to heal or to serve, but to touch."

"I didn't think so then, Captain, I'm not sure I think so now." She held out her hands. "This is what I brought to the Church, Captain, a pair of hands. This is the gift I laid on God's altar. And this is the gift God found unacceptable."

"You're chanting, Sister. You're not explaining what happened to you, you're making a service out of it." He stood and grabbed her arms. "Face up to it, Sister. You bitched it. Like me. And the others—Sister Agnes, Sister Mary, Sister Roberta. Did they bitch it, too?"

"No. Sister Agnes teaches, Sister Mary nurses, Sister Roberta—no, they—" The hands formed a basin, as if to catch and hold a rain of fire.

"And in contrast we have you, a registered nurse, delivering a septic kitchen of blue hamburgers and hot chili." Shamed by her passivity—or enraged by it—Sterling put both hands on the bodice of the uniform and jerked it open. "And giving the male customers a peek at something that isn't on the menu, but can be obtained— at popular prices—in the alley yonder." Shaking, as if chilled, he turned away from her.

"You're not easily appeased, Captain. Fully clothed, I irritate you. Half-naked—" she looked down at her exposed right breast with its half-dollar-size nipple—"I frighten you. Where is your middle ground?"

"Come away with me."

"I must lock up."

256

"I'll get a taxi. We can go to my place."

"Your friend must be expecting you, Captain."

"Letty Peebles isn't expecting anyone, Sister; she's giving God His instructions for tomorrow." Turning, seeing her breast, he took off his jacket and put it around her shoulders. "We'll go to a hotel. Or your place. We'll get a bottle of Scotch. Two bottles. Where's your coat?"

So be it. "In back."

She took him to her room and sat with him while he talked and drank steadily from one of two bottles of Scotch he had insisted on buying. He spoke to her of Letty Peebles. "I could tell you some stories about that spider that would boil your blood, Sister. Really dry up your sinuses. But don't laugh her off; she's got more workable brains than the faculty of U.C.L.A. and no moral inhibitions to slow them down." He laughed, refusing to share what he knew about Letty, at the same time unwilling to have her believe he had nothing to share. "She's scared, though. Sometimes, late at night, I can hear her motor running. Clear across the city. Like a big diesel."

He stared at her, as if he suspected this did not interest her. "You and I, Sister, we bitched it. Why? Goldman didn't. It wasn't in his nature to bitch anything. That doesn't make him any better or stronger than we are; it makes him different." Sterling sat and lit a cigarette. "We shouldn't have stopped at that monastery. We should have gone on. When you stop you make a target out of yourself, you attract aggression. The roving people, the nomads, the raiders, get very irritated at squatters. I understand that, Sister. There's a special kind of arrogance about people who want to occupy the earth instead of living off it. I've been thinking about Lewis lately. You remember Lewis? The mountaineer?"

"Not very well."

"That's an outright lie, Sister. I haven't been thinking about him. Or no, no, I have. A little. That goddamned peninsula." He stared at the pin holding together the torn bodice of her uniform. "Why do you go around like that, Sister? Don't you wear a slip?"

"Too hot, Captain. Besides, it's not done."

257

"You disgust me. Take that rag off and put on a proper dress. Or no, don't. I'm sorry. I'll buy you a new uniform. What do they cost?"

"You needn't, Captain. We don't own the uniforms. They belong to the laundry."

"The laundry? What laundry?" Sterling had taken his wallet from his pocket and now sat looking at it, puzzled by an autonomous gesture of the body to which, suddenly, he had no mental link. "You find me any different, Sister?"

"A little older."

"Well, I'm no enigma, but you are. You're not married, are you? No, of course not. Well, do you have a man? Any man?"

"No, Captain, I don't."

"Do you want one?"

"No."

"If Goldman were here now would you go to bed with him?"

"I don't think he'd want to."

"Would you? If he wanted to."

"Why don't you stay here tonight, Captain? A friend of mine will put me up."

"I've got a home, Sister. I've always been able to find it—on the darkest night. You think I'm too drunk to drive?"

"Aren't you?"

"I'm never too drunk to drive. I just get too drunk to live."

"Why don't you cry, Captain? I have towels."

Sterling laughed. "One thing I learned on the peninsula, Sister, and learned fast—either you'll get it or you won't. From their side or from yours. In back or in front. Above or below. We're inspecting this village one day and I pass this poor pathetic beat-up kid, all sores, flies, and wounds. As I pass him I pat him on the head. The famous American love for children. I take three steps and something—out there you develop instincts you never knew you had—jerks me around. This kid is pulling the pin from a grenade. I shot him and yelled at Goldman, who was off to my left, to hit the ground. We had one killed, three wounded. The slower ones. No,

258

Goldman was no better than that kid or any of the other kids or women I had to kill. Or killed accidentally or ordered killed. Sure, I'm going to cry in my cups, but not because of something I know as well as that. It's what I don't know, the thing out there in the darkness at the end of the stick I'm holding, that scuttles me."

Sterling poured and drank more Scotch, leaning in the chair at all angles to himself. He spoke clearly and easily but his muscles appeared to have stiffened. Now and then he shuddered slightly as if cold or spastic. "Little sleepy, I guess. Suddenly, no more to say. Bottom of the well." He yawned, gasping for breath.

"Would you like to use the bathroom, Captain?"

"What for?"

She pulled the bed down from the wall, releasing the clamps holding the mattress to the springs, folded the bedspread, and pulled back the blanket and top sheet. Sterling was unexpectedly heavy. Or, not heavy, muscled. But then, she was not accustomed to handling such patients. Having stripped him to his shorts she put the sheet over him and took one pillow and the blanket for herself. As she settled on the couch, Sterling sat up and put his feet on the floor. "Bathroom," he said. "Lost the goddam bathroom. Sixty square feet of tile and fixtures and I lose it. Shit." He found it finally on his hands and knees, used the toilet noisily, and crawled back to bed. He began to sing "Waltzing Matilda," got as far as the third Matilda, and broke off, snoring.

He slept badly, twice waking her by screaming obscenities in his sleep. He would grip the thin metal slats behind the pillow, tense his muscles, and scream. She could not wake him. At six thirty she dressed and phoned the restaurant to say that she would not be able to work that day. She made coffee in the kitchenette, an alcove containing a two-burner gas range over a small electric icebox, and a cupboard for dishes and silverware. At seven thirty, drinking a second cup of coffee, she saw that his eyes were open. Crossing to the head of the bed so that she looked directly down into his face she asked him how he felt.

"Like hell, Sister."

"So you remember."

"Some, some."

"There's a razor in the bathroom cabinet but no shaving cream."

"Thanks."

"Would you like an egg?"

"Coffee."

While he showered and shaved, she made the bed and pushed it up into the wall, and set up a card table in front of the couch. The perils of domesticity: card tables and folding chairs, split china and nonpolishable spoons, paper napkins and place mats, dented saucepans and a paper-thin skillet, no toaster, but a fine glass orange-squeezer and one semiblue egg cup. She made breakfast for herself, one three-minute boiled egg, one piece of bread browned in the skillet, the juice of one fresh orange, a thin slice of margarine (she could not bring herself to buy butter), black coffee. As an afterthought, the nurse-nun forbidding her to make more judgments when tending her patients, she placed the half-empty bottle of Scotch beside Sterling's cup.

"A little stick?" he asked, when he appeared.

"Shall I pour it for you?"

"Please."

She put approximately an ounce and a half of Scotch in his cup and poured coffee over it. After he finished that she poured him another and lit two cigarettes, bypassing the shaking hand to put one cigarette between his lips. Using the paper napkin, he wiped the sweat from his face and arms. Neither the napkin nor her mouthwash did anything for the heavy smell of whiskey that hung around him like an atmosphere.

"What would you like to do, Captain?"

"I take it you slept on the couch?"

"Yes."

"I didn't—?"

"Make a pass at me, Captain?"

"You know the lingo. Only I wasn't thinking of pass."

260

"Nothing like that happened. In the first place, you were in no condition for such demanding exercises, and in the second place, I wouldn't have permitted it."

"When I woke up I was positive something like that had happened. And I was powerfully ashamed of it. I don't look too red-eyed, do I?"

"No, but you smell."

"Like what? Give me a hint. Like a bottle?"

"Nothing so fresh."

"Like what, then, Sister? Science demands."

"Like a soiled diaper."

Sterling nodded. "That's about right, I guess. Do you drink?"

"A little."

"Do you date?"

"Occasionally, yes. Captain—"

"I hear you, I hear you. Morbid curiosity. Let's get out of here. Joints like this depress me. I always hear rats in the walls. I don't suppose you own a pair of shorts or a bathing suit, do you?"

"No."

"I'm thinking of the sun."

He drove her to the place in Laurel Canyon, and, after changing his clothes and using a half-bottle of mouthwash, left her, saying that he would be back at two. "We'll have a goddam picnic—what's your civilian name, Sister?"

"Margaret."

"And what did your parents call you?"

"Middy."

"All right, Middy, two o'clock." He showed her a bedroom and bath off the kitchen. "Maid's room. I know you wouldn't want anything grander."

After inspecting the house and the patio (the wooden bridge across the dry brook enchanted her) she stripped, washed her stockings, bra, and pants, hung them from the shower rail to dry, put on a white wraparound she found in the broom closet and began to clean house. She started with the two bathrooms, scrubbing

261

the tile floors on hands and knees, disdaining handled mops. She vacuumed the living room, dining room, den, and the three bed-rooms, emptying and cleaning ash trays and wiping down the Venetian blinds with a damp cloth. As she worked she hummed parts of arias, duets, and instrumental passages from the operas she had heard on the radio in the last few months—Rodolfo's lovely narrative, the waltzes from *Der Rosenkavalier* (what a lovely image, rose-bearer), Carmen's seductive music as she writhes in the square outside the tobacco factory, Walther von Stolzing's hymn to secular love, Cherubino's glorious arias—secular music with the secular heartbeat and the gritty secular passions, secular pain and secular nostalgia, the nightingale (though of course she did not recognize the image) with its small feathered chest pressed to the prick of the thorn. She immersed herself in a secular pool of bathos and yearning, thinking, quite coolly, of a calendar image of a bare-breasted island girl squatting under a waterfall.

She waited for the stern internal interdiction of the nun. It did not come. She thought instead, He intends forcing me; what shall I do? I don't want him, but how can I tell him that? Does not wanting him prove that I am not a woman? And why should this, this act I can't properly visualize or put in meaningful rela-tion to an orderly existence, why should this one act be the test? Am I to accept, in perfect obedience, judgments—or, if you will suggestions—handed down by those who are no longer my superiors and can offer neither effective comment nor forgiveness?

Mother Church, the sublime arachnid, sat at the center of her international web and awaited the renegade's return. She felt the pull of the sticky radial threads that communicated her presence on the circumference of the web and drew her, subtly and with an unbreakable persistence, toward its center. God? Could one only serve Him by removing Him as a critical force in human affairs? Not by postulating a gorgeous and irredeemable absence, but by confirming a total independence from extraterrestrial power. For-bidding eternity to enter into time. Freeing the mortal from the punishing and degrading threats of immortality, the curse of the Western conscience. A return to Paradise? No, a demolition of the nightmare of Paradise, whose horrors enabled the few to manipulate and subdue the many.

On her knees on the kitchen floor, scrub brush in hand, she debated the point—had she assumed the posture of prayer or did she mock it?

CHAPTER XXVI

BISHOP HAVEMEYER STARED AT FATHER SERRANO, the administrator at the business of managing his diocese and prodding and curbing reluctant or stubborn priests. The stare, he knew, had little effect on the guileless and the unambitious, two qualities that make a man hard to hold. A lecture on the value and scarcity of money? Perhaps. Serrano would not know what money could buy, but he would certainly be able to tell you, with maddening simplicity and charm, what it couldn't.

"The thing to do, Father, is to accept Letty Peebles as a benefactor and leave me to regard her as a liability."

"I can't have her interfering in parish business, Excellency."

"But does she? Interfere in parish business." Damn the man's spurious incorruptibility. Couldn't he see where it would take him? "You surely aren't going to tell me the case of Margaret Westlake is parish business. Have you forgotten? We have a qualified man from Rome handling that."

Father Serrano, indifferent to the rich appointments of the Bishop's study (did he realize that the heavy silver crucifix on the wall to his left had a monetary value half as great as his yearly budget?), moved two steps closer to the Bishop's desk, getting a better view of the Bishop but also letting the Bishop get a better view of him. Someone should tell the good Father his pants needed pressing. "Two private investigators came to my office yesterday, Excellency. Hired by Letty Peebles. To find Margaret Westlake. I showed them the door."

"Did you? Would you rather the police found her?"

"I haven't reported her missing."

"Why not?"

"I'm not her guardian, Excellency. Not even her confessor. Nor is she a member of my church."

"I suppose you also showed Monsignor Kramer the door, Father. Why?"

"You ought to know, Excellency, that I've refused any further assistance from Miss Peebles. I can't in good conscience accept it."

"So she told me, Father. Well, where do we stand? You have a most urgent need of proper quarters for your delinquent girls. Yet with your building half finished you refuse to accept any further help. The trade unions won't work free, Father. Nor will the wholesalers give you unlimited credit for supplies. Church construction is always a good risk, but I've found over the years that those people you're dealing with can smell the difference between a good risk and a bad one. You see, Father, the lumberyard has to pay the mill on the spot for deliveries of wood, cement, nails, insulation, et cetera. And as they sell to you they must replace these goods and again pay on the spot. And the smaller the yard the greater its need for prompt payment from its retail customers. Now, a contractor usually takes care of these bills himself. He borrows money from the bank, puts it into the job and presents you, after the job is finished, with one large bill. Which you pay promptly and in full. Or perhaps not so promptly and not in full. But the way you have this construction set up—and this is partly my fault— you're constantly being dunned by small contractors, subcontractors, and wholesalers, and paying in dribs and drabs but always paying. Most unbusinesslike, Father."

"I'm afraid my zeal outsped my good sense, Excellency."

"Then it must also outspeed your very reasonable distaste for the likes of Letty Peebles. Or, failing that, let me assume full responsibility for the warehouse."

"I don't like burdening you with this—Leviathan, Excellency."

"I have a special fondness for Leviathans, Father. Now, I try as much as possible to let the help proceed on its own. But when I do have to jump in I do so with both feet. So first thing in the morning I want you to send me all bills, agreements, contracts, and whatever, and spread the word that all future deals concerning the warehouse must be made with this office. Agreed?"

"Thank you, Excellency. I apologize for my—inexperience."

"Now to the important thing. I'll take private charge of Letty Peebles, but you must promise me that for the present you'll overlook—I don't say condone—actions you may not approve of but can't really condemn on moral or theological grounds. You may even have to put up with a plaque on your institution's outer door, 'Letty Peebles Home.' But greater evils will befall, Father, so persist."

The possibility that Letty Peebles had the power to hurt or to exploit Margaret Westlake shocked Father Serrano, so profoundly in fact that his bruised sensibilities had sent him to the Bishop. Or, as he felt, sent him crawling to the Bishop. He did not doubt that she suffered. And nothing so small as regret or remorse. He knew the wounds underlying apathy and inaction, he could detect under indifference the raw smell of suppuration. God in His infinite mercy often extended to those who had willfully or helplessly separated themselves from His presence and love the temporary benediction of a relief from pain. Christ, too, had been extended an opiate on the cross, and what is offered to one cannot be beyond the reach of all.

Several days later he received the good news that the father of Inez Parraga's impending child had been granted an emergency furlough, and would be in Los Angeles, if he caught the right plane, in twenty-four hours. This persuaded him to think charitably of Letty Peebles. Her habit of having her secretary phone him at any hour to discuss the warehouse or the disappearance of Sterling and Sister Esther annoyed but no longer depressed him. The

Bishop, he felt, could handle her. Then one evening, while he was discussing the case of Margaret Westlake with a sour and sarcastic Monsignor Kramer in the study at the rectory, Letty Peebles walked in with Joe Sterling. Sterling was, possibly, forgivably drunk (his breath stained the air), but Letty was coldly, even icily, excited.

"I've got one of them, Father," she said, nodding at Kramer.

"All right, Letty," Sterling said. "We're here. Now do you know where she is or don't you? Goddam it, just give us a yes or no."

"Well, she isn't in her room or with Miss Quando or at the restaurant. My guess is she's headed here. That is, if your story of her walking out on you is true, Giuseppe."

"I fell asleep. When I woke up—" Sterling gestured.

"All this took place in one bed, Father," Letty said.

"At last a union of differences," Kramer said. "Or perhaps each of them in his own way has overcome his prejudices."

Sterling lit a cigarette shakily. "The inquisitive inquisitor himself, gents. Flying in for the burning at the stake."

"In Southern California, Captain, everyone cooks out," Kramer said.

"You sadistic bastard, what myopic obstetrician put you on your mother's teat instead of at her throat?"

"At last he understands the importance of my office."

"Do you, Monsignor?"

"Mr. Sterling, there's a bottle of brandy in the lower drawer of my desk," Father Serrano said. "Will you help yourself?"

"Thank you, Father." Sterling sat at the desk Father Serrano yielded and drank from the bottle. "A last grapple with the grape."

"You took Margaret to your house, Captain?" Kramer asked.

"A waitress. With a full head of hair and a scar on her belly."

"Are you joking, Mr. Sterling?"

"No, Father, I'm not joking. I commiserate with Monsignor Kramer here. Just a hot pair of pliers and a lighted candle and he might have saved her. And what couldn't he have done with a box of kitchen matches and a bottle of castor oil."

"More brandy, Mr. Sterling?" Father Serrano asked.

"Reduce me to an alcoholic, Father, which is to say a spoiled child, and my objections to the medieval Monsignor Kramer's methods of interrogation become ludicrous."

"She told you, Captain?"

"Enough, enough. Am I drinking too much, Father?"

"Every man has his drug, Mr. Sterling," Father Serrano said. "For example, I cannot exist without copious daily drafts of prayer and meditation, far more dangerous drugs than alcohol."

"Only to those who know how to use them." Sterling laughed. "You can't imagine the cunning of the wounded human beast. An animal's only thought is to protect himself—animals, I'm told, die with great dignity and restraint—but a man, a human being, all he thinks of, Father, is revenge. And it doesn't matter who—from whom he gets it. The awful thing is the innocent will do—sometimes a little better than the guilty. That's my speed, revenge."

"You disgust me, Captain," Kramer said.

"Curb your dog, Monsignor."

"Excuse me, Monsignor." Letty moved to stand over Sterling. "What happened at Laurel Canyon, Giuseppe?"

"An aging whore, a molting she-hawk—"

"Giuseppe—"

"Got up like a flamingo. Listen, I'm just saying my litany."

"Where is she?"

"You can leave now, Letty. We all know you. You've identified yourself."

The phone at Sterling's elbow rang, causing him to jerk away from it. Answering it, Father Serrano listened, nodded, and said he would be there in ten minutes.

"Margaret Westlake?" Letty asked.

"At the warehouse, Miss Peebles."

"I'll drive you."

"Shirley says she's in a highly nervous condition. I think it would be best if I saw her alone."

"What do you mean by highly nervous?" Sterling asked. "She hasn't a nerve in her body."

"You know, do you, Giuseppe?"

"I've got to see her, Father. There are things—unfinished things—"

"Then leave them, Captain, unfinished and unsaid," Father Serrano answered.

"We're down to the last veil, Monsignor. Do you want me to quit now?"

"But first I must see her alone, Mr. Sterling," Father Serrano said. "After that—"

"Can you walk, Giuseppe?"

"I must ask you to stay here, Miss Peebles. Or to go back to Hollywood."

"I won't be in your way, Father. Actually, I might be able to help."

"I don't know you, Miss Peebles, I will never know you, I have no desire to know you. Nor do I know what you want or why you're so interested in staging—yes, staging—a meeting between Captain Sterling and Margaret Westlake. I assume you have some idea of using the tragic events in the Far East to your advantage. To me such an idea is repellent. I will oppose it without reservation. I hope Monsignor Kramer agrees with me."

"You have my support, Father. I can also promise Cardinal Bellini's support and, indirectly, the Holy Father's."

"All that ecclesiastical talent lined up against poor me. I suppose even the Bishop's getting hostile. But you know, Father, I'm used to having the donation grabbed out of my warm palm and the door slammed in my face. But you end up with the money without doing either."

"You're right, Miss Peebles. This is not only mean and uncharitable but a shocking discourtesy. But the giver must be content with his giving and not expect to follow up his good deed with intrusions that dishonor it."

"I know my catechism, Father."

"But do you know your place, Miss Peebles? In the sight of God."

"You're really set against me, aren't you, Father? This isn't just dislike; this is opposition. And why must Margaret Westlake's

268

story be used to my advantage? Couldn't it be used to her advantage? What is she that you're so delicate of her? Not a saint, Father. Not even a very great sinner. Just a bitched-up she-animal crawling toward a darker hole. And you, Father, are you helping her? Or prosecuting her? Give me a few honest answers and I'll go my honest way, filthy to the core."

Father Serrano clasped his hands and extended them to Letty, a gesture so perfect in its simplicity that it cut beneath manner and theatricality and touched, perhaps, the raw edges of the spirit. "If I have offended you, Miss Peebles—and I believe I have—I ask your forgiveness."

Letty stepped backward, hand out, her face locked in a grimace also perfect in its simplicity. "Please—"

"It is easy to confess our faults, Miss Peebles, but often very hard to have the courage to see them. Will you forgive me?"

Letty backed to the door, the defensive hand still out. "Keep away from me, keep away—" With her hand on the doorknob she relaxed abruptly, as if realizing that what she saw in Father Serrano could not be in pursuit of her. Sterling, staring at her, only half comprehending her reaction, remembered that though she touched people, as when she had put him to bed, she rarely permitted people to touch her. Even in sexual passages she allowed no embrace or interlocking; she demanded that her lovers approach her from the rear, like animals. Remembering this—rather, having it thrust at him (the computer whirred and handed him a card)—he turned his attention back to himself, and so did not hear her say, "Good-bye, Giuseppe. You're fired. Be smart, use the little pill."

When she was gone Kramer tapped Father Serrano's shoulder and suggested they leave for the warehouse.

"That poor woman," Serrano said. "I'm afraid I've misjudged her. I must go pray for her."

"Not now, Father," Kramer said.

"It's possible she rejects being thanked, her generosity being greater than her need for praise."

"Shall we *go*, Father?"

269

"Yes, yes." Serrano stood, noting that Sterling's head now lay on the desk, surrounded by his arms. "Asleep, do you think?"

"Passed out. He'll keep, Father."

The warehouse, a large square wooden building, stood at one end of a dark semiresidential street next to the small factory (now closed and shuttered) that had once used it for storage of its products. Though considerably changed in appearance by the additions of windows and a canopied porch and entrance, the building still looked like a warehouse, one insufficiently converted into, say, a dance hall or a roller-skating rink—a triumphal arch, Kramer decided, to charity and impracticality. The interior, however, was charming, that is, the finished parts. Though the staircase rising from the central hall reminded him of Cardinal Bellini's thirty-seven steps (he felt them in his knees), the lounge to his left, almost a small auditorium, presented him with a picture of advanced modernism marching backward toward Colonial chic. The only religious symbol visible was a small statue of the Virgin in a niche to the left of the door.

Five girls, all clearly pregnant, occupied the room. Three sat before a television set at the front of the room, two danced to a record player at the rear of the room. In the center, the truce line, sat a massive female nurse, the bulldog matron of a thousand nursing homes and private hospitals, the handmaiden who attends love after love's eyes have opened. After greeting his girls (four did not look at him; one gave him, with grace and finality, the upraised middle finger), Serrano led Kramer through an unfinished office to the right, through connecting cubicles, into a large kitchen-refectory, also unfinished. You could feel, in the semidarkness overhead, the industrial combination of steel trusses and spiders and you could hear (or imagine you could hear) in the newly surfaced walls the running of the rats. In other words, the bright and the ghastly laid over the dull and the ghostly. Margaret Westlake and Shirley Quando sat at a table drinking coffee, a situation so flagrantly female (if not domestic) that Kramer, expecting passion and pornography, found himself watching apple pie. Compassion derailed into revulsion.

"I owe you some money, Father," Margaret said. She took an envelope from her pocketbook and laid it on the table.

"Severance pay, Margaret? You know Monsignor Kramer."

"I did, yes."

"We've just left Sterling," Kramer said. "He's in bad shape."

Margaret shrugged. "I was just telling Shirley, Father, that I'd like to thank you for helping me, when I really needed it, and to say good-bye."

"That means I haven't helped you, Margaret."

"It means I'm persuaded finally that I don't belong here doing what I'm doing and thinking what I'm thinking."

"Why not come in with me?"

"Or with me," Shirley said.

"Why not with Captain Sterling, Sister?" Kramer asked. "Of all of us, surely his need of you is the greatest. As, Sister, is his claim."

"I must be stupid," Shirley said. "You're not a Southerner, are you, Monsignor?"

"Southern Pennsylvania."

"Then why do you call Maggie Sis—my God, so that's it."

"Please, please—" Father Serrano, engaged with Margaret, could not feel genuinely indignant at Shirley's efforts to put her own questions on the agenda, but he could feel disturbed at her timing. Having accepted Margaret Westlake's history, he had forgotten the rich and ironic hours that preceded acceptance.

"An ex-convict I could take," Shirley said. "But an ex-nun?" Feeling that she had accepted a fact without checking its credentials, she added, "Is this true, Maggie?"

"Is it important to you, Shirley? And if so, why should it be?"

"Where does that leave us? It is true."

"If you like, Shirley."

"Well, it is or it isn't, goddam it, and if it is—oh no, no, no—"

"Now, Shirley," Father Serrano said, "you know very little—"

"You had a child when you were a nun?"

"Yes."

"By osmosis, of course. You wandered into the gent's room by accident—"

"I should have told you, Shirley, but how?"

"How?"

She was being judged, she knew, and not by the Church, which she could challenge, but by her peer, whom she could only petition for understanding. For the first time in her life someone, a person, demanded that she reciprocate in an act of love—and she could not. Surely the smallest of all challenges and the one most easily met, one for which she needed no training, not the lap of the parent or the bosom of the Church or the arms of Sterling. She felt it, then, the great club crashing against her skull, not to stun, but to awaken her. Stand up, Middy, the cheapest of all demands—and she could not.

"Shirley, please—" Please? An act of cruelty that stupefied her. Please?

Shirley answered her, so simply and effectively, that the act had no immediate meaning, that is, none Margaret could react to. Shirley leaned forward and spat in her face. After which she left the room. When Margaret became aware of Father Serrano kneeling beside her and wiping her face with a handkerchief she twisted her head from side to side, like a child avoiding a washrag, and wondered why he should bother. It wasn't blood, the martyr's gold, only the mucous lining of the throat of a fellow being, expelled in defense of that being's integrity, the ultimate raspberry, audible and wet.

She let Father Serrano lead her to one of the cubicles off the unfinished office and persuade her to lie on a couch. She slept, dully, achingly. When she awoke she heard Sterling's voice in the kitchen-refectory, where she had sat with Shirley, countered by Father Serrano's soft tenor and Monsignor Kramer's baritone. Like a Verdi trio, she thought, each member of which mouthed his own betrayal. At the door of the cubicle she saw that if she moved quietly she could pass through the office and out of the warehouse unobserved. At least by the three men in the kitchen-refectory. She could go to her room, pack, and take a bus to—San Francisco? Kansas City? Home? She did not have money enough to reach the East Coast in one leap, no, but she could go to Denver, then to Kansas City, then Chicago—or she could rent a room in another part of the city, call home, and wait for her father or one of her brothers to pick her up or—yes, she could wire her mother for money. What else?

Standing there in the semidarkness of the cubicle, she went through her list of choices once again (again came to the question: What else?). In the convent you accepted the imposition of rule and restriction to become totally yourself, the highest of freedoms. You gave up your personality, little by little, as a soldier on a forced march rids himself, often reluctantly, of nonessentials, and in time you saw that personality was only a set of superstitions peculiar to yourself that family, society, and nation, for reasons of continuity and consistency, forced you to accept and practice. To execute a criminal the law must identify him with an act of homicide and demonstrate, logically and conclusively, a personality to fit the act. The personality is deduced and constructed from the act, which represents a limitation of choices. As Margaret Westlake, waitress and ex-nun, she had bonded herself to a mythical creature whose choices were limited to running and hiding.

Not a very large or attractive truth, she thought, or a very subtle one, but at least a clean attempt to admit a truth. Could she say that she waited? Ah, but if she did could she be sure that that kind of waiting was not a euphemism for timidity? Or a simple if unprovable lie? To lie is an attempt to enlarge yourself while actually undergoing a process of reduction. Did she not stand now on the point of disappearance? "Christ, that my love were in my arms—" The remembered line startled but did not displease her. Could she face Sterling? That macabre scene in Laurel Canyon—no, she could be stripped and assaulted but she could not be forced. She had known what he intended—dear God, had she consented in appearance (simply by not leaving him) to force him to prove, on her body, what she could be certain of beforehand? But had she been certain? Motives were indeed queer things, only to be uncovered or interpreted after the act they impelled, and then only partially, incompletely, often only as self-accusations, the true justifiers of conduct. She—would leave. Parraga's "You're a coward and a fraud, Miss Westlake" was the true bill. She would call her mother in Rye. My beloved daughter. And why not? She left the cubicle, trying to shut out the raw sound of Sterling's voice. Father Serrano, walking fast, intercepted her in the hall. "You must help me with Sterling," he said. "I'm afraid he's—becoming ugly."

"I can't, Father."

"You're going, then, are you?"

"I have to."

Father Serrano nodded, approving her decision to leave simply by accepting it. "You'll need money, Margaret. I'll stop by the church—"

"I have plenty of money, Father. Good-bye."

"Good-bye, Margaret. Write me."

She got as far as the sidewalk outside the warehouse before she turned back. It was not the nun in her that turned her back, but the woman.

CHAPTER XXVII

SHE SAT AT A TABLE in the kitchen-refectory rejecting Sterling's pleas to come home with him while a sardonic Kramer and an anxious Father Serrano stood by.

"I'll get a taxi," Sterling said.

"No, Joe—"

"Goddam it, you're coming with me. That's it, nothing else."

"Under the circumstances, Captain," Kramer said, "you can hardly expect to summon Miss Westlake with commands a dog would resent."

"I meant it, Middy. My wife won't contest a divorce. We can go to Nevada. In six weeks we can be married."

"You don't stand on the rim of despair, Captain, you boil in its depths. Remember your prejudices. Or were you waiting till the meat had become sufficiently putrid to become acceptable to you?"

"I think that's a little strong, Monsignor," Father Serrano said.

"Not for the situation, Father."

Sterling swung around to Kramer, strongly but a little unsteadily. He had perhaps underestimated the probable effects of straight brandy. "She's out of the system now, Monsignor, with no possibility of a return. She's disqualified herself. With my help."

"Sexual, I assume."

"The dirty little mind leaps to its dirty little conclusions."

"Necrophilism, Captain. Violating the dead."

"That collar of yours is a sanctuary, Monsignor, only so long as you keep your neck in it. Stick it out and I'll clobber you."

Margaret stood. "Good-bye, Joe."

"Good-bye? My wanting you means nothing to you?"

"You want me, yes, but how badly? And for what purpose?"

"I've offered to marry you."

"Without loving me?"

"What do you want, a certificate as well as a license? You have become a woman, Sister."

"Yes. Why should I ask you for promises when I'm unable to keep any of my own?"

"Then promise nothing."

"Please don't treat me as an object, Joe."

"Are you anything more than an object now, Sister? With certain symbolic meanings, of course."

She sat at the table, feeling not too lightheaded to stand but too displaced. "As Bolton would say, you touched me—"

"You'll marry me, then."

"I thank you for the offer, Joe. You can't have a very high opinion of me—"

"Is that important?"

"Under the circumstances, no."

"Children aren't everything, Middy. If you really want them we can adopt."

"Adopt?"

"If it will make you feel more of a woman—"

Had he freed her finally? "I often wonder what Job sitting in his ashes said when he saw, coming toward him, a swarm of mosquitoes. Did he say—"

"Middy, Middy—"

"Did he say, I ordered snakes and He sends me these? I expected maybe the kitchen sink and He delivers the plumber's friend?" She was not crying so much as releasing tears. "You see how far apart we are, Joe. That scar on my abdomen isn't the result of a hysterectomy but of a Caesarian section. I don't quarrel with your lack of medical knowledge but with your assumption that having misused a woman's most precious organ I couldn't be trusted with the possession of it."

"That doesn't change anything, Middy."

"Whatever its faults, Joe, Catholicism, the only religion I know well, isn't a pantywaist religion. It doesn't remove the temptation; it insists on it. And it knows the curative properties of doubt. When other rocks were available on which to found His Church why should our Lord have chosen quavering Peter?"

"This isn't you talking, Middy, this is Kramer and his slave-owning superiors. Don't you realize what's happening to you? You're becoming an echo chamber, a tape recorder, a—"

"A person, Joe. It would be very stupid of me to reject my beliefs because I can no longer operate in the system that promoted them. I am what I always was, Joe. I suffer to be."

"At last you identify yourself, Sister," Kramer said.

"To you, yes, Monsignor."

"Perhaps you needed only a change of occupations."

"A change of occupations, Monsignor, doesn't represent a change of nature, but an assertion of that nature. I will serve—but how?"

"Serve?" Sterling knelt to take her hands. "How serve? By killing what's human in you in the hope of saving what isn't?"

276

"You diminish yourself, Captain," Kramer said. "As a seducer of corpses you have a gamy desperation that is very nearly heroic. As a theological critic you can express yourself only in dribbles."

"Not so long ago, Middy, you acted as if you loved me."

"I offered you what I had, you took what you wanted. And if you have the right to say that the little you took is enough, I have the right to say that what I offered isn't."

Sterling pulled her to her feet. "Middy, to the Church you're a disposable item, easily replaced, calmly discarded. Another pair of worn-out hands and broken knees—"

"And what am I to you really, Joe? A fetish?"

"Only someone I need. That's my claim on you, Middy. A simple crying need."

"Good-bye, Joe."

Expecting pleadings, violence, tears, perhaps, she saw instead a ghastly evacuation of the spirit. The hands on her arms were those of a corpse. The face became that of a child, losing all mark and imprint of adult passion. This was the youthful Sterling she remembered, turning toward her that morning on the hill above the monastery. She smelled, in the alcoholic's breath, an odor of shaving lotion. She must reach him, quickly, but how? Without conceding what she had refused to give him.

"The Virgin," Sterling said. "I've got to find the Virgin."

"I think we should call a doctor," Father Serrano said.

Sterling turned and left the room, followed after a moment by Father Serrano. She could hear their voices in the office but not what was being said. She leaned against the table, having foreseen what she could not prevent, indifferent to both the horror of what could come and her contribution to it. She marveled at the departure of purely personal passions and wondered how she had tolerated them. Hadn't she, really, forced them on herself? How real were they?

"I once asked you to help me, Monsignor."

"We all have our moments of self-pity, Sister. I'm glad to see you survive yours."

"We are born to pity ourselves, Monsignor. Otherwise, why should God provide us with the gift of grief?"

"You found that you couldn't accept Sterling. After offering to."

"A woman can't be penetrated against her will, Monsignor."

"You permitted the necessary preliminaries but withheld consummation. A greater sin, I believe, than actual fornication."

"You take an iron view of situations you'll never be involved in, Monsignor."

"You miss your chains, Sister."

"Because I thought they contained my freedom."

"One may always hope for a special dispensation from the Holy Father, Sister. There have been cases of renegade priests who have been permitted to resume their religious duties after having, in effect, renounced them. Usually, certain conditions are attached to these dispensations."

"Conditions."

"Conditions, Sister, are the prizes of pride."

"And the penalties of pride, Monsignor?"

"You know them well. Do you wish to make a formal request to resume your vows?"

"Would I be permitted to?"

"I will write your request and submit it to Cardinal Bellini. Who will then use his influence with Cardinal Andreani and perhaps with the Holy Father himself."

"But do you think this is the right and proper thing to do, Monsignor?"

"You mock me, Sister."

"And why not, Monsignor? You make such a show of helping Sister Esther that I begin to think you're really closing the files on her."

"I have my orders."

She laughed, then, as much at herself for having cringed before his interrogation in Italy as at him for having confessed the true nature of his assignment. "I forgive you your embarrassment at being forced to crawl after such an unimportant backslider as Sister Esther, Monsignor. I shall write Cardinal—"

"You exceed yourself, Sister."

"I shall write Cardinal Bellini a letter relieving him and his office of any further obligations toward me. I shall declare, as plainly as I can, that I have no further need of helpful monsignors."

"May I remind you, Sister, that beyond and above 'helpful monsignors' and aging cardinals is the spirit of the Holy Father himself?"

After a moment, after gauging the man's audacity against his need, she said, "This has nothing to do with me, Monsignor. Good-bye."

When she reached the hall of the warehouse she saw, first, the big matron trying to hold back the five girls from the object lying on the floor under the statue of the Virgin, secondly, Father Serrano praying over the object, thirdly, the object itself in a position so familiar, so apt, so commonplace, that she expected to hear Goldman's voice naming a burial detail. "Don't dig it too deep, Bolton; he's got to make the Second Coming." What allegiance did Goldman and Bolton owe to the God that had abandoned them? It is in the nature of God to permit suffering. In whose nature is the power to encourage it?

"Now, now, girls," the big matron said, "you've all seen a man die—"

"He's dead?" one girl asked. "Man, I thought he was just passed out."

They went back to their television and their dancing, having been cheated once more of a promised spectacle that might have removed, temporarily, certain inexhaustible anxieties concerning bread and love.

The matron took Margaret's arm. "At first I thought it was a heart attack. Or a stroke. You know what it is, dear? Cyanide. Listen, we're lucky he didn't cut his throat or stick his head in a fan. You all right?"

"Yes, thank you."

"You'd better lie down, honey. Come on over here."

"I'm used to this, nurse. In the Army."

"One of those, huh? Well, I was stationed at Halloran not so long ago—"

Over the matron's confidences came the expressed piety of Father Serrano, who, she knew, would pray for anyone *in extremis.* This tardy dispatch to God might or might not reach the throne room, but it would be sent, and in case of detention by the staff of the decoding section there was another recipient who received all appeals directly, at any time, from anyone—*Ave Maria, gratia plenis*—yes, the Lord is indeed not only with Thee but of Thee. And at Thy feet the fruit of another womb.

"Would you call it suicide?" Kramer asked at Margaret's shoulder. "Or a necessary and forgivable sacrifice?"

"Blasphemy, Monsignor."

"Such rebukes are a fundamental part of teaching, Miss Westlake. Will you teach?"

"It's as if we had all been thrown into an arena—armed—with instructions to kill each other. And to the survivor—I don't say victor—freedom. But freedom, Monsignor, only from the arena."

"From killing, Miss Westlake. Now you know how you must serve. Will you?"

"Shall I be permitted to serve?"

"Such permissions are never granted, Miss Westlake; they are seized, taken by force, torn from the reluctant, the arrogant, the favored. Even as God damns the bold He must take a secret pride in them. If sin is not an ultimate exercise of godhood there is no God. What I'm trying to say, Miss Westlake, is that the Church will be very happy to oversee your damnation. If you will make it worth the Church's while."

Sterling's wife flew west to claim the body and succeeded in having it interred at the National Cemetery in Arlington, as befitted a combat infantryman, an image she preferred to the civilian portrait, one she wished to preserve for her children. Shirley Quando did not marry her Jack or any of his successors, but she did stand as godmother to Inez Colby's legitimate children and as foster mother to Father Serrano's girls. To Father Serrano's astonishment—and not altogether to his delight—he found himself in charge of an active and extraordinarily triumphant program. In time Cardinal Brooker, through Bishop Havemeyer, granted his request to be relieved of his administrative duties and put him back on the streets, among his beloved gutters and their misdirected inhabitants.

Letty Peebles, who had really wanted to make a religious picture, hired a number of writers to do a script based on the lives of a group of nuns in Central Africa, but after several years and many, many versions shelved the script. "Garbage," she said to her good friend Bishop Havemeyer. "So be it," the Bishop said, and called her attention to plans for a new foundling home to be built in South Los Angeles. Funds to start this necessary project would be granted by the Letty Peebles Foundation. Funds to complete it would be raised by popular subscription. "For all creeds and colors," the Bishop added, "needless to say."

Inspired by Sterling's death, feeling that this event ended a period of frustration, to begin a period of constructive action, Monsignor Kramer initiated the first of a series of artful and positive moves that would close (forever, he imagined) the file on Sister Esther.

The Return

CHAPTER XXVIII

THE BIG JET AIRLINER APPROACHED the landing strip from the ocean, setting down at 4:11 P.M. Mrs. Cora Draper met her at the airport, saw her through customs, and drove her to an air-conditioned office in a building whose cornerstone had been laid while Dr. Westlake was in Italy.

"Not much in the way of local color, I'm afraid, Dr. Westlake," Mrs. Draper said. "But you'll get plenty of that in the jungle. I know you're tired and probably want a bath, but I think we'd better have a briefing session first. Now, the hotel where you'll be staying—the phone very probably has a tap on it. I don't know about the room itself, but it may have a concealed microphone."

"But why?"

"May I ask how you got your passport, Doctor?"

"I see."

"Some, but not all. Officially, I represent a private agency. My job is to recruit doctors, nurses, public-health people, and various medical and other technicians. Unofficially, I represent the State Department. We all do. We can't help it. You, Doctor, whether you like it or not, will also represent the State Department. I don't know what you were told in the States, but the political situation here is hot and getting hotter. Years of fighting, truce, and no peace." Mrs. Draper, a handsome woman in her late forties, pointed to a map of the peninsula on the wall. "One country, Doctor, divided into two parts. On the map a very clean line between north and south. As you can see, the southern section—us —is separated from its neighbors on the west by a river and by mountains. Those neighboring countries are officially neutral. We're told that their borders are guarded and patrolled. They may be. Recently, however, there has been guerrilla action in the mountains. Officially, these guerrillas are a few die-hards left over from the last insurrection, the polite word for those who don't like war. You understand, Doctor, that I speak off the record."

"Yes."

"You know, we weren't expecting a woman doctor."

"I can travel as light as a male doctor, Mrs. Draper."

"Good, good." Mrs. Draper turned a photograph on the desk toward her. "My late husband. He was assassinated by the anti-imperialists, another nice phrase. I don't know why—except that he was an American. Last month there were three such murders. We expect more."

"Are you advising me to leave the peninsula, Mrs. Draper?"

"I would, Doctor. In your place. Or no. No, I wouldn't. But I would strongly advise you not to go into the mountains. I doubt if we have enough American troops in the country to do more than protect our military bases and major cities. And they are scattered all over the map. It would be downright silly of you to tell me you're not afraid. Even if you weren't afraid, Doctor, that has never been—and never will be—a proper reason for taking unnecessary risks."

"Do you think there will be an invasion?"

"We already have infiltration, Doctor. When the number of hostile units becomes large enough, we'll call it an invasion. Officially, we're here to neutralize a native paramilitary force whose aim is to prevent a peaceful settlement of this country's political problems. And we're trying to do this principally by building a native army with sufficient strength to keep us out of the shooting and to support a popularly elected government—the hell with it, you get the picture."

"Officially, then, we're not at war, Mrs. Draper."

"Cora. Officially, we're at peace and we're going to stay at peace. Of course, during the last few months we've shipped and flown home several hundred American wives, children, civilians, and other nonessentials. For health reasons. And you can guess what that covers. Actually, we do have a strain of malaria in this country that's a killer, Doctor. You've studied it, I trust."

"What's known of it, yes. I expect to get in touch with the public-health people—did I understand you to say I'm to be assigned to a clinic in the mountains?"

"That was the plan, Doctor. However, before we send you anywhere we'll have to clear it with the American Embassy. They take a dim view. Which is why I wanted to talk to you first. After all, we recruited you and ultimately we're responsible. How *did* you wangle a passport?"

"Influence, Cora."

"Dear, dear, I've really stuck my neck out."

"Not political influence, ecclesiastical."

"Bishop Key?"

"Indirectly, yes."

"Then I guess the Embassy can't touch you." Mrs. Draper picked up a ruler and went to the map on the wall. "Now, here is where we were planning to send you. It's a clinic in the mountains. You're to replace Dr. Ralston. We wanted you to assist him. Unfortunately, he has to return to the States for an operation. Neither the civilian nor the army doctors will touch it. Are you qualified in surgery?"

"Barely."

"You'll be expected, of course, to travel. And you'll give one day a week to the convent—here. That's about fifty miles from the clinic. Or four hours by jeep. The nuns are American. So there'll be no language barrier. Have you studied the local dialect?"

"Yes." So soon?

"Good. But you'll have plenty of interpreters. Almost everyone speaks a little pidgin. Well, I've said about all I can say. No use rambling on, is there? However, there is one thing I'd like to add —doctors are very valuable people here. They rank just below the military. To the enemy—whoever he may be—they rank *above* the military. Will you remember that, please?"

"Assassination, Cora?"

"That wasn't what I had in mind, Doctor. The clinic is only a few miles from the border— Well, let me help you get settled. Sorry about the hotel, but despite all the building you see going on and the people who have left the country, we're horribly cramped. By the way, if you get lonely there's an army post not too far from the clinic."

"I'm not much interested, Cora."

"No? Something happens to the American woman out here, Doctor. Despite the heat. Or maybe because of it. Either you dry up totally or you can't get enough of it. But there's one good thing—what you do out here won't affect you at all in the States."

"Sorry, but I came here to work."

"I'm not a whore, either, Doctor. You might say I'm a victim of the unwritten rules."

Dr. Westlake expected to leave for the clinic at the end of the week. After three weeks of pointless appointments, broken appointments, official delays, interviews with the wrong people, pleas of no authority in the matter, she appealed to Bishop Key.

"No one wants the responsibility of sending you into an unprotected area, Doctor." Bishop Key, half a head shorter than she, explained that the various mountain tribes, despite intensive American propaganda and technical help, were loyal only to their tribal chiefs and that the chiefs disliked and distrusted the national government. "The American missionary nuns, however, have great influence with them. Are you a Catholic, Doctor?"

"A very bad one, Excellency."

"Yes. Well, you will hear the story. You must be very careful in dealing with these people, Doctor. Most of them have been converted to the Catholic Faith but the Catholicism they practice is heavily infected with tribal myths, morals, and customs. I can do very little for them. When I visit them, which I try to do at least every three or four months, I must accept an homage that horrifies me. Idolatry, Doctor. And this despite the fact that I myself am a native and a city man. I sometimes think they perform their acts of homage in sincere mockery. But of course I can only urge them to pray and to learn their catechisms. They are great carvers, these people. When they hear that I am coming—and they always know, despite all precautions for secrecy—they remove my statue from the church and place it in a post of honor near the chief's

288

house. After I leave—and they know if I plan to turn back and surprise them—they return my likeness—it is an excellent one—to its niche in the church. Father Phillips hangs a cloth over it when saying Mass. He explains that if he did not it would be very unpleasing to God, Who is a jealous God. Do you see, Doctor? Fortunately, they love and respect Dr. Ralston, though they often reject his medicine. Sometimes, if you'll forgive me for saying so, quite rightly. Have I offended your medical honor?"

"No, Excellency. If anything, bolstered it."

"A woman doctor. This is a fine, a splendid thing. I salute you, Doctor." Bishop Key paused, possibly to indicate that if she had any other credentials to offer he would be glad to accept them. "As I understand it, Doctor, you came here under the sponsorship of a civilian agency."

"That is correct, Excellency."

"And this civilian agency cannot—or will not—fulfill the promises that lured you to the peninsula."

"I had hoped to proceed without your help, Excellency."

"And without the help of his Eminence Cardinal Brooker. Put it this way, Doctor—you wish to fly your own banner."

"As far as possible, Excellency."

Bishop Key picked up a letter from his desk. "His Eminence writes that while he disapproves of your presence here, Doctor, I am to give you all possible assistance. This is a request, Doctor, not a command." Watching her, noticing the clasped hands, Bishop Key added, "You know that a word from me to the military will cancel your plans for going into the interior. Should I speak that word?"

"Please, no, Excellency."

"Must you persist?"

"Yes."

Bishop Key simply looked at her, neither expectant nor impatient, waiting her out. After perhaps fifteen seconds he said, "Very well, then, go. With or without God."

"Thank you, Excellency."

"Actually, it will be a very great relief for the twelve American nuns to be examined by a female doctor. No, don't smile, Doctor. These nuns are a stiff-necked group. Imagine, a nurse who will forgo physical examination till she drops. I must warn you about dealing with them. You must be extremely firm. I will give you a letter to Mother Teresa. I doubt if she will do more than read and file it."

"I'm shocked, Excellency."

"Oh, they submit, Doctor. You should see them when I visit the convent. Twelve of them kneeling in the dirt outside the gate to the compound, six on one side of the road, six on the other. I dislike this kind of homage intensely. And their faces. Like twelve white doves. My goodness, they honor me. And they will not get off their knees till I dismount and extend the episcopal ring, which they kiss with such fervor and simplicity that if I were not so brown I would turn a glowing red. Like one of your American Indians. Tell me, are they really red?"

"Not very, Excellency."

"Well, well, I must abandon another of my illusions."

Of course they would love him, she thought. They would adore him. His presence, intelligence, simplicity, and wit would enliven and enrich their long drab unsparing day and give them something precious both to look forward to and to look back on. The Bishop is coming. What an honor. And the happy, happy preparations. And in each breast the unspoken question: Will he like this? Will he be pleased by the gay wreath on the door? And the flowers, we must flood the place with flowers. She remembered the ritual of his last visit—how many years ago?—the Mother Superior herself appearing with a bucket and brush to scrub the steps and porch at the entrance to the convent proper, the cooks and the bakers outdoing themselves in the kitchen, the nurses decorating the wards and cleaning and dressing their patients in flowered bed jackets, the gardeners fervently tidying up their vegetables and flowers—yes, this group of nuns, these twelve new people, loved him as much as she and her group had. He would not, of course, recognize her; Kramer's dispatches had not identified her. She had been assured that none of the present nuns knew her or had served with her. She was, as she wanted, Dr. Margaret Westlake, internist, obstetrician, pediatrician, surgeon, pathologist—an old-fashioned general practitioner.

Three days later an army helicopter flew her to an army base at the foot of the mountains and a squad of soldiers in a jeep and two armored trucks drove her to the clinic. As the sergeant in command of the small convoy said, "We don't expect any trouble, Doctor. We just want the people to know we're interested in you." Dr. Ralston, assisted by native nurses and technicians, showed her the clinic, a U-shaped one-story building, the offices of which led across a roofed boardwalk to a small bungalow. "Your quarters," he said. The tropics had gotten to him, by the age of fifty-six, the tropics or the enormous frustrations of his solitary vocation. "Watch out you don't become a loner, Doctor," he said. "That's my trouble. There's lots of companionship here, but you've got to find it, work at it." In his bungalow he pointed to the library, the phonograph and record albums, the chess set, and the desk on which lay the unfinished manuscript on the ecology of the country. "An important work, Doctor. If it had been published ten years ago."

He said that the operation for which he would have to leave the country "is for a double hernia, Doctor. You could do that easily here, couldn't you?"

"Well, that would depend, Doctor."

"They want me out of the country, and that's their stupid excuse. I'm a threat to American propaganda. At the Embassy they dismiss me as a crank and a bore. I'm always screaming for medical supplies, drugs, assistants, a new plant—I'm doing nothing here, Doctor, but holding the line. And that's what you'll be doing. But not for long. Well, don't let me scare you."

"You don't, Doctor."

"One of those, huh? Well, you're not so goddam young, Doctor. Where did you get all this dedication?"

"In self-defense."

"Yes. That's true. It *is* better out here. Not closer to God, Doctor—that's a particularly stinking piece of sentimentalism—but closer to the people. That's *never* a sentimentalism. Listen, you might as well know, I have a native wife and two children. But don't worry, I've sent them away, they won't embarrass you. I've made my peace. At least I think I have. Well, come on. I'll take you around to the villages. Introduce you. You've got one problem, though, that I can't help you with. About fifty miles from here is a convent staffed by twelve Catholic nuns. They also run a clinic— of sorts. And a school and a farm and even a small dairy. You're supposed to help them out once in a while. They get a lot of shrapnel cases. How? Where? I'm damned if I know—and they simply won't tell. Oh, they claim 'old bombs, booby traps, that never went off as planned.' There was a lot of action in this area not so long ago. The people are supposed to report these things to the army post up the line, but they never do. They just show up. It's bad enough in the adults, but wait till you see the kids—"

After Dr. Ralston left she made her plans—first, a vocational school for children and adolescents (she would need instructors but she would find them); second, an intensive training program for nurses and midwives; third, a massive though subtle attack on native standards of sanitation; fourth, the foundations for a real hospital (just the foundations; nothing so shocks and irritates the bureaucratic mind as the naked underpinning for a structure that should be there but isn't); and fifth, the necessarily cautious but remorseless campaign to win the respect, loyalty, and devotion of the tribal chiefs. To them she was a doctor, yes, but she was still a woman, and one could not talk man to man with a woman. Where was her husband, her lord? Ah, did no man want her? Or had she driven away men with her medical totems and her powerful hands? To a woman blood was a sorrow and a sign of loss. Could the doctor overcome the woman in her? A nun was a woman, but a special kind of woman, a priestess, God's servant, to whom His temple was always open. They knew nuns; they did not know women doctors.

The call from the convent came on the fifth day of her residency at the clinic. There had been a bad accident, would she come? Of course. She sat at the desk in her small office and told herself firmly that she did not believe in premonitions, hunches, or fore-bodings. Nor did she believe, really, in the direct intervention of God in human affairs. She stared at the two-way radio (a gift from the Army) over which the call had come, by relay from the army post equidistant from convent and clinic. There was no doctor at the army post; she was the nearest surgeon. She felt herself relapsing into superstition, which in turn phased into inevitability and fatal-ism. She had gone so long without prayer, that floating and in-visible barrier between consciousness and unconsciousness, that for a moment only reason, the thin product of a thinner intelligence, stood between her and panic. And reason was like cheesecloth, a filter but hardly a barrier. "But I just arrived," she said aloud.

What was the feeling? Fear alone? Panic? Yes, panic. Not the modern panic where the being becomes a human torch of burning nerves, but the ancient madness, the goat-frenzy, ecstasy. She felt it, she knew she felt it, she controlled it, she banked it. Let it burn; it would not consume. She packed quickly, one small suit-case for her personal things, an instrument case as well as her medical bag. When she called for the one jeep that served the clinic she was told by one of the native nurses, whom she did not as yet know well, that there was no driver.

"In that case," she said, "I'll drive myself."

"Better not to go," the nurse said. "Too dangerous." She pan-tomimed firing, perhaps from cover. "Pat—Pat—he come back."

Hearing the old word for the enemy, she smiled and said she would check it out with the army post. And then remembered that the call had been relayed through the post. "I'll drive myself," she said again. But how could she get there without a guide? She sat on the veranda of the clinic and pretended to check her bags. Her first test, and she could not cope with it. "I'll need a guide," she said. Not to the nurse, but to the general environment, as if she still controlled it. "No guide," the nurse said. She took a stick and drew a rectangle on the ground. By leaning on the railing she could see it clearly. "The clinic," the nurse said, poking a hole in the ground. "The army." Another hole. "The convent." She then drew rough snaking lines between the three holes. "Only roads. No can miss." And then the explanation that summed up the total situation. "Army roads. Bang-bang roads."

In the highlands, for the first two hours, the road was rough but no real impediment to the jeep's oversize tires and four-wheel drive. The country appeared to be made up of patches, a large patch of grassland, dry and dusty, with groups of trees and secondary growth, a thick patch of tall stiff grasses reinforced by giant sheaves of bamboo, a park of conifers, and, as she dropped down from the plateau, the jungle itself, thick, pungent, abundant with flowers and ferns. The birds delighted her, particularly an Oriental pheasant, brilliantly colored, that thundered up from her wheels and ruffled the steamy air with its passage to safety.

She drove carefully. Too large holes in the road she filled with branches, stones, and dirt, using the ax and the shovel she found in the tool compartment built across the back of the jeep. She noted also a sickle, a spade, a rope, chains, large spikes, a block and tackle, a saw, tire-changing equipment, a trench tool, and a small drum of aged water. In the dashboard compartment she found screwdriver and pliers, wrenches, a flashlight, water-purification pills, army rations, and a flare pistol. With such splendid equipment, she decided, you did not need companionship, you needed only a free and well-stocked mind.

In the fourth hour the road turned back toward the foothills, rising slowly and snakily toward drier, cooler, less congested-by-nature country. She saw few villages, perhaps two in the first hour of travel, one or two in the second, three or four in the third. The road did not run through the villages but past them, as a highway bypasses a community. She knew that the farmers and hunters she passed saw her, particularly when they refused to acknowledge her. "A bad sign," Sam had said. "When they go into the tents of neutrality, you go onto the slabs of the morgue." Dear Sam, the world's most consistent pessimist. He knew, as his men said, the score. And it was always a thousand and one against you. The men summed it up with consummate lyricism and finality. "We're fucked, royally fucked, and we know it. So cease the shit, Rollo."

A grubby lot, she had thought at first, dirty, coarse, profane, blasphemous, and totally oriented toward survival. Yet, as she saw later, survival on their own terms. They would not leave their wounded. When possible—and sometimes when not—they buried their dead. Though they reviled each other in the plainest and most sincere phrases, often with a ferocity that astounded her, they worked as a team, leaving no man unprotected, exposing no man unnecessarily. Self-defense, of course. You scratch my back and I'll scratch yours. Simple and self-explanatory. And Sterling. "The trouble with that guy is," she had heard Corporal Plinnett say, "he has no self-respect." He moved among the men with an ease and a familiarity that puzzled her. He said that he was a snob. He made no effort to talk down to the men or practice their mores or make friends. He would dig his own foxhole (under prevailing conditions, granted), but he would also help carry the wounded, feed them, fetch ammo when needed, ask for advice, bum cigarettes, share his rations, grab an end of a tarpaulin and help fold it—yet though the men said he was no soldier, they liked and respected him. Now, of course, he was dead, unexpectedly, shockingly, unforeseeably, meaninglessly dead. Could you be said to have lived a meaningful life without dying a meaningful death?

She began to pass through villages now from which she could see small farm plots, vegetable gardens, the special brand of tough tropical cattle the nuns had imported to improve and strengthen the local breeds. The villagers bowed and nodded. Few waved, though, and the children seemed less curious and exuberant than she remembered. Again, a bad sign. She recognized certain landmarks—the cleft in the hills to the west, the bend in the river to the east. Others, such as the Buddhist temple and roadside shrines, she looked for but didn't see. At the peak of the last rise in the road overlooking the valley she stopped the jeep and dismounted. Why should she not expect to see the convent and its adjacent buildings intact? And what appeared to be the original structures. Yes, she thought, when you have undergone a personal, internal destruction you must be given, in compensation, a comparable amount of exterior destruction. And what had the present nuns done—or what grace had been given them?—that they should inherit the works of her hands, knowing nothing, feeling nothing, sensing nothing of the history of these works?

Enough, enough. The gates of the convent compound were open and unattended. Driving through them, she saw the sergeant and six men from the army post standing by two armed vehicles talking to, obviously, the mother superior, Mother Teresa. No other nuns were in sight. They would be told in time what they needed to be told, the spare verbal spurs for action—in the meantime there were the hospital and routines of work and prayer.

"Where the hell did you come from, Doctor?" the sergeant asked as she got out of the jeep. He did not, she noted, look at her legs.

"From the clinic." She turned to Mother Teresa. "Where do I scrub?"

"This way, Doctor."

"Just one bleeding minute, ladies." Why did he remind her of Sam? Ah, that look, that tone, that attitude of perpetual exasperation.

"We have lives to save, Sergeant, not to bargain with."

Mother Teresa scrubbed with her, explaining that she herself and two other nuns would assist. There were three cases—Margaret Westlake did not really hear Mother Teresa or the nun-nurse who briefed her. She had had no experience with shrapnel or grenade or bomb fragments but she had operated on construction workers (one with cable fragments in his chest and abdomen), victims of automobile accidents, knives, gunshot wounds, and other perforants. She could handle it. But why had they enlarged the scrub room at the expense of the storage closet and the ward next to it? You would think that with these new sinks (what a waste of money)—and, ah, that special mirror that subdued glare—how much had that cost? And how about that magnificent statue of the Blessed Virgin in the hall outside the chapel, carved from a single block of wood and painted in gold and blue? And the new furniture in the waiting room to the right of the entrance—where had *that* come from? Of course, these things had been needed, in her day badly needed, but such grandeur. She supposed the nuns had new beds in their cells, with real springs and fine cotton pallets instead of the old box stalls whose boards were always breaking, dropping the sleeping person's posterior to the floor while retaining her feet and neck. What grandeur, what magnificence, what needless—

"But these are bullet wounds," she said over the uncovered patient.

Mother Teresa's eyes stared at her over the surgical mask. "Would you like to lie down for fifteen minutes, Doctor?"

She replied by putting her hand palm up for a probe. By God, they had better be good, these nun-nurses, or she would kick them, one by one, into the hall and do the whole job herself.

CHAPTER XXIX

AS SHE WALKED ACROSS THE COMPOUND under the light of a setting moon, accompanied by the young nun whose name she had not heard spoken, she marveled at a profession that could give her such intense satisfaction without giving her a sense of joy or celebration. She had loved nursing. Why should she not love the practice of medicine? Especially since she could live it so completely that it protected her from such stinging questions as a possible reconciliation with God (what a phrase) and belittled such stunning demands on her conscience as what of the future. And if satisfaction was the most any reasonable person in her position could hope for, why should she expect it to take that final leap toward celebration?

In the moonlight the compound dropped its familiarity and became one of the wayside caves in which the soul kept its appointments. Coming out of the scrub room with Mother Teresa, she had pretended not to see the slight hand signal from the nun who now walked beside her and, of course, she had willingly excused the Mother Superior, who without seeming to hurry had disappeared quickly into her office. A call from the outside, possibly from the army post. Did it matter?

"You have quite a plant here, Sister."

"The Bishop has been very generous, Doctor. Spiritual backing can give one a magnificent lift but sometimes only money—"

How old was she? Thirty, thirty-two. No more, certainly. Lighting a cigarette, feeling a need to use her hands, she pointed to a series of windows at ground level on the west wing. "You have an extensive basement?"

"Yes. We have almost half as much space in the basement as we have on the first floor. We use this space for classrooms, storerooms, clothing and sewing rooms, recreation—yes, and leading out of the basement—you can't see it from here—a basketball court."

"For you, Sister?"

"And the children, Doctor. Not every boy and girl wants to be a scholar, but they all like games. So in the one hand the bitter, in the other the sweet."

She stopped at the gate in the south wall of the compound. "And that, Sister?"

"Our graveyard." The young nun made no move to open the gate, nor did she move away from it. The doctor had requested a walk to clear her head from the fumes of the operating room; the young sister had been detailed to accompany the doctor.

"Taboo, Sister?"

"Heavens, no. We are proud of our sisters who lie there awaiting the glory of the Resurrection." She opened the gate. "The last thing we want, Doctor, is to make a shrine of a simple burial place. Please."

Dropping her cigarette and putting her heel on it, she preceded the young nun into the graveyard. The seven black wooden crosses stood in a row to her left, other smaller stones and crosses stood in clusters to her front and right. As she turned to the seven crosses, she saw behind them, near the fieldstone retaining wall, backed by a line of trees, the life-size statue of a nun holding in her over-size hands a not quite life-size basketball, which by separating the hands appeared to place them in an attitude of benediction rather than prayer. And the face? The moonlight struck the coiffed head behind the left (of course invisible) ear, empowering the face with the inscrutability of darkness.

"Our people carved it in honor of our seven martyred sisters, Doctor. I suppose you know the story."

"Most of it, yes. Is this a likeness, a composite, or an abstract?"

"It's quite a definite likeness, Doctor. Carved from memory, of course. But which sister it portrays we don't know. The hands, you see, are the clue. But whether they represent saintliness, skill, tenderness, or simply largeness—the carver died soon after completing the likeness. Most of his contemporaries are either dead or blind—some years ago an epidemic of conjunctivitis swept this section of the country—and the life-span is not long—" The young sister brooded, caught in the legend.

"How do you know it is a likeness, Sister?"

"Because of the popular native belief that she—note the singular —she will come back and perform great works for the people. Principally, we understand it, healing. Of course, we can't have this, Doctor. Your kind of healing, yes, but miracles?"

"It should be easy enough to identify the nun, Sister. You have photographs, surely."

The young nun smiled. "I'm afraid you don't understand the life of the religious, Doctor."

"Some. For example, certain European communities observe a vow of silence from—oh, whatever your last service is—"

"Compline?"

"Till morning. You don't."

"No. But then we don't permit ourselves to be photographed riding bicycles or dancing around Maypoles, Doctor."

"Your passports?"

"Our mother superior handles those, Doctor. Besides, we found very little left in the buildings when we came here. The rebels stripped the place. Even the chapel—" She could not, apparently, put this sacrilege adequately into words. "And what the rebels didn't take, our people did. They offered to return what they could, but we insisted that they keep it. We do know, though, that the statue is intended as a likeness of one of the seven you see here."

"Why?"

"Because there is no possibility of the others return—" She broke off abruptly, stunned by her indiscretion. "You must be hungry, Doctor. Shall I bring you some sandwiches?"

"Please."

"Iced tea?"

"Yes."

In the guest room of the convent, a remodeled room where in her day visiting doctors stayed overnight, she sat at the desk writing the reports of the operations until Mother Teresa herself brought the sandwiches and tea. Time, that famous laggard who slept at your back and then in one leap overtook and obliterated you. Time, the great proof offered by a planetary species that it could count. Computers, evidence that man could improve on his fingers but not dispense with them.

"I must tell you, Doctor, that we have been ordered to evacuate the hospital," Mother Teresa said. "You will leave under escort at 0900 hours. Nine A.M. civilian time."

"And you, Sister?"

"That is our business, Doctor. The Army, for some unexplained reason, cannot send helicopters. We must make do with trucks and ambulances. And, I suppose, weapons carriers."

"I've just seen your graveyard, Sister." (Best not to use the title "Mother.") "I've heard a little about your predecessors. Or do you believe in the old proverb about lightning?"

"Nothing like that will happen again, Doctor. I wish to thank you for coming to us when others could not. You have marvelous hands. I'll leave you to your supper."

"I'm afraid I'm not very hungry."

"Oh, but you must eat, Doctor. Something, at least."

"Have you had any earlier warnings, Sister? Please, if I'm to be in the middle of a fracas, I ought to know something about it. I gave you the letter from Bishop Key. Have you read it?"

"Have you, Doctor?"

"I should think it comments on your reluctance to schedule physical examinations for your company."

"It does, yes. And you, Doctor? When was the last time you had a vaginal smear taken?"

"Sister, I share your distaste for vaginal examinations, but I must insist on the importance of the Pap test. You're a nurse. Must I tell you?"

"I'm also a nun, Doctor. I know the stupidity of cutting short a working life. As well as the waste of valuable human material. But out here a doctor's time is so valuable we think it ought to be given to our patients. Who have far greater need of it."

"Such pride, such dedication."

"Are you an atheist, Doctor?"

"I'm not that close to God."

Mother Teresa smiled. "May I sit with you a moment, Doctor?"

Was it the hope of a conversion? Or something else? "Morning cometh, Sister. You probably have services."

"The bells will ring, Doctor. Besides, after so many years I have the rhythm of the canonical hours in my heart. It quite literally suspends a stroke thirty seconds before the clapper strikes. You could probably give me a sound reason for this."

"Not I, Sister."

"You seemed shocked—or, no, unprepared for bullet wounds, Doctor. Had you expected shrapnel?"

"I was told to expect shrapnel, yes."

"I'm afraid the Army is quite jealous of our bomb disposal unit."

"You have one, Sister?"

"A very good one. Sister Anselm. She's quite expert on all makes, sizes, and national origins—American thousand-pounders, Russian fragmentation bombs—all makes, British, French, Czechoslovakian, Chinese. Fortunately, these are older bombs and shells. Some of the newer ones, I'm told, are very difficult to disarm."

"I'd forgotten that people like you existed, Sister."

"Forgotten, Doctor?"

"The missionary complex."

"Oh, but it's more than that, Doctor. Much, much more. You yourself, Doctor. Why are you here?"

"To practice medicine."

"But you can do that much more profitably and comfortably back in the States."

"You're mistaken, Sister. I can't."

"Oh?"

"About these bullet wounds. What does it mean?"

"We're being urged not to panic, Doctor. We're also being urged to evacuate. The Army—you must understand that its orders come from very high up and very far away. What is seen—to use an abominable term—in the big picture doesn't always fit what's seen in the little picture. At the moment neither the native Army nor the U.S. Army is prepared to defend this section of the country. There are, undoubtedly, excellent reasons for this negative response to our local problems. We will learn them in time."

"Fatalism, Sister."

"But a working fatalism, Doctor. We do not crouch under God's shadow waiting for what must happen. We move beyond it, confident that it will follow us. May I ask, is surgery your specialty?"

"Has one of my patients died?"

"No, no. But you do practice internal medicine."

"Also obstetrics, orthopedics, pediatrics—a smattering, Sister, but necessary, I was told, for the remoter places on this planet."

"What I'd like to propose is this, Doctor: Why not make this hospital your home base? Or is it court? We are much better equipped than—forgive me—your clinic. And Bishop Key himself —I won't say he suggested it, but he did think you ought to make better use of our facilities than Dr. Ralston did."

"But you have your own doctors, Sister. Ralston has gone back to the States."

"How many patients have you treated so far, Doctor? In the short week you've worked. And for what major illnesses? We have ten or fifteen times the number of people to draw from, better roads, a sure supply of electricity, good communications, the trust of the people, trained nurses—and here, Doctor, you could teach. Imagine, in a few years we could be turning out not only native nurses but native doctors."

"You exceed yourself, Sister."

"Do I? Yes, I do. But we could at least prepare our students for entrance into medical schools. That, Doctor, is no dream."

No, but it presented, if she permitted, one of those irrevocable concessions, often granted from politeness only but accepted with iron purpose, that lead by the nature of pressure and demand to other larger concessions, and finally to a surrender of the will. Those who ask you to concede, to give, to withdraw objection, do so not to obtain an objective, but to destroy or render you impotent to oppose them. They are not interested in swapping, in offering you something in return for money, good will, properties, or services; they are interested only in subjugation, removal of will, and neutralization. She doubted that Mother Teresa had the above in mind (or even under mind), but she believed firmly in what she had often observed as a nun—that the religious have fewer scruples and inhibitions (in certain areas, of course) than habitual criminals. God's umbrella is larger than any yet erected by His manic children. Margaret exaggerated. Exactly. The normal response to pressure.

"That's out of the question, Sister. To be truthful, I'm thinking of expanding the clinic. When you want something—and there's no other way to get it—you set a trap for it. For example, this plant. You have better facilities for diagnosis, treatment, and postoperative care and convalescence than some of the hospitals in the coastal regions. If you have the facilities you will attract the doctors. But I refuse to be a medical captive. I prefer my clinic. Furthermore, I intend setting up other small clinics in even remoter areas. Like the old-fashioned country doctor, I'll ride the circuit."

Be careful, she warned herself, and saw immediately that it was too late. But it was time for the bell to ring for matins. Why didn't it ring? To free herself from the older nun's stare, she got up from

303

the desk, yawning, and lit a cigarette. The bell sounded, massively in the humid air. She felt its vibrations against her skull. Persistent old woman. Rhythms in her heart? What odd types the religious life promoted.

"I applaud your ambitions, Doctor, but question your good sense. Together— Is anything the matter?"

"The bell—"

"The bell? Oh no, that rang thirty seconds ago, Doctor. I saw it ringing in your face."

She turned quickly away from Mother Teresa. "Are you reading my lips, Sister?" She turned back and repeated the question.

"It has been the custom of our Order, for more years than anyone remembers, to respond to the bell with a whispered 'Laudamus Deo.' Yes, Doctor, I read your lips. I have one very bad ear and one not so good one. Soon I will have to report this to our Reverend Mother in the States and then my tour of duty—in this land—will be over."

"That explains your distaste for physical examinations."

"My child—"

"I've worked with nuns, Sister, I know when the bell rings for chapel."

"To within thirty seconds, Doctor? I see you're not wearing a watch. Is it possible that the rhythm of our devotions is still in your heart?"

"I'm exhausted. Please—"

"A double trap, Sister. Sister Anselm, a strict follower of the rules, was most upset by my order to delay the ringing of the bell, especially since I gave no reason for my shocking action. And I read—on your lips—the 'Laudamus Deo'—the second trap. Sixteen years a nun, Sister—no, one never forgets, one cannot forget."

"Am I never to be freed of Monsignor Kramer?"

"Kramer? I know no such priest, Sister. You forget the sharp inner senses of the nun. We are not easily deceived, especially by our own. And then—do you see?—the people here are very rarely wrong on psychic mysteries. They said—she will come back. And

304

she has. Won't you acknowledge me, my child? For one precious moment?"

She sat at the desk, aware that traps are set only where there is evidence of game. "That statue—"

"It is your likeness, Sister, yours alone. What a scandal! The people set it up originally in the basketball court, where they intended making a shrine. We persuaded them finally to move it to the graveyard, where, very properly, it could serve as a monument." Mother Teresa stood. "But we must get you away from here. The enemy knows the legend of the Sister of the Hands and wishes, I'm sure, to convert it to their purpose."

"Then there is some danger of attack."

"Very little, Sister. But I cannot risk the possibility that you came back only to put yourself on trial, to test yourself."

"As a doctor?"

"As a nun. There are many unsettled areas in this distressed world where you could pit your skill as a doctor against a primitive economy, but only one where you could hope to prove to yourself that submission was not the act of a coward."

"I'm not sure I believe it is, Sister."

"What do you search for, then? Death? A disgusting suicide that you hope will be mistaken for martyrdom? Are you jealous of the bayonets your sisters received and wish one of your own? After having rejected it?"

"You almost convince me, Mother."

Mother Teresa knelt beside the chair. "Why did you go out, my child? Why when the others elected to work out their salvation in the blessed arms of the Church did you choose to leave?"

"Do you think that can be answered, Mother?"

"Possibly by the very processes you use to evade it, Sister."

She shrugged, certain that what the years had not yielded moments would withhold. "I must have realized—though when, I don't know—that what preserved me during those astonishing months wasn't the God in me but the woman." Her head ached, her chest hurt, her eyes itched—as if shedding an old membrane? "Even before I became pregnant—" She had walked the flat of the knife, could she walk its edge? "Even before I became pregnant I began to look forward to a new order, a new logic, a new progression. Not new to a woman, but unthinkable to a nun."

"The flesh, Sister?"

"Of course. I put myself back—not consciously, not willingly, but as if I had been compelled by the release of certain new and powerful hormones—into the secular world of secular cause and effect. Instead of accepting a timeless suffering I marked my pains on a calendar. I measured my degradation by a tape from a woman's sewing basket. There was no longer a life to be given or taken according to God's will, but a life to be preserved against any idea or person, sacred or profane, that threatened it. Pride, Mother. I put this sheerly physical pride against our divine Mother's holy grief and refused to believe that my crown of slops was the lesser wreath. That, I think—I can't say know—is my sin, one that cannot, at least in my present condition, be forgiven."

"All sins may be forgiven, Sister."

"All known sins, Mother, known so fiercely that they can be sincerely and absolutely repented. Mine is neither. To the unknown God, the unknown sin."

"If you believe that, Sister, you are lost indeed."

"That, Mother, is no longer important."

"But there is one thing that is important, Sister. You—not God—abandoned Sister Esther. You owe her the chance to confess herself and receive absolution for her sins, even for those unknown to her. They can, after all, be reached for, if not grasped. After which, Doctor, you may carry on your singular war with God freed of Sister Esther's guilt and anxiety—till He concludes it."

"In whose favor?"

"Yours, Doctor. In such hand-to-hand combats the soul never loses. Ask yourself, Doctor, have you the right to hate Sister Esther? Are you the barrier between God and her soul? Will you keep them apart?"

"May God, if He so wishes, damn Sister Esther. With my unswerving assent. But I refuse to hate my loathsome twin and I shall never abandon her. No, either God takes me completely—the compelled whore with her dishonored vagina as well as the scientist with her scalpel—or He takes me not at all. It may be that He shall—it may be that He shall not. I leave it to Him. Thus ends the lesson for today."

"In speaking to you, Sister, I have broken an important rule of our community. For which I shall do penance." Mother Teresa paused, perhaps out of respect for what she had to say. "Spiritually, you are beyond my help, beyond even my experience, and, in truth, beyond my understanding. But I can do one thing for you, and that is to see that you are sent back to the States as quickly and as quietly as possible. We have good and powerful friends at the Embassy. And there is, as you know, Bishop Key. Good night."

Margaret put out the light and lay on the bed, staring at the padded darkness below the ceiling. Was it over? Or was it beginning?

CHAPTER XXX

SHE LAY TENSELY ON THE BED, unable to move. No weight pinned her, no ropes or chains restricted her, no sheet enclosed her—yet she could not move. She lay on her back with one leg raised at the knee, straining to sit up, to turn, to sidle, to spring. The sweat burst from her face and trickled down between her breasts and over her belly, forming a stream along the major axis of the scar, taking with it the warm waxes of her navel. The leg in contact with the sheet sweltered in the salty fluid. Ah, there it came, from the pit of the diaphragm, up the esophagus, over the larynx—the scream—it hit the hard palate and ricocheted off her teeth to the uvula, gagging her.

She awoke, repossessing her body-mind. Voices, movement in the compound, a sound of metal—she went into the bathroom (the visitors got all the luxuries) to empty her bladder, wash, and brush her teeth. Her escort? Although she had left her watch in the scrub room (could that be right?) she knew that it wasn't yet nine. Mother Teresa acting on her threat. After giving her short hair a quick brushing she packed (a two-minute procedure) and checked the desk for loose pens and papers. Mother Teresa opened the door without knocking and entered the room, escorted, she observed, by a native soldier with an automatic weapon. Pat.

"You are to follow me, Doctor," Mother Teresa said. "No, leave your things."

Outside in the compound the eleven nuns were lined up like some weird military unit in full field uniform standing at ease. Ten-shun. Port basins, order swabs. Off to one side, a little out of the picture, the convent porters and messengers knelt in an un-disciplined circle, their hands clasped behind their heads, guarded by more soldiers. Facing the nuns, an officer (obviously an officer) wearing a holstered pistol (yes, very much an officer). As she ap-proached him she thought, If he says, "Dr. Westlake, I presume," I'll spit in his eye. When she saw him smile she realized that she herself was smiling. Or was this the famous idiotic grin, a reflex of the palsied ego, that people took into such situations as the only weapon?

"Dr. Westlake, yes?"

"I'm Dr. Westlake, yes. And who, may I ask, are you?" She would bring it off, by God, she would. Dear Blessed Virgin, those children in their white tropical habits. No, no—

"Good. You do not panic."

"Am I expected to, Captain? Shoot me and you shoot my skills."

"No one is going to be shot, Doctor. Not even those—" He pointed at the crouching natives.

"Traitors, Captain? But if they're traitors how did you get into the compound without firing a shot?"

He came close to stare at her then, his deep-brown eyes with the yellow-shot whites (malaria?) against her (hot?) gray eyes with the white whites. "This is the face of your enemy, Doctor."

"And of our wounded patients, Captain."

"Very true, very true." He stepped back to speak to Mother Teresa, having, she observed, not challenged but simply assessed her. Or perhaps checked her against the information (it would be correct) he had been given. How accurate their statistics, how mendacious their assessments of the American temperament.

"Article one," the officer said to Mother Teresa, "we take with us all medicines and medical equipment." The pomposity of command did not cancel the threat or make the proposition ludicrous; it pointed up the simplicity of power and its naked application.

"Agreed to in principle," Mother Teresa said, "but only on this condition—that you leave us enough medicines and medical equipment to treat our patients till we can procure further supplies."

"To relieve you of such responsibility I propose to treat your patients myself. Article two, those who resist us will be shot immediately. That is, now."

"If you will permit me to talk to our people, Captain, I will urge the stupidity of resistance and order that none be offered. Provided that nothing beyond nonviolence be asked of them."

"Article three, we will take with us such of your personnel as we think will be useful to us."

"Only if those you select go with you freely and openly."

"And how would you enforce this unrealistic objection, Sister?"

"By leaving you no choice except to kill us, Captain."

"That I can do any time." The Captain removed an American-made forty-five from its holster and pointed it at Mother Teresa. "Now, if you wish."

"I have no wish to die, Captain."

"You will not suffer. One bullet—or don't you wish to be deprived of suffering?"

"Please—"

"The doctor. Yes. Your escort, Doctor, has been eliminated. We will take its place."

309

"I'm needed here, Captain. For the present."

"You must not waste my time, Doctor. I have said that I will take care of your patients." The Captain looked up at the small plane circling the area around the compound. "Your observation planes are out, Doctor. Next, your bombers. They have lost you Asia and will one day lose you South America."

"What personnel do you need, Captain?"

"You find the arts of indoctrination dull, Sister. In truth, so do I. I'll want your sturdier males—to act as porters—the strongest of your nurses, including your younger nuns. And, of course, the doctor."

"And if I refuse to go, Captain?"

"You must know how badly we need your skills, Doctor. Not only to heal—and this is very vital—but to teach."

"But if you have me why do you need the others?"

"I don't have you yet, Doctor. Which is the reason for this conference. Ordinarily, I don't dicker, I take."

"You can always kill me, Captain."

"Another offer to die. You talk like a nun, Doctor. I have had some experience with nuns. Years ago. But you must understand that I kill only for effect, never for pleasure, and never from anger. Anger is a waste of reason. Anger cannot build, it can only destroy. And I, Doctor, am a builder. But you must understand that I am willing to torture, burn, pillage, and kill when such tactics become necessary. And no one, Doctor, is too high, too low, too weak, too strong, too young, or too old to be excepted from this golden rule. The test is a simple one—is this person useful to our program? And how is he most useful, dead, half-dead, alive, half-alive, blind, hamstrung?"

"I will come with you freely and openly, Captain, provided you do not touch or abduct the others."

"By others you mean your fellow whites."

"I mean my fellow man."

"I could prove that you don't, Doctor, if I wished. However—" He pointed the pistol at Mother Teresa. "Do you wish to pray,

Sister? It will be simpler for me to shoot you in a kneeling position."

"I kneel to God, Captain, not to man."

"Bishop Key? He is no man?"

"A mark of respect for his office. Certainly not idolatry."

The Captain knocked Mother Teresa down with the pistol, a calm, thoughtful, and precise piece of business. "If you won't kneel, lie."

"I withdraw my objections, Captain. I will come with you. Willingly. But what do you gain by killing or abducting these nuns?"

"You see how easily your position can be changed, Doctor. You blow hot, you blow cold. And this is good. Very realistic. But you must not concern yourself with these priestesses. They have different rules. When I kill them I send them to—let me see—Paradise. But you, Doctor, what is your address in the next world?"

"They're strong, these women, because they believe in a loving, just, and merciful God. And, like you, Captain, they have a distinct, a unique program."

"Not all these women are strong, Doctor. Like you they will suddenly lose their faith in a loving, just, and merciful God—at the point of a bayonet."

"But I am not at the point of a bayonet, Captain. I hope to save lives that these nuns are prepared, if necessary, to lose."

The Captain pointed to one of the soldiers standing before the line of nuns. "The cord." Forcing Margaret to her knees the soldier put a cord around her neck and twisted it. She put her hands to the cord but did not pull at it. "Loosen it. We kill from necessity, Doctor, not from spite. I must know that you understand this, physically as well as intellectually." She nodded, trying to draw air through the constricted passage to her lungs. The Captain stepped forward and put a thumb to her left eye. "And this, Doctor?" She nodded. "You don't protest? No?" At a gesture from the Captain the soldier pushed her on her back and lay on top of her, his hands moving up under her skirt. She screamed then, pushed, twisted, shoved—till she became aware that the soldier had gotten up and that the Captain leaned over her, smiling and nodding, proud of his pupil as well as of his teaching skills. "You will serve now with no doubts and conditions, Doctor?"

"Yes."

"In whatever capacity I wish?"

"In whatever—" She lifted her hands. "With these, Captain."

"They are now, Doctor, the most useful part of your body. To us."

Seeing Mother Teresa trying to sit, Margaret got up to help her. A slight bump above the temple but no blood, at least none trickling from under the coif. The other nuns, patient, silent, only their eyes moving, watched, possibly having received a signal from their superior, possibly aware that any gesture of aid or comfort would be countered by physical assault.

"We will need registered nurses," the Captain said.

Every nun looked at her superior, each from a personal as well as a collective viewpoint. Dr. Westlake, unwilling to observe Mother Teresa too closely, saw no sign. Two nuns, however, stepped forward a pace and bowed slightly to the Captain.

"These are registered nurses, Sister?"

"They are."

"And the others?"

"There are six registered nurses in all, Captain."

"Six."

No one moved, no one spoke. Thirty seconds (she counted them in her heartbeats), a minute, two minutes. She had done what she could; now the others must accept what they must. There was nothing threatening in the Captain's appearance. He might have dozed, as soldiers do in periods of waiting, knees locked, arms moving imperceptibly to counter the limp sway of the torso, the lids half down on the eyes. The Captain clearly numbered and tested his choices. Which would prove the most useful? She believed him when he said he killed only from necessity, political as well as tactical. It would not do to argue the murderous doctrines of his politics or the crudeness of his tactics. He had a program. What advanced that program was good, what hampered or halted it was bad. A most pragmatic and endearing ethic, neither the worst in history nor the last.

Finally, after perhaps ten minutes, the Captain said, "You have been here before, Doctor?"

"Yes."

He stared at her hands. "And the others. What happened to them?"

"One has had to be confined—a working confinement—one died in childbirth, the others survived."

"I was only a common soldier then and the experience meant nothing to me. Actually, I only pretended to participate. I consider the use of whores a degenerate practice. A companion, yes, but—"

"You separate yourself, Captain. Isn't that a sin against your ideology?"

"You can't lift others to your level by descending to theirs, Doctor." He smiled at her. "You think us inhuman? Or nonhuman?"

"My son is human, Captain. That is all I ask."

"Very practical." He turned to Mother Teresa. "The doctor and these two, Sister. And your male orderlies."

As she learned later from Captain Quong (the only name he gave her, the title replacing or dominating the Oriental Sam or Joe or Theodore), the tribal chiefs, in return for a promise that their villages would not be burned or their men shot, had yielded the convent to Quong's raiding party. Some weeks later their villages *were* burned and their men *were* shot (those men who didn't escape into the mountains), but that was in retaliation for giving forced succor to government troops, another act entirely. The march to the border took only two days, the trails having been freshly cut for the expedition by forced labor, which also set up the hospital in the neutral country across the river. The main attack, Quong explained, would come from the north, but there would be continuous activity along the border in both company and battalion strength.

The two nuns, Sister Cecilia and Sister Barbara, who had

changed into army fatigues and heavy shoes, were offered both respect and kindness, possibly because Quong had explained to his soldiers that the white devils had become their white sisters. The whiteness of their bodies when exposed at toilet enchanted and amused the soldiers. To put a stop to this childish voyeurism Quong had the two nuns strip to their underwear and show their skins to his men. The tan faces and the hands were like the markings of, say, a species of baboon, causing some distress and unease among the soldiers, as well as admiring laughter. No sexual advances were made, in either sign language or direct physical contact.

"It is hard on them," Quong said to the doctor, "but they are soldiers, and abstinence is a part of the soldier's life. Once we establish a permanent base we'll be able to bring in teams of whores occasionally to give them some relief. Masturbation is forbidden and must be confessed, but it goes on and we don't try very hard to stop it. Sodomy is punishable by death, but it, too, is practiced, mostly on long patrols and on duty in remote places where there are no women."

To her astonishment Quong did not try to indoctrinate her. He spoke to her as his intellectual equal, confided in her, asked her advice in the construction and layout of the hospital. He wanted to be an engineer, but because of continuous military service and advancement he had not been able to study as intensively as he thought he should. Her first operating room was a tent, her second a long shed open at the sides and divided into sections by partitions of bamboo and grass mats. She wanted the operating room sealed and detached from the wards, but Quong, charming and pliable on most issues, refused. "You must wait for a permanent building," he said.

The number of casualties appalled her. Yet she knew she never saw the very badly wounded. Those cases were diagnosed in the field and treated with great speed and efficiency. Operating twelve hours a day with her two nun-nurses, she had little time for reflection, none at all for nostalgia. The abdominal cases disposed once and for all of the famous theory of the Oriental indifference to death. The usual anesthetic was a half-bottle of rice wine or, when available, the powder from a root she suspected might be a native cousin of Rauwolfia. She also used the blood of the soldiers and the laborers, and even tapped the teams of whores sent down from the north at bimonthly intervals. It testified to the practicality of the regime that everyone of any significance, including the joy girls, knew his or her blood type.

One day, after she had treated three cases of syphilis, she showed Quong an open can of penicillin. "Contaminated," she said. "Cut with some kind of powder, root, or stalk."

"Exactly, Doctor. American."

"Shipped from America, sold in the black market, opened by your people, cut, and resealed."

"Can it be used?"

"Not by me, Captain. Or my nurses."

"I'll report it, Doctor. That's all I can do."

She had learned to read his round face, and what she saw there now saddened her. Though he could be pompous, orotund, magniloquent, he was no demagogue. He did not fear his doubts, he detested them.

"This is the face of your enemy, Doctor."

Of course. But it was also, she reminded herself, the face of God, a notorious fact, she was glad to see, that both Sister Barbara and Sister Cecilia understood.

Quartered with the two of them in a small tattered tent, she exacted, in the beginning, the respect properly accorded a medical doctor by nurses. Sister Barbara, a big handsome woman with enormous breasts, which she bound grimly every morning and loosed with a belly sigh every night, had the outgoing nature of her physical type and a pungent sense of humor. Sister Cecilia, slighter, something of a mystic, with a fine hawk's head, kept well within herself till she felt she was needed and then gave of that cool self with dedication and strength. She could not be certain that either of them knew she had been a nun (that scene in the compound with Quong), but she learned very quickly that revelations and comment would have to come from her. Clearly, they admired her skills. And they thanked her for teaching them, as she operated, what they could do not in her absence but in her stead. Like her they demanded of themselves a spontaneous and ungrudging service that could not be defined as love (though it was certainly passion) and would not be contained in charity.

Why had these two volunteered for this outrageous appointment? She could not have said, though she knew. Not I, but I in Christ. And not in the mystical Christ (yet that, too), but in the Man-God Jesus, flesh born of flesh to act out a knowledge of suffering that God knew but must show, to His skeptical and officious children, that He felt. For without a visceral god no salvation is possible. Diffident at first about praying in her presence, the two nuns, at her urging, recited their offices and prayers at length in the evening, briefly in the morning, at any time at all during the day. Though they could not observe the canonical hours, they could recognize their passage by short whispered prayers, over perhaps an amputation or an extracted bullet. Infection and not sin was the enemy. Without electricity they constructed charcoal pits over which they hung great iron kettles for a steady supply of boiling water. Quong, at her suggestion, taught the dozen old men and women who had come out of the jungle to live off the invaders to make soap and candles.

"Where," she asked Quong, "are the nurses I'm supposed to be training?"

"You have men, Doctor. Later I will find you women."

One afternoon Quong brought her an emaciated American flier his men had found lying in a stupor near one of the semihidden trails leading north, a simple case of exhaustion. As she examined him he stared at her dully, as if comprehension had been accomplished but could not be expressed. When she visited him briefly the next day, accompanied by Sister Barbara, he refused to answer her questions.

"Name, rank, and serial number, Doctor, that's all you get from me."

"I'm not sure that I want anything else, Major."

She nodded at the guard by the bed. "He has orders to shoot if you attempt to escape. And he can't be bribed."

"You, Doctor, are the lowest thing I have yet encountered in my young life. And I've seen them low and slimy."

"You can talk, then."

"I'll talk a lot when I get back to my outfit. Dr. Margaret Westlake. I'll remember."

"Would you please remember me, Major?" Sister Barbara added. "I'm Sister Barbara of the Order of the Sisters of St. Luke. My diocesan superior is Bishop Key."

"Christ," the young Major said. "Oh, sweet Jesus Christ." And he began to cry.

Later, Sister Barbara said that she had tried to explain the complexities of their position but that the Major, who saw what he saw and knew what he knew, could not be persuaded to re-examine his viewpoint.

"Perhaps you weren't too convincing, Sister."

"I'm serving the children of God, Doctor, where God placed them. That's all I ask."

"You are also betraying your country, Sister."

"I know." Sister Barbara smiled. "Isn't it dreadful? Sometimes I feel so ashamed of myself. And then I see those awful wounds and those poor brave men suffering under our supposedly healing hands. We kill as many as we save."

"On the other hand, Sister, we save as many as we kill. Neither you nor Sister Cecilia seems to miss your habit."

"We're the new breed, Doctor. You'll be hearing more of us in the future. Because we're coming after you, and you can't stop us. Dear, dear, I'm proselytizing. And it isn't necessary, not at all."

"I think this has gone far enough."

Sister Barbara took her hand and kissed it. "I know a believer when I see one, Doctor. And so does Sister Cecilia. Well, here comes a fresh consignment of beef."

After three and a half months, after a second light shelling by American mortars from across the river, Quong moved the hospital north.

"You would think that the American observation planes had reported the crosses painted on our roofs and tents."

"Probably rogue pilots, Captain. Anyway, we're close enough to the border for all kinds of military mistakes."

"But how can they violate this country's neutrality?"

"Well, aren't we?"

"Give and take, Doctor, give and take. No, here we're all right. But a few miles farther inland—"

She saw his point. And she was not at all astonished that he ordered the immovable wounded placed just across the river under the guard of the forced labor.

"The Americans will take care of them, Doctor. Of course, if our imperialist brothers find them first—" The two nuns offered to stay with the abandoned wounded, promising that they would follow Quong later, provided he blazed a trail for them.

"You'll excuse me, Sisters, if I say that I don't understand this aspect of the American character."

"You know that we cannot lie to you, Captain," Sister Cecilia said. Seeing that she had offended him, she added, "I do beg your pardon, Captain."

"You chose, Sister. I honor your choice. To release you now would be a most grave disservice to you. Come."

On the route north they passed a giant chain of porters, each of which carried his weight in matériel. They also passed combat units, trucks, and lighter vehicles. Once they were stopped by an officer obviously superior to Quong who pointed to the two nuns and the doctor and nodded toward the troops he commanded. Quong, vehemently deferent, argued in a dialect she could understand very little of, a man solid in the righteous possession of valuable articles and unmoved by another's anxiety to share them. Glancing at the two nuns, the oblique flick of the eye that mastered so much for so little obtrusiveness, she saw that they understood the subject of the conversation and that they had withdrawn into that semicontemplative state where the conscience searches itself while continuously being fed information by the alerted ego. No, you do not know what you will do, you cannot know what you will do—and, worse, you dare not visualize what you may be forced to do. Your throat is always ready for the knife of Jesus but your eye (external or intuitive) is rarely focused to recognize it. What, she thought, would she do? With the kiss of Sister Barbara on her hand and the shy smile of Sister Cecilia in her heart, she knew very well what she ought to do and felt, with a cutting sincerity, that she might very well do it.

But the incident closed itself with the saliva of the superior officer on Quong's face and the sullen passage of the combat unit. Quietly, she took and pressed Quong's hand and kissed the damp cheek, taking on her lips, she hoped, the savage cut of the rebuke and the immediate pain of Quong's humiliation, well aware, of course, that he might shoot her and the two nuns or place them precisely in the category or class the superior officer had instantaneously proposed for them. He did nothing, beyond lower his head and turn away from her. Except that he did not interpret her action as a desire for physical intimacy. Or perhaps he did and was ashamed of her for offering such a detestable gift, the lewd indecently popping up through her surgical skills to remind him after all of the fatty sentimentality of humanity and its infantile urges to please itself. It might have been that turning away he, she, and the two nuns executed with grace and ease (and no comment) when a soldier, his body outraged and corrupted by a willful and unnatural continence, stepped off the trail during P halt to relieve himself, first dreamily, then savagely. In God's order, room for man's disorder.

Twice they were attacked by American fighter-bombers, once massively, a hideous fifteen minutes in a centrifuge of steel and fire. Only one soldier was killed outright, five suffered superficial wounds. Though opium and its derivatives were available in quantity, Quong refused to use them except in extreme cases. "The poppy," he explained, "is for export." They came, finally, after ten days, to a plateau in a low range of hills, one that reminded her of another in which she had lived and suffered. In the center of the raw bulldozed earth stood a hospital complex perhaps three-quarters finished, a gift, Quong said, "from our good neighbors to the north." On examination the buildings themselves seemed firm enough, the machinery workable, but the supplies— "I estimate we have a year's supply of tongue depressors but not a single bed sheet," she said to Quong. "Furthermore, while we have over a hundred carts, none of them are usable. There are no nuts to hold the wheels on the axles."

"We'll flatten the ends of the axles with a hammer, Doctor."

"I've spoken to the architect. He refuses to use lead shielding in the X-ray rooms."

"Unnecessary, Doctor. We have immense supplies of human material."

"Trained?"

"We'll make use of what we've been issued."

"Good. We'll convert the stomach pumps we have in storage to retractors, which we don't have in storage."

Quong spoke to the commissar in political charge of the construction. The commissar, a smiler who spoke English in bursts of three or four words, assured her that in a few weeks the hospital would be fully stocked with the most modern conveniences of the finest quality. She pointed out that the only bathrooms she had seen were equipped with urinals. After he had finally understood her complaint he said, "All use same bathroom. Any further questions?"

"These complaints, Doctor," Quong said, "are not worthy of your genius. You are here to help us, not to criticize us."

She apologized, explaining that all medical doctors, especially surgeons, function by demanding the impossible, both of men and of material. She had observed before that while he could detect sarcasm, he could recognize neither wit nor irony. In time the proper supplies did arrive and, with them, the first corps of student nurses. Expecting reserve and hostility, she found instead great respect and eagerness to learn. As Quong said, "They love the American people, Doctor, especially those that come to help. You, Doctor, are the great volunteer. They worship you." Aware of Quong's insularity and geographical and observational limitations, she saw that he spoke the truth. The great question—"Are there no graves in Egypt that thou has led us out into the wilderness to die?"—burst into fragments, a stone struck shrewdly and sharply, she realized, by the hammer of God, a revelation she rejected consciously but one that embedded itself in her gut, a most benevolent and useful tenant.

In the second year of her residence at the hospital, Sister Cecilia, who in addition to her nursing duties taught children and adult evening classes, died of a particularly virulent form of malaria for which the Orient at least had not yet established a proper course of treatment. Sister Barbara read the service over her grave; the hospital's chief carpenter made a wooden cross that no one objected to, neither Buddhist nor atheist nor Quong himself. Dr. Westlake and Sister Barbara, along with several promising student teachers, took over Sister Cecilia's classes, extending their workday from sixteen to eighteen hours. Quong's dictum, a paraphrase of Mao's famous indiscretion—"Let a hundred nurses bloom"—sufficed for Sister Cecilia's epitaph and justified the longer workday.

Sometimes, pacing the terrace outside the solarium for a fifteen-minute break in her schedule, Dr. Westlake would stare over the low range of hills to the southwest, as if at a forgotten anchorage, and remind herself that she was a prisoner pressed into labor as well as a doctor giving aid and comfort to the enemy, and that while the first could be rationalized and accepted, the second could not. Except that it so clearly was. Undoubtedly, she was doing one hell of a job, so good, in fact, that Quong spoke of a decoration, perhaps, she thought, the order of the pot-holder with moist palms. Where was her discontent, human, semihuman, semidivine, divine? She did not demand of herself an accounting of her satisfactions and accomplishments; she asked, Where, Doctor, are your frustrations? Sexually, she either did not exist or existed so fully in her work that this dynamic power-complex fulfilled itself, converting the energy it created into the fuel it consumed. She saw her nature so delicately balanced on itself that she was no longer aware of it. She had found the climate, by whatever incredible and dishonorable means, for which the Church and her ordeal (and her stubborn and irreconcilable selves) had conditioned her. The hand that im-

pelled her, that rank and terrible paw, could be either God's or
Satan's. Or one laid on the other in tandem push, with just
enough of an overlap to make the image valid. She did not care,
that was the point, for angelic beast or bestial angel—let John
Milton with his exquisite tensions decide.

Or Father Serrano, that beautiful man-priest, who had returned
to her thoughts lately. His letters, more than Monsignor Kramer's
manipulations, saw her through medical school, his insights into
the commingling of flesh and spirit sustained her. He had not re-
converted her; he had not intended to. He had reassured her, in
secular or philosophical rather than religious terms, that is, rather
than the familiar Catholic language. "Man," he had written, "is a
religious animal. His politics stem from a passion either to embrace
God or to reject Him. I assume, you see, that God is a staple. His
Presence is a fact; His definitions are the theories." She understood
that this was a prologue with which, on her own, she would have
to provoke a second, possibly a third, act. In the human experience
a dialogue is a speaking tube speaking to a speaking tube. The
ear is there, but atrophied through disuse. In offering this idea
Father Serrano apologized for his skepticism. "That and an indifference to medical doctors have kept me alive to question that
and an indifference to medical doctors. I say that the more gently
one treats one's brothers, the more response one can expect from
them. A kick is often answered by a pulling in of the horns, help-
lessness responding to power. But a kiss, a pat, a hug, is answered—
and rightly—by a knife in the chest or evisceration. Between the
two falls the shadow of God—shall I say a Christian God, the Son
crystallizing the unutterable and unreachable majesty? Does this
sound brutal? Perhaps. But there is little tenderness in truth. What
tenderness there is lies in our response to truth."

"The shadow of God." Precisely. Not a shield, but a gauze
curtain; not lead, but paper; not a turmoil of invincible atoms, but
a darker, thinner, penetrable breath. This unlikely correspondence
she saw later as a tapering-off process, the addict to be given smaller
and smaller doses of his drug till he could function successfully
without it. Yet when Father Serrano spoke of the "romance of the

missionary" he spoke to a hunger that surpassed addiction, that hunger for excellence that may be traced to a neurosis but cannot be reduced to or confined by it. Science cannot describe the Amazon by giving an astonished planet the chemical formula for water, nor can Menninger forfeit the works of hairy and smelly saints by pointing out that these bearers of sanctity had in common a hatred of the mother. No, her training as a scientist could never quite demolish her respect for the all-for-nothing life Father Serrano had suffered in Africa, for, as he put it, "personal glory, my dear Margaret. Here, at the church and the mission, I suffer not at all and accomplish far more. I have learned to distinguish between dedication and commitment, the two poles of the religious, and find in commitment the riches I demanded—and didn't get—from dedication." Precisely. Dedication is the intent, commitment the action. Once committed, as she felt she was not committed, the liturgical routines and contemplation could be discarded. At the peril of her soul, of course. Again, precisely. Because that and nothing else is the definition of human life at its most acute and most perceptive. "You are already lost, my child." Yes. Had she the arrogance to do the Divine Shepherd out of His job?

By the end of the second year the war had intensified. Or, in the new jargon, escalated. She put on her gown and operated, sometimes for eighteen and twenty hours without rest, a cigarette intermittently held for her by a nurse while she changed gown and gloves during a short recess. Cut, probe, extract, stitch. Next? Napalm burns. Or a shredded leg to be amputated above the knee. Or a case of a missing jaw. As she operated, she could hear the giant steps of bombs coming toward the plateau and feel the floor in sympathetic vibration to the powerful foot. The Americans were after the storage depots and bridges to the east, laying their bombs as accurately as a hen its eggs. "Do they know this is a hospital?" she asked Quong.

"Yes. And they know we have their fliers here."

She had been presented with her second American flier a few weeks earlier, at the beginning of the bombings, and then another only the day before—the one in traction with a compound fracture of the right femur, the other nastily pierced by the tines of a farmer's fork. Visiting the guarded ward set aside for them, she conducted her examinations as quickly as possible and spoke only when necessary. The boy in traction, a Captain John, had questioned Sister Barbara but had said nothing at all to the doctor. He looked at her, looked away, answered her few questions with grunts and monosyllables, and seemed ashamed not of her but of himself. Quong's presence apparently inhibited him. On a day when she came without Quong and without Sister Barbara he said abruptly, "You're not an Oriental."

"No."

"Then what are you doing here?"

"Hasn't Sister Barbara told you?"

"You're really a prisoner?"

"Technically, yes."

He nodded at the heavily sedated flier next him. "He's in bad shape, Doctor."

"Does he bother you, Captain?"

"Call him lucky. Are they going to hang me with this leg or without it?"

"I shouldn't think they'd hang you, Captain."

"Decapitation?"

"I don't know. Is that any comfort to you?"

He lit a cigarette, quite steadily, she noted. "You wouldn't give me a little pill, would you? In case."

"No."

"Against your principles, Doctor?"

"I believe you'd be happier following the consequences of your actions to their logical ends."

"Communism."

"Oh, no, Captain. Christianity."

"How did they do it, torture? Or did they just talk to you?"

"Why don't you ask Captain Quong?"

"You're safe enough, Doctor. But I don't think I'd want that kind of safety."

"Are you afraid you may have to choose it, Captain?"

"I said I don't want that kind of safety."

"Then why did you ask for the little pill?"

"You're a doctor, you figure it out."

"I think you're more afraid of giving in than you are of dying. But whom would you be giving in to, your captors or yourself?"

"Don't pin me down. What the hell, I'm not a specimen."

"There's your fear, Captain, that you may be."

He stared at her. "What kind of lousy remark is that?"

"I'll ask you one, Captain. Shall I have Sister Barbara pray with you?"

He put down the cigarette and shut his eyes. "I don't know much about your patients, Doctor, but you've just lost one."

"That means you're getting well, Captain, that's all."

"Shove off. You're breathing my air."

In the mirror of the scrub room she noticed that she was smiling. She had shaken young Captain John, she felt that she could talk to him, she felt that she *wanted* to talk to him. Had she regained the human touch? Modify that. Gained, since she could hardly regain what she had never had to lose. Behind her the native nurses, those she herself had trained, prepared themselves to assist her. Sister Barbara, now, there was the human touch. A squeeze, a pat, a hug—or a smile, a nod, a hand gesture—she knew exactly which to administer when. The new breed. Or the old. Think of the marvelous humanity of, say, Mother Vincent. True, only rarely physically expressed, but there, copious and enduring, even in rebuke. Still, seeing the smiles in the mirror, clearly in return for her own, she decided that she had scored an important point. Or had it been scored in spite of her, she rushing toward the basket where she herself stood in defense, the ball moving upward over the great hands to bounce against the backboard and drop through the net?

Dear God, that statue of the nun in the graveyard. The oversize hands. Was *that* what the artist intended? She warned herself against the stultifying clichés of sentimentalism. Her badge, she told herself primly, was service. Now that she no longer smiled, the smiles in the mirror would be gone. But she was afraid to check. Or, no, she was afraid to let her nurses see her face. She did not want to see it either. Something had entered it that should not have, not something from outside her, but something very much inside her, the thing, the— She bent over the sink, washing, scrubbing, gnarling her body into one great resistant fist. The attack, however, the revolt, the rebellion, came from within, thrusting from the center outward, putting the faltering provinces of her body to the torch. The Rose, the Rose, fiery and incensed—Lord, I am not worthy—Lord, I am not worthy—Lord, I am not— The lines of science held for a moment and then broke, the accusatory "a full-blown psychosis" blasted as it formed.

Lord, I am not worthy—Lord, I am not— Yes, well, there was the patient in whose abdomen she probed for the piece of metal that lay just beyond the retractors, the sponges, the clamps— She heard the giant stepping toward the plateau, each step a nearer explosion, and saw Quong's face briefly over the table between her and Sister Barbara—his violation of the sanctity of the operating room shocked her. The altar of God to be desecrated twice in her small lifetime? An attack by American bombers? So? She shook him off, as a puppy shakes off water, jerking her head to indicate that the giant had crossed the plateau and would not be back. When he returned, step by step, she was so deep inside her patient that she refused to hear him, the last of her major dissents and the one she could neither dissemble nor plead.

In What Stream?

CHAPTER XXXI

THOMAS PAUL KRAMER, AUXILIARY BISHOP of Los Angeles, had been in Rome only thirty-one hours when the call came from the villa of Ottavio Cardinal Bellini. Would Monsignor Kramer be so kind? My privilege, Monsignor Vassallo. His Eminence usually receives important visitors in the late afternoon, after a short nap. Would Monsignor Kramer defer to the Cardinal's wishes in the matter? Monsignor Kramer would. Vassallo. So Cinotti was gone, possibly to a higher post. Good. Kramer had never liked Cinotti. He had not disliked the man, no, but there had been that in Cinotti's character, a definite strain of cynicism—or, no, not cynicism. How should he put it, to be exact? Yes, Cinotti was a man who knew his place a little too well.

After a brief audience with the Pope, a new pope, who did not seem too interested in California, Kramer looked up his old friend Monsignor Arturo Licciardi, still bony and ugly, still occupying a niche in Giorgio Cardinal Andreani's Congregation of Religious.

"Your Excellency is looking very well these days," Licciardi said. "Very photographic."

"A little fat, would you say, Arturo?"

"Most impressive. That touch of gray—"

"The first frost."

Licciardi laughed. "No, I'm very pleased to see you, Tom. You carry authority very well."

"What there is of it to carry, Arturo."

They spoke of old times, as old friends will do, till Licciardi, with his fine Roman sense of what to sacrifice to the clock and what to preserve for the calendar, said that he was leaving for Prague the day after tomorrow but that if there was anything he could do to enliven his friend's stay in Rome—

"Prague?"

"Well, Athens, really. But if there's something you'd like in Lisbon, Tom—"

Kramer laughed, acknowledging Licciardi's perception but annoyed by its presentation. "Still the naïve American, Arturo. As you see."

"Only a small man would refuse to become his office, Tom. And you *are* your office."

"Leaving aside the tailored clericals and the silver cigarette case."

"Externals, Tom. And very proper ones. I suppose you'll be paying your respects to his Eminence Cardinal Bellini. Or have you?"

"I shall, of course, call on his Eminence. If he'll receive me. I've heard he isn't very well."

"Nearly ninety. When he submitted his offer to retire to the Holy Father—have you heard the story?"

"Arturo, the States are another world."

"It's said his Eminence made a gesture only and wasn't too pleased to have it so promptly—though graciously—accepted. No, the old hawk isn't at all well. But then, it's a marvel he isn't dead."

"Is the bite still there, Arturo?"

"On occasion, yes. Depending on the issues. If you want to pass the time with him you'll find him—according to gossip—little more than a vegetable. But if you bring him something raw and red—bloody, Tom—in your talons—"

Kramer could think, in the Vatican limousine that took him to the old Cardinal's villa, that despite Licciardi's gently ironic jibe at a man becoming his office he, Kramer, *had* become his office. Simply to assume an office or to represent one without pouring yourself into the mold readied for you by your predecessors is a piece of false humility, a breaking of your promise to uphold the duties of a position assigned to you by your superiors in full expectation that you are the man—and the one man—fittest for the job. Nevertheless, he could use Licciardi's flawless sense of time as well as his depthless view of history. He remembered once, years ago, asking Licciardi (jokingly, of course) what had become of the Romans. "Very simple, Tom," Licciardi had said. "They became the Italians."

Getting out of the car at the rear entrance of the villa, Kramer stood for a moment facing the three shallow steps leading to the portico and then turned, as if by a suggestion planted years earlier, and walked the depth of the building to a place from which he could see (he trusted, unobserved) the great staircase with its thirty-seven stone steps. He had bled on those steps, more, he thought resentfully, than Cardinal Bellini knew, more, perhaps, to be truthful, than he himself knew. Enough, enough. He had climbed those steps once—in a certain position. He need not climb them again—in any position.

Monsignor Vassallo, a younger priest than he had expected, escorted him up the stairs to the Cardinal's bedroom, leaving him at the door. "His Eminence's nurses are across the hall," Vassallo said. "Should you need them, knock." Entering the Cardinal's bedroom, Kramer walked the distance between door and bed on one breath and knelt to kiss the Cardinal's hand, a piece of business that might have impressed Bellini, but who could tell? The old hawk had become the old mosquito, the great nose rising above the terminal cheeks not like a beak but like a stinger. Bellini lay with a pillowed bolster at his spine, at an angle that put Kramer three-quarters back from the headboard of the bed with his right leg touching the coverlet.

"Very thoughtful of you to accept my invitation, Thomas," the old Cardinal said.

Thomas? "I'm very glad to see your Eminence, particularly looking so well."

Kramer did not want to open up until he saw what he had to deal with, an old man's sentimentality and petulance, a broken memory, disconnected thoughts, or simply a physical and mental fatigue. Or, possibly, a sharp and contentious challenge from one too close to death to consult the feelings of the living. He could not say that he would have called on the old Cardinal without an invitation or sent a card or telephoned his secretary. And how had

Bellini known he was in Rome? Kramer's patron, Cardinal Brooker, would certainly have sent a note or have given Kramer a letter to deliver by hand, but Brooker was dead and the new man neither well known in Rome nor well connected. Nor, for that matter, well attached to his auxiliary bishop. Still, time, time—

"On the table, Thomas, a letter. From Bishop Key. Perhaps you ought to read it."

"As your Eminence wishes." He picked up the folded paper and began to read it.

"The news of Dr. Westlake's heroic death has not yet been released to the public. Perhaps it never will be released. In detail. And I'm not sure that it should be. In detail."

"This doesn't say much, does it?"

"A simple announcement. Bishop Key is a cautious man, not inclined toward sensation. The Mother Superior, however, of the convent where Sister Esther once served—" Bellini suddenly switched from Italian to Latin, as if the latter were the required language for the subject he wished now to discuss—"wrote me a long, long report that I intend sealing and placing in my files. I'm thinking of putting your name on the envelope, Thomas. After my death, which should come reasonably soon, you shall read this report and decide what to do with it."

"Your Eminence puts too high a value on my judgment."

"No, no, Thomas. This is a confession of weakness, not a pejorative estimate of your powers of reasoning. I feel that I—in my present state of health—am not competent to judge this report fairly or dispose of it with the proper imagination and courage."

Had he walked into a trap? The mind that scanned him from behind that death mask had certainly not lost its edge, at least for a short interview.

"Does his Holiness know of Dr. Westlake's death?"

"You hearten me, Thomas. When I ask where are the future leaders of the Church I see you ransacking the closets of power with just that mixture of insolence, deference, and boldness which always marks the coming man. What is needed, Thomas, if one does not have the strength of the lion—or the opportunity or position to

332

use such strength—is the tenacity of the rat. I do not say the character of the rat, I say the tenacity."

"The rat, Eminence, is a rodent."

"And the eagle, Thomas, is a bird. Have you not wished now and then for its eyesight?" Bellini spoke in Italian. "I am a dying man."

"We are all dying men—" Nothing to do now except acknowledge Bellini's maneuver. "I beg your Eminence's pardon."

"For what, Thomas?"

"For insulting him with this unctuous platitude." Would that be enough?

"For the present, yes."

It took Kramer a valuable moment to realize that Bellini had answered his thought rather than his apology. But why should the old predator bother?

"This Mother Superior, Eminence—"

"A most knowledgeable and perceptive woman, Thomas. In her report she states that she told Dr. Westlake that Sister Esther used her ordeal as an excuse to renounce her vows rather than as a proof that she was unworthy of them. Had you this charming insight?"

"I thought I knew Sister Esther better than that, Eminence. As for Margaret Westlake, I can say that having procured entrance for her into medical school I felt that my job was done. But I can say this: her intelligence, perseverance, and character astonished and impressed everyone she came in contact with. Unfortunately, she refused to fly the Catholic pennant."

"Which pennant did she fly, then, Thomas?"

"Such powerful questions ought not to be answered without divine guidance."

"Which you lack?" Bellini grimaced, perhaps in pain. "Have I said that Dr. Westlake died the heroic death?"

"I believe so, Eminence."

"Good. But you realize, Thomas, that without Sister Esther this death would have little meaning."

"To rush into death like a young girl to the arms of her lover is hardly heroic, Eminence. Romantic, yes."

"I have a romantic spirit, Thomas. I depend on you to sober it when it reels through the cosmos unchecked and unnoticed. Nevertheless, Dr. Westlake's achievement impresses me. She had only two years. In this short time she made herself a legend among a people who have no reason to love Americans and every reason to hate them."

"A legend, Eminence?"

"An exact statement, Thomas, not hyperbole or the metaphor of an old romantic. Her trial this time was hardly as spectacular as the first, but it sufficed." Bellini gave Kramer a brief sketch of Dr. Westlake's two years in the peninsula. "We have, you might say, an eyewitness. A one-legged nun who survived the bombing of the hospital and was released by her captors, probably to secure a prosthetic device unavailable in the north. She babbles of a promise to return north. According to her, Dr. Westlake, though ordered to the basement by her captors, refused to leave the operating room, probably because her patient was a farmer with American shrapnel in his belly. Thomas, when I received this news I cried. Joy for the soiled but unconquerable spirit, grief for the heinous but skillful flesh. Then I felt such an intense exasperation—not really anger— that I put myself to bed. To conserve my strength for the spiritual vigil I intend holding in Sister Esther's honor."

"May I point out that his Eminence's health will not permit such a vigil?"

"His Eminence's health will last long enough for his Eminence to clean the dust off his soul. That's the curse of administration, Thomas. In the precise embraces of statistics and numbers one forgets the inexactness of the human touch, its badly distributed pressures, its crude power, its claws, its hairiness, its bad smell. There is another thing—Dr. Westlake was a traitor to her country. She defected, Thomas, as she defected from the Church."

"May I question Dr. Westlake's spiritual state at the time of her death, Eminence?"

"You'd like to hear that God as well as the State Department had revoked her passport. Or perhaps only to hear that she begged God to forgive her killers or rose to the dignity of that marvelous line "into Thy Hands I commend my spirit," a line that once electrified the world but that now does not have the power to light a single candle on the altar of God."

"Your Eminence is ill."

"That, I think, is an even more wonderful line. You dismiss a truth by discounting its speaker, as if the bearer of a truth must be worthy of what he delivers. You attended the death of Socrates, Thomas, and you were certainly a spectator on the Hill of Skulls. In you I behold myself. But however much we revere Sister Esther, there is still Dr. Westlake. No, we have evidence that she died as stubbornly and as hardheadedly as she had lived. With her hands in her patient's abdomen rather than in his pockets." The old Cardinal shut his eyes, as if to conserve his energy.

"But we cannot know this, Eminence." Kramer had begun to sweat. "She may have refused God's sacraments, pronouncing herself unworthy to receive them. But have we any proof that she refused His mercy?"

After a moment Bellini opened his eyes. He seemed to have difficulty speaking. "It was I who urged on you the possibility of the odor of sanctity, Thomas. Will you throw it back in my face?"

"I say we cannot know or dare believe that she died unreconciled to her Redeemer. There are her actions."

"Always, Thomas. But they are quite outside our jurisdiction. Are we to canonize the Department of Public Works because it keeps our streets clean? And if, as you say, she ran to her death like a girl to her lover, what is the Church to make of this?"

What precisely had the old Cardinal in mind? Since we can't have it more than one way, Kramer decided, we must accept that way and forgo speculation and theological quibbles. Besides, he was more than a little annoyed by the old man's hammerheaded sarcasms and more than a little repelled by the old man himself. Should he mention that the room stank of corruption and bodily functions? Of bad breath, strange oozings, and flatulence? And was Bellini aware of those little rumblings inside his sagging gut? "I can only plead the reverse of Dr. Westlake's cause, Eminence, to prove to myself—and to others"—he could not control the rise of voice—"that Sister Esther can now be wiped off the Church's rolls like a name chalked on a blackboard."

"Or like a symbol on a gravestone?" The old Cardinal moved his eyes toward the table under the windows. "There is a gift sent me from the Far East, Thomas. Through Bishop Key. One of the officers who captured and detained Dr. Westlake, or one of my powerful brothers, thought I might be grateful to have these souvenirs of her activities. In the service of her country's enemies. The note was brief, the sentiment cool, the message clearly understated."

"Her cross?" Impelled by the Cardinal's stare, Kramer went to the table and opened the lid of a wooden container the size and shape of a shoe box. Bellini would have his theatrics. "Christ in Hell." Kramer backed away from the box and fell against the bed. "What savages!"

"What poets. Notice that it is her scalpel, the final symbol of her usefulness, and not her cross, that lies in the rack of thumb and forefinger." Kramer slipped to his knees, a hand on the bed, the safe position. "Has she touched you at long last, Thomas?"

"She lives—"

"A common hallucination. You see her now quite plainly. In a moment she will be gone."

"Never—"

"She has sunk her teeth into your heart, Thomas. And into mine. Is it possible she withdrew from the Church to spare it the embarrassment of her martyrdom?"

"It's even more possible that I, in my ignorance and pride, drove her from the Church."

"But not from God, Thomas. She is hardly an ox to be goaded peaceably from one pasture to another."

"Is, Eminence?"

"Her people—mind you, her country's enemies—think she is very much alive. As do many friendly to her country. Should some extraordinary event fan this strong and sullen spark we might yet have annoying proof of Sister Esther's vitality. In which case your agitation is premature."

336

"I ask only that it arrive in time to enlighten me."

"Now who is being romantic?"

"I begin to question myself, Eminence."

"A test you will pass *magna cum laude*. No, if you want less than a score of perfect, question God."

"I must know, Eminence—did you smell the odor of sanctity?"

"The proper question, Thomas, is, was it there to smell?"

"But surely, Eminence, from your immense experience—?"

"In such cases as these, Thomas, we have no experience, we have only noses. And very short ones at that. But why such stupendous remorse? The militant spirit fires itself on adversity. She did not choose to crawl to salvation or its flaming opposite, a stand we must honor. Take a spark from this spirit, Thomas, don't try to quench it with your tears."

"I burn to know, Eminence."

"You will burn whether you know or not, Thomas, in this world and very probably in the next. Why not pray for her? This is all we know of wisdom—and all we need of love—to pray—" Bellini shut his eyes, perhaps because he had nothing more to say, perhaps because he had a great deal to say but lacked the means to say it, perhaps because his old man's body had shut the gate on a hunter's mind that had shot down—and bagged—the hostile and implacable wing of every error that flew in its preserve and at last had lowered its gun on a perfectly empty field. Silenced by this majestic withdrawal, Kramer left the room.

On the first floor, attended by the Cardinal's secretary, Vassallo, Kramer indicated that he would leave by the front door. The thirty-seven steps descended before him, a majestic fall, one worthy of his oscillating bones. He had climbed up them on his knees, he could climb down them on his knees. Or, no, no. The time for such gestures had passed—and would come again—but it was not now. "Lord, I am not worthy that Thou shouldst come under my roof, but speak the word only and my soul shall be healed." Yes, the best way to meet your God face to face is to turn your back on Him, to place yourself in a position to see not the object of your adoration, but the subject of His attention.

337

Which is always less than perfect, and, being human, never less than foul. Had God washed His hands after He created Adam? And, if so, in what stream? Kramer got into the limousine and permitted himself to be driven back to the Vatican. Such questions were important—perhaps necessary—at least relevant—but not for him to answer. Speak the word only. Had He?

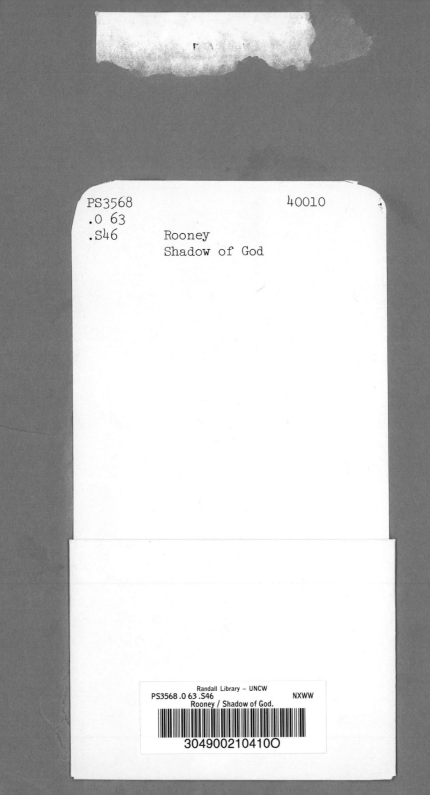